The Boxer & the Poet
Something of a Romance

The Boxer & the Poet
Something of a Romance

James Thayer

Black Lyon Publishing, LLC

THE BOXER & THE POET:
SOMETHING OF A ROMANCE
Copyright © 2008 by James Thayer

Our books may be ordered through your local bookstore or by visiting
the publisher:

www.BlackLyonPublishing.com

Black Lyon Publishing, LLC
PO Box 567
Baker City, OR 97814

Cover Model Back: Cody R. Givens
Cover Model Front: Cody R. Givens and Kerry A. Jones

This is a work of fiction. All of the characters, names, events,
organizations and conversations in this novel are either the products
of the author's vivid imagination or are used in a fictitious way for the
purposes of this story.

ISBN-10:   0-9793252-9-3
ISBN-13:   978-0-9793252-9-8
Library of Congress Control Number: 2007942742

Written, published and printed in
the United States of America.

Black Lyon Literary Love Story

This story is for my beloved wife Patti,
our daughters Alex and Annemarie,
and my mother Buryl.

Part One

"No person can be a poet, or can even enjoy poetry, without a certain unsoundness of mind."
-Baron Macaulay.

1

She was a sorceress or a witch or a mesmerist, or maybe some nameless mix of them all. When I accused her of possessing otherworldly powers she would reply, "I'm only a poet," and then laugh in her throaty way.

I look back now, and believe that her laugh—deep ribbons of sound from the back of her throat, usually coming when she had me locked up in her gaze—was a source of her power over me. One of the sources. There were others, as you will see shortly.

She was there when I surfaced from the black. I heard myself breathe, a ragged, thick-tongued gasping. Then I tasted the blood and salt. Wood was against my back, so I wasn't still on the canvas, but was laid out on a bench. My lip was split. Blood had trickled into my right ear, filling it, making me feel like I was under water. My right eye was swollen shut, and there was pressure all along the right side of my face. Then came a searing sting from that same eye. My eye teared over, and the tears squeezed themselves out between the swollen tissue.

I had been wrecked. Bad this time.

Cranking open my good eye took some effort. I blinked, trying to bring things into focus, expecting to see chipped green paint and a bare bulb, the usual in these joints. Instead, she slowly formed above me. My swollen right eye felt as if it were on fire.

Her hair was as black as a crow's wing, and fell to her shoulders in wild ringlets and waves. The light bulb was above her, and the few rays of light that worked through her wilderness of hair made it sparkle with golds and whites, and cast her face in shadow so that for a moment—me in my grogginess trying not to cough, lest a rib was broken, which has happened to me before, and feels like a shiv is being slipped between your ribs each time you take a breath—I couldn't make her out, just a shadow framed by roiling dark hair.

Then her eyes switched on as if a current had been put through them, blue and gleaming, at once exotic and amused, slightly lidded with sweeping eyelashes and set wide in her face. I closed and opened my good eye. Her lips were painted red, and the lower one was more full than the upper, a slight mismatch suggesting mischief.

She smiled as she stared down at me. Her teeth were large, a shiny white grill. I had no clue who she was. I licked my lips, still lying there on the bench. My attempt to say something came out a groan. Still smiling, she leaned closer, strands of her black hair falling off her shoulder. She cocked an ear toward me.

"Please." My voice sounding like the rasp of a wood file. "Get some water. Throw it into my eye." My words were garbled. My lips had been puffed up, too.

"Water? In your eye?"

"Please," I begged. "Quickly."

My right eye felt like a wasp was sitting on the pupil, piercing it again and again with its stinger. I moaned.

She disappeared. I moaned and licked my lips. I hadn't shaved for three days, so I had some stubble, which helped prevent cuts. My mouth guard was missing. I suppose it had been punched out of my mouth but I had no memory of it, nor of hitting the mat. My eye burned and tears poured down my cheek.

She returned, moving into my vision, blotting out the bulb's light again. She held up a paper cup.

My words were shaky. "Pry open my eye and pour the water in. Hurry."

She tentatively put two fingers on my face. She prodded a bit.

My voice rose uncontrollably. "Don't mess around. Shove back my eyelid and dump the water in."

This time she wrestled open the swollen tissue, then poured the water into my eye. The pain loosened its grip. I blinked. Water trickled down the sides of my face onto the tile floor.

She grabbed one of my elbows and helped me sit upright. She steadied me as I sat there slumped over, my mouth opening and closing like a fish. My eye felt better. I would live, I decided vaguely.

"What was in your eye?" Her voice had a purr to it, a hint of the feral.

"Pepper sauce, probably."

"How'd it get there?"

"His corner man sprayed it onto his glove in the third. He blinded me, then he laid me out." I shifted on the bench. "I've been hurt worse, though, I suppose."

"Isn't that cheating, using pepper?"

"Yeah." I turned to stare at her with my good eye. "It's cheating."

"Didn't you tell the referee?"

My voice carried more emotion than I intended. "This isn't Madison Square Garden."

Indeed, it wasn't. Bowder's Hall in the swamp town of Xanadeaux, Louisiana belonged to the Masons, and they rented it out now and again. The Southeast Boxing Federation had taken over the hall this night, and had put together an exhibition of three fights. My bout had been last on the card.

The Southeast Boxing Federation was owned by Billy Dupree, and consisted of him, his eight-year old Cadillac and his cell phone. He visited any given town twice: once to put up the posters and rent the hall, and the second time on the day of the show. If he had four hundred paid admissions, Dupree counted it a success and bought himself a fifth of Jack Daniels instead of his usual Big Swipe Corn Liquor.

If the Masons were to get any rent from Dupree, they got it up front. Town citizens most likely never saw him again, nor did the local police, though they often had questions for him. Dupree always stayed on the two-lane roads, never too far from the cypress and tupelo gum trees, the egrets and alligators. He claimed to be from the bayou, but he could shift his accent here and there. When Dupree took his show into Texas, he called himself the East Texas Boxing Association. Sometimes I went with him.

She asked, "Don't you have someone who takes care of you?"

"I take care of myself."

She laughed then, and that's the first time I heard it, that rope of deep musical notes. "I mean, after a fight. Shouldn't someone be in here cleaning you off? A trainer?"

Some of a moan escaped me but I clamped it off with my jaw.

She left the bench to search the room, then returned with a wet towel. She dabbed my cheeks. I closed my good eye. She wiped away blood, cleaning it from my nostrils and chin. Ring chalk was heavy on my cheeks, some of it streaked with the tears my eye had pumped out due to the pepper. She gently washed away the chalk, and was careful with my swollen eye, cleaning it with a corner of the towel. Then she touched the towel to her tongue to re-wet it, as if I were a child, and cleaned my split lip. I felt the gentle press of her fingers.

I could not remember the last time I'd been offered tenderness. And I had not often been touched by someone whose interest in my face coincided with mine. My brain was still puddled from the beating, but not so much so that I wasn't suspicious. This woman wanted something.

She asked, "Your name is Sonny James?"

"Today it is. Last week it was Kid Deutsch. I was billed as the Return of the Blitzkrieg."

She hesitated. "The poster out front says Ring Magazine ranks you number six in the heavyweight division, and that you'll fight for the WWM championship next fall."

I laughed as best I could, more a ripple of my shoulder, which hurt my chest. "That's the promoter's idea of a joke. WWM, Wonder What that Means. Ring Magazine has never heard of me."

She stared at me, as if she were a bidder at a horse auction judging lineage and musculature. Maybe she was going to roll my lips back to look at the length of my teeth.

She said finally, "Perhaps I've made a mistake."

"That's for sure." My voice was still ragged. "How about helping me out of my gloves before you go."

She dug at the knot on my left glove, me sitting there. She smelled of lilacs. I braved another look at her. She wore a ring on her right hand, a gold band with a ruby in it, a large red stone with numberless facets. On her necklace were three diamonds mounted on platinum. Her black slacks were tight, and she wore a black blouse under a black leather vest. She wore black boots with one-inch heels.

Working the knot, trying to loosen the Everlast glove's ties, she said, "You smell like a corpse, by the way."

Every inch of me hurt, even my hair. I deserved to be surly. "You try getting the hell beat out of you for seven rounds, you'll smell like this, too."

"Three rounds. I was there."

"Yeah, well, it felt like seven." I sighed, something I don't like people hearing me do. "It felt like seventy."

Her brows furrowed in concentration, working the lace. When

it was loose, she awkwardly pulled off the glove. Protective tape was thick around my hand. She moved to the other side of me, trailing her scent, and began with my other glove.

"I'm looking for a fighter," she said.

"Let me know when you find one."

"Someone who will do what I tell him." She plucked at the ties. "And not ask a lot of questions."

"You want someone beat up, you've got the wrong guy."

"I didn't say that, and ..."

"I'm not anybody's hired muscle."

She looked up at me, raising those eyes. "Is it the beating you just took, or are you always goofy?" Her eyes were fathomless and arresting, a blue unique to the universe, a new and mysterious blue. She pulled at the laces.

I again studied her face with my mono-vision. Her cheekbones were so high they threw shadows on her face below. A slight notch was on the point of her chin. Her long Gallic nose gave her face purpose, though I was clueless as to what that purpose might be.

Billy Dupree walked into the locker room, his shirttails most of the way out, and his tie loose around his neck. He never paid more than ten dollars for a tie. His belly always preceded him by a good measure.

"Nice fight tonight," he said.

I didn't say anything.

"For the first twenty seconds," he added. "Then it went downhill."

He carried a wad of bills in his fist, and flipped through them. He had a blood pudding of a face, the skin mapped by adipose tissue and burst capillaries. His nose resembled a potato left too long in the field. His little eyes were sunk deeply and were always bright with self-interest. His shoes were scuffed to raw leather, and he wore a fraternal ring on his right pinkie.

He eyed the woman on the bench who was tending to my glove. "Who's the babe?" He had a cigarette voice.

"My fiancée." Maybe I could make her laugh.

Billy eyeballed her top to bottom, then scoffed, "Dennis, you've got more chance of marrying me than you do her." He peeled off several bills. "Here's your three hundred." He pronounced it *hunnert*.

I protested. "You said it'd be a three-fifty, Billy."

"Had to deduct a fee for the cut man."

"Then where is he? I could use him."

He chuckled, sounding like a truck trying to start. "After the fight he told me your face was beyond his skills, so he left."

It was a lie, of course. Sometimes the so-called fee was for towels, other times for the ride to the hall, sometimes for ring clean-up, sometimes to grease a deputy sheriff—always something. The only time a boxing promoter tells the truth is when he calls another promoter a liar.

Then, the damnedest thing. The lady smiled grandly at Billy Dupree, rose from the bench and moved toward him, more a glide than a walk, sort of a sashay. Her smile could've peeled paint off the wall. Her eyes were merry and inviting. She had taken on the look of a coquette.

She sidled up to Billy, put a hand on his arm, went up on her toes and leaned close, like she wanted to share her perfume, and for a moment I thought she was going to nibble his fleshy earlobe, a revolting thought. He seemed paralyzed by her approach, as if he'd never before been close to a woman who didn't have gin blossoms on her nose or a black tooth.

Still smiling, she whispered something into his ear. Then she stepped away from him, bracing him with her gaze. She opened her hands, a gesture inviting understanding.

Billy's red face got redder. He chewed on nothing a moment.

Her smile narrowed, and this tiniest movement of her lips hardened her face to granite.

Billy sputtered, his wet mouth working, indecision on his face along with a touch of fear. Then with a sharp inhale, he withdrew several more bills from his wad and threw them on the bench next to me, pivoted on his heels and left the dressing room as fast as I'd ever seen him move.

She returned to the bench and my glove. "Return of the Blitzkrieg, what's your real name?"

"Dennis Jones."

"A prizefighter named Dennis?" She laughed. "First time in history."

She finally worked the laces loose and gripped the glove, but before she yanked it off, her gaze came up. She drilled me with those eyes. "I haven't stumbled upon a loser, have I?"

She might have, all right. I tried to growl, but my voice was still serrated. "Once you've got my glove off, don't let me keep you from the rest of your life."

She nodded, more to herself. She pulled the glove from my hand, and was about to rise, and I knew I'd never see her again, but then she looked at my taped fist.

"What's that in your hand?" she asked, pointing.

"It's ten dollars," I replied.

She reached over to open my fingers. Then she lifted out the roll and held it up like a trophy. She sounded like a district attorney. "It's a roll of quarters."

"Like I said, ten dollars."

She exclaimed, "You had a roll of quarters inside your glove."

"Didn't do me much good, did it?"

Her laugh rolled out of her, pouring over me and filling the dressing room. And then she stared at me some more. Up and down, my shoulders and arms, my legs, my belly, my battered face.

Her expression was of a schemer. "Maybe you'll do, after all."

I heard a crackling, as if electricity were jumping pole to pole, a sound that raised the hair on my neck. The air around the woman began shimmering and sparkling, throwing off tiny crimson and sapphire and gold particles, small lightning bolts and tiny comets. The air was shot with undulating colors, an aurora borealis surrounding her. The tang of ozone curled under my nostrils. She smiled at me and currents played about her face. Her eyes blazed blue.

I was hallucinating, surely. I had just taken a terrible beating to my head.

"Where are your clothes?" she asked, breaking the spell. The electric charges and colors faded to nothing. There she was again, just a woman, however peculiar.

When I nodded toward a locker, she opened it, took out my duds with two fingers like they might be contagious, then threw them back into the locker, keeping only my wallet.

She pulled me to my feet. "You come with me."

I tottered, pain coursing up and down, but she leaned into me, my arm over her shoulder, and she worked me toward the exit to the parking lot. She pushed open the door with her butt, then pulled me through. Weaving under my weight, she guided me across the lot.

She propped me up against her car, a black Mercedes sedan, then opened a back door. She shoved me inside. I hurt too much to resist. I sank into the seat. The smell of leather enveloped me.

She slid into the driver's seat, started the engine and off we went, the wheels squealing as we pulled away from Bowder's Hall and onto Xanadeaux's main street.

I was being rescued or kidnapped. I didn't know which.

2

The stairs creaked, even though I climbed slowly, burdening each step with my weight only after testing the plank.

The stairwell was meagerly lit by a smeared glass window that overlooked the Mississippi River. One of the panes was shattered, leaving a jagged edge of glass stuck in putty at the bottom. The windowsill was knobby with dead flies. Spiderwebs hid much of the inclined ceiling. Squeaks from my footfalls were amplified by the narrow stairway. Surely the men upstairs could hear me coming.

"Don't let them hear you coming," she had told me. "They'll run away."

"Will they kill me first before they run away?" I had asked.

She had flicked her hand as if tossing aside a useless fragment of the conversation. Her name was Isobel Autrey, if I haven't mentioned.

I slowly climbed the last few rickety stairs, my hand on the peeling wall for balance, passing graffiti in black paint that read Aints Suck, which referred to the New Orleans Saints.

The place smelled of cat spray and mold. I hesitated at the door. Isobel Autrey had given me an envelope with money in it, a lot of money in hundred dollar bills, for the gentlemen at the top of the stairs. It was in my back pocket.

I stepped up to a door, which was half open, revealing only darkness inside. The ancient lock had been kicked in decades ago, judging from the rotted wood. With my fingertips I carefully pushed open the door. The hinges scraped loudly.

I didn't like this business. My heart was in my throat, banging away. I stepped into the room, then waited for my eyes to adjust to the darkness.

The Rousseau Street Dock, downriver from the French Quarter

a quarter mile, and near a sand-and-gravel pit with its barges and push-boats, had once been the terminus for the New Orleans and Inland Steamship Line. Edgar Degas first set foot in News Orleans at this dock, it was said. The steamship company had folded, so then over the years the building had been filled with bales of hay, barrels of molasses, bags of pecans, and whatever else Louisiana farmers shipped out. The three-story structure hung out over the river on pylons. From the street and railroad side, the clapboard building was dappled with blisters that revealed generations of paint.

This floor of the building was above the main warehouse. I walked into the room, high stepping so I wouldn't trip over anything, a hand out in front of me to ward off a pulley on a cable or a fallen beam or whatever else might be dangling from the ceiling. Several broken windows were in the wall, too far away to do me much good. I moved around a pile of barrel staves, then a stack of rotting gunny sacks, and I avoided a dumbwaiter's hole in the floor that went through to the main warehouse below. I angled toward a door at the end of the room.

The light was better as I neared the door, with the windows at that end of the room allowing in weak light. The scent was of dead fish and creosote. I tried lightfooting it, rolling my feet heel to toe, but the wood floor still yelped as I crossed it.

I had asked Isobel Autrey what would happen if I just took her envelope of money and disappeared with it. She smiled at me and said with acid sweetness, "I swear to you, I will hunt you down even if it takes me five years, and then I'll shove an ice pick into your eye some night when you are asleep." So I didn't give that plan any more thought.

I came to the door. The warehouse's office lay behind it. The deep rumble of a passing freighter, headed down the Mississippi to the Caribbean, filled the warehouse and rattled the walls. The door had an iron latch rather than a knob. I gripped the latch and opened the door.

Grimy windows lit the room inside, and in that powdery light I could see two men, one standing over a printer and the other sitting behind a computer monitor. They looked up from their work. The one at the desk smiled at me under his mustache.

His computer rested on a battered desk. Two rusted metal file cabinets were along a wall. A table and four chairs and a three-legged milking stool were also in the room, all of them worn out and dusty. I had a particular interest in the furniture, is why I took note.

"Cops usually come in teams," the man at the desk said. His narrow face was full of sharp angles, an ax-face.

"I'm not a cop," I said.

"Then what do you want?" the other man demanded, the one at the printer. His porcine eyes seemed lost in his full, bloated face. He had shaved his head and was as bald as a peeled egg. A skull was tattooed on his forearm, a bad job, maybe a prison tattoo. His belly hung out of a Hooter's T-shirt and drooped down over his belt. His arms were fleshy, and his skin had a sallow tinge.

"I want to make a deal with you." I steadied my voice by speaking slowly.

On the old desk were paper samples and a cutting board, a digital camera and a loose stack of cards, all of them forest green. These men were counterfeiting green cards.

"You wearing a wire?" the tattooed counterfeiter asked.

"Like I said, I'm not a cop. I'm here on a pure business deal."

"Yeah, right." And so saying, the mustached counterfeiter pulled a pistol from an open drawer and pointed it at my belly. No weapon had ever been pointed at me before—other than fists, of course—and I learned then that some law of physics dictates that a pistol looks much larger when the muzzle is pointed at you.

I lifted my hands away from my body, showing them they were empty. "All I want to do is buy something from you."

The balloon-faced counterfeiter stepped away from the printer. Then he reached down and withdrew a thin knife from his boot. Same law of physics. It looked like a cavalry saber. I was sweating freely.

Looking down the barrel of his gun at me, the mustachioed counterfeiter asked, "What do you want to buy? A green card?"

I shook my head, a small motion. "Your furniture."

His predatory eyes narrowed. Then he laughed crazily, and waved his pistol, a signal. The fat one walked toward me, his knife in front of him.

The gun-wielding counterfeiter said, "This furniture ain't worth five bucks, the lot of it. It's a bunch of old broken crap. The hell you talking about, buying our furniture?"

"I'm just here to make an offer for your furniture," I said feebly. "The chairs and desk and such like."

"Cut him some, Soapy." The gunman rose from his chair to keep me in his line of fire as his partner approached. "Maybe he'll tell us why he showed up here, talking about the furniture."

Soapy came toward me, a grin on his face. He had a snaggle tooth. How that registered on me I don't know because my eyes were on his blade. He held the pointy end of the knife near my face..

He said, "I'm going to start here, at this eyeball. This is going to hurt, I'll bet." And then he moved to cut me.

•

How I got into this fix is worth a mention.

Isobel Autrey had driven me from Xanadeaux to her home in the Garden District. My skull was still filled with cotton from the fight, so she guided me up the porch stairs, through the heavy double doors and into a first-floor room where she lay me out on a sofa and threw a blanket over me.

I didn't wake until the middle of the next morning, and when I did—my face still pumping pain into me—the first thing I saw was a wiener dog gazing at me from three inches away, one of those two-dog-long, half-a-dog-high ratters with the pointed muzzles and the blank brown eyes, just looking at me like I was a hamburger patty.

"Beat it, dog." I brushed him off the sofa. "That's all I need, some wiener dog staring at me."

"They are called dachshunds," Isobel Autrey said, some frost in her voice.

I struggled to sit up. My nylon boxing shorts were still on, and my ring shoes. I felt like hell, like I always do the morning after a fight. "They give me the creeps, wiener dogs do."

She was sitting at a wrought-iron soda fountain table in front of a bay window, a silver tea service in front of her. Out the window, magnolia leaves drifted in a slight wind.

I brought my hand down as if it were a towel over my face. The swelling had lessened so I had the use of both eyes. My mouth was chalk dry. "I need some water. Will you tell me where the kitchen is?"

She pressed a button on the table, and a maid appeared at the door. I didn't think anybody had maids anymore. The maid was wearing a navy blue dress and a white apron. About forty, I'd guess.

"Mr. Jones would like some water," Isobel said. Then she asked me, "I'm having cinnamon toast for breakfast. Would you care for some cinnamon toast?"

"No, thanks."

"Anything for breakfast?" she asked.

"Ten eggs, scrambled, heavy pepper. A package of bacon, four pieces of buttered toast, no cinnamon, and two quarts of milk."

She stared at me. "It'll take the cook five minutes. Can you wait?"

I nodded.

"And please bring him one of Charles's sweatshirts and a pair of work-out pants, will you?"

The maid disappeared. Across the room, a grandfather clock—mahogany with a beveled glass door and massive brass cylindrical weights—bonged the hour. On the wall was an oil portrait of some old guy wearing an ascot and holding a bronze-tipped walking stick. On another wall was an oval mirror in a carved and gilded frame, could've been two hundred years old. A satinwood display cabinet was filled with Vaseline glass. My wallet was on a pedestal table next to the sofa.

I didn't see the need for pleasantries. "Why am I here?"

She bit into a slice of toast and chewed delicately, her eyes still on me. In the morning light her ebony hair had auburn accents. She lifted a china cup to sip her tea. The wiener dog sat at her feet. It wore a red rhinestone collar. It didn't like me. No wiener dog ever did. Some dogs do, though.

Finally Isobel said, "I want you to get something for me. It takes some explaining."

"Doesn't matter how much explaining you do, I'm not going to commit a crime for you."

"I want you to go to an old warehouse on the river and retrieve a piece of furniture." She poured herself more tea from a delicate pot.

"Why don't you hire Bekins?"

"The two fellows who own the furniture are low-lifes of some sort. Maybe criminals, maybe gang members, maybe something else. I haven't been able to find out."

"If you want to buy some furniture from them ..."

"It's a desk," she interrupted.

"Then why don't you make them an offer for it? No low-life turns down cold cash." Believe me, I know.

"The desk is dilapidated, little better than firewood. Of itself, it is worth nothing. If I offer them money for it, they'll be instantly suspicious and they'll tear the desk apart. I cannot have that."

"Something is inside the desk? Is that what you're trying to get?"

A fellow walked into the den, crossed the carpet and pecked Isobel on the top of her head. He wore matching jogging pants and jacket, and Nike running shoes.

He asked her, "Is this our champ?"

She raised her eyebrows at him. She didn't know if I was her champ yet, I suppose. He smiled at me. His teeth were small but perfect. His lips were curved deeply, and would be considered sensuous on a woman. His nose was straight with a small bulb at the end that made it flippant and his cheekbones were finely-planed. I could see his mother in his face. His walnut-colored hair had touches of gray at the temples.

He didn't wait for an introduction. "How old are you?" he asked, helping himself to a slice of Isobel's toast.

"Thirty-four."

"Little old for the fight game, aren't you?"

People who've never done it like to call it a game. I asked, "Who are you?"

"This is Charles Brooks, my fiancé," she said.

"I'd shake your hand, but I'm perspiring from my jog." He chewed his toast.

Some people perspire. Others, such as me, sweat.

She caught his eyes. Some understanding passed between them. They were conspiring, that was plain.

She said, "I cannot deal with the men, those fellows—I don't even know if there are two or three or four of them—who possess the desk. I approached them once and they chased me away before I spoke a word."

"So why doesn't your fiancé here, Charlie, do it? Is it Chuck or Charlie?"

He cleared his throat. "It's Charles, which is more appropriate in my professional life."

Isobel looked at me over the rim of her tea cup. "Charles is a medical doctor, a dermatologist. I can't ask him to retrieve the desk. He is a person of the mind."

I said, "I thought a dermatologist was a person of the skin."

She stared at me in cold surmise. "I need someone who is tough, someone they won't fool around with."

Charles Brooks drew himself up stiffly. "I'm tough enough, in my own way. Try looking at leaking pustules for a living."

Isobel ignored him. "I need someone who has a certain look, and can be a messenger, someone who projects a certain image."

She rose from her table. She was thin and supple, and moved with unthinking grace like a cat. She was wearing a black blouse and a slender black skirt that reached her ankles. She was barefoot and her toenails were red. She crossed the room to the gilt-framed mirror.

"Come here, Dennis."

I pushed myself off the sofa, hurting in most joints like always after a fight. "You have any Advil? I always have to take a couple. Didn't when I was younger."

She didn't answer me, so I stood next to her, looking at her in the mirror. Once again, I swear her royal blue eyes were illuminated from within. They glittered. She came up to my chin. Her thicket of hair brushed me as she nudged me sideways so I had to look at myself in the mirror, something I've never found profitable.

She touched my right ear. "What's this?"

"My ear?"

"I mean, what're these lumps in the skin, and the folds?"

"It's called a cauliflower ear," I replied. "I don't know why I don't have two of them, as I get hit on each side of the head about evenly."

"And this?" She tapped my nose.

"It's a bump." I wanted to add *What the hell does it look like?*, but I was determined to be civil until I'd eaten my breakfast.

"So you've broken your nose?" she asked.

I shrugged. "About twenty-five times."

She glanced over my shoulder at her intended. He had helped himself to a cup of tea from the silver service. He added three teaspoons of sugar.

"And what about your eyebrows? They're sort of large, aren't they?"

"Some scars and calluses."

The maid returned with a heaping tray and placed it on a coffee table near the sofa. The room filled with the smell of bacon.

"And this?" She drew her long fingernail along my cheek, not an altogether unpleasant experience.

I turned my head toward her, but she gripped my chin and yanked it back to the mirror, nothing pleasant about it.

"Pay attention," she ordered. "What's this scar along your jaw bone."

"Some guy up in Joplin at the Civic Center had a screwdriver in his glove. Laid me open like a fish belly. Hurt like hell, I don't mind saying."

"Your plastic surgeon didn't do much of a job," Charles Brooks said. "I can see the cross-hatching on the scar from here."

I looked at him at him in the mirror and laughed. "Like I could ever afford a plastic surgeon. I did it myself, with a needle and some fishing line."

"And who does your hair?" Isobel asked.

"What do you mean?"

"Your stylist?" When I hesitated, she added, "Your barber?"

My blond hair is cut almost to the skull, the chemotherapy look.

"I do it myself. Sometimes I enter tough-guy competitions."

"Pardon?" she asked.

Those are anything-goes brawls. Kicking, eye gouging, strangling —and my opponents are usually small-town bullies who think because they've got a pot-belly or because they can lift a beer keg they can fight.

I explained, "In some fights, hair-pulling is allowed so I keep my hair short. I don't need a barber to sheer myself."

Isobel was wearing dangly silver earrings that swung back and forth when she nodded. "So, Dennis, look at yourself and tell me what you see?"

"I see me."

She looked at me in the mirror as if I might be a moron. "What I see is a frightening visage."

"My eggs are getting cold." I tried to turn toward my breakfast but she pulled me back to the mirror. She had some strength in those slender arms.

The maid returned with clothes, laying them on the sofa. Then she left the room. She could walk without making a sound.

"Your face looks like a gnawed bone. It's tough. And your arms are big, and your stomach is rippled. You're just what I need."

"For what?"

"To meet with those guys who have my desk." She released my arm and turned back toward her chair and table. "I need someone who can deal with them on the only level they understand. Someone who is hard and mean."

I put on the sweatshirt, then lowered myself to the sofa and pulled the coffee table closer. The eggs were a four-inch mound covering the plate. A second plate held a side of bacon, and a third the toast.

"Don't get between me and this breakfast," I said by way of humor. "It'd be too dangerous."

Nobody laughed. They watched me shovel eggs for a while. I was now the wiener dog's best friend. He planted his butt right next to my shoe, his head going up and down as he followed my fork.

"So what's in the desk?" I asked around a mouthful of eggs.

"I cannot tell you," Isobel said flatly.

She was watching me eat, too, with the same attention the dog was giving me. She was fascinated by my eating, it looked like. Hadn't she ever seen anybody fill his belly? I shoved a couple pieces of bacon into my mouth. I kept my face above my plate, lest any crumbs fall. I didn't want to foul her rug.

She said, "I didn't just happen into the Mason's Hall in Xanadaeux last night, Dennis. I had done some research about you."

I looked over at her. "There's not much to discover about me."

"How many fights have you had?" She again lifted her tea cup. She didn't sip. Maybe she used the cup as a prop.

"All told?" I asked. "Counting tough-guy events?"

She nodded.

"Counting bare knuckles?"

Charles Brooks smiled with the benevolence of superior knowledge. "Nobody fights without gloves any more. Bare-knuckle matches were outlawed eighty or ninety years ago.

"Whatever you say, Doctor," I replied.

I just needed to get to the end of my meal, then I could take my leave. Why argue with a dermatologist about anything? Life's too short.

In tiny towns, some hicks will put up money for a bare-knuckle fight. Trouble with those bouts, though, is that after two rounds your hands swell up like pillows and you stand there toe-to-toe flailing away without doing much damage, but the rubes think they're witnessing the greatest thing since Uncle Jeb knocked a horsefly out of the air with tobacco spit.

"So how many matches, Dennis? Counting everything."

"More than six hundred, I suppose."

Brooks exclaimed, "Impossible."

"Sometimes six a night." I wiped my mouth on the sweatshirt sleeve.

She inhaled sharply through her teeth. "You are just the person I need. You are tough, and you must be cunning to have survived all those fights."

My plate was clean except for the last piece of bacon, which I tossed to the wiener dog, who caught it in the air, shook it to make sure it was dead and swallowed it, taking all of one second. He ate like I did.

The dermatologist said, "Meat gives the dog bad breath."

"I won't be around for it." I rose from the sofa. "Thanks for breakfast."

Isobel Autrey held up her hand like a traffic cop and commanded, "Sit."

Down I went, back onto the sofa. She already had a peculiar power over me. The wiener dog sat down, too.

"You box because you have no other skills," she said. "And yet, you attend college?"

She had indeed done some research. "I recently spent a quarter at LSU. I'm a junior, I think."

She smiled. "And how long have you been a junior?"

She probably knew the answer, so I didn't fudge the truth, "About three years."

"And before that?"

"Four or five years of being a sophomore, some at McNeese State, some at Delgado Community."

"And?"

I rubbed my skull to warm a memory. "Before that, I was upriver in St. Louis, at Washington University. Before that, let's see—"

"An epic struggle to gain a college degree," the doctor said. "It's admirable, truly."

He had probably shot through college like grain through a goose.

I asked, "What'd you tell the promoter, David Dupree, that made him fork over my money?"

"I said I was the Xanadeaux police chief's daughter, and Dupree was going to be in jail in ten minutes from that moment if he didn't pay you all your money."

"You lie pretty well, sounds like," I said.

Isobel looked down at the table as if she had notes. "And speaking of jail, as far as I can determine, you've spent about ninety days behind bars, all told."

"County judges and JPs put me in the slammer once in a while for boxing without a license. It's part of the cost of my doing business. I do my two or three days, eat everything they serve, and leave. No problem."

Once again I rose from the sofa. This time I wasn't going to let her push me back down with the force of her personality. I boldly stepped around the coffee table.

"I'm going to make you a deal," she said.

And she brought up her gaze. Her straight and untamed blue eyes bored through the back of my eyeball sockets and into my skull, and stirred my brain to uselessness. Must have, because I stood there like a fence post rather than making my escape. I ordered my legs to work but they were listening to her, not me, so there I stayed on her carpet, the wiener dog next to me as if it were suddenly my dog.

"I must have that desk." Her voice rose like a storm. "It is more important than you can imagine."

"I'm sure, but—"

"It's not just for me," she said. "The entire world needs the contents of that desk."

"I'm sure." I looked out the den door. The hallway and the front door to the street and freedom lay just beyond.

"I have spent six years looking for it." Her words crackled like electric sparks. "It will make me famous, and the entire world will be grateful. I will be able to assume my rightful position."

"Well ..."

"And now you are going to retrieve it for me. I can't do it myself."

"Well ..."

I was fairly stammering. I hadn't noticed any mental deterioration due to boxing over the years, but she had quickly turned my mind to porridge. I couldn't answer her, could hardly follow her, while she had me bound and gagged with her gaze.

She leaned back, and her face softened. "You haven't even asked what's in this deal for you."

"This could get me killed," I said. "You've got some crazy plan, and the sum of it is, your errand boy, who you hope to be me, is probably going to be killed."

The doctor said, "Nonsense."

"You don't have enough money to tempt me to get myself killed," I said.

I tested my legs. They were working again. I made for the door, passing a cherry wood fern stand. The idiot dog followed me.

"I'm not talking about money."

I paused. "Then what?"

"You are clueless about life," she said, not unkindly. "You are trapped, like a fly against a glass window. You don't know the way out. You are thirty-four years old. You are trying your best, but you simply don't know how."

There was some truth to what she said.

She continued with her indictment. "Not in all your adult life have you lived in one place for more than three months because you can't ever make the rent."

I wondered again where she found out all this stuff about me.

"You enter these crummy freakshow bouts in jerkwater towns because every time you've gone up against a respectable, ranked opponent, you've been beaten."

"Well ..."

"You are Pavlov's bell," this Isobel Autrey said. "Good boxers see you step into the ring and they drool."

"There isn't enough money in the world to make me risk my hide, and—"

She cut me off. "If I paid you money, you'd go out and buy a Lincoln Continental or something."

"What's wrong with a Lincoln Continental?"

"So here's my deal." She leaned forward to place her elbows on her knees, resting her chin on the points of her fingers. She spoke slowly, I suppose to let each word sink into my head. "If you get that desk for me, I will manage you for one year."

"Manage me?" I laughed harshly. "I've never had a fight manager who didn't steal from me."

"Not manage your fights." She increased the wattage in her eyes. "Manage your life."

I stared at her. "My life?"

She nodded, a knowing smile hanging from her cheekbones.

"My life?" I'd never heard of such a thing. "Everything? For one year?"

Maybe I indeed had been hit in the thinker too many times over the years and was punch drunk, because just then air in the room coalesced and shimmered and hardened, and the sum of my existence formed out of the ether. I gasped. It was ghostly, filling the room, demanding I look, making me peer at myself and my long and tortured journey.

All the dead-ends. All the frustrations. All the pain. The stupid choices. The hopes and dreams abandoned. The potential gone sour. A day late and a dollar short, every damned time. My whole life— the entire three-downs-and-I'm-out saga—there in front of me, a dark and sordid montage of failure. It was ugly.

I blinked. The foul cloud of memories vanished. And there again was Isobel Autrey staring at me, inveigling me with her smile.

Manage my life?

I said, "You've got yourself a deal."

•

Before I return to that warehouse over the Mississippi River and to my predicament—one knife and one gun pointed at me—let me put things in perspective.

Prize fighting is a skill learned in increments over the years, much like learning to be an architect. I was no Muhammad Ali, sure. And I was no Tug Johnson, the current heavyweight champ. But I had fought more than six hundred times in the ring. Lots of bums and street-toughs, but some real boxers, too. I had won about two-thirds of my bouts, and only had to cheat in a few. Well, a few dozen. I had kayoed maybe a hundred opponents and TKO'd maybe another hundred. I had learned to take a hellacious punch and to give one of the same caliber. Calluses on my knuckles were half an inch thick and had the texture of bark. I had some stamina and strength and skill.

These two counterfeiters were chumps. The fat one, the one named Soapy, moved his blade slowly toward me probably hoping I'd cry out in terror.

Boxers know the hand is quicker than the eye. If it weren't, no boxer would ever get hit, not once. In a blur, my left arm swiped sideways like a windshield wiper, smacking Soapy's arm and knocking the knife into the air.

He didn't even have time to change his surly expression before I hit him again, this time square on the chin, a pile-driver blow that rocked his head back. He blacked-out instantly. The knife landed in a corner.

I rushed half a step forward and grabbed Soapy by his belt and shirt before he could fall, his head rolling around on his neck. I clean-and-jerked him, spun toward the gunman and threw Soapy at him. The mustachioed counterfeiter spilled backward, his unconscious partner weighing him down and spreading him across the floor, a tangle of arms and legs.

The counterfeiter still had a pistol, and I could be sure he was trying to wrestle it from its entanglement. I sprinted toward the door.

The flat clap of a gunshot filled the room, and the doorframe near my shoulder splintered. Another shot came, and the bullet singed my earlobe as I passed through the door.

My legs churned. I ran passed the barrel staves and sacks, then down the stairs taking them three at a time.

I made it out onto the street, the steep sun making me squint. I checked over my shoulder. Nobody was following me. I touched my earlobe. It smarted, as if it had been skinned. I turned toward the Quarter.

I was going to have a chat with Isobel Autrey about our deal.

3

Isobel was standing in front of her students, turned toward the windows, gesturing widely with her slender, golden arms. Her hair was like obsidian, gleaming and black. She wore a black silk dress that had small scarlet accents. Her lips were painted the color of blood. Her silver earrings threw sparks. Flowing into the room and around her like a current, the sun was possessive of her, washing her in livid colors. Everything else in the classroom was faded to dun and gray.

I had taken the streetcar from the CBD out St. Charles, my ear stinging all the way, and had slipped into her classroom in the Norman Mayer building at Tulane.

She asked the sun, "Who can read these lines by Keats and not be stirred?" With a grand flourish, she turned to her class and commanded them, "Listen to my voice. Tune out everything but my voice. 'That thou would wish thine own heart dry of blood.'" Her words were silky and full. "'So in my veins red life might stream again.'"

The class was as silent as a cemetery. Nobody moved. Nobody coughed or yawned or tapped a pen on a desk. The air in the room was thick.

"Can you listen to these words from Keats and not be filled with yearning?" Isobel's face was flushed. Her skin glowed and a fine line of perspiration was on her forehead. Her lips were moist and when she breathed deeply her delicate nostrils flared like a race horse's. Had she not been standing in front of a roomful of students, I would have sworn that she was in a state of pure sexual arousal.

"Keats is offering you his flesh and his blood in these living lines of poetry." Her lips puckered slightly and she breathed again. Her words were serrated with passion. "Can you feel the tension?"

Damn straight they could. The place shimmered with it. Every male in the room, and it was mostly filled with males, was transfixed.

The guy sitting next to me was massive, with a full belly and ham-hock thighs. He hung out over his chair in all directions, probably on the Tulane football team. He wore a sweatshirt with a red T on it. Watching Isobel Autrey, he and the other men were in steamy trances.

Then Isobel spotted me. At first her expression was rapturous, staring at me, thinking I had been successful. But my grim countenance quickly told her otherwise. Her face collapsed and she spun away from her class and gripped her desk for support. She shuddered, her shoulders heaving. A moment passed, her students exchanging glances, dumbfounded Then she straightened as if rebar had been inserted down her spine, and she turned to the class.

Rather, she turned to me, sitting about six rows back. The counterfeiter had missed with his pistol shots, but had his aim been better, it would've felt just like her stare at that instant. Her eyes hammered into me, nailing be to the back of my chair.

Her face was as cold as a carving. "You have failed."

As if a drill instructor had barked, "Eyes right," every student in the room turned to me. They had no idea what she was talking about, but I felt the weight of their sudden hatred. I was Satan sprung from the netherworld, shrouded in fire, horned and hooved, and dealing only in evil.

Isobel wouldn't relent with her gaze. Finally, she said, "Perhaps you should leave our classroom, Mr. Jones."

I was feeling aggrieved, and I was feeling duped, and I hadn't stopped shaking from being fanned by two bullets. And sometimes when I get agitated, my mouth works on its own.

I said, "You mean, they give college credit for poetry?"

She reacted like I'd thrown a pail of cold water on her. She stood there shaking with rage. The room was utterly still.

Then the football player turned in his chair toward me and put a scowl on his face. He had a surprisingly birdlike voice for so big a fellow, and he spoke loudly for all to hear. "Miss Autrey asked you to leave. Get your ass out of here."

I leaned toward him, shoving my knobby, much-abused face right into his and I gave him my ring stare. "I want you to look at me, sonny. Look closely." I held up a fist, heavy with calluses. My arms were like hawsers, my neck like a fire hydrant. "Do I look like I take orders from a 300-pound Pillsbury Doughboy like you?"

He studied me a moment, then his face blanched and his mouth opened and closed, and then he turned away to face front again, the back of his neck flaming red.

I was fuming. Isobel Autrey had played me for a sucker. Sent me into a run-down warehouse on a deadly errand. Manage my life? What sort of idiot falls for that pitch? I'd known her for less than a day and she had talked me into being a pistol target, and I'd bet she and her skin doctor boyfriend last night sipped their Chardonnay and laughed at the dummy they were tricking into doing their chore.

I am cursed with a touch of credulity, and that's the hell of it. It has brought me misery more than once.

My muscles were constricted I was so angry, and I had to argue with them to let me rise from my chair. I slowly stepped along the wall, passing the students, the weight of their gazes on me. Isobel's head turned with the mechanical motion of a tank turret. I could almost hear her hydraulics. Her flashing eyes followed me.

I arrived at the front of her class, turned to look at them, meeting their stares, making their eyes drop. Then I looked at Isobel. Her arms were crossed in front of her, and a hip was shifted forward. Her chin was up, a stance of utter contempt.

So I stepped to the blackboard, facing it, my head half a foot away from its surface. I whipped my head forward, right into the slate blackboard, a bull's blow, my forehead crashing into it. The sound was of a vase shattering. Same thing I've done to many opponents when the ref wasn't looking.

The blackboard shattered, cracks appearing instantly, radiating away from where I'd hit it with my head. Two chunks of fractured slate fell to the floor.

I looked at her again, and this time I was able to hold her gaze. "That's a better use for a head than learning poetry."

I walked out of the room. She said something to my back, but I was already in the hall and couldn't make it out. That'd be the last I'd ever see of Isobel Autrey, with any luck.

•

I have never been lucky. My next fight was a real one, not one of those freakshows for bumpkins promoted by David Dupree, and unlike Dupree's Southeast Boxing Association, the American Boxing Association was a legit outfit that ranked fighters and sanctioned fights. I stood in my corner, moving side to side to keep warm while the ring announcer introduced me and my opponent.

He didn't spend much time with me because, while I had cleaned up my record as best I could listing only sanctioned fights, I was still an over-the-hill canvas back, and there wasn't much the announcer could do to disguise it, standing there in his tuxedo like this was the big time.

My opponent, Darnell "Sonny" Smith, doing his warm-up dance over in his corner, was another matter. He was a rising star, ranked sixteenth by the American Boxing Association, a twenty-three-year-old ripped and buffed hellion from Biloxi, Mississippi.

Sonny Smith was ticket punching, and I was his bum of the month. As a rule, the ABA allowed a boxer to compete against one of its top five fighters only if the boxer had twenty wins with fewer than five losses. And though Sonny Smith had won dozens of amateur fights and a silver medal in the Pan American games, he was only seventeen and zero in his professional career. I was scheduled to be number eighteen.

Hell, I didn't mind. I'd take home six hundred dollars, the loser's share. I had hired a local cut guy for a hundred dollars. His name was Arturo Lopez, from Mexico, and if he spoke English I never heard it. He stood in front of me to smear Vaseline on my face.

We were at a municipal gymnasium in Lafayette, and I guessed there were fifteen-hundred people in the audience. Not a single press camera was ringside. The gym smelled like popcorn. The ring announcer slipped through the ropes. My opponent chatted with his trainer, smiling, then laughing at some joke. He didn't honor me with a look, hadn't yet recognized my existence. He had four guys around him. Twenty-three-years-old, seventeen pro wins, and he already had an entourage.

The referee called us to the center of the ring. Now Sonny Smith glared at me, giving me the look, like a dog does a biscuit, his brows down, his lips curled into a sneer. I winked at him. I was going to give it my best, but I wouldn't last four rounds, probably. That's six hundred dollars for twelve minutes' work, is one way to look at it. I didn't have the financial luxury of factoring into my equation that I'd be receiving considerable damage during those twelve minutes.

The ref walked toward the timer and was about to give him the signal to ring the bell when a voice behind me said in a lilting voice, "You'll put him down in the first round, Dennis."

Someone's idea of a joke. I looked over my shoulder.

Isobel Autrey stood right below my corner, gazing up at me. I wouldn't have been more surprised had it been Dwight Eisenhower. She smiled at me, giving me her entire dental array.

"Beat it," I growled. "I'm done with you."

She was wearing a white cotton cardigan and khaki twill pants, and she gripped a turnbuckle and climbed right up to the mat, her sable hair flowing behind her. Hoots and wolf whistles came from the audience. She braced herself against the ring post and leaned over the top rope and—the damnedest thing—with one hand she grabbed my jaw, her fingers and thumb digging into my cheeks so that she was cupping my chin. Now the crowd laughed, really howling, and it wasn't the first time I've been laughed at in the ring, by the way. Her fiancé, Charles Brooks, was in a ringside seat near my corner and next to him was an African American lady wearing a maroon turban and a pair of slacks of the same color.

Isobel snared me with her eyes and she intoned, "Sonny Smith won't last a round."

The bell rang. A smattering of applause came from the audience.

She squeezed my chin with such force that her red fingernails cut my skin and drew beads of blood. Electric currents ran from her arm into my face, it seemed. "Go out and destroy him. Do it for me."

That must have been her idea of a joke. Do it for her? I wouldn't look out a window to watch Isobel Autrey fall into a manhole.

When I shook her hand off, I spotted a flash of color near my feet. I looked down. The woman in the maroon turban was standing next to my cut man, and she was sprinkling something under my ring stool. I bent for a closer look. The stuff looked like ashes—gray and slivery. The lady fanned them with her hand so they blew against my feet. Then she looked up and smiled. I didn't have a clue who she was or what she had just done, and I certainly didn't have time to think about it. I turned for my beating.

Most of my ranked opponents rush across the ring, eager for

their short workout. But Sonny Smith took a few steps and had inexplicably slowed, his hands up, waiting for me. I put up my fists, and circled the ring to the left. Moving to the left means your opponent's left jabs meet a retreating target, and I'm always for that. Sonny pivoted to follow me but his feet seemed leaden.

I closed in and popped him with a jab, then another. I was startled by my own speed. Never had I been quicker. Smith countered but I brushed his glove aside and jabbed him again. I was snapping his head back, solid hits, carrying more freight than my jabs usually do. Sonny Smith stepped back. His expression suggested bafflement. He had a real opponent.

Smith threw a right. I slipped inside and sank my fist into his belly so far it bounced off his backbone. He folded like a jackknife. As he was falling, I hit his ear with left cross, as solid a blow as I've ever delivered. Sonny Smith found the canvas and there he stayed, his feet and arms splayed out in all directions. The crowd booed Sonny.

I went to a neutral corner until the referee counted Smith out, and at ten his manager and trainer and cut man climbed through the ropes and rushed to him. I trotted to my corner where Arturo Lopez already had his hand out for his hundred dollars, like I might've tucked the bill into a glove for him.

Isobel Autrey was waiting for me at the edge of the ring, her grin rivaling the ring lights. "What'd I tell you?" she asked sweetly.

"What happened?" I asked, looking back to see Sonny Smith still on the mat, his people bent over him.

"A one-round victory over a ranked opponent is what happened," she said, laughing in her deep mellifluous way. "Just like I said it would."

That strange lady in the maroon turban who had spread ashes below my ring stool was standing at Isobel's elbow. She was grinning, too.

My voice was low. "Yeah, but what really happened?" I hadn't even worked up a sweat.

Isobel climbed up to the mat, grabbed a towel from Arturo's bucket and began wiping the Vaseline from my face. "You've got to learn to trust your manager, Dennis."

She lifted the rope so I could step through. I jumped down, and she followed me, headed for the dressing room. Arturo came with us, still hoping for his hundred. The next fight was being introduced and spectators ignored me as I walked along the aisle. Isobel followed me.

"I don't have a manager." I had just somehow beaten a ranked opponent. My mood was a mix of wild elation and intense suspicion.

"Yes, you do," she said behind me, keeping up with me, vast humor in her voice. "You've got me, and we've still got our deal."

•

Isobel took me to her father's home to show me off, I think, like a cat brings home a mouse or a mole or a shrew, just to show its owner it doesn't spend the day on frivolities.

His home was only three blocks from Isobel's. It was one of those Garden District houses that resembles a mausoleum, huge in every proportion and forbidding in every aspect. Gripping my arm, Isobel brought me up the steps, across the porch and through the front door. She entered without knocking, and we wound our way around and eventually entered the old man's den. He was bent over a table, making some adjustment with an outstretched arm.

"I dumped the dermatologist, so meet my new boyfriend," she announced gaily, maybe to test her old man's heart.

He straightened himself slowly, his eyes finding me. I can't say his face registered anything pleasant.

"My daughter has always been the funny one in our family." His white hair was carefully combed over his bald spot. His eyes were jackdaw blue, surrounded by webs of deep wrinkles. His chin was pronounced, and was heavily wattled. Sun spots dappled the back of his hands, and a few liver spots were along his forehead. He was wearing a blue sports coat, a blue and red regimental tie, and sharply-creased black slacks. He was thin, and his clothes hung on him as if from a hanger. He was in his seventies, and he projected energy and power.

He said, "I have always adjudged your dermatologist friend to be a bit of a milksop, Isobel."

I would learn that's the way he often talked, using two-dollar words when cheaper ones would do.

"He's more than my friend," Isobel replied. "He's my fiancé."

He looked at me but talking to his daughter as if I were deaf. "If there is an inverse correlation between the appearance of physical ruggedness on the one hand, and intelligence on the other. And I believe there is. Then, your new friend here is a moron."

I am occasionally called a moron and have never taken to it kindly.

Isobel introduced us. Without any hesitation, he extended his hand and I shook it. His hand felt like a fistful of twigs. He kept on staring at me, amusement in his eyes. His name was Lawrence Autrey. Nobody ever called him Larry, Isobel told me later.

He was standing next to a table on which were three thousand or more soldiers, all of them an inch tall. Civil War soldiers in blue and gray. Cannons and infantry and cavalry, a few houses, many trees. Some of the soldiers were arrayed in long lines, the rank and file marching forward. Each piece seemed unique, made of lead and intricately painted down to the mustaches and boot laces. It was a vast diorama of a battle set on a table.

Lawrence Autrey asked, "Do you know anything about miniature soldiers, young man?"

"I gave up toys when I was eleven or twelve," I said. "I haven't given them any thought since."

He cleared his throat. "This is the Battle of Gettysburg." He grandly swept his hand above the battlefield, lest I miss any tiny part of it.

"You can see here," he said, "General Lee is trying to break the center of the blue coat army on Cemetery Ridge."

The table was molded, with contours representing hills and valleys. Along one end was a road with tiny fences bordering it.

"Lee chose his freshest soldiers and placed them under the command of Major General George Pickett."

I looked around as if I'd gotten off the bus at the wrong stop. Another diorama was to one side, this one of a more recent battle featuring a bridge over a replica of a river with buildings on both sides of the bridge. Tanks and armored cars were approaching the center of the bridge. Tiny balls of cotton represented blasting shells. Miniature soldiers were on the bridge's parapet and in slit trenches and weapon pits on the bridge embankment.

Along the den's walls were mahogany display cases with glass fronts. Inside were thousands of soldiers, some with swords, some with kilts, some with bows and arrows, some with tall black shakos. There were horses and oxen, landing craft, howitzers, tanks and mine flails, pike men and lancers. In the corner of the room was an elaborate desk with a hand-tooled leather top and ball-and-claw feet. On a stand behind the desk was a cigar humidor. Next to a bookcase was an enormous yellowed globe, so old that the west coasts of the Americas were left blank.

The old fellow bent over the table to point. "Pickett is charging, trying to pierce the enemy line—you can see here—but the Union soldiers are repulsing them, with terrible casualties inflicted on the Confederates. See, some of the horses and men are down. I've even got tiny viscera here on the ground."

Everything in this room was foreign to me. The cigar and wood scents. The leaded glass windows on the bookcases. The buttery leather on the chairs. The thick Persian carpets. The green-shaded banker's lamp shining down on a sterling silver pen and pencil set. The long and sweeping velvet drapes with cords and tassels. The antique oak apothecary cabinet with brass pulls on the drawers and brass hinges. The solidity and permanence and wealth and breeding of it all. With my cauliflower ear and faded jeans, I stood out like a half-driven nail.

The old fellow again pointed at his toy soldiers, at his meticulous reconstruction of the chaos of battle. "Pickett's charge was valiant, and it was doomed to failure."

"Let me help General Pickett." I walked over to his other diorama—I would learn later it was a reconstruction of the battle for the Arnem Bridge in World War II—and I plucked three tanks from the bridge ramp and walked them over to Gettysburg, flicked aside several downed horses, and placed the Panzers at the head of Pickett's line.

"Nothing like tanks to help an infantry charge," I said.

Isobel laughed, musical notes forming in her throat.

For a moment, I thought the old guy was going to spit his bit, but he took a long breath, and then his eyes narrowed in amusement. "A problem solver, are you? I can see why my Isobel has brought you home."

Lawrence Autrey was formidably starchy, standing there, old and autocratic, surrounded by all his shiny possessions.

He asked, "What sort of deal has Isobel made with you?"

She spun the huge globe. She had the inward look of one scheming. "A good deal."

"I don't doubt it." He chuckled. "A good deal for Isobel."

I said, "May I ask you something, Mr. Autrey?"

"Go right ahead, young man."

"Is your daughter a nutcase?"

He glanced at her. "She may be, alright."

Isobel laughed again. I liked Lawrence from that moment.

She sat in a leather Williams rocker, then crossed her legs. "I haven't told Dennis what is in the desk drawer, Daddy."

I didn't want to talk about that damned desk, the one that had almost gotten me killed. "How'd you make all your money, Mr. Autrey?" No point in being subtle.

"My father was a rum-runner."

I hesitated. "A weimaraner?" I don't hear too well out of my cauliflower ear, what with all the scar tissue filling the passage.

"My father imported spirits to New Orleans from Cuba," Lawrence said. "No tax stamps required that way, you see."

"Wasn't that illegal?"

He replied, "It certainly was, and that's why my father made so much money at it."

"Well, New Orleans has never been known to turn aside liquor."

"My father died of lead poisoning," he said.

"He was shot on a Magazine Street sidewalk," Isobel clarified. "Three bullet holes. One in his chest, two in his back."

"Doesn't sound like an accident," I said by way of penetrating analysis. "Did the police ever solve the crime?"

"The police didn't think it was much of a crime," Lawrence said. "And they didn't do much to solve it. The price of a martini in New Orleans rose considerably upon pop's death, though."

"So you've never had to work for a living?" I asked.

"Let's just say that I carried on my father's businesses, and expanded them. It was work, believe me."

"How about you, Isobel?" I asked, glancing at her. "You ever had to work for a living?"

Her only reaction was a tick of her eyes. "Teaching poetry is work."

Her father laughed, and she looked sharply at him.

"I also write poetry." Her eyes were glacial. "I've been published in the *Southern Poetry Review*, the *American Poetry Journal*, and many others. Maybe you have read some of my poems, Dennis?"

"I limit myself to limericks," I said.

"I am also a literary critic. My latest article is 'Feminist Intertextuality in Emily Dickenson.'" She raised an eyebrow. "I don't suppose you've read that, either."

"Read it?" I said blandly. "I wouldn't sneeze into it."

The muscles on her jaw worked. Then she demanded, "Do you read, Dennis? Anything at all?"

"The back of my box of Fruit Loops at breakfast."

"Children, children, children," Lawrence Autrey intoned. "We are here on business. Apparently Isobel has made some sort of deal with you, Dennis."

I don't know why Isobel Autrey could annoy me with such ease, maybe because hers was the cultured voice on the other side of the fence. She was born to diamonds and I was born to gravel, and every little thing she said reminded me of it. She was lavish cheekbones, turned ankles, a universe of black shimmering hair, and sculpted red lips. Her voice was mellifluous and her smile brilliant. She was dignified and intelligent, and she was elegant in even the smallest gesture. I was an assemblage of scars and bony protuberances and spiky hair, inept in small things and a failure at large ones. When I was around her, I felt as common as a mongrel. And my cheap clothes made me itch.

"I'm his new manager," she said. "Maybe mentor is a better term."

"A mentor?" her father asked. "What do you need mentoring in, son?"

"Everything." Isobel cut me up with her eyes. "You can tell just by looking at him."

"I want to know how I won my match with Sonny Smith," I demanded. "He should've been able to beat me wearing a straightjacket."

She laughed but didn't volunteer any information.

My voice sounded like I was tattling. "Your daughter has proposed some crazy deal, and now she thinks she owns me."

"Isabel tells me you just defeated a ranked opponent." Lawrence walked to a side-bar and reached for a crystal decanter and two goblets. "Doesn't sound like too bad of a deal to me."

"And tell me what's in that desk in the warehouse." I put on a look of ill-usage. "Otherwise, I'm not going to volunteer to be almost killed again."

Lawrence poured amber liquid into both goblets, then handed one to his daughter and one to me. Then he returned for a goblet for himself. He said, "In all likelihood, nothing is in that desk."

"That's not true, Daddy. I know precisely what is in the desk."

He raised his glass to me, then took a dainty drink. I usually throw back whatever liquid I get my hands on, but I sipped, too.

It was fiery. I inhaled through me teeth. The liquid ate its way down my throat.

He said, 'Thirty-six-year-old single malt scotch whiskey."

She held her scotch but didn't drink it. "I've proven what's in the desk, and you know it, Dad."

"So you keep saying, Isobel. I can only hope you are correct."

I asked, "So what's in the desk?"

She looked at me, weighing my very existence. Her voice cool and low, she said, "I'm about to reveal to you the most important thing in my life."

I nodded.

"It's my great secret and my great ambition," she said in the tone of a prayer. "It is the thing that keeps me alive. It's my soul." She finally sipped her scotch, eyeing me above the goblet's rim. At last, she said, "It's a poem."

"A poem?"

"It's pronounced *poem*, not pome." She raked her hair with her fingers. "Why is my life filled with imbeciles?" She looked heavenward. "What have I done?"

I asked, "I almost got shot for a poem?"

"It is Edgar Allan Poe's lost poem," she said. "It may be the finest poem ever written by an American."

"Poe?" I asked by way of a dig. "I think I've heard of him."

But she wasn't listening. Isobel had been caught up in her own passion again, just as she had been in front of her class. Her face gained a scarlet hue, and her glittering eyes were on the middle distance. Lord only knew what they were seeing. "Not just the finest by an American. It may be the grandest working of the English language ever in history."

I took another drink of scotch. It had the faint scent of oak. I could get used to drinking this.

Her voice took on the hypnotic pulse of a southern radio preacher.

"No one has ever seen this poem, except the man who wrote it, Poe, and the man he sent it to. It took me six long and grueling years, but I've found it. It is literature for the ages. It is priceless."

"The poem have a name?" I asked.

My question startled her. She had forgotten anyone else was in the room. Her eyes whipped around to me. She appeared feverish. "The Lost Land."

"I dare say you haven't found it yet, dear," Lawrence said.

She pointed at me as if I were a stick of furniture. "That poem is as good as mine if I can get this big lump to help me."

Her father asked, "Why not enroll Charles to help? He's a bright boy."

She laughed derisively as she rose from her chair and walked toward me. She reached for my goblet.

"May I borrow this?" she asked sweetly.

She lifted the glass from my hand. It was now mostly empty. "Father, watch this." With that, Isobel gripped the stem, and cracked the goblet against my skull. The goblet shattered, and glass shards clattered off my shoulder and fell to the floor. Drops of the whiskey slid down my face.

She said, "I love my fiancé, Charles, but that would have killed him."

I hadn't even flinched. I'd been hurt worse by ring opponents' stares. She walked over to Lawrence, and they spoke awhile, scheming, me forgotten again. I wiped whisky from my face.

I was left standing there, puzzling more about Isobel Autrey. I was teasing when I had asked her father whether she was a nutcase. But I was beginning to think I had been accurate. A nutcase, pure and simple.

4

"Have you ever rowed a boat before?" I was sitting on the stern plank.

"Plenty of times," Isobel Autrey whispered.

"Have you ever rowed one in a straight line? I'm going to be the first person in history to get seasick on the Mississippi River."

She pulled on the oars. Her black pants and black sweatshirt, black shoes and socks were her version of a Ninja outfit, I suppose. A small wind spread catspaws in front of our boat. The river reflected red and yellow lights from streetlights and warehouses and offices.

The moon was high overhead, and its reflection on the water was brassy and shimmering. Upriver, the ferry to Angiers was making its last run of the day. Filled with conventioneers, the sternwheeler Delta Queen was midstream, heading back to its moorage.

We were approaching the Rousseau Street Dock, gliding toward the pylons that held the warehouse over the river. A flashlight was in my pocket. Our boat was a twelve-foot-long lapstrake flatbottom. Isobel worked the oars like a landlubber, and the rowboat slid along irregularly, but after a fashion the old building loomed overhead, blotting out the peppering of stars. The warehouse floor was above us. Isobel's oars cracked loudly against wood as she maneuvered us among the grid of pylons. Small waves lapped against boulders on the shore. The water was black.

"It's this one," I whispered. "Here's the ladder."

Not a ladder, but one-by-twos hammered onto the pylon at the corner of the warehouse, probably used by carpenters in the past. Several of the rungs were missing, and a few looked wobbly. Isobel backed the boat so the stern bumped the pylon.

I tugged a rung. It seemed secure.

I asked in a low voice, "Nobody's up there, right?"

"Right."

"Then why are we sneaking around?"

"I can't be certain nobody is up there. I did my best."

I had described the counterfeiters to her, and so she had spent the day in her car, parked fifty yards from the Rousseau Street Dock, binoculars in hand. She saw the counterfeiters leave the warehouse's street-side door carrying a printer, which they loaded into the back of a Dodge minivan.

They made several other trips back and forth, loading cartons, but not furniture. The counterfeiters were moving quickly, fleeing the building, Isobel had said. Maybe my visit had spooked them. But they had not taken any furniture, not a stick of it. The counterfeiters had sped away in the van. So the desk was still in the warehouse. She had remained in her car, watching the warehouse the rest of that day. The two men never came back, at least, not while she was watching.

She had come to me and had said, "We can peak into the warehouse from the river side. There's a ladder on a pylon. You won't have to go through the front door."

So there I was, rising in the unsteady rowboat, then lifting a foot over the transom to place it on a rung. Isobel didn't compensate for the shift in weight with her oars, and I had one foot on the rung and one on the aft bench, and the boat drifted away from the pylon, so I hung there above the water, my legs spread like a wishbone, water below me.

"Row backwards," I whispered fiercely. "Hurry."

She dug at the water with the oars. The boat slowly returned to the pylon. I tested a higher rung, then stepped up to it. I slowly climbed the pylon as Isobel tied the boat to a rung. I reached the warehouse deck. A loading platform stood out twelve feet from the riverside wall of the warehouse. I climbed up a wobbly outside set of stairs up to the windows on the second floor. Isobel followed me. Her face had gained a feral cast, closing in on her prey.

At the top of the stairs was a landing that led to a door. I knelt below window level and pulled out the flashlight. If they were in there, we were going to scramble back down the ladder and come up with another plan, so she had said. I brought my head up to peer through the dingy window. Too dark to see anything. Isobel climbed up to the landing. I flicked on the flashlight and quickly scanned the room.

"Nobody inside," I said.

She twisted the door knob. "It's not locked."

She reached for my flashlight, and in she went. I followed her. The place smelled of tar and rot.

The flashlight beam found a mound of splintered wood in the center of the room. A hundred pieces lay there, piled haphazardly.

"Oh, God," she said. "It's the desk. They broke apart my desk."

And on the pile of fractured wood was a piece of paper, tacked to one of the desk's legs. I lifted the wood leg and brought up the note to our eyes. She pointed the flashlight at it.

She read aloud. "'We have what you were looking for. Bring $20,000 to the front door of St. Louis Cathedral Sunday at noon. Mess with us, and we'll destroy it.'"

St. Louis Cathedral was the ancient house of worship on Jackson Square in the French Quarter.

"How do you know that this pile of splinters is the desk you are looking for?" I asked.

She aimed the flashlight back and forth on the pile. She pulled out a piece of thin leather the size of a blotter. "Here's the leather inlay. Take a look." She aimed the beam at a corner of leather rectangle. "Here's an embossed swan." She held up the note, studying it. "Twenty thousand dollars? Not a problem."

"You going to call the police?" I asked.

"The poem is a bargain at twenty thousand. I'm going to pay the ransom."

"How do you know they'll give you the damned thing after you hand over the money?"

She brought her gaze around to me. "They'll give it to you. You'll make them."

I put my hands up. "Not me. They almost killed me the first time. I'm done with them. And now that I've brought you to your desk, I'm done with you."

Once again, she lit into me with her eyes. I don't know how she did, this peculiar effect: my intelligence—such as it was—began to escape me.

She said, "Dennis, I'm going to transform your miserable life. You don't dare turn aside what I can offer you."

The force was entirely gone from my voice. "I'm done with you."
She led me to the door. "You think?"

•

Isobel gripped my arm as if it were a life ring, and we stepped
into Jelly's on Decatur Street in the French Quarter. Zydeco washed
over us, that magnetic combination of a squeeze-box, fiddle, guitar
and rhythm section.

The dance joint was lit by neon beer signs and stage lights, and
it was crowded with dancers and drinkers, both working hard at
their tasks. Jelly's was several blocks off Bourbon, so the patrons
were mostly locals. This was a Friday evening, and the place was
hopping.

"You come here often?" Isobel asked me over the roar of the
band.

My voice was nicely prim. "After a day studying Edgar Allan Poe,
I find it a refreshing release."

She dug her nails into my arm, and I don't mean gently. She
looked around, entirely out of her element. "I mean, what do you do
here?"

"I drink beer."

She said, "That sounds like so much fun."

The band's name was the Swamp Soul Kings, and they were
playing a crowd favorite, From the Indies to the Andes in his Undies.
The drummer was earning his living, banging his hides and throwing
sweat in all directions, and the guitar player's back was wet with it,
the stage was so small. The washboard player had thimbles on his
fingers. Working a four-string Fender, the bass player was in a coma,
like most bass players, but was laying down the groove anyway. The
accordionist danced to his own music, grinning at the audience and
singing into a microphone in a smoker's voice.

The song ended and the MC leaped onto stage to shout into a
mike, "Give it up for the Swamp Soul Kings. Give it up."

The audience applauded and the dancers returned to their chairs.
A barmaid passed a hat. Preserved in all its fierceness, an alligator
was hung above the backbar, its mouth open and its villainous yellow
teeth all business. The bar and backbar were more than a hundred
years old, and featured ornate moldings and beveled glass, still
grand though they had been nicked and chafed over the years. On a
backbar shelf was a cobra wrapped around a mongoose, the cobra's

neck in the mongoose's jaw, one of those taxidermal nightmares sailors brought back from the Pacific after World War Two.

As we walked toward the tables, a couple of men at the bar leered at Isobel Autrey, but I gave them my ring stare and they quickly dropped their eyes. A beat-up face like mine doesn't have many advantages but that's one of them.

The tables were close together, and we found an empty one near the street window. A neon Miller Lite sign on the window made Isobel's skin seem translucent and her hair as dark as oil. She glanced around like a tourist. Jelly's might have been Timbuktu.

A waiter came over. "Hi, Dennis." He put his hand on my shoulder and gave it a squeeze, the gesture saying, *Wow, where'd you get the girl?* "Something for you and the lady?"

Isobel said, "I'll have an Annabel Fizzer, please, but go a little light on the raspberry syrup."

The waiter stared at her.

I said, "Two Buds."

When he had gone, Isobel said, "If I'm to help you, I need to complete your profile."

Yes, I had renewed my deal with her. My theory is that she had hypnotized me.

I said, "Just get me a fight against another ranked opponent, and then do whatever you did last time against Sonny Smith, whatever you did to make me win."

"Getting you another fight doesn't reform you."

"To hell with reforming me. I'm not going to meet those two counterfeiters and get your poem unless you already have a fight lined up."

"My goal is to complete your personal evolution, from you as you sit there tonight, to human being." She touched the tip of her chin, as if exploring a bruise. "As I see it, Dennis, your problem is that you have— How may I say this? An insufficiently developed concept of taste."

"What does that mean?"

"The difference between the Three Tenors and the Three Stooges eludes you."

"So what?" I asked.

"An appreciation of certain refinements would add much joy to your life."

I gestured to encompass the dance joint. "Good beer, good zydeco music, a goofy conversation. What could be better than this?"

"Point out one refined item in this bar." She spread her hands. "Select something that isn't drenched in tawdriness."

I looked around. Three young ladies were sitting at a table to one side of the stage, near the bassist's amp. They knew they were drawing glances, and they were laughing and gesturing in an exaggerated manner, their drinks in front of them.

I nodded toward one of them. "Her. The blond. She's nicely refined."

Isobel affected a look of mortal shock. "Why don't you just kill me, Dennis, rather than torturing me every minute?"

"What's wrong with her?"

"Well, let's just see." She held up her fingers to count them off. "Her eyelashes peel off. She bought her fingernails in a store. Her hair is a color only a severe chemical reaction can produce, and then she spent hours teasing it to get that perfect grenade-explosion look. She's wearing so much makeup her head is about to drop forward and bang the table from the weight. And her bosom has been pneumatically enhanced in some clinic."

"She's perfect, is what you're saying."

"You are missing some synapses in your brain, is what I'm saying."

Our beers arrived. I took a few gulps, glad to have something to do with my mouth other than to talk with Isobel.

"Where are you from, Dennis?" she asked. "You aren't from around here, are you?"

I wiped my mouth with the back of a hand. "From Port Angeles, up in Washington State, if I'm from anywhere."

"Everyone is from somewhere."

"I left Port Angeles when I was fourteen. Haven't been back. I hardly remember the place."

"Your parents moved somewhere else?"

"My father moved to hell, is what happened."

She looked at me, waiting for me to say more.

"He was a logger and a drunk in about equal proportions. One day he went out on a log raft without his caulk boots, and he slipped into the water between two logs, and the logs drifted together, and popped his head."

"You didn't get along with him?"

"He wasn't too bad when he wasn't beating me. He'd come home drunk and he would teach me to box, so to speak." I drew off the last of my beer.

"And your mother?"

"I don't have any memory of her. Not of her face, anyway."

"Did your dad talk about her?" Isobel asked.

"If I asked about her, he'd cuff my ear. Sometimes when he was swearing, he'd use her name. I've never seen a photo of my mother."

"Well, I wonder ..." Isobel's words faded. She touched the corner of her eye, and if I didn't know her to be tough, I'd have thought she was wiping away a tear. No chance of that, I suppose.

Her voice a little grainy, she said, "Well, let's hope your mother didn't look like you."

I signaled for another beer.

She asked, "Where did you go when you left Port Angeles?"

I shrugged. "I drifted around. Couple of foster homes. Went to school when I could. Worked when I had to. Tried to be a prize fighter, but you've seen how that turned out."

"We don't know how it turned out." She smiled at me. "Not yet we don't."

I was suddenly angry, her asking about things I try every day to forget. My worthless father and vanished mother. But I wasn't angry with her. With me.

My voice was tight. "I just can't get any traction, damn it, Isobel. Thirty-four years, and I can't seem to ..." I cut myself off. A guy with a cauliflower ear shouldn't be heard to whine. I rallied with, "Your old man is a cool dude, although he talks like he misplaced a cork. What about your mom?"

Isobel looked away, and when she turned back her face was vulnerable. "My mom is in an institution. It's a home, nicely staffed with the finest doctors and nurses, all of which Dad can afford. But it's a home for people with mental problems."

"An insane asylum?" I asked.

"They aren't called that these days."

"A nut bin? What?"

She explained to me like I was four years old, "My mom is a schizophrenic."

I resisted the urge to say at least Isobel came by it honestly, willing to spend $20,000 to ransom a poem.

"Mom has been at the Sunlight House for years," Isobel said. "She is taking a battery of new medicines."

"Do you ever see her?"

"Three times a week."

"Will she ever come back to your dad's home?" I asked.

"Maybe this year."

"So she's making progress?"

Isobel replied "It's been at least six months since she has mistaken me for Druida, Queen of the Plague."

The band drifted back toward the stage. The drummer climbed up and placed himself on the throne behind his kit, lifted his sticks and gave himself a rim shot. The bass player put his guitar strap over a shoulder.

"But I'm here to talk about you, Dennis, and to enroll you in the School of Isobel."

I laughed.

She said in the slightly hectoring tone of a schoolteacher, "We begin tonight, teaching you about the finer things in life. That's our first step."

"You get me a good fight, and I'll try to get your poem. That's our only step."

The washboard player climbed up to the stage and put his rig over his head so it rested on his shoulders. The guitar player ran off a lick.

"Our first lesson is: quality, not quantity," Isobel said. "Got that, Dennis? Quality, not quantity. Follow me."

She rose from her chair and stepped between tables toward the stage. I trailed after her.

Halfway to the stage, she turned and said, "Don't say anything, no matter what happens. Keep your lips zipped."

She walked up to the table where these three young ladies sat. The one with the blond hair and pneumatic chest, as Isobel had called it, smiled invitingly at me.

Isobel said, "My brother, Dennis, and I are having an argument. Would you help us settle it?"

The blond said, "Sure," and so did the other two, game for most anything.

These were three nice looking women, out for a fun night.

If Isobel would go away, maybe I could join them, dance a while though I dance like I box, which is to say, not well. We were near the bandstand, and stage lights threw colors on us.

"He has been cloistered since he was eighteen," Isobel said.

"What's cloistered mean?" asked the blond.

Isobel stared at her, her smile fixed as if it had been varnished. "He is a monk at the St. Angina Monastery in Port Angeles, Washington."

"Wow, a religious person." The blond removed her hand from her scotch and soda.

"I'm trying to talk him out of going back to the monastery. He's wasting his life."

One of the other ladies said, "He doesn't look like a monk. He looks like he uses his head for a hammer."

"It's a tough, tough monastery," Isobel explained.

She was talking nonsense, of course, but her words and gestures and expressions carried the weight of sincerity and truth. She was utterly convincing. She was a good liar, is what it was. I'd have to remember that.

"Brother Dennis has no idea what he is missing," Isobel said, worry and hurt on her face. "No talking, no music except chanting, no television, porridge twice a day, and—" She paused a beat. "No women."

The girls quickly looked among themselves.

Isobel said, "Not once, ever, if you know what I mean."

One of the other young ladies said, "Hey, this sounds like a con to get one of us to take your brother home for the night."

Isobel held up a hand. "I wouldn't think of suggesting it. Such a night—" She looked meaningfully at the blond. "Would kill Dennis. He is in a fragile state, his awareness limited by all his praying, all that kneeling on cold stone floors."

"What then?" asked the blond.

Man, could she fill a blouse. I stood there, mute.

"Just a kiss," Isobel said. "Not even a long one. Just a good one, to give him something to ponder during his last night in New Orleans."

"A kiss?" the blond asked. "Just a short kiss?"

"And maybe he won't get on the Greyhound tomorrow morning," Isobel said.

"Why not?" the blond gushed. She rose from her chair.

The squeezebox player stepped by us to jump up to the stage.

"Burn Brother Dennis up," encouraged one of the other girls. "Show him what you're made of."

The blond looked at me like I was the last piece of bacon on the platter. "Brace yourself, Brother Dennis."

She stepped forward, all breasts and hips, bountiful and lush, and applied herself to me, toes to forehead, her arms gathering me in and pressing me into her. She planted her mouth on mine, and her lips were living things, moving all round, grinding against my teeth, her tongue like an eel in my mouth. Startled, I took a half-step back, but she clung to me like a vine, reaming out my mouth with her tongue, moving her hips against me until she had to take a breath. She finally stepped back.

Then she looked at me, waiting for my judgment, coy smile on her much-exercised lips. I'm sure my expression resembled a stunned carp.

"That was indeed a powerful smooch," Isobel said. "If anything will keep Brother Dennis from a life of contemplation and good works, it was that kiss."

Isobel turned me by the shoulders so that I was square to her, and she once again—I'll never understand the mechanics of it—bored into my brain with her eyes, and abruptly the blond and her friends and everything in Jelly's ceased to exist, leaving only those glittering blue orbs that somehow paralyzed me.

"Pay close attention, Dennis," she said in a low voice.

Then she leaned toward me, rose on her toes, brought her lips to my ear—my good ear, not my cauliflower ear—and I'm not sure what happened next.

As best I could reconstruct it later, she did these things in this order: she lightly, on the verge of imagination, drew her damp lower lip along my ear, then she breathed her hot-house breath into my ear, and then she sank her teeth into my earlobe, unleashing some force within me that raised the hair on my neck and stopped the breath in my throat and made neon colors dance at the edge of my vision. My knees shook and my fingertips went numb.

She had short-circuited me, put too much charge through too thin a wire, is what happened. And when my eyes could find her again, she was under the beam of a stage light that turned her skin red and added a fiery auburn sheen to her hair. And at that instant, the band kicked in with their second set, and the bass rumble from the speaker enveloped her.

The noise from the amp came in grinding punches. The sound was a bottomless rumble, loud and deep waves that coursed over Isobel and rippled her hair and clothes and skin.

I touched my earlobe and came away with dampness. She had drawn blood. I shivered. She was staring at me, her teeth shiny and red under the stage, her hair writhing as if it were reptilian.

She leaned toward the blond's ear and said loudly over the band's noise, "You've given Brother Dennis much to think about."

Isobel took me by the elbow and guided me through the tables, the young ladies giggling behind us. The band was playing If My Nose Were Full of Nickels, I'd Blow It All On You, and the squeezebox player was doing the singing. I was still having trouble catching my breath.

As we neared Jelly's door, she asked above the music, "So tell me, Dennis, which was better? What Blondie did—her big hip-shaking, tongue-mashing, slobbering smack. Or what I did?"

I touched my ear again. "What did you do, exactly?"

She laughed lightly. "Tell me, which was more fun?"

"It wasn't fun," I said. "Having someone draw my blood with her teeth isn't fun."

"Then which was more intriguing?"

I wondered if I was being asked to incriminate myself. "Yours, for sure. More intriguing."

We stepped out onto Decatur Street. A fellow wearing a T-shirt reading *Show Me Your Bazoos* passed us.

"So you see?" she asked. "Quality, not quantity."

"Isobel, may I ask you something personal?"

"No."

Sometimes I listen to her, sometimes I don't. "You and your fiancé, the skin doctor?"

"Charles. Yes?"

We walked around a street performer playing a harmonica through a bullet microphone and a small, battery-powered amplifier.

I said, "I mean, I presume you and he are ... are close."

"We are—" She paused to imitate my awkward timing. "Are

close, yes."

"How does he survive it?"

Her laugh came from her belly. "Oh, Charles survives it." We took a few steps, then she added gaily, "But it's close."

5

The skin doctor, Charles Brooks, you'll remember him. Isobel's fiancé. I saved his life twice—*twice*—within sixty seconds, and he never thanked me once, that being the nature of ingrates.

The Knights of the Arcadian Peacock needed a bartender, and Charles Brooks thought of me. Two hundred bucks plus tips to pour drinks. I couldn't pass it up. I make some of my living as a bouncer on Bourbon Street, and sometimes I have to step behind a bar and mix drinks, so I know vodka from beer, but not too much else. I had to sign a document saying that I would keep secret whatever I witnessed at the Knights of the Arcadian Peacock event

Louisiana has more secrets than anywhere else in the United States. I'm convinced this is true though I don't have hard evidence, such being the nature of secrets. It's a combination of French and African and Spanish and Anglo heritages, swamp gas, heat and humidity, the meandering river, the eerie dangling moss, the feathers and masks, and the Lord only knows what else.

I had never before heard of the Knights of the Arcadian Peacock, and I first thought they were a New Orleans krewe, one of the groups that builds and rides the floats for Mardi Gras, tossing bead necklaces and shiny doubloons to the spectators, but no, the Knights were no such thing.

I hopped a ride with the other bartender for the event, out into the low country west of New Orleans. His name was Johnny Dykes and he drove a yellow 1988 Cutlass that had the back seat removed so he could put more boxes of liquor in the car. Bartending was his business. Rust spots the size of maple leaves covered the Cutlass. We drove down a country lane, the beat-up Cutlass sounding like it needed the Heimlich maneuver.

Johnny Dykes was as thin as a hose, and his white cotton shirt hung loosely on him. He wore his black hair in a bouffant, with sideburns down to his earlobes. He was missing two lower teeth. His face was pinched and disillusioned.

He always spoke out of the side of his mouth as if he were telling you some great confidence, didn't matter what he was talking about, could be about the weather. This time he said, "You ain't seen nothing like this outfit."

He turned the Cutlass off the country road onto a long driveway. We stopped at a gatehouse but the guard waved us through, recognizing the dilapidated car. We drove under a canopy of live oak, then came to the clubhouse—I learned later they called it the grand lodge, an enormous Greek Revival structure with eight white columns in the front and the same number on the other sides, each column with a circumference of eight feet. A wide veranda surrounded the house behind the columns, and above the veranda was a balcony. Black fretwork was on the balcony between the pillars. The roof had many dormers.

A doorman stood on the veranda. Two valets waited at their stand, but they didn't casts a second glance at the Cutlass rustbucket. We drove along the side of the lodge to the rear, passing a walled-in swimming pool and two tennis courts, finally reaching the service buildings.

"Costs two hundred big ones to join this club," Johnny Dykes said. "And then you pay forty grand every year in dues."

"I'll stick with the Old Al's gym," I said. That's where I worked out.

"Most people in New Orleans never heard of the Knights of the Arcadian Peacock. Only five hundred members." Dykes lowered his voice, as if there were someone listening in the back of the car. "Five years ago, Hugh LaBlanc, the sugar cane heir, hung himself two days after he was blackballed here."

We passed a carriage house, now used as the kitchen. The buildings were surrounded by lawn dotted with maple and oak trees. Flower beds were laid with precision. An animal, maybe a water buffalo, had been carved from a huge bush. I think it's called topiary.

Dykes parked the car in the staff lot and led me into a small brick building that had once been a smoke house and was now a supply shed. A number of white coats were on hangers. We sifted through them until we found ones that fit. They looked like lab coats, except that stitched medallions were over the hearts. The medallions were of a blue and green peacock, the Knights' mascot.

We picked our way between banks of lilac bushes to the pool area, and spent a few minutes setting up the bar, pulling bottles from their cartons and filling the ice bin, slicing oranges, setting out olives and miniature onions, and such like. The pool had no slide or diving board, nothing for children or teens. Four gold peacock statues were at one end of the pool, issuing streams of water from their open mouths into the pool. Lounging chairs were stacked to one side. Under the water's surface, the sides of the pool were tiled with green peacocks on yellow fields. Stone planters marked the edges of the pool area, and were filled with white freesias which accounted for the heady jungle scent all around.

The band entered and started setting up. Six guys carrying crates. Then I noticed they were all drummers, putting up kettle drums and snares and tom-toms and cymbals. Not a guitar or a trumpet in the lot of them. Trays of hors d'oeuvres began arriving and were displayed on a table next to ours. Day was fading quickly, and a staff member walked around the pool area lighting enormous brass torches fueled by propane.

Johnny Dykes said, "This club is two hundred years old. Five Louisiana governors and eight senators have been members, though they don't put it on their resumes."

Bobbing in the pool was a papier-mache peacock, its tail in full display. It was painted emerald green, except for its feathers which alternated blue and red and green. Also in the pool were floating torches that threw wavering light on the papier-mache peacock.

Dykes tapped an aluminum keg, then poured and discarded several glasses of foam until beer started to run. Rimming the pool area, flags displayed crescents and moons, peacocks, palm fronds, triangles, the letter eight, and a fleur-de-lis, and I suppose they all symbolized something, but I hadn't a clue.

Then the drummers began an intense rhythm, all of them beating their skins and cymbals. The door to the lodge opened, and out marched two lines of rainbow-colored turkeys. At least, that's what I first thought, a mass of yellow and red and purple feathers, coming through the door in a loose march. They weren't turkeys, but were men with feathers all over them.

As they drew closer, coming toward the pool in their procession, I saw the costumes were similar to Mardi Gras attire; peacock, pheasant, ostrich and turkey feathers arrayed from headdresses and garters and arm bands and belts.

There was more to these costumes than feathers. The man at the head of the column wore a crown, which included a white fur miniver along the forehead, a silver circlet and imperial arches. In his hand was a crosier, which was a long staff on which was a silver orb.

Some of the knights wore silver chains across their feathered breasts. Others wore green sashes, I presumed indications of rank. Their slippers were adorned with rosettes. One knight carried a scale of justice. Six knights marched with medieval halberds. Charles Brooks told me all these costume terms later.

The feathers had been dyed vivid colors: blood red, loud purple, bright yellow, ocean blue. The costumes of the Knights of the Arcadian Peacock didn't really resemble peacocks, but rather peacocks as viewed through a kaleidoscope by someone on drugs.

Four of the knights carried a palanquin on which sat Charles Brooks. He took gulps from the tumbler of scotch he carried. The sides of the palanquin were adorned with peacocks carved in relief, and painted blue and green. Brooks was dressed like all the others, in feathered finery, but every one of his feathers was white, flowing from his arms and down his back. He wore an expression that mixed solemnity and high humor. He was clearly the man of honor.

The procession made its way toward us, moving slowly, rounding the pool. At one end of the patio was a bronze school bell suspended from a wood arc, the clapper visible just below the bell's rim. A rope hung from the clapper.

Johnny Dykes was mixing bourbon and water one glass after another, and he set the amber drinks in a row on our table.

He ordered, "Pour some scotch and water."

I complied, putting a shot and a half into each glass.

Dykes said out of the side of his mouth. "They do this couple times a year, whenever one of the knights is about to get married."

"Do they always dress in feathers?" I asked.

"Only for the important ceremonies, like tonight."

The procession of men slowly passed our table, some of their feathers brushing the white table cloth. Many of the marchers reached for the drinks we had lined up. Some of the knights were unsteady. I gathered that the ceremony had begun inside the lodge, accompanied by much libation.

The grand marshal—the fellow with the crown, raised his orbed staff and called out, "Corpulas mutatis loci."

My Latin is rusty, so I can't translate. The parade fell out, and the knights rushed the bar, clearing away our stockpile of mixed drinks and grabbing them from us the instant we poured more. Turning on a spit above a brick-lined pit was a pig, the entire sorry animal from snout to curly tail.

The knights had been silent during their entrance to the pool area, but now they laughed and hooted. Knights who hadn't as yet greeted each other engaged in a handshake involving two pumps then locking the little fingers together.

The palanquin was lowered, and Charles Brooks unsteadily stepped to the ground. A knot of knights surrounded him, patting him on his feathered shoulder and nodding encouragement. The line at the bar was four deep, and I worked quickly. One of the knights handed Brooks another scotch and water, and the doctor drained half of it in one quaff.

The knights liked fire, that was clear with all the torches and the barbecuing pig. But there was another blaze going, one I couldn't account for. It was an open brazier resembling a barbecue, but it was on the lawn at the edge of the pool. One of the knights tended it, sliding kindling onto the fire. Protruding from the fire was a length of iron. The percussionists maintained a driving, hypnotic beat. I poured drinks in rhythm to the drums.

Johnny Dykes leaned sideways. "Charles Brooks is getting married soon."

I nodded.

"I hear his fiancée is a real piece of work. You ever met her?"

"Nah." I didn't want to talk about Isobel Autrey.

Dykes spoke just above the persistent sound of the drums. "So when a Knight of the Arcadian Peacock becomes engaged to be married, he gets a reminder of where he came from." Dykes laughed. "That's what this big hoe-down is all about."

Two knights asked for beer, so I turned to the spigot. The place was loud, what with all the laughing and drumming. I passed schooners to them.

Dykes said, "The guy who just took the beer. He's the son of Lawton Remler who owns Remler Lines, the container ship company. And the guy he's talking with—the fat fellow smoking the ten-inch stogie, is Reg LaPierre, grandson of the founder of First Louisiana State Bank."

LaPierre's huge peacock feathers were attached to his belt, and the tips of them brushed the ground.

"What's a skin doctor doing in this crowd?" I asked.

Pouring steadily, Dykes looked at me from the corner of his eye. "Charles Brooks? He's the son of Fairfield Brooks, founder of Brooks Chemical with those big plants on the river at English Turn and upstate in Baton Rouge. Those yellow mounds you see coming down the river on barges—the sulfur? That's all from Brooks Chemical."

I asked, "If Charles has so much money, what's he doing lancing boils every day?"

Dykes shrugged. "Gives him something to do, I suppose."

The chief poobah rang the bell five times. The drums fell quiet. Many of the knights grabbed one last drink from our table before forming a circle. The poobah placed himself in the middle of the circle, and he was joined by the knight carrying the scale of justice, and another knight I hadn't seen before, one wearing the same feathers but also a red hood. Only his eyes were visible behind slits in the cloth.

"That fellow with the red hood is called the Grand and Royal Artisan," Dykes said.

The Grand and Royal Artisan held his feathered arms aloft. He loudly called, "Sir Charles, step forward if you dare and meet your fate."

Brooks handed his bourbon to another knight. With inebriated confidence, he walked to the center of the circle to stand in front of the Grand and Royal Artisan, who placed a hand on Charles's shoulder. Charles rocked up on his toes, grinning widely.

The Incubator announced, "The Knights of the Arcadian Peacock gather today to reaffirm our eternal links with Sir Charles. He will soon take upon himself the bonds of holy matrimony."

Some snorts and snickers and chuckles, and a few amens. The knights had been consuming prodigious amounts of alcohol, and it was beginning to show.

"But a knight of the Arcadian Peacock cannot ever leave our brotherhood. His oath of obedience is unto death."

A tipsy knight near our table said, "Isobel Autrey? You lucky SOB, Charles."

Another chimed in, "How'd you ever talk Isobel Autrey into marriage with you, Charles?"

More laughs.

The Incubator banged his staff on the ground. "No knight must forget his oaths."

I poured more bourbon, passing them out to knights who broke ranks to rush the drink table.

"So every knight of the Arcadian Peacock submits his flesh to a permanent reminder of our eternal commitment," the Incubator said loudly.

The knights with chains across their chests stepped forward. Two of them ceremoniously removed Charles's shoes, breaches and stockings, exposing his legs. His thighs were muscled from his jogging. He was wearing boxer shorts, which the dukes left on him.

Charles extended his arms, and each was gripped by a duke.

"Have you prepared yourself, Sir Charles?" the Incubator asked.

He tried to make his voice solemn, but he giggled. "I have."

"Do you submit your flesh for mortification?"

"I do."

"Dukes, secure Sir Charles to the earth, just as he is secured by his oath," the Incubator ordered.

Their feathers rippling, two dukes knelt to spread Charles's feet, exposing his thighs. Each gripped an ankle with both hands, and held that position. Charles stood there, anchored to the ground..

"Mort ignitious el grecco," intoned the Incubator. "I call upon the Grand and Royal Artisan to do his duty. Excalibur duo nundus."

Moving with the slow and deliberate step of a flower girl at a wedding, the Artisan moved toward the open brazier, the crowd of knights parting in front of him. When he reached the fire pit, he raised his arms toward the moon and wiggled so that his feathers shimmied. Then the Artisan reached down to pull out the rod that had been heating in the fire.

He held it aloft like a prize. The tip of it glowed. It was a brand.

The drums began again, this time with an insistent ONE, two, three, four, ONE, two, three, four, a victory rhythm, an ancient call to dance around a fire holding scalps high, trophies from that day's battle.

"They're going to brand Charles?" I asked.

"These sissies?" Dykes said out of the side of his mouth. "Are you kidding? It's all a big pantomime."

The Grand and Royal Artisan walked back through the circle of knights, the glowing brand held in both hands like a broadsword. All the knights began shaking their arms and legs, making their feathers shimmer and shake. The Artisan stepped up to Charles Brooks. The heated metal faded from red to purple.

The Incubator's words were delivered with a liturgical cadence. "Never must Charles forget that he is once a knight and always a knight and ever a knight."

The knights shimmied their feathers. "Grand and Royal Artisan, apply the eternal reminder."

The Artisan knelt before Charles Brooks, who was still in the grip of the four dukes. The Artisan held the brand in front of Brooks' eyes a moment so he could study it. The burning tip was about the size of a fifty-cent piece. I couldn't make out the design. The skin doctor's smile was steady.

Down came the brand to Brooks' leg. The drum beat quickened.

"You, Charles, must never forget," called out the Artisan.

And with that, instead of applying the brand to Charles, the Artisan made a small stabbing gesture at the air with the rod, and all the Knights, every one of them, hissed loudly between their teeth. *Hisssssssss*, they all went. But the brand never touched Charles. It was all pantomime, just as Dykes has said. Every feather on every knight was shimmied. *Hisssssssss*.

The knights began circling Brooks and the Incubator and Artisan. They chanted, "Krinkton maybo, sobolay, hiyamana," over and over, in time with the drums. Maybe it was Creole or Spanish, or maybe their own secret language. I didn't know.

Brooks bowed low, accepting congratulations. A knight passed him a full glass of bourbon. The drums rolled and thundered. The knights twitched their feathers and stomped their feet, slowly walking in their circle, calling out their mantra, some knights staggering under their burdens of bourbon and scotch and beer.

Then a knight lurched into one of the propane torches. It teetered on its base. The knight tried to catch it but it was a drunken, clumsy effort, and the torch fell sideways, the fire flaring. The torch fell onto Charles Brooks.

Instantly his feathers were on fire, from his knees up to his shoulders, all in a flash.

Some knights gasped. Others laughed, maybe thinking it was a new twist to the ritual. The Incubator frowned, puzzled at the human torch standing next to him.

I leaped around the table, charged through the ranks of stunned and soused knights, grabbed Brooks by a wrist, dragged him through the feathered crowd—him resembling the burning bush—and body tackled him into the pool so hard that I fell into the water alongside him.

Brooks had only been on fire five seconds, and it was all over in less time than I just took to tell it. I'm quick on my feet, what with all that boxing I've suffered.

I surfaced and dog-paddled to the side of the pool to lift myself out. The drums were still beating. Many of the knights were still shivering their feathers. Others nodded vaguely at what they had just seen. It had happened so quickly, I don't think it registered on most of them. Dripping water with every step, I returned to the drink table, and Dykes handed me several bar towels.

I looked for Brooks to emerge from the pool but he didn't. I waited, wiping water from my face and arms. Dykes told me to return to the outbuilding for a dry jacket. Charles Brooks still remained in the water. I wondered why.

I stepped back to the pool. There he was, lying on the bottom of the pool, some of the scorched feathers slowly floating up.

I dived in and swam to the pool's bottom and grabbed his collar. I kicked to the surface, bringing him with me. Then I pushed him to the pool's side. Some of the knights had gathered their wits, and they pulled Brooks from the pool, rolling him onto the patio. He coughed and sputtered. His eyes opened. The knights helped him sit up.

I climbed out of the pool again.

Brooks was covered in blackened feathers. He hadn't been burned much, just his feathers. The back of one hands had been charred, and his right ear was pink.

"Too much scotch to swim, I guess." He slurred his words.

Ash from the ritual thumbprint dripped down his forehead and along his nose. Several knights helped Brooks to his feet, then guided him toward the lodge, supporting the skin doctor by his arms.

Once again I returned to the drink table, and once again Johnny Dykes handed me towels. The knights were already lining up for more bourbon and scotch, laughing and chatting about the spectacle they'd just witnessed. Not one of them cast me a glance other than to locate my hand to grab a drink from it.

I imitated Dykes, speaking out of the side of my mouth. "I've always wanted to be wealthy, to have a rich father who left me a lot of money."

"Yeah?" he asked.

"Now I'm not so sure."

6

"Don't say anything to upset her," Isobel whispered, standing on the stool in her wedding dress. "Coral Thibideaux makes only twelve gowns a year. She does the beading by hand. She won't be rushed. The waiting list is always months and months."

I sat on another stool near a sewing table that was covered with bolts of satin and silk and a bobbin rack. An ancient treadle sewing machine was on the other side of me, near half a dozen yellow measuring tapes hung from a peg.

Isobel said, "Coral is the fourth generation Thibideaux who has made wedding gowns. When a Garden District daughter gets engaged, her mother immediately calls this shop to see when the wedding can be scheduled, and it's whenever the gown can be finished."

The tiny shop was on the second floor of a hundred-fifty-year-old stucco building on Ursuline Avenue in the French Quarter. A restaurant named Remoulade occupied the first floor. The only street-side evidence that wedding dresses were made above the restaurant was a small wood sign at the corner of the building that said Thibideaux. Hung from beams above the second floor balcony were baskets of ferns and orchids, and those baskets and the iron scrollwork on the balcony beams and railings were the view through the seamstress's windows.

Isobel shifted on the stool. "I didn't want to bother with a Thibideaux dress. I'm no twenty-year-old debutante, but Daddy insisted. Mom was wearing a Thibideaux when she and Dad were married."

Her white silk dress was sleeveless with scalloped pearl details on the neckline. Hand-embroidered flowers decorated the bodice. The train wasn't yet attached to the dress, but was hung over a nearby chair. Even though she was on a stool, the dress flowed almost to the floor because it had not been hemmed. The dress was still in several pieces, hung together with pins. Isobel's obsidian hair fell to her shoulders.

"How did you get me a fight with Antoine Doaks?" I asked.

Isobel grinned mischievously. "I called in some IOUs."

"How do you, a professor of literature at Tulane University, have any IOUs with the twelfth-ranking ABA heavyweight?"

"Ah, Dennis." Her voice was light and airy. "This must forever remain a mystery to you. Just like the multiplication table."

"Yeah, well, I've seen a video of Doaks' last fight. He's going to kill me."

Her look of mischief had turned to a look of devilry. "You never know, Dennis."

I looked around. "What kind of dressmaker burns incense sticks in every corner of her shop?"

The place was gamy, crowded with scents, almost unbreathable. Smoke from the incense sticks and the old lady's brazier crawled along the ceiling.

Isobel said, "She burns frangipani for friendship, rose for love, and sandalwood for protection."

I gestured toward a table. "What's all that—"

"Don't call it junk," she whispered fiercely, glancing through a door into a side room where the proprietress had gone to fetch something. "It's an altar."

"Candles and flags make an altar?"

Fifteen little flags were arranged around a table, each on a small stand. The flags were of many colors and designs, and most had sequins sewn onto them. The flags were surrounded by a dried branch from a bush. Dozens of silver and brass thimbles hung from branches by threads.

Isobel explained, "The flags honor the deities commonly known as Voodoo. And the branches and thimbles mark the boundary between the living and the dead."

"And what about the big candle?" I indicated a large, dripping mound of red wax that had seven lighted wicks.

"That's called a seven-knob candle. Each knob represents a wish, usually involving passion or romance."

"Voodoo gives me the creeps. And how come I have to sit here watching you get pinned up, and breathing these smelly fumes?"

"You asked how I know Edgar Allan Poe's poem was in that desk. So sit here while I tell you."

The room was filled with other candles, smaller with only single wicks, more like votive candles. They were all lit, the flames motionless because the air in the room was still and thick.

Coral Thibideaux entered with a grand swoop, moving quickly, her clothes trailing after her. She was wearing a Guinea brocade and damask skirt and a matching blouse with loose and flowing sleeves. The fabric was glossy purple, and the repeating embroidered pattern was cream-colored. Her head wrap was the same shiny purple.

This was the woman who had tossed a handful of ashes under my ring stool at the Sonny Smith fight. I hadn't let on that I recognized her, and didn't have the courage to ask what in the world she had been doing. Were they really ashes? Ashes of what?

"Let's work on the hem, Isobel." On Coral's wrist was a pincushion. "Then we'll look at the shoulders. I think it's still a little loose there." She glanced at me and said with a grin, "Maybe you'll learn something, Dennis, and you won't have to use your fists to make your living. Get yourself an honest job."

Coral had a mouth full of teeth, and her grin had enough wattage to power a small city. Her skin was the color of a chestnut, and her lips cranberry. Huge silver hoops hung from her ears. Isobel had introduced me by saying, "Dennis thinks he's a boxer." Coral bent to her work, pinning the dress at the right length. Her husband, Lou, was a mate on the Delta Queen, Isobel had told me.

Only then did I notice an old woman in a corner behind Isobel. The old lady was sitting on a low stool with a brazier at her feet. Coals glowed on the brazier's grate. She was so close to the fire that her dark skin, which had the texture of pine bark, glowed orange. She poked the little fire with a darning needle, tossed a handful of dried twigs onto the flames, then reached into an leather pouch for a pinch of something, and when she tossed them at the fire, licks of flame leaped up and sparked red and green.

The old lady's arms were as thin as rebar, and her fingers were long and bony, resembling talons. Her ankles were the diameter of my thumb. Wisps of her sparse white hair flitted above her scalp, hovering like insects. In her loose cotton dress, the old lady looked like a sack of bones.

"Hello?" I said.

"This is my aunt Bea," Coral said. "She doesn't talk much."

When Bea's black BB eyes found mine, my brain went blank, as if my cranium were being stirred with a spoon. She returned her attention to her little fire, and a few thoughts returned to me. Carol and Isobel acted as the old lady wasn't there, as if an ancient husk of a lady stirring up a fire in a seamstresses salon were entirely normal. If they could ignore her, so could I.

Isobel asked, "Did you know that Edgar Allan Poe was a boxer?"

"Yeah, and I wrote Gone With The Wind," I replied.

"Poe boxed at the University of Virginia and later at West Point. He was quite accomplished."

"Then he and I have something in common."

"Yes, you do have a little in common with him," she admitted. "But not much. At age thirteen, Poe was reading Cicero's *De Officis*, while you were reading Little Lulu comic books."

Coral laughed around the pins she was now holding between her lips.

"One of Poe's great themes was that nothing stays buried. You can see it in *The Fall of the House of Usher*, *The Tell-Tale Heart*, and many others."

"Just because I'm going to get your Poe poem doesn't mean I have to endure learning anything about him," I said.

Isobel looked at me as if I were a bug. "This poem's history reflects Poe's lifelong theme. *The Lost Land* wouldn't stay buried. It has surfaced. I've found it." Her face took on that rapturous expression I'd seen before whenever she talked about the poem. My face looked like that once when I found a twenty dollar bill lying in the street.

"Stand up straighter, girl," Coral ordered.

"Poe's *The Raven* was published in 1845, and Poe was instantly a celebrity."

"A celebrity? For publishing one poem?"

"Times change, Dennis. Poe was suddenly as famous as a rock band that has a number one hit today."

I was still skeptical.

A half dozen leather bags were arranged at Bea's feet, and she opened their drawstrings one by one, pulled out small amounts of their contents and pitched them into the fire. Sometimes the fire reacted with crackling and sometimes with hissing.

Isobel said, "That same year, 1845, he went to New York. He had been desperately poor all his adult life, and he wanted to secure his future by becoming a publisher. So he planned to purchase a literary magazine called *Broadway Journal*, a weekly."

"But he had no money because— Why? He was a drinker."

She looked at me again. "You do know something about Poe."

"I know something about drinking." My father, don't you know.

"The *Broadway Journal*'s owner said he would sell the magazine to Poe for $2,000, a huge sum back then."

"It's a huge sum even today," I said. "I have to get beat up four or five times to make that much money."

Coral chuckled. Isobel never laughed when she was in one of her Poe trances. The seamstress lifted an edge of the dress, revealing Isobel's legs up to her thighs. Coral worked on the dress while I stared at Isobel's legs.

"The *Broadway Journal*'s owner offered Poe the editor's job until Poe could come up with the $2,000 to buy the Journal," Isobel went on. Her engagement ring, a diamond the size of a .38 slug, glittered in the light.

"I'm done with the hem," Coral said. "Now put your shoulders back, Isobel, like you are at the altar listening to the minister. Shoulders back, chest out."

"My chest is out."

Coral's laugh reminded me of a steel drum. She gently pulled the dress a few inches off Isobel's shoulders, exposing her long neck and a shoulder. Her skin was frost white. The old lady must have put some herbs or something into her fire because the heady scent was now more dense, so that it caught in my throat. I've never liked strong smells. My father would go through a bottle of Old Spice every week. Some he wore. Some he drank.

The little old lady, Aunt Bea, opened a Mardi Gras fan and wafted the smoke in my direction.

I asked, "Coral, do you and your husband do voodoo?"

"We both do."

"You and Lou do voodoo?"

"We do."

"You do?"

"Sometimes it's called hoodoo."

"Hoodoo?"

"Lou does hoodoo, too."

"You do?"

"Hoodoo. Voodoo. We do."

With a chalk, Coral made a few slight marks on the fabric of the dress. "Now put both arms in the air."

Isobel Autrey was no athlete, but she possessed the grace of a natural-born dancer. Her slim arms rose like a fountain. Dressed in silky, clinging white, she was one long undulation, from her elegant hands to her small feet. I tried for another breath, but the cloying odor of sandalwood filled my mouth and nose. And it was warm in that room, what with the New Orleans heat and all those candles and Aunt Bea's fire and too many people in too small a room. My back was suddenly damp.

"Prentice Archer was a wealthy New York contractor," Isobel said, arms still aloft. "He built the York Hotel on Fifth Avenue, and the New York Bank and Trust Building on Wall Street. He contacted Poe in July 1845, just after publication of The Raven. Archer commissioned Poe to write a poem."

Coral moved around the stool and gathered fabric at the dress's back. She pulled it taut so that the smooth silk pressed against Isobel's breasts and stomach. I wiped new beads of sweat from my forehead. The room was like a hothouse. Isobel and Coral didn't appear to feel the heat. Aunt Bea fanned her smoke.

"During the last three months of 1845, Poe was working fourteen or fifteen hours a day," Isobel said. "I know this because I've found a letter from the owner of the Broadway Journal, Thaddeus Richards, to Richards' wife, who was in Philadelphia visiting her parents, complaining that Poe works all day and into the evening but doesn't accomplish much. The reason, I can only assume, was that Poe was working feverishly on The Lost Land."

"Shoulders back a little more," Coral said.

"Where'd you find that letter?" I asked. I didn't give a damn about the letter, of course. But I knew that Isobel wouldn't object to me staring at her because she was oblivious to all around her when she was talking about her Poe poem.

"Scholars have long been puzzled by Poe's lack of writing in those months after The Raven was published. So I dug around in the Broadway Journal's business records with no luck, but then I searched the personal correspondence of the owner, Thaddeus

Richards."

Coral said, "Okay, you can put your arms down, Isobel."

She complied automatically. She stood there under the light, shimmering in her wedding dress, supple and willowy, her mad black hair setting off her luminous blue eyes. I shifted on my stool, trying to get comfortable.

Isobel said, "The letter from Richards to his wife had been referred to several times in studies of Poe, but none of the scholars knew what to make of it, and they just concluded that Poe was too busy editing the *Broadway Journal* to do any writing. The letter from Richards to his wife was originally found in the archives of the New York University business school, not by me, but by earlier Poe scholars."

"All right, turn this way," Coral ordered.

Still on the stool, Isobel turned her back to me.

"Now I'm going to unpin the shoulders, Isobel. Hold up the front of the dress."

Isobel crossed her arms in front of her to keep the silk in place while Coral pulled away the back of the dress, revealing Isobel's back, the delicate knobs of her spine visible. Her waist was so narrow I could have circled it with my hands, not that the thought occurred to me.

I asked, "Is there a window I can open somewhere, Coral? Get some air in here?"

"My windows are already open." She laughed at something.

Isobel said, "So I looked again through the rest of the *Broadway Journal*'s business correspondence, boxes of it, mostly letters to and from contributors and to suppliers, that sort of thing, looking for something—anything—I had missed the first time."

She shifted her weight, accenting the curve of her posterior. I tried again for breath, but the viscous odors stopped me up, like I was smothering.

"I found another letter." Isobel's back was to me. "One from Thaddeus Richards to Prentice Archer in which Richards demanded in that Archer 'desist from importuning the *Broadway Journal*'s new editor.' Those were Richard's words: 'desist from importuning.' Richards was of course referring to Edgar Allan Poe. It was now obvious to me that Archer had made Poe some kind of offer. And what would desperately poor Poe possess that anybody would want, other than the product of his literary brilliance? Nothing."

"Dennis, there's some cold water in the fridge in the other room if you need it." Coral glanced at me, a knowing expression on her face.

"So it took me months to locate the descendants of Thaddeus Richards," Isobel said. "There's only about half a million Richards in this country."

"Dennis, do you like my work here?" Coral asked. "How does the neckline on Isobel's dress seem to you." Coral slowly, very slowly, drew her brown hand along Isobel's shoulders, pressing the skin lightly. Coral looked at me. "Does it seem right to you, how I've done it?"

I cleared my throat, twice. "It looks good, sure."

"After months of searching, I found Prentice Archer's great-great granddaughter, Millie Donovan, living in Chicago. She had retained her family correspondence, passed from generation to generation. I searched through Prentice Archer's letters."

Then Coral lifted aside Isobel's hair to reveal the back of her long neck. The seamstress said, "I toyed with a putting a collar on the dress. But then Isobel has such a graceful neck, I thought I'd leave it exposed." She drew her hand slowly along the curve of Isobel's neck. "Did I do it right, you think, Dennis?"

"Good choice." I drew my tongue along my upper lip.

"And in Millie Donovan's boxes of family items," Isobel said, "I found a letter from Prentice Archer dated June, 1863. It was written by Prentice on his death bed, telling his son that the most valuable thing Prentice Archer ever owned was hidden inside his desk at his office, a document titled *The Lost Land*, tacked to the inside of the desk's left pedestal."

"You see," Coral said, "a collar would press down on the nape of her neck and along the curve of the throat." She pressed skin the under Isobel's ear, then smoothly drew her hand down her neck to her shoulder. "Have you ever seen such a curve as this one, Dennis?"

"Collarless is the way to go, for sure." My voice was husky.

"Archer's son was killed at Gettysburg," Isobel said. "This letter was among the son's possessions returned to his family. By then Prentice Archer was dead and the war had ended. I don't know if anyone in the Archer family ever read the letter. Maybe they were grieving too much to do so."

Looking at me, her eyebrows up, Coral slowly ran her hand along Isobel's shoulder.

"Prentice Archer must have been eccentric," Isobel said, "because once he had Poe's poem he never did anything with it, never sought to publish it. He apparently kept it to himself, like some art collectors will buy a painting and put it on a wall at home, and gain great pleasure from looking at it and even greater pleasure from knowing no one else can look at it. That's just what Prentice Archer did, I think."

"A talented seamstress doesn't let the dress press here or here or here." Coral's hand stroked Isobel's shoulders, slowly pressing the firm flesh.

"Prentice Archer's construction firm lasted for thirty years after his death, run by his second son," Isobel said. "But then the company went bankrupt in the panic of 1893. The desk was manufactured in Boston in the 1840s by Barry and Fields, and it had a leather inlay on the writing surface, with a swan embossed in a corner of the leather. It was listed among the items to be auctioned at the bankruptcy sale. I've seen the court records, which describe the desk, including the embossed swan. At the bankruptcy sale, the desk was purchased by a young lawyer, Clancy Latrobe, who used the desk in his law office for the next thirty-five years."

Aunt Bea added a pinch of dried leaves to her fire, and pushed the smoke toward me with her fan.

Coral asked, "And what about here, Dennis?" She brought her hand down to the base of Isobel's back. "Getting the correct fit around the waist is difficult." She pressed Isobel's skin at the small of her back. "I mean, the dress can't be too tight, like something she'd go dancing in." She moved her hand along Isobel's lower back, pressing the skin and drawing her fingers along. "It can't be too tight, here or here or here, if you see what I'm saying."

I managed, "Where's that water, did you say, Coral?"

"Latrobe's granddaughter showed me old photos of Clancy Latrobe sitting at the desk in his law office," Isobel said, apparently carried away by her account and not hearing Coral's discussion about dressmaking. "And the reason I know Clancy Latrobe used that desk all his career is because when he died in 1928, his three other partners purchased his office furniture and law books under terms of their buy-out agreement. The granddaughter still has the forms used for the buyout. She showed them to me. The buyout inventory lists that very desk."

Coral lowered Isobel's dress two inches to reveal the dimple just above her derriere. "And you can't have the dress's waist too loose because otherwise nice features go unnoticed. A bride should look enticing on her wedding day."

Isobel said, "The law firm disbanded in 1981, and the desk and several other pieces of furniture were sold to the Vickers Cotton Brokers." Isobel was gesturing to the wall, as if she were delivering a lecture to her students. "I discovered this when I interviewed John Jacobs, who was the firm's managing partner when it folded. He still had all the firm's records, including the bill of sale for the desk."

Coral pressed her fingers into the skin around the dimple. "Do you see what I mean, Dennis? Being a seamstress is harder than it looks."

Sitting on that stool was harder than it looked. I think back now, and realize that my mind had loosened its grip on reality, because just then candle flames all around Coral Thibideaux's room seemed to grow so that the candles threw flickering yellow and orange light across Isobel's skin, and cast quick shadows on Isobel's dark hair, making it seem to twist and curl as if alive. I was drenched in sweat.

Isobel said, "I spoke with Arnold Jernegan, the last Vickers Cotton Brokers manager. He clearly recalled the desk at their Rousseau Street Dock office, and said it had become battered over the years, so much so that it didn't have any value as an antique, and was used mostly by clerks. When Vickers stopped doing business five years ago, they just left the desk and some other worthless furniture in the office at the dock."

"Isobel, is this too much pressure?" Coral pressed the skin at the top of Isobel's rump. "If the dress were this tight, would it be too much?" She kneaded the skin there, staring at me. "Would it be too tight here and here and here?" She pressed and released Isobel's flesh, pressed and released it. Then she slid the dress down a bit more, exposing much of Isobel's rump. The shadows danced around.

I gripped the edge of the stool. My lungs had shut down entirely. It must've been the incense. I was suffocating.

"Pardon?" Isobel was dragged from her recital by Coral's question. "Too tight? No, that feels fine. It's comfortable."

"Then I've got all the measurements I need." Coral returned the dress to its proper place across Isobel's back, pinning it quickly. "You can step down, Isobel."

I couldn't get a breath, and sweat from my forehead ran down the side of my nose. I rose unsteadily from the stool and without a word I fled through the door and ran down the steps to Ursuline Avenue, Coral's laugh chasing me all the way. I gulped air. My pulse was in my temples. I clung to a lamppost, collecting myself.

Across the street was a house made partly from boards taken from Kentucky keelboats that had come down the river two hundred years ago. Next to it was a brick building that had plaster over it, and the plaster was scored so that it looked like stone. Remoulade, the restaurant under Coral Thibideaux's shop, was serving red beans and rice, and I could smell the onions, garlic and smoked pork.

Isobel came down the stairs and walked out into the sunlight. She was wearing gray slacks and a maroon blouse. A small purse was over her shoulder. "What was your rush?"

"It was a little close in there." I drew my hand across my forehead, bringing away dampness.

"I'll bet you are now satisfied that Edgar Allan Poe's *The Lost Land* was in that desk." She smiled at me. "What do you think of my detective work?"

"What detective work?"

Her face registered astonishment. "What I just told you up in Coral's shop, about how I found the desk."

I stepped along the sidewalk and she followed. I was back to normal, except the back of my shirt was still wet and was chilling me.

"I fell asleep on that stool," I said. "And I didn't hear a word you said."

She glared at me, then she punched my arm. I've been punched harder in my life, but not by a woman.

"Let's get a sandwich somewhere." I led her along the sidewalk. "I always get hungry after a nap."

•

"We need to build your resume," Isobel said. A Cobb salad was in front of her, though she hadn't eaten any of it.

"Why?"

"It's part of my relentless effort to polish the spittoon, as it were."

We were in Jasper's, a place on Royal that was only open for lunch, and did a brisk business. Our table was tiny, and our foreheads almost touched when I leaned forward to bite into my sandwich. I was having a muffuletta sandwich. A pint of Samuel Adams was next to my plate.

"What jobs have you held in the past," Isobel asked.

"Never one for long."

"Well, name some of the work you've done."

"I was a heavy equipment operator for several months, driving scrapers and loaders and trucks, working for a highway road crew in western Montana. I've worked the king crab season up in Alaska a couple of winters, launching crab pots off a boat deck in the middle of winter out in the Bering Sea."

She made a note. "That's a good job for a resume. It sounds romantic."

"That's because you've never done it."

The work I had done, odd jobs here and there, had always been so I could earn enough money to return to school or to hold me over until I found a fight with a purse. These jobs weren't anything that would put a shine on a resume. And Isobel was so earnest about this project of hers, rehabilitating me. Earnestness has its place, but not while I'm having a beer.

I said, "And for a while I was a pepper tester for the Smith Spice Company."

She looked up from her notebook. "What did that involve?"

"At their testing lab, I would sniff up my nose a dozen or so grains of pepper, then count the seconds it took me to sneeze. The quicker the sneeze, the better the pepper. I'd write the results down on a pad of paper. I'd do this about once a minute. Sniff, count, sneeze, write down the seconds." I took a bite of my sandwich. "At the end of the day I'd have quite a headache."

She stared at me, then she folded up her notebook. She wore a trace of a smile. "So you don't want to talk about your past."

"Tell me about Coral Thibideaux. Don't you find her voodoo stuff creepy, those alters and the smells and the candles in her place? And her aunt, Bea? What's with her?"

"Coral is the best wedding gown designer in Louisiana."

I asked, "Was she just joshing me about voodoo, you think?"

"No."

"What about those ashes she threw under my stool at the Sonny Smith fight?"

She shrugged and smiled.

"Isobel …"

She said, "Coral is a direct descendant of Marie Laveau, the Queen of the Voodoos, who was born about 1800."

"This is your way of saying I shouldn't invent stories about working in a pepper testing lab."

"I'm serious." She finally tried her Cobb salad, eating a slice of hard-boiled egg. "Marie Laveau's tomb is in the St. Louis Cemetery on Basin Street. Coral is …" She counted with her fingers. "Her great, great, great, great, great granddaughter. Marie Laveau's family came to America from the west coast of Africa from the Yoruba tribe, with a stop in Haiti." With her fork she lifted a cube of ham. "They didn't come here of their own volition."

"Does Coral do those bizarre rituals and all?" I sipped the beer. "Or are the candles and incense in her shop the extent of it?"

"She changes her clothes three times a day, in the event an enemy has applied a potion to her garments. She gathers her fingernail clippings after a manicure and her hair after a hair cut lest they fall into the wrong hands. She wears a small gris-gris around her neck. It's a sachet holding powders and certain animal parts."

"I'd better not upset her." I wiped my mouth with a napkin.

"Coral has come up from nothing. Her mother was a seamstress back when it didn't pay much, and her father was a charcoal burner in a turpentine factory. But she makes six figures every year designing and making wedding gowns."

I asked, "Why does she dabble in voodoo, then?"

"It's more than dabbling. It's her destiny, she says. Many folks in New Orleans call Coral a Voodooienne, a voodoo queen. Coral has terrariums where she keeps lizards and snakes. Her garden contains fifty different herbs, maybe more."

I finished my beer.

Isobel said, "I visited the St. Louis Cemetery once with Coral, to see Marie Laveau's tomb. Coral showed me how to use a stone to mark the tomb with an X to appease wandering spirits."

"I don't believe in any of that stuff," I said, too harshly.

We were done eating. I paid the tab and left a tip. Isobel gathered her notebook and purse. We walked between the tables, and stepped out onto the sidewalk. The sun was behind a tree, and the street was patterned with wedges of light.

Isobel said, "Men tend to fear voodoo rather than practice it."

I looked at her. "You don't practice it, do you?"

She laughed, more a scoff. "I'm an Episcopalian."

We walked along the sidewalk, heading toward her car.

She said, "Of course, Coral the voodoo priestess has asked me to bring her an item that belonged to you, and that you have used and discarded."

I stopped cold on the sidewalk. "What item?"

She smiled. "It was just a little something."

"Isobel, you are weirding me out here."

She opened her hand to reveal a crumpled paper napkin. "It's the napkin you just used to wipe your mouth. I'm taking it to Coral."

I yelped, "Give me that napkin."

Isobel turned and ran down the sidewalk. I chased her a few steps until she stopped, laughing too hard to run, and I was laughing, too. We got into her car and she drove me to my apartment, both of us laughing much of the way. I said goodbye to her, and she smiled and said she would see me soon.

Only when I got up to my apartment did I realize she hadn't given me that napkin.

7

I stepped out from under of the Cabildo's shaded arches onto the cobblestones of Jackson Square, the heat lying over me like a blanket. I carried a manila envelope in one hand. Inside the envelope was $20,000.

I made my way toward the Cathedral of Saint Louis, its triple steeples looking down over the grass and palm trees and the Andrew Jackson statue in the park. Tarot card readers were separating tourists from their money. Watercolor artists had leaned their works against the iron pike fence that ringed the park. A band was playing on the St. Peter side of the square, a tuba player at one end of the bench and an upright bass player at the other, and assorted instruments in between. A young couple was dancing the Lindy Hop to the music. Pigeons scooted aside for me as I walked.

My wristwatch said noon. Right on time. I walked a few more paces along the Presbytere to look down St. Ann Street, which was bordered by the Pontalba apartments, and which resembled a train station. At the far end of the square, on the river side, mule-drawn carriages awaited customers. I returned to the cathedral, standing a few yards from its front door.

The counterfeiter—the one at the warehouse who had tried to cut my face with a knife—came round the corner of the Presbytere. He was wearing the same Hooter's T-shirt. He glanced at me, then looked over his shoulder, then down St. Ann, then at the crowd watching the band. The counterfeiter's shaved head reflected the sun. His eyes were far back in his head, lost amid his moon face. He approached slowly.

"Here's the money." I held up the envelope. "Where's the document?"

His porky face creased into a grin. "I've got a new proposition for you."

"The hell you do. Here's your twenty thousand. Give me the document."

He held up his meaty hands. "I want to talk to Isobel Autrey."

My chin came up involuntarily. How would he know her name?

The fat man laughed, reading my thoughts. "You don't think someone can sit a block away from our place of business—the Rousseau Street Dock—and not have me notice, do you? I ran her license plate by a friend at the Department of Motor Vehicles. Got her name that way."

"She's not here."

He laughed, a peculiar clattering, like a stick dragged along a picket fence. "She wouldn't trust you out of her sight with her twenty grand." He looked at the Presbytere's arches, then into the park, then at the crowd around the band. "Call her out here. Otherwise, she'll never see her piece of paper." He rocked back on his heels, grinning meanly at me, exposing his snaggle tooth.

If I walked away from the chance to obtain that damned poem, Isobel Autrey would push me in front of a truck, first chance she got. I signaled at the Cabildo, which had been built by the Spanish two hundred years ago. Isobel immediately came out from under the masonry arch. She walked swiftly, her eyes locked on the counterfeiter. She was wearing a jersey top with black and white stripes, a long black matte skirt, and black sandals.

She walked right up to the counterfeiter, sticking herself in his face. "Give me my document." She grabbed the envelope from me. "Here's your money."

Startled, he took half a step back. "I don't want your money, lady."

Isobel's face was pulled taut and her teeth showed. She brought up a hand, so I moved forward, separating them.

"Give me my document." Her voice was stainless steel.

I said, "Isobel, we don't even know if they have it." I turned to the counterfeiter. "If you found a piece of paper in that desk, tell me what it says."

The counterfeiter said, "It's a poem called *The Lost Land*."

Isobel inhaled sharply.

"It's by a guy named Eap," the counterfeiter said. "You ever heard of him? I Googled him and went to Wikipedia, but couldn't find no poet named Eap."

She stared at him, her face unreadable. After a moment she said levelly, "He was my great great grandfather, Horace Eap. He only wrote one poem, and it's been lost for a long time. The poem means a lot to my family. The poem is all we have left of him."

Horace Eap? She was a good liar, as I've said. EAP were Poe's initials, of course. He often signed his name that way, Isobel told me later.

The counterfeiter nodded, his double chin ballooning like a frog's. "Like I said, I want to make a new deal. Keep your money."

"What sort of a deal?" Isobel asked.

"I found out who you are. A teacher out at Tulane." He pronounced it TWO-lane. "I went out there and visited one of your classes."

Her brows shifted together. "You've never been to one of my classes."

He grinned, his teeth the color of the dirty cobblestones we were standing on. "I slipped in, sat behind a big guy, one of your students."

"What's your name," Isobel asked.

"Ted Fay. My friends call me Soapy." He held out his hand to Isobel.

She ignored it. "What were you doing in my class?"

"You were going on and on about some poet, Shelly or Shealy or somebody, and were sort of sweating and bumping your hips and stuff. You weren't looking at anybody, your students or me or anybody. A bomb could've gone off."

"I don't bump my hips when I lecture," she said stiffly.

Yes, you do, I replied in my head.

"Your lecture about that poet makes me wish I'd gone to college. Makes me wish I'd gone to high school, too."

"Give me great-great-grandpa's poem," Isobel said, her voice rough.

Soapy Fay eyed Isobel up and down, and wiped the corner of his mouth with his hand. "You ever heard of Moe Barnes?"

Her eyes searched his pockets for evidence he might be carrying the poem.

Half circles of sweat stained Soapy Fay's shirt under his arms. His belt buckle was hidden beneath his belly. "He's got a joint in

French Town, out in St. James Parish."

Moe Barnes owned a club and did some loan sharking. He was a small-time hoodlum by New York standards, a guy wearing a short tie and a fedora in many of the photos of him on the walls of his club. Billy Dupree had occasionally gotten me on the Friday night fight card at Barnes's place. Fights from eight o'clock to ten, strippers from ten to three in the morning.

The counterfeiter said, "I owe Moe Barnes a favor, a big favor, and he never lets me forget it. I was facing ten to fifteen over at Oakdale but Moe Barnes fixed it for me." He laughed gleefully. "The prosecutor had me cold. Passing hundred dollar bills that leaked green ink if they got wet. But the jury acquitted me, and I walked out a free man. Never thought he could do it, but now I owe Moe Barnes big time."

"What's that got to do with me?" Isobel asked.

"Moe Barnes ain't a man who carries a chit lightly."

"Give him the twenty thousand in this envelope," Isobel said. "And give me my poem."

"Twenty grand ain't going to do it," Soapy Fay said. "That's cigar money for Moe Barnes. You ever been to Moe Barnes's club? The Pink Lady in French Town?"

She stared at him. Soapy Fay's face had a peculiar yellow complexion, as if he'd taken an overdoes of anti-malaria tablets.

He said, "The sign out front of Moe Barnes's club says *The Choicest of the Choice*."

"Choice what?" Isobel asked.

"Moe Barnes likes classy chicks dancing at his joint. And it's a class joint. Even the G-strings have sequins."

"Dancing? G-strings?" Isobel might've been hearing a foreign language, so incomprehensibly vulgar were these words.

"Barnes prides himself on the Pink Lady's class. His business card has *Choicest Chicks in Louisiana* printed right under his name."

Her voice was low. "So what do you want?"

"Moe Barnes told me to find him a classy dancer. A lush babe. And he would cancel my marker. You're plenty choice. If you can light the fuse under a group of college boys while talking about poetry, imagine what you'll do dancing at Moe Barnes's club. You'll pack them in."

"What's your deal?" she persisted.

"You dance at his club, three nights a week for four weeks, and I'll give you your poem."

She was aghast. "I am a professor of literature at Tulane University.

I added, "She's no stripper."

"Let's see," Fay said, holding up his hand to count on his fingers. "Three twenty-minutes shifts a night, times twelve nights. That means you get your poem back for twelve hours of work. Sounds cheap to me."

Isobel stared at the Presbytere, her face hard with calculation.

Soapy Fay added, "You'll get your poem after your last performance."

She said, "And otherwise?"

"We make a deal right now, or I signal Donnie up there in that window." Fay turned to point at the Pontalba Apartments. "And he sets the poem on fire with his lighter. You'll see the ashes float down to St. Ann Street."

Fay's partner Donnie, the mustachioed counterfeiter I had last seen at the Rousseau Street Dock, waved from the window.

"How about the twenty thousand dollars?" Isobel offered.

Soapy Fay shook his head. "I want to do this for Barnes. It means more than twenty grand."

Isobel chewed on her lip, indecision on her face.

Fay held up both his hands in the air, like the French. "Donnie is looking at me right now. If I put my hands together, he'll put the fire to your great-great-granddaddy's poem. Do we have a deal? Tell me right now. I clasp my hands together and your poem is gone forever, or I put them down by my side and you'll get your poem. Make your choice."

She hesitated. Her mouth worked, then stopped, then worked and stopped again. Finally she said, and there was iron in her voice, "I won't be rushed on such a decision."

Fay lowered his hands. He barked out, "What?"

Isobel replied, "If you insist on a yes or no from me right now, go ahead and burn the poem. I won't make an instantaneous decision of such importance while I stand out here in the hot sun talking to a maggot."

This took courage. Isobel's hands was hidden behind her back because I suspect she knew they were shaking.

Donnie sucked on his tooth. "Okay. We'll give you twenty-four hours to decide. Be here same time tomorrow." He turned to go. Then he called back over his shoulder, "And don't worry about your costumes, the G-strings and feathers and stuff. Moe has plenty."

Isobel stood there, wearing an infantryman's thousand-yard stare. I turned her by her shoulders and led her back to her car.

•

"Don't use any of those words you use," Isobel instructed me. "This is a mental hospital."

"What words?"

"Funny farm, bat house, booby hatch, rubber room."

"I've never used any of those terms," I protested. "Only nut bin once or twice."

"Schizo store, acorn academy, bug house, banana plantation, ding tank, flake factory. They are all rude."

I had never said any of these things. They were from Isobel's own head, her own dealings with her mother's condition. We were in a hallway at Sunlight House about to visit Kathleen Autrey. I admit to being nervous.

"And don't say anything about her hair," Isobel said.

"I wouldn't do that."

"During a Monica, Mother Mermaid of the Mediterranean episode, she dyed her hair green. Most of it has grown out now, though."

An attendant walked by. At Sunlight House the staff wore street clothes, nice outfits, every one of them. No white pants or sturdy nurse's shoes.

"Where are all the straight jackets?" I asked. "I haven't seen a single one."

"This is a combination hotel and hospital, Dennis. No bars, no padded cells, no electrodes."

The hallway's floor was veined green marble. On several cherry-wood stands along the walls were large Japanese vases filled with flowers. The lighting was hidden and indirect. Instead of the Pine-Sol smell I had expected, the scent of a summer meadow drifted along the hallway.

Isobel said, "Most of the time when she's not in the grip of her disease, my mother is the wisest person in Louisiana. She'll help me decide."

Isobel squared her shoulders, then rang the doorbell. I'd never before been in a hospital where interior rooms had doorbells. After a moment, the door opened. Standing there, looking at Isobel and me, was another Isobel, plus thirty or so years. The resemblance—the dark hair, the keen blue eyes, the elevated cheekbones, the lush yet impish mouth—was remarkable. Isobel's mother had a few wrinkles and her hair was shorter than Isobel's. And, yes, the ends of her hair were green, but otherwise the two women were reflections of each other.

Her mother smiled and held out her arms to Isobel. Until that moment I had thought Isobel could carefully control her emotions, that she could put them on her face like masks in perfect control, one after another, handily switching them when required by the situation. But at the sight of her mother, Isobel shuddered, then sobbed and fell into her arms.

Kathleen stood there woodenly for a moment, clearly surprised by her daughter's collapse. Then an expression of love and sadness came to Kathleen's face. She patted Isobel's back and said in a low voice, "Now, now, now. Everything will be all right."

Mrs. Autrey glanced accusingly at me, as if I might be the cause of this tribulation, then she guided Isobel into the room, Isobel sobbing and leaning heavily into her. I wasn't invited to follow but I did anyway. Kathleen guided her daughter to a leather chair in the main room.

The mother's digs at Sunlight House consisted of a sitting room, a bedroom, a bath and a small kitchen. The furniture was modern and stylish, mostly light wood and glass. Photos of her family were on a small grand piano in the corner of the main room. The carpet was a red and purple, and Isobel later told me it was from Daghestan on the Caspian Sea.

Kathleen lowered Isobel into the chair, then rushed into the kitchen for a bottle of water. She poured it into a tumbler, passed it to Isobel, then hurried into her bathroom for a washcloth.

She returned to the main room, dabbed Isobel's face and murmured, "There, there, there." Kathleen looked at me as if I had sprung from a wanted flyer at the post office.

"I don't know what to do, Mom," Isobel burbled. "I've got a dreadful decision to make and I don't know what to do." She took the washcloth and used it to touch the corners of her eyes.

Kathleen sat on the ottoman in front of Isobel. She held her daughter's hand. "Maybe I can help."

Isobel breathed with little hiccupy noises. She shaded her eyes with a hand, hiding her tears. Maybe she thought this was weakness, and she didn't want me to see it.

She said, "I don't know what to do. I must have that poem. It's all I live for." She swallowed. "It's my entire future. It's everything to me, and I can't …" She wiped her eyes again. "I just can't seem to get my hands on it."

Kathleen asked, "How can I help, Isobel. Tell me what I can do."

An unheeded tear dripped onto her shirt. She inhaled in long drafts for a moment. Her mother squeezed her hand, smiling tenderly at her.

Isobel managed a brave smile. "Mom, this is Dennis Jones."

From the ottoman, she held out her hand, and I stepped forward to shake it.

Isobel sniffled, then said, "If you are looking for clever rejoinders, timeless epigrams or ironic aperçus, you've got a better chance of getting them from your kitchen stove than from Dennis here."

Well, Isobel was returning to her old self. She grinned feebly at me. Tears had left tracks on her cheeks. She pressed the washcloth to her face.

"I get enough of those clever rejoinders when you bring Charles by." Kathleen smiled at me. "At least you don't smell like cologne, Dennis. With Charles, you've got to stick your head out a window after a couple of minutes."

She had the same voice as her daughter, too, that silken contralto that was usually about turn to laughter. I couldn't see any of Lawrence Autrey in Isobel, only her mother. Kathleen was wearing a blue-and-white plaid Irish linen shirt and creased linen pants of the same color blue. Around her neck was a pearl necklace. She motioned toward a chair, so I sat down.

"Dennis is my comparison," Isobel explained.

Kathleen looked me up and down, "A comparison?"

"Every time I introduce Dennis to someone, that person realizes how lucky I am to be engaged to Charles."

Kathleen laughed. "You must have a good measure of resilience, Dennis, putting up with Isobel for any length of time."

I grinned. "I'll bet your husband also has some resilience."

Kathleen turned back to her daughter. "Now, tell me, sweetie, what troubles you?"

Her voice was just above a whisper, and her mother leaned toward her to hear better. "A couple of hoodlums have my Edgar Allan Poe poem."

Isobel described how the two counterfeiters had come into possession of the poem. Her mother nodded and squeezed her hand. When Isobel came to the counterfeiters' demand that she work as a stripper at the Pink Lady in French Town, Isobel couldn't say the words aloud and had to lean toward her mother to whisper.

I give Kathleen Autrey credit. Her eyebrows didn't rise. Her jaw didn't open. She didn't exclaim, "You've got to be kidding." None of these things.

Her dilemma set out, Isobel sighed. "I don't know what to do."

I expected her mother to raise issues such as the Autrey family honor, Isobel's standing in the community, her professional reputation at Tulane and in the literature world, and her self-respect.

Mrs. Autrey said, "I know exactly what you should do. I'm as certain of it as I'm certain the sun will come up tomorrow."

"I knew you would." Profound relief swept over Isobel's countenance. "You always do."

Kathleen said, "Your happiness depends not on a dermatologist or getting your next poem published in the *Southern Poetry Review*, but rather on obtaining that missing work by Edgar Allan Poe."

Isobel nodded.

Her mother went on, "From what you tell me, the only way you will get the poem is if you learn to dance."

Isobel and her mother stared at each other, right into each other's eyes. Kathleen had the same charged, faceted, pure blue eyes as her daughter. Who knew what pyrotechnic reaction occurred to the dust motes in the air midway between them when their eyes were locked on each other.

Kathleen broke the silence. "To save what you prize most, you must risk what you prize most."

Isobel's face was blank, as if the tasks of registering her mother's advice and moving her features into an expression were too exhausting to do at the same time.

"Do you understand, Isobel?" Kathleen asked.

Isobel blinked. "I understand that you are suggesting your daughter become a stripper."

"More than that. You need to be a powerful argument for your own cause."

Isobel shook her head, a slight, tired motion. "I don't know what you mean, mom."

"You must compel this gangster, this Moe Barnes, to give you the poem by the force of your nature, which will be made clear to him by your brilliant performances."

"What are you saying?"

"You must make him want to give you the poem. He must be certain you have earned it."

Isobel was silent.

Kathleen said, "So you work to be the best dancer he's ever hired. You've got to dazzle. And, besides, Isobel, you've never been able to do anything in half measures. If you want to succeed and make that gangster want to give you the poem, you'll have to throw yourself at this project."

Isobel pressed her fingers against her temple as if fighting a headache.

Her mother added, "I'd do it for you, but the bunion on my left foot aches all the time."

Isobel rose from her chair. She stood there a moment, her gaze cast down at the carpet. Her mother reached for her hand.

Isobel muttered, "I just don't know. I just ..."

"But you do know, sweetie," Kathleen said. "You know what you want and you know what must be done to get it. And I know this about you: the things you do well at are those things you give one hundred percent to. Anything less than that, and you might fail in your quest."

"I just can't picture myself ..." Isobel's words were almost inaudible. She drifted toward the door. "A professor of literature just doesn't ..."

Kathleen opened the door for us, then looked at me. "I hope you visit again, Dennis."

I shook her hand goodbye. "Lawrence Autrey has good taste, that's for sure."

She beamed. "Oh, you." She tapped my arm playfully. "Isobel, I think— Isobel?"

Her daughter had wandered down the hallway, past the elevator where she should have stopped to press the button, and was walking slowly as if in a trance along the hallway toward the fire exit.

Kathleen said, "You'd better go get her, Dennis."

I started after Isobel.

Before she closed the door, Kathleen called after me, "You take care of her. Will you? Baby sit her a little?"

I hurried along the hall, gently took Isobel's arm, then turned her back to the elevator.

I said, "Take care of you? That's your mom's idea of a joke. Right?"

Isobel stared at the elevator door. Her lips were moving but she was making no sounds. She was entirely lost inside her own mind.

When the elevator door opened, I helped Isobel inside. Then I said, "You need baby sitting like Lennox Lewis needs baby sitting."

This wisecrack was as good as I ever managed but Isobel wasn't listening. I walked her toward her car, hoping she would pull out of it before she got behind the wheel.

•

"No, no, no," the old man said. "In chess, you don't jump your opponent's pieces unless you are moving the knight."

"What about crowning me?" I asked.

Isobel's father asked, "Crowning me?"

"If I get a piece all the way to your side of the board, don't I get to stack two of my pieces together? They don't seem to stack too well." I tried to balance one of my pawns on another pawn. I knew how to play chess, but I was teasing him.

Lawrence Autrey said, "Let's start from the beginning, Dennis. Let's wipe your slate clean, not that we'll perspire doing so."

The old guy was wearing a paisley smoking jacket, gray slacks, and leather slippers. On a table next to his chair was a scotch and water. The chess board was made of Italian elm root, he had told me, and the chess pieces were carved of ebony, with leather bases. We were in his den, the one with the battlefield tableaux.

Isobel paced in front of the bookshelves, her hands in the pockets of her workout pants, walking back and forth, staring at the floor. The shelves were filled with military miniatures and a few books.

She abruptly reached for a leather-bound volume. She held it up. "This is what I know. Poetry. It's my milieu, my life blood, my entire existence. But now I'm going to be an exotic dancer?"

Charles Brooks was in a leather chair in front of the fireplace, reading a copy of the *Journal of the North American Academy of Dermatology*, a yellow high-lighter in his hand.

"Here's an interesting statistic," he said. "In any given year, a dermatologist has a .006 chance of catching scabies from a patient."

"You got me into this, Dennis." Isobel started pacing again. "It is entirely your fault."

"My poor, malleable, impressionable, docile little daughter." Lawrence Autrey chuckled. "Shame on you, Dennis."

A knock came from the study's door.

Lawrence's maid stuck her head in. She was wearing a strychnine expression. "A Bambi LaTour for you, Miss Autrey."

The maid was brushed aside by the dancer, who barged into the room on long legs. "That's my stage name. When I've got clothes on, I'm Jenny Blake."

She had an athletic bag over a shoulder and was wearing green sweats and a black headband. On her feet were Nike cross-trainers. Her smile swept the room. Her blond hair was piled on her head, and was kept in place by a tortoiseshell clip.

She held out her hand to Isobel, who tentatively reached for it. Then Isobel introduced us all. Charles Brooks placed the dermatology journal on his lap, and turned in his seat to watch.

Jenny Blake took out a CD from her athletic bag, then tossed the bag into a corner. "Cool battle stuff," she said, indicating the Gettysburg and Arnem dioramas.

"Thank you, I'm sure," Lawrence Autrey replied. He was staring at her, no longer interested in teaching me chess.

Isobel put the CD into a stereo system on the bookshelf.

"Have you loosened up?" the dancer asked Isobel.

"Stretching, just like you told me to."

With one swift motion, Jenny Blake removed her sweatshirt and threw it onto her athletic bag. She was wearing an athlete's halter top. She was all curves.

Brooks pushed himself back in his chair. Laurence Autrey cleared his throat, apparently in some confusion.

Jenny Blake's mouth was wide, and her eyes were leaf green. She was wearing little make-up. She had a scrubbed, healthy look, nothing like any dancer I'd ever seen onstage.

Next she whipped off her sweatpants and piled them onto the bag, revealing a modest pair of running shorts. But she filled those shorts nicely. Her waist was narrow. Her naval was pierced with a piece of metal. I couldn't make out the design. Charles's medical journal slid from his lap to the floor.

Earlier that day Isobel and I had met the Soapy the Counterfeiter in Jackson Square. Isobel had agreed to the deal. She had said little to me or anyone else since.

"Do you want to start with pole work?" Jenny asked. "Or open floor?"

"What's pole work?"

"You dance around a pole, trying to turn it on."

Isobel blurted, "Open floor."

Jenny pressed a buttons on the CD player. David Rose's The Stripper came from the speakers.

Jenny spread her legs wide. "Let's try the basic straddle." She bent over at the waist to touch her left foot.

Isobel did the same.

"Now you have to raise your chin to look at the audience."

"Why?" Isobel looked up, still bent over.

"To let them know that even though you are alone on stage, you are dreaming of them. Dancing is communicating. And wouldn't it all be a better world if we just communicated more?"

"Now what?" Isobel asked. "I can't hold this position much longer."

"Now rise to you full height, keeping your legs spread."

Isobel rose.

"Way too fast, Isobel." The dancer was still bent over, her head at knee level and her tush provocatively in the air, fingers on her Nikes. "Nothing about exotic dance is fast. Do it slowly."

Isobel bent over and rose again. This time she placed her hands on her hips as she stood.

"Try again," Jenny urged. "Bend over, and draw your fingers up along your calf and then your thigh, all the way up."

"Why?"

"It's all about communicating, Isobel. And as you draw your hand up your thigh, move your butt in a slow, small circle. And smile at the audience." Jenny displayed the proper form.

"I'm not sure I can do all those things at once," Isobel

complained.

Charles Brooks was so still he might've been epoxied to his chair.

"Give it a try. Move your butt to the beat. Ba-boom da, ba-boom da, ba-boom da. Around and around your butt goes. Keep it high and tight. And now up comes your hand. Slowly, as if your leg were a mile long. Oooh, feel my thigh, it's so smooth and wouldn't this be wonderful if you could touch it like this, is what you're communicating to the audience."

I turned back to Lawrence Autrey and reached for a bishop. I was playing black. "And this piece can only go diagonally? What sense does that make?"

He ratcheted his gaze around to me. "You aren't interested in exotic dancing, champ? Parts of that young woman are highly exotic."

"Sometimes I work the door at strip joints," I said. "After a couple days, all the girls look alike, and all their teasing moves look alike. A grocery store receipt is more interesting."

"I've always believed Isobel could do whatever she put her mind to," the old fellow said. "But I'm not sure she has the wherewithal to be a stripper."

I said, "You've never seen her lecture about poetry, maybe."

He reached for his scotch, then leaned forward, "The Isobel of high school is not the Isobel of today."

"What do you mean, Mr. Autrey?"

"I thought I'd lost her there, for a few years." A flap of long hair was over his bald spot, and was combed with such precision it looked wet. "It began about the time her mother started having her health problems, her mental problems. Isobel didn't understand it, and began drinking and carrying on, this was when she was sixteen and seventeen, hanging around with hooligans. She would disappear for three or four days. Wouldn't go to school for weeks at a time. Got arrested a couple of times, and I don't even want to mention what the arrests were for."

I looked over my shoulder at Isobel, who was trying to imitate Jenny Blake's posterior wiggle without much success. Jenny's bottom moved in time to the music. Charles Brooks stared unabashedly at the dancer.

Lawrence Autrey said, "We tried several different schools and counseling, even a psychiatrist. Nothing worked. Isobel was on a downward slide and there was nothing her mother and I could do. We were afraid for her."

"What happened?" I fingered a rook.

"She showed up in class one day, against all odds, and her English teacher gave her a copy of *Two Centuries of American Poetry*, and asked Isobel to take it home and browse though it."

"And she did?"

"She went up to her room that day—" Lawrence pointed at the ceiling in the direction of her room. "And didn't come down for a week. I checked in on her now and then, bringing her some food, and found she was bent over that book night and day, underlining passages and making notes."

"The poetry book changed her?"

Lawrence nodded. "Transformed her. At the end of the week, she went back to school and didn't miss a day until she graduated. Then she got into a junior college, stayed there one year, and based on her record there and several poetry criticisms and a small book of poems she had written, she entered Yale for her sophomore year."

I smiled at him. "Maybe you should've thanked the teacher who gave Isobel the poetry book."

"I sent the teacher a note, which said, 'Isobel would like to keep *Two Centuries of American Poetry* that you loaned her, but allow me to pay for the book in proportion to how much it has meant to her.' I enclosed a check for $100,000."

Jenny Blake punched the remote control and the music ended. She said, "Isobel, you aren't sending messages to your audience. You've got to emit."

"Emit what?" Isobel asked, lifting a leg and holding her foot behind her with a hand to loosen the muscles.

"Your lush sensuality. Make each man in your audience fantasize that you are the world's biggest tramp who is just waiting for her music to end so she can take him outside to his pickup truck and climb into the cab with him."

"Yuck," Isobel said.

'Well, exotic dancing isn't for everyone, and maybe—"

"I can learn," Isobel interrupted. "Let's keep going."

"Yeah, keep going," Charles Brooks said.

Jenny fingered the remote, and the pulsing music again filled the den. Lawrence Autrey sipped his scotch.

"Not like that, Isobel," Jenny said above the music. "Use your biceps to push up your breasts, then put sheer ecstasy on your face. The audience spends as much time looking at your face as your boobs."

I asked Isobel's father, "How come Isobel's never been married? Does she love poetry too much to bother, maybe?"

He pursed his lips, then said, "My daughter has a strong personality."

I laughed. "You mean, she wears her boyfriends down to nothing, then tosses them aside."

He nodded, but didn't smile. "Something like that, yes."

"Charles must be tougher than the others," I ventured.

"I don't think so. He puts up with more than the others. He is like a puppy in that regard."

"Isobel, you're too stiff," Jenny said over the music. "You are dancing like a mummy. Put some lust into it. It's not called bending and stretching, it's called bumping and grinding. Give us some heat."

"I don't know how," she protested.

"Do this." Jenny thrust out a hip, swung it slowly around, then did it again. "Push that curve out there."

Charles was transfixed.

"I can't do that," Isobel said.

I rose from my chair. "Sure you can." I reached for the volume of poetry she had held aloft, and then quickly leafed through the index. "Here, Edgar Allan Poe's *Lenore*. You know it, Isobel?"

She scowled at me. "I can recite it verbatim."

"Keep the music going, Jenny," I said. "Isobel, you listen to this."

Jenny narrowed her eyes, surely puzzled.

I held the book up to the light and read, "Ah, broken is the golden bowl! The spirit flown forever! Let the bell toll! A saintly soul floats on the Stygian river. And, Guy De Vere, hast thou no tear? Weep now or never more!"

Poe must have been a lot of laughs. I loudly read more lines of this incomprehensible ditty, trying to syncopate my words with the beat of The Stripper coming from the speakers.

"Wretches!" I read. "Ye loved her for her wealth and hated her for her pride. And when she fell in feeble health, ye blessed her—that she died!'"

Jenny began to dance, thrusting her chest out, turning slowly, sticking her bottom out, running her hands up and down her body, eyeing her student, hoping Isobel could mimic her.

"Go up to God so solemnly the dead may feel no wrong." Reading junk like this always makes my face hurt, but I was determined to help Isobel.

Isobel closed her eyes and pushed out her lips as if they were begging to be kissed. She slowly moved her hips side to side, then shifted her weight provocatively, and ran her hands up her sides to gather her hair, then released it.

"That's more like it," Jenny exclaimed. "Keep it up."

I read, "The sweet Lenore hath gone before, with Hope, that flew beside ..."

Isobel brought her elbows together, pushing out her chest, then slowly slid her hands down her hips. Her cheeks had acquired a soft pink hue. Her mouth was parted, and the tip of her tongue touched her upper lip.

"You're a natural, Isobel," Jenny said.

"'The life upon her yellow hair but not within her eyes.'"

Isobel's eyes were now half open, and she pursed her lips again, a pure bedroom expression. She moved her shoulders and her hips, and her hands sensually caressed the air.

"'And I! Tonight my heart is light! No dirge will I upraise. But waft the angel on her flight with a Paean of old days.'"

I closed the book and placed it on a shelf next to six tiny General Grants. Isobel slowed, then stopped. She opened her eyes like it was morning.

After a few seconds, Charles blurted, "Isn't there more to that poem?"

Jenny hit the stop button on the remote, then grabbed Isobel's arms. "You see? All you needed was the proper stimulation. You'll knock them dead, Isobel."

Isobel looked around, her face registering bewilderment.

Jenny said, "I've got to run for my club date. May I call a cab?"

Isobel's father said, "Charles will drive you to the club, young lady." He nodded at Charles.

The skin doctor leaped off the leather chair. "More than happy to."

Isobel and the dancer made arrangements for another lesson the following day. Still acting bit dazed, Isobel left the study, escorting Charles and Jenny to the door.

Lawrence Autrey poured himself and me more scotch. He clucked his tongue. "A father should never live to see his daughter dance like that."

8

My fight with Antoine Doaks was at the Slidell Community College gymnasium, and we were third on the card. Tarpaulins had been placed on the hardwood basketball floor, and metal folding chairs were on top of the tarps, so the chairs wouldn't ruin the wood. Pretty good turnout, maybe eight hundred fans. I had hired Arturo Lopez as my cut guy again, figuring maybe he was lucky. This time he wanted a hundred and a half.

Antoine Doaks was in full steroid bloat, his pecs huge, his stomach rippled and his arms like hams. His brows were low and his thick chin was out in front of his mouth. He was an African American, with a shaved head. He didn't have any hair that I could see, none on his chest or arms or legs. Maybe he shaved everywhere.

On the elastic waist of his white trunks was printed The Doaks Express. His gloved fists looked to be the size of basketballs. This guy was going to beat me like a rented mule. I was afraid.

The ring announcer introduced me quickly, then my opponent, wringing out Doaks's name like a towel. "Number twelve ranked in the entire U. S. of A, Aaaannn—twaaann Dah-oooooksss." The words echoed back and forth in the gym. Doaks raised his gloves, acknowledging the applause.

I looked down at Isobel, who grinned brightly at me. The gym was overly air conditioned, and she had buttoned up her black wool bomber-cut jacket. Her slacks were white gabardine. Charles Brooks was at her side in a coat and tie as if this were a nice restaurant. He gave me a Churchillian victory sign, then, maybe thinking that insufficient, changed it to a thumbs-up. The back of his right hand, burned during the Knights of the Arcadian Peacock ceremony, was still pink.

Then I saw Coral Thibideaux, the seamstress, standing next to

Arturo right below the corner post. She reached under the rope, and with one pass of her hand spread something on the heel of my shoe, some shiny substance resembling Vaseline. She turned away, walking toward Isobel.

The bell rang, and Antoine Doaks came at me like a bull released from a chute. Some fighters are as silent as an ambush, and others are full of noise. The bare-knuckler John L. Sullivan was a famous examples of the latter, huffing and grunting and cursing as he destroyed you. Doaks was of that ilk. He sounded like a locomotive, blowing and hissing and snorting, and he crossed the ring in a straight line and snapped my head back with a left jab and then sent a right hook into my ear. Down I went, five seconds gone in the first.

I've been on the canvas before, and am quite comfortable there. It's like a second home. My head was ringing like a gong. I was flat on my back, and Antoine Doaks raised his arms as if he were king of the world, him skipping around, figuring he'd just won his twenty-first pro fight. The crowd clapped politely, most of them waiting for the main event. The referee waved him to a neutral corner, but Antoine was having too much fun dancing around the ring, gloves high over his head, so the ref had to push him toward the neutral corner. Then the ref came back and began his count.

"Get up, Dennis," Isobel called. "You look silly, lying there with your shoes on."

I'm better at taking punches than giving them. Nobody ever accused me of having a glass jaw. I waited until the ref reached five, then climbed to my feet. I didn't feel too badly, all things considered.

Doaks's face registered vast surprise, which, along with my seven-hundred-dollar share of the purse, would make getting beaten to a pulp almost worth it.

The ref rubbed my gloves on his shirt, then waved the two of us together again. Doaks sent a jab my direction, but I slipped it. He tried again, and it glanced off my shoulder. He stalked me, moving forward, trying to corner me. Man, he was fast, with pro footwork, side to side, in and out, not giving me even the ghost of a target.

Isobel caught my eye, her sitting there happily next to her fiancé, me trying to avoid being killed dead. Then she let me have it with her gaze, sending a thousand kilowatts into my brain. I never figured out how she did it, but I was abruptly energized. I danced forward, and sent my first punch of the match at Doaks, missing him, but startling him nevertheless. He growled in rage at my impudence, and came at me again.

Then, the damnedest thing. All the wristwatches in the arena must have begun to act crazily. Time began a peculiar accordion-like expansion and contraction, something to do with Einstein and his space-time continuum, whatever he said. I sped up, and Antoine Doaks and the rest of the universe slowed down. Maybe someday they'll write a physics text about this phenomenon.

Doaks slowed. Not a lot, still faster than anybody on the street, but slow for a ranked contender, just a little off his sharp edge. The spectators slowed, too, it seemed. And I seemed quicker and sharper, as if I'd just had six cups of coffee.

I sent a fist at his face. It found his forehead and he half-stepped back. His eyes opened wide. He was alarmed and confused.

He threw a left and a right, but they seemed in slow motion. I ducked and dodged, and all he found was air. I countered hard to his belly, and he nickered like a horse. He tried an uppercut, but I was already back and standing. His fist missed, and all I felt was the wind that trailed after his glove.

Doaks stepped forward again to try another jab, brushing my ear. I clinched with him, tucked my head into his neck, and lay three solid blows into his midriff. The old boxer's saying: kill the body, the head will die. He grunted and tried to step away from me but I followed him, keeping my head safe against his ear, and I pumped my arms, sending uppercut after uppercut into his belly. He would be peeing pink for a week. He tried to retreat, but I was on him like I'd been applied with a putty knife.

His back was now against the ropes, and I kept it up, my arms driving like pistons slamming his stomach again and again. He groaned and slid sideways along the ropes. I was right with him, pummeling his belly, my fists a blur.

The ref slipped his arms between us to push us apart.

Doaks fell forward, landing on his knees, then toppling face down onto the canvas, too insensate to break his fall with his hands There he stayed during the full count.

The ref raised my hand. Arturo Lopez climbed up the turnbuckle and put his hand out for his pay. I walked over to my corner and looked down.

Charles Brooks was standing and grinning and applauding mightily, reveling in my good fortune. I was beginning to like that guy, even if he was a skin doctor and a knight of the Arcadian Peacock.

Isobel Autrey sat there, her arms folded across her chest, a slight smile on her mouth, looking up at me with her blue eyes. She had the knowledge of the world in those eyes. Then she and Coral Thibideaux exchanged triumphant glances.

I had just defeated the twelfth-ranked ABA contender, an event as unlikely as finding a mustache in China.

I put my gloves on the ropes and leaned over, and asked around my mouthpiece, "Isobel, what happened?"

"When?" She smiled slyly.

"Just now, out in the ring."

Her eyebrows arced, and she asked in a honeyed voice, "Whatever do you mean, Dennis?"

Suspicion tugged at me like a dog on a bull's nose. Had Isobel somehow fixed the fight? No way. A fighter who takes a fall wants to do so without getting hurt, wants to get his bribe without paying physically for it. I had beaten Doaks down, punished him severely. Not many redwoods could've taken the blows I had sent into Doaks's belly. I stared at Isobel and she stared right back, her expression that of a rascal. I looked over at Coral. Her smile revealed nothing.

Antoine Doaks was standing now, but bent over, his trainer and cut man supporting him. His mouthpiece was on the canvas. The fans were still applauding. I looked around. They were clapping for me, of all people. I hesitantly raised my arms over my head, the boxer's bow.

Why shouldn't I gather in the applause? When would I ever be able to do that again? I danced a little victory jig, just like Joe Louis and Muhammad Ali and Tug Johnson. I blew the audience a double-gloved kiss. Man, this was fun. I looked back over my shoulder.

Isobel was laughing. Maybe at me.

•

On Isobel's third weekend of performances, I couldn't stand it any longer so I decided to visit the Pink Lady out in French Town just to see how she was doing. Isobel had told me her stage name was Lizzie but hadn't volunteered anything more. She was utterly spent after each performance, and slept much of the next morning, barely making it to her classes at Tulane. So I thumbed a ride out to French Town, having to change cars three times because the town is on the road to nowhere.

French Town is a country hamlet southwest of New Orleans, not quite within commuting distance of the city. The Pink Lady's gravel parking lot was filled with beaters and pickups, many with rifle racks. A jowly bloodhound stood in one truck's cargo bay. Another pickup sported a bumper sticker, Let's All Eat More Spam. A couple guys over by the dumpster were making some deal, bent toward each other and talking quietly.

The Pink Lady had begun life fifty years ago as a service station, and had been added to many times over the years during its business reincarnations so that it was a rambling structure with several kinds of siding and a roofline at several levels. On the big reader-board above the Pink Lady was *Dr. Lizzie, the Professor of T&A, Live Tonite. $20 Cover.*

A dozen guys were outside the front door waiting to get in. Two bouncers blocked the door, one holding up his hand to request patience. One fellow in the line was waving several twenty dollar bills at the bouncers, trying to bribe his way in.

I walked to the rear of the building, rounding several corners, to the service entrance. Two busboys were standing there smoking and leaning against the wall.

"Remember me?" I asked. "I've fought here a couple times. How about letting me in?"

They may or may not have remembered me, but people look at my face and I sometimes get what I want without a lot of discussion.

One of them said, "No problem," and pulled open the door.

Walking through the kitchen, I could smell red rice and beans. None of the cooks or waiters looked up. I passed through swinging, leather-padded doors into the Pink Lady's main room. The stage was off to my right, hidden behind a corner. Hundreds of men were in the room, gazing at the stage, grinning, banging ashtrays on the tables to the music. The audience was jammed together, tables no larger than inner tubes, six and seven guys to a table, the tables covered with beer bottles. More men were standing at the back of the room, ogling the stage, whistling and clapping.

The music was thunderous, the bass cranked up to shirt-rippling level. A crap game—illegal as hell—was set up at a table in a corner of the room, but the players had stopped the dice to watch the performance. Pool players were leaning on their cues, watching. Waiters and waitresses slipped between the tables, doing their jobs, but nobody was ordering. The crowd was staring at Doctor Lizzie, cheering for her, urging her on to new horizons of bumping and grinding.

How can I say this and have you believe me? I had gone out to the Pink Lady to take a good look, to see Isobel shake everything she had. But as I walked further into the room, just as the stage lights came into my view, I suddenly averted my eyes. I looked at the floor, then the bar, anywhere but at her up there on the stage.

I liked Isobel Autrey, sort of. Isobel was my manager, so she claimed. I liked her fiancé Charles. I respected Isobel's father. I had no business looking at Isobel in a G-string, is what I'm saying. So I didn't. I stepped along the bar, keeping my head turned.

But I was the only person in the room not gaping at her, some of the men wiping spit from the corners of their mouths, damn them. Most of the gawkers wore dozer caps, and many had greasy shoulder-length hair. A lot of scruffy beards were in the room. A few of the patrons were missing teeth, so their leers were gap-toothed. Lots of big guts and rolled-up sleeves. Copenhagen cans showed through the fabric of many shirt pockets. The far wall was veiled by cigarette smoke. The patrons cheered and hooted and whistled.

Sitting at a table near the bar was Moe Barnes, who I recognized from my fights at the Pink Lady. He was a stocky man with a blunt face. He was leaning back in his chair, thumbs hooked in his belt, grinning hugely.

Next to him was a fellow with a laptop computer, probably tallying the gate. I would learn later that he was Barnes's nephew, the only son of Barnes's beloved sister. The nephew's name was Steve Sprague, but he'd been known since he was a kid as Spazz. He was his uncle's flunky and bodyguard, putting in his apprenticeship, maybe hoping to take over from his uncle some day. I didn't know it then, but Spazz Sprague would inflict on me a ton of hurt, and more than once.

Usually the Pink Lady didn't charge for admission, making their profit on the liquor. Dr. Lizzie was a big draw. I kept my eyes down, about to make my retreat, go back to the city.

A guy at the bar yelled, "Shove it out there, Lizzie."

Shove it out there? Isobel? I was abruptly enraged at these mossback voyeurs. Something snapped in my brain is my only explanation for what happened next.

I stepped up to the fellow, a wiry runt wearing a cowboy hat and pointy boots, and I grabbed him by the shirtfront and lifted him to his toes, and snarled, "She's got enough out there already, buddy. Got that?"

I was just presuming Isobel had enough out there. I hadn't looked.

He stammered, "What ... what'd you say?"

"Keep your mouth shut."

He was about to say something more, but he surveyed my face and his jaw closed quickly.

The music boomed. Further along the bar, a fellow inserted two fingers into his mouth to wolf whistle and then yelled, "Take it all off, Dr. Lizzie."

I rushed up to him and put my face right into his. "She's got enough off, pal." I didn't know, but I presumed she did. I wasn't thinking too clearly, you can tell.

He leaned back against the bar. "Who the hell are you?"

I pressed my finger into his breastbone, and I can do it so it hurts. "Not another word from you, loser."

The music thumped, and a spinning disco light sent shafts of color across the room. The crowd cheered and stomped. Dr. Lizzie was working them into a fever. The bartender signaled somebody, but I didn't pay attention because I was fueled by rage.

A guy at the nearest table whooped, "Strut it, Lizzie. Strut it."

I grabbed him by the back of the neck and lifted him out of his chair. "Where's your manners, jerk?"

He hung there, his eyes wide, a beer in his hand. He managed a squeaky, "Hey, this is a strip joint."

"Watch your mouth." I threw him back into his chair.

At the next table a guy in a Hawaiian shirt was gaping at the stage, and making comments to his buddy sitting next to him, and making vulgar cupping gestures with his hands.

I was so angry the corners of my vision were tinted red. I grabbed his fingers and squeezed. I rasped at him, "You do that any more, and I'm going to tear off your fingers and feed them to you. You got that?"

A hand grabbed my shoulder and turned me. I glimpsed Spazz Sprague, a crooked smile on his face and a blackjack in his hand. He brought the sap down across my temple. I don't remember hitting the floor.

•

Spazz Sprague knew how to clip someone, because one minute I was raging against this swampie in the Hawaiian shirt, and the next thing I knew I was in the garbage dumpster behind the Pink Lady. The bouncers had carried me outside—probably to the cheers of the crowd—and had thrown me into the dumpster.

"Dennis? You there?"

I groaned, my head filled with nails.

"Dennis, are you in the dumpster?"

It was Isobel's voice. I sat up unsteadily, amid damp, sour garbage. I blinked the flies out of my eyes. After several seconds I could crawl over to the dumpster's lip. I stared down at her.

"Are you okay?"

"No, hell, no, I'm not okay." My throat was dry.

I crawled over the rim and dropped to the ground, which sent pain circling in my head. I was a mess with filthy clothes, garbage hanging from me. Isobel was dressed in a black jogging outfit, and was carrying an athletic bag. She pulled a towel from her bag and wiped garbage from my face. The towel was still damp from her post-performance shower.

"You look like a bog monster," she said.

"Drive me to my place, will you?"

"I don't have a car. Charles drove me out here to French Town tonight."

"Then he can drive us both back."

She looked around the Pink Lady's parking lot. "Jenny Blake was in the lineup tonight, the girl who gave me the dance lessons. Her set was done before mine, so Charles volunteered to drive Jenny home. He said he'd be right back, but I don't see him yet."

A cantaloupe rind was stuck to my elbow. I pulled it off and flipped it back into the dumpster. I smelled bad enough to gag a maggot.

"Call a cab, then." I touched my temple, sending pain from my head down my neck.

"It's not safe to leave my purse at the club, so it's in Charles's car. Do you have money for a cab?"

I shook my head. I never have money, not more than a few dollars in my pocket. I wiped grime from my wristwatch. It was two in the morning. A huge, indifferent yellow moon was above us, and the air was still, so I stood in a stubborn cloud of garbage stench. I could hear music coming from the Pink Lady, but the show was over, and parking lot was now only half full.

"I passed a biker joint down the road a bit," I said. Even talking made my head hurt. "We can get some money there."

"What do you mean?" she asked.

I walked across the parking lot, and she followed. We passed a mini-mart and a quick-lube store. Neon beer signs were visible in windows of the one-story building up ahead, the biker bar. The town had no sidewalks. I guided Isobel around puddles at the side of the road. It had rained that evening.

She said, "I saw you come into the Pink Lady while I was up on stage."

I touched my temple again. "Big mistake on my part."

"You were averting your eyes from the stage. Why did you do that?"

I shrugged.

"Well, it was sweet of you, Dennis."

The bar was a concrete block structure with a satellite dish on the roof. Eight Harley Davidson motorcycles were parked in front of the place, all of them big 94s, several with extended front forks. One of them had flames painted on its gas tank. Leather saddlebags were over rear wheels. The handlebars on all the Harleys were a foot above the tanks, and the frames were low-slung. Chrome on the bikes glittered malevolently in the neon light.

"Your performances have almost caused riots," I said. "Each night police are called in from the neighboring parish, men trying to get into the Pink Lady, trying to crash the gates. I read about it in the paper."

She laughed lightly. "Professor Lizzie is becoming famous around here. Moe Barnes has offered me five thousand dollars a week to continue dancing at the place."

"I went to a library," I said.

"You? I'm astonished."

I ignored the jab. "I searched old copies of the *Times-Picayune*."

"Why?"

"I was researching my manager."

"Ah," she said. "And I'm your manager. So what did you find?"

"Your father was mayor of New Orleans twenty years ago. He was on the board of Children's Hospital, and was the founder of the New Orleans Children's Fund. And he was an organizer of the Bring the NFL to New Orleans Committee, and for several years he chaired the Louisiana Boxing Commission. And so your family got a lot of press coverage."

"More than my father wanted."

"Your first engagement—what was the fellow's name? Jeffrey Danworth—was the talk of the town. Parties left and right, big coverage. He was the son of a successful real estate developer."

"I think I remember."

"And then, nothing. You never got married. At least, I couldn't find a mention of it in the newspaper."

"I called it off."

"Why?"

"That's probably none of your business."

"You burned Jeffrey Danworth down until there was nothing but ashes, is my guess."

She laughed from the back of her throat.

"And then there was your engagement to William Lejune, the wealthy investment banker who was twenty years older than you. Same huge press coverage, all the festivities. And then no marriage."

"Another mistake on my part."

I said, "He had no stamina, is my guess again."

A sign in the window identified this joint as Buddy's Tavern. Another sign said Cold Kegs To Go. A dog, all black and white patches except for brown ears, a pure mutt, sat on the seat of a Harley, eyeing me. I stayed clear of the animal.

I pushed open the door and was met with raucous laughter, a bank of cigarette smoke and ZZ Top coming from a juke box. Isobel followed me into the place, keeping tight against my shoulder, her mouth turning down as she surveyed Buddy's joint. Tattered naugahyde on the bar stools had been repaired with duct tape. A gallon jar of pigs' feet was on the bar. Hanging from the ceiling, horses and a wagon circled endlessly inside a plastic Budweiser bulb. At the other end of the bar hung a blue bug light. Cigarette butts littered the floor. Craters marred the wall near the men's room, probably the result of thrown billiard balls.

Bikers were slouched around a table, where a pill helmet was next to a vast array of empty schooners. Two others bikers were playing pool. The bartender was lining up glasses, ready to fill them. No one else was in the bar, maybe chased away by the bikers.

They looked over at us, invaders on their turf. They were wearing their colors, black leather jackets with devil emblems on the backs. Some of the jackets were sleeveless, more like vests. A few of the bikers wore black leather chaps. Filthy hair and huge guts, skull tattoos, jackboots, torn jeans, bad teeth—the usual biker uniform. To a man, they leered at Isobel.

I stepped to the juke box and pulled the plug from the wall. When the music suddenly quit, all the jabbering and laughing also stopped.

The great heavyweight Jack Dempsey spent his impoverished youth in Colorado and Utah mining towns. Beginning at age sixteen, he would enter hard-pan saloons filled with miners and gamblers and blacksmiths and farmers and loggers—callused, big-armed, no-nonsense men, the lot of them—and would proceed to earn his living in the precise manner I was about to do so at Buddy's Bar in French Town, Louisiana.

I turned to the bikers and announced loudly, "I can beat any son of a bitch in the house."

Time and again, Dempsey used those exact words. They were irresistible then, and they were irresistible now.

Gape mouthed, the bikers stared at me, at this spectacle of suicidal impudence just come in through the door. Isobel gripped my arm. Then the bikers hooted and cursed and banged the table, and then they looked at me some more and laughed, and then they looked at each other, determining who among them would be their champion.

The biggest fellow rose from the table, and did so slowly and ponderously, pushing back his chair, and rising and rising. He must've weighed three hundred pounds, about evenly distributed between muscle and fat. His walrus mustache hid his grin, but amusement showed in his eyes. He had an out-of-kilter nose, a blocky chin and tiny coffee-black eyes.

"Two hundred dollars says you don't last three minutes," I tempted him. I didn't have ten dollars in my pocket, much less two hundred.

He chuckled, and his mates guffawed and called out things such as, "You'll kill him, Deacon." They dug into their wallets and gathered the money, passing it to the big guy.

Deacon placed the pile of bills on the bar. He was wearing black leather half-gloves, which left his fingers exposed. A blue bandana was around his head, and his pony-tail hung below it. Fifty keys were on a chain suspended from his belt.

His voice was low and rumbly, like he was speaking into a bucket. "My cash is on the bar. I don't see yours, sucker."

I half turned to Isobel, keeping my eye on the big biker, and said, "Take off your engagement ring and put it on the bar."

I give her credit. She didn't hesitate. She tugged off the ring and placed it next to the bikers' grubby pile of bills. She was looking at me, not the bikers.

The big biker squinted at the ring. It sparkled, reflecting neon light. He nodded, and maybe a small measure of doubt creased his face. He could buy a new Harley for the price of that ring. We were willing to wager a big diamond against two hundred dollars? Something might be wrong with this wager, probably entered his alleged mind.

Too late now, though. His friends rose from the table to gather around us, leaving about ten feet of fighting room, some leaning against the bar, some sitting on tables. They heckled me, using the standard junior high school stuff. I gently pushed Isobel away from me. Under his leather coat, the big biker was wearing a Ted Nugent Full Bluntal Nugity T-shirt.

"My chick's going to dig that ring," Deacon boasted. He had a wad of tobacco behind his lower lip. "Let's get it on, sucker."

He brought up his arms and balled his fists. The bikers cheered. Deacon viewed me between his fists, then lumbered forward.

Let me interject some knowledge here. A lot of big fat guys think they are tougher than regular guys, when in truth they just take up more acreage and produce more sweat. And if you need to hang around in a pack, such as this bunch of bikers, you are revealing your secret that you can't stand alone. And further: Deacon, like most amateurs, thought his opponent was going to play slappy-face with him for a while, have a little playground brawl, push and shove and swing away. He was mistaken on this point. And another thing, we fistic scientists know that the throat is the most vulnerable, least mobile target on the human body, and that amateurs seldom lower their chins to protect their throats.

I didn't even wait for him to try a jab. I feinted at his belly with my left, and when he dropped his guard—all laymen will drop their arms; it's as predictable as the morning sun—I sent my fist into his Adam's apple. The sound was of a cue stick snapped in half.

Deacon dropped to the floor like a steer at the slaughterhouse. He sputtered and clutched his throat, and his face turned red. Some of his buddies bent down to try to help. Deacon coughed and gagged. Something new in their eyes, a couple bikers looked at me and then quickly looked away.

Isobel grabbed the ring and the cash, and we quickly left Buddy's Tavern. We headed back toward the mini mart to use the pay phone. Now we had money for a cab.

As we walked under the big moon, Isobel said, "You know, ever since I met you, Dennis, I've been to one crummy beer joint after another."

"Yeah." I looked at her. "It's been great, hasn't it?"

Part Two

"Poetry makes things happen, but rarely what the poet wants."
-Poet Howard Nemerov.

9

I was nodding, nearly napping, and suddenly there came a tapping, a rapping at my chamber door. I blinked, then sat up in bed. Someone was gently rapping, rapping at my chamber door. I coughed. 'Tis some visitor tapping at my chamber door.

"Who is it?" I yelled.

"Your tutor," Isobel called through the door.

'Tis some visitor entreating entrance at my chamber door. Only this and nothing more. I still had my pants on, so I stood up and lifted my shirt from the back of the chair and pulled it over my head. I rubbed my eyes with my hands, then opened the door.

She stepped in, but slowly, surveying my little place. After a moment, her nose curled, she asked, "You live here?"

"You're another C. Auguste Dupin."

Her eyes widened. "You've been reading Poe? *Murders at the Rue Morgue*. I'm impressed."

I nodded smugly. "What do you want?"

"It's time for more School of Isobel."

"No, I'll tell you what you want." I took four steps to my sink. "Saturday is your last night at the Pink Lady, and you want me there to make sure you get your poem." I squeezed Crest onto my toothbrush.

"How can you live in this dump?"

"Not enough maids and wrought-iron ice cream tables for you?"

"How many species of vermin live in your rug, do you think?" She stepped around it, staying close to the wall.

I brushed my teeth. She examined my desk, then the top of my chest of drawers, running her finger along its battered top, then checking her finger as if this were a barracks inspection.

She lifted a photo frame. "Who is this?"

I hesitated. "My mother."

"You said you had no memory of your mother, and had never seen a photograph of her." She looked at it more closely. "This isn't a photo. It's been cut from an old magazine."

A moment passed before I said, "When I was ten or eleven, I decided I ought to have a photo of my mother. I didn't have one, so I just clipped one out of a magazine. It's been with me ever since. When I think of my mother, that's the face I give her."

She glanced at me, then gently returned the frame to the dresser. "A man's possessions shape his character."

She turned half a circle, still taking in my room. The landlady hadn't insisted on a damage deposit because everything was already damaged. Every stick of furniture was nicked or gouged or scraped. Everything else was faded: the curtains, the blanket, the lampshade, the print of Marylyn Monroe on the wall, standing over the heating grate. The smell of cat urine was thanks to a former renter's pet. And the place was small, so I couldn't ever get away from the stink.

She opened a three ring binder that was on the dresser. "What's this?"

I spit into the sink. "Help yourself to all my stuff, why don't you?"

"It's press clippings from your fights. They are mostly old and yellowed. And what's this?" She held up a cube of clear plastic. "It looks like a tooth. A broken tooth."

"A souvenir of my last heart-to-heart talk with my father. He came at me, so I knocked him down and sent that tooth skittering across the floor. I picked it up, put it into my pocket and left. I never saw him again."

"And you had it preserved in a polyurethane block?"

"If I'm ever disposed to think a kind thought about my father, I look at that cube, and it quickly chases the thought away."

Isobel returned the cube to the dresser, then stepped to the closet. She opened it.

I rinsed my toothbrush. "Who gave you a license to be so nosy?"

"I'm your manager. It comes with the job. Where are your clothes, Dennis?"

"What're those in that closet, if they're not my clothes?"

She looked at me. Her thicket of black hair was pulled back by a tortoise-shell clip. She was wearing a crested navy blue blazer over a white shirt and white Capri pants. The blazer's sleeves were pushed up her arms.

"Your life needs a make-over, Dennis. That's why you have me."

She stepped to the sink cupboard. She fished around a moment before pulling out a black plastic garbage bag. Then she plucked every shirt—all three of them—from the closet and tossed them into the bag.

I sat on the one chair in the room. It was tipsy, with one leg too short. "They don't need to be laundered."

She said, "I should've worn a surgical mask and gloves."

"Those clothes are clean."

Then she pulled my three pairs of pants from the hooks and threw them into the bag. Then my three pairs of shoes.

"These aren't going to the dry cleaners," she announced. "They are going to the dump."

I made to rise, but with surprising strength she pushed me back into the chair. "Dennis, sit."

Out came another garbage bag from under the sink. She opened the dresser. She pulled out my two towels, and into the plastic bag they went. She opened the next drawer, and lifted out my socks and my underwear, making a big production of using only two fingers to do so. Then she threw in my two belts and my one sweater, and my Arizona State sweatshirt, not that I ever attended school there. So now every item of clothing I owned was in the garbage bags, except the clothes on my back and my boxing trunks and shoes, which she had left alone. She opened another cupboard, and into the bag went my two dishes and two drinking glasses.

A snapshot was on the mirror above the dresser. She pulled it off. "Who is this? Your girlfriend?"

"An ex-girlfriend."

"She dump you?" Isobel raised an eyebrow.

I searched for a suitable explanation, one that didn't make it seem like I'd been gelded, but being dumped is being dumped. "Yeah. She dumped me."

She studied the photo. "What's her name?"

"Lisa."

"Lisa looks like a tart. Ronald McDonald wears less make-up." She moved the photo toward the bag.

I held up my hand. "Hey, that's a keepsake, the only thing I have left after a nice couple of weeks with her."

"Dennis, you can't be anchored to your past. Lisa and the French Revolution have this in common: they are history."

So into the bag went Lisa. I squeezed the bridge of my nose. Isobel opened the medicine cabinet above the sink. The toilet and shower were down the hall, shared by the three rooms on the floor. The only appliance in my room was a hot-plate the landlady had lent me. I once had a microwave, but two weeks ago someone had jimmied my door and stolen it.

"That's my private stuff in the medicine cabinet," I said.

"As a manager, I insist on complete disclosure, Dennis. You can hide nothing from me, not even the intimate contents of your cabinet." She picked up things, one after another, and returned some items to the shelves and tossed some out, saying things like, "This dental floss is an inferior brand," and "They still make Butch Wax?" And into the bag they went along with my toothbrush and my bar of Ivory soap.

Then she balled up the blanket on my bed and shoved it into the bag. She did the same thing with the sheets and pillow case.

She said, more to herself, "Honestly, I've never been so disgusted."

And now you ask, why didn't I jump up from my wobbly chair and stop this crazy woman from cleaning me out? Well, that goes back to her peculiar power over me, that stupor she could put me into, maybe produced by the spectacle of her sheer audacity. Boneless, I sat there, incapable of defending my room against her pillaging.

"Where'd you win this?" She lifted my trophy from the dresser.

"Gold Gloves when I was a kid." It was a cheap trophy, plastic and flaking, and much abused in all my moving from place to place. My name wasn't on it, just *Second Place, Welterweight Division*. I weighed less back then.

She returned it to the dresser, to my relief. But she swept into the bag my pencil and notepad, not even looking into it to see if I might've written something interesting. And my old Timex, and my black plastic comb, not that my hair is long enough to need a comb. She picked up a biography of Muhammed Ali and returned it, but my *Sports Illustrated* went into the bag. Then a rabbit's foot and a ball of rubber bands. When I see a rubber band in the street, I always pick it up. She picked up a nose hair clipper with two fingers and said "Ugh," as she dropped it into the bag.

She opened a drawer, lifted out a thick manila envelope, and asked, "What's in here?"

"My academic records." I put on socks and shoes.

Isobel dumped the documents onto the dresser, then sifted through them. Some were yellowed. She held up a University of Illinois transcript to the window light as if she were checking for a forgery. I had lived in Urbana for three months. "Why don't you just keep going to college until you finish?"

"Easy for you to say with your father mailing in the checks."

She turned a slow circle. "Where's the rest of your stuff, Dennis?"

"I travel light."

She spread her arms. "You are thirty-four years old and this is it?"

"I draw strength from an uncluttered life."

Carrying the trash bag, she walked to the room's back window and yanked it open. Below was a tiny, weed-choked courtyard, the location of eight garbage cans, half a bicycle, a small pile of bricks, and usually a skinny cat or two. She dropped the trash bag out the window. I heard it hit the cobblestones.

"You are what is yours," she announced. Then she tossed out the other bags, all my old stuff. One of the bags must have hit a garbage can as I heard a rattle and clang. "Your personality is much better than it was ten minutes ago."

"I don't feel different."

"It's differently. You are how you speak."

"I thought I was what was mine."

She crossed the room to the door and opened it. "Follow me, Dennis."

I did as told, pushing myself up from the chair. Why did I obey this woman like some dog?

In the hallway, she laughed. "Dennis, you are how you follow orders."

•

Toulon's Fine Clothing, on Loyola Avenue in the CBD, had a bouncer, just like a French Quarter Club, except he was wearing a tailored suit and three-hundred dollar shoes, and he sold clothes on the side. But his main duty was to see that people like me didn't wander through the beveled glass door.

I pushed my way into the store, and he was moving toward me before the store's chilled air had fully enveloped me. The suit, no matter how well tailored, couldn't hide the fellow's muscles. His black hair was slicked back and pasted to his skull. He hesitated only a step when he saw my face and the slope of my shoulders, but he did his job, coming up to me, blocking my way and asking, entirely rhetorically and with hints of menace and contempt, "May I help you?"

The store smelled of rich leather and exotic wood, and the bouncer was wearing too much cologne. I stood there in my sweats.

"I need some clothes, I guess."

"If you are looking for Pants-O-Rama, it's over on South Rampart." He touched my elbow, trying to guide me back to the door. "I'll point out the way."

Isobel Autrey had been outside feeding the parking meter, but now she walked in, grand and grinning. She had a way of moving, utter confidence in every step. She was wearing a dusty rose-colored silk jacket with a notched collar over a silk sweater of the same hue. Her white slacks had a bold peony print, the flowers matching the jacket. Open-toe sandals were on her feet. Her earrings were pearls on tiny silver chains, and they swung when she moved her head.

She said, "Anthony, I see you've already met Dennis Jones."

On seeing Isobel, Anthony removed his spine, collapsed his chest, and generally made himself smaller. He put a smile of ingratiating servitude on his face.

"Miss Autrey, what a pleasure to see you again." Anthony's voice was now a full octave higher. He gently shook Isobel's hand. "Did you bring your fiancé Dr. Brooks for another fitting?"

Isobel turned to me. "I help Charles buy his clothes. He trusts my judgment."

I nodded. "I can see your influence."

"What does that mean?" she asked sharply.

"Compared to Charles, the Prince of Wales dresses like a hobo."

Isobel nodded as if this were a compliment. To Anthony, she said, "I need a range of attire for Dennis here."

"Of course, of course. Let me get Gerard."

Anthony briskly walked toward the fitting room. The shop was intimate, and the atmosphere was of a London club. Prints on the wall were of fox hounds and horses. My shoes were sunk in the carpet up to the strings. Burgundy leather chairs were here and there, next to small tables on which were copies of that morning's *Wall Street Journal.*

Out came the tailor, a tape around his neck. He bowed to Isobel. The tailor's forehead was half his face, ending on top with curly tufts of white hair. He was over-featured, with a nose that had a rosy knob at the end and a wide mouth filled with dark teeth. A stick of chalk was behind one of his large ears. Suspenders held up his pants. He gripped me by the elbow and led me to a seven-foot-high mirror.

He asked, "What do we need today?"

"Well, a shirt, maybe," I said.

Isobel and Anthony had followed us. I could see them in the mirror.

She asked, "Remember those French-blue cotton dress shirts we ordered for Charles? Several of them for Dennis, I think."

"Excellent choice," Anthony purred. A small notebook and pen were in his hands.

Gerard wrapped the tape around my neck. He whistled appreciatively, and said, "Going to take a lot of cloth just for the collar," then made notes on a pad of paper that was on a table that had an elephant's leg as its base.

"And Dennis would look good in your scalloped-collar twill shirts, three or four in different shades," Isobel directed. "And several white pinpoint button-down shirts."

I said, "I can only wear one shirt at a time, Isobel."

Deep in concentration, Isobel touched her chin with the point of her finger. "And for casual, several of your Largo short-sleeve poplin shirts, and three or four twill button-down shirts. You know, the kind Charles favors."

"We certainly do," Anthony said.

"For pants: some cotton chinos, and also several pairs of stretch flat-front pants, maybe in khaki and taupe and charcoal, the usual variety. And toss in a pair of light blue twill trousers, and a pair of plantation silk pants."

"I favor those plantation silks myself," murmured Anthony.

"How about some jeans?" I said. "You threw mine out the window, Isobel."

"Two cashmere blazers, one black and one navy, each with two buttons," she said. "And a three-button tweed sport coat. And slacks to go along with the blazer and sport coat, maybe six pairs."

"Six pairs?" I exclaimed. "Isobel, we aren't outfitting an army battalion here."

"Half with cuffs, half not," she said. "You choose the ties, Anthony, about a dozen. And shoes. Half a dozen pairs. What's the size, Dennis."

"My feet? Twelve."

"It'll be my pleasure." Anthony was taking notes at a rapid pace, his expression one of rapture.

"Did I throw out your underwear?" Isobel asked. "I can't remember. Maybe I've repressed the memory."

After a moment I replied in a low voice, "Yes." Was I the only person in the room embarrassed by talk of my underwear?

She said, "You fill in the order for accessories, Anthony. Shoes, belts, underwear, socks, and so forth."

Gerard was on one knee, measuring my inseam. "How do you hang, sir?"

"Pardon?"

"Your, ah, privates," the tailor explained. "How do you hang?"

Mystified, I looked at Isobel in the mirror. One of her eyebrows was up, and she wore an expression of refined amusement.

Then the tailor's meaning hit me, or so I thought. I cleared my throat. "Down, most of the time."

Her eyes clicked to the ceiling.

"Left or right," Gerard explained. "I make accommodations in the pants accordingly."

I had to think. Then I whispered down toward him, "Left."

He rose to make a note on his pad. "All done, then."

"Anthony, can you assemble all this by, say, 4:30 this afternoon?" Isobel asked.

Anthony hesitated only a fraction. "Of course."

Anthony escorted us to the door, a hand on my elbow. "We look forward to your next visit, Miss Autrey," were his parting words.

We walked out onto the sidewalk. I had lived in New Orleans half a year, and had never become accustomed to the slap of heavy wet air when you step from an over-air-conditioned building out onto the street. It felt like a barber's towel had been draped over my head.

"I can't afford a leather belt at that place," I said. "Who is paying for all those clothes?"

"The syndicate," she replied.

Isobel led me to her car, the big Mercedes. I've never owned a car that didn't argue with me when I wanted to open the door, creaking and groaning, afraid I might actually request that the engine start. The Mercedes' door seemed to anticipate me, opening softly and silently before I had squeezed the handle.

I slid onto the seat. "What syndicate?"

"Up-and-coming pugilists are often sponsored by a syndicate. Charles and daddy and me. A syndicate of three."

I was wary. "What percentage of my purses does the syndicate get?"

"Zero percentage. You simply continue to help me." She started the engine, then reached for her sunglasses. "Toulon's will send me the bill, and you are not to worry about it."

We shot out of the parking spot onto Rampart, the car not making any noise that I could detect.

"Cashmere blazers?" Talking more to myself. "Twill shirts?"

"Don't worry, Dennis." She grinned. "You won't be the first boxer in history who dresses better than he fights."

•

"How is it possible you are thirty-four years old and don't know how to dance?" Isobel asked, leading me onto the small floor.

"I can dance just fine." I stepped between tables. "Play some rock or blues or zydeco. I'll knock your socks off, my moves are so good. But the waltz? Who needs that?"

She said over her shoulder, "Sunday evening, meet us at Nola at seven o'clock in the evening. I want to make an introduction. And we'll celebrate my last day of work for Moe Barnes, and getting my poem." Nola was a restaurant in the French Quarter.

"An introduction?"

"You heard me."

"A girl?"

"No, a rash." She rolled her eyes for my benefit. She loved doing that. I saw it a lot. "Of course, a girl."

"I don't need your help. Anytime I want to meet a girl, I go to Jelly's."

"And your first words to her are, 'So, how's your first day back in society?'"

"I like fun girls, girls with big laughs, girls who know how to eat crayfish and hot sauce, girls who know how to make the seven-ten split."

"Honestly, Dennis, you have the horizon of an ant."

"Girls who don't call me a bug."

She led me to the middle of the dance floor. We were at the Fortune Club where Isobel's dad spent much of his spare time, which is to say, much of his time. The club was in an old mansion at the edge of the Garden District. It had no athletic facilities, but served its members with a restaurant and bar, a library and a card room.

The club had the musty scent of an ancient sanctuary, sealed off from the rudeness of commerce and politics and the media. This was an early Wednesday evening, the club's midweek dance night, and seven gray-haired couples were on the floor, moving to a five-piece band. The seniors creaked and shuffled across the floor, the men eyeing Isobel and trying to stand straighter.

At the edge of the dance floor, diners finished their meals. At the bar, a couple of old gents were leaning toward each others' hearing aids. Propped against the backbar, the bartender appeared to be sleeping on his feet. Isobel's father and Charles Brooks were going to meet us here in a few minutes.

I said, "I've been to funerals that were more lively than this place."

"You are here to learn, not to have fun," Isobel said primly. She turned toward me and stepped close. "Put your right hand on the small of my back."

I carefully put my arm around her. "Your back is nicely bony."

"You have more bone between your ears than I have in my entire body." She took my hand. "Her name is Alison Karl. She likes to dance, and she's good at it. I want you to impress her."

"I can slow dance," I protested again. "I've done it all my life."

"Slow dancing in a tavern—you and some tramp pasted to each other, writhing away, embarrassing any sober spectators—is not dancing. It's some reptilian mating ritual."

"What've you got against fun?"

"I put my hand in yours, like this." She was close to me. Smelling of lilacs, her thick black hair was at my nose. She was wearing a khaki silk crepe tank top and a long black skirt with a khaki floral print, and black leather sandals that had an inch of heel. She looked up at me, her blue eyes huge. Her hand was a cool, slight presence in mine. She lightly placed her other hand on my shoulder. "Now, remember, there should be air between us."

"Can do."

"Keep your shoulders straight."

"Can do."

"And keep your hips above your feet."

"I always do, except when I'm taking a nap."

"Follow my lead, first your left foot forward."

She stepped back, and I went with her, then she went sideways, and I followed.

"Piece of cake," I said.

Then I stepped on her toes. She winced.

"Sorry."

"That's okay," she replied. "I walk on them, too. Now follow me."

Five seconds later I landed on her toes again, and I said, "Maybe it's these new shoes. I've never owned a pair that weighed so little. They're throwing off my rhythm." I was wearing some of my new duds.

She smiled up at me. "A lifetime swinging vine to vine should have made you more graceful."

"Who is Alison Karl?"

"She is one of my graduate students. She is working on her Ph.D. dissertation, the Dialectic of Intersubjectivity and Intercultural Dialogue of Austen's Prose."

"Won't we have fun chatting, then?"

"She is smart and funny and lively."

I waited, but finally had to ask, "And?"

"And what?" Isobel's tone was accusing.

"Usually when I hear some girl is smart and funny and lively, it means she's been run over by the ugly truck a couple of times."

She dug her nails into my shoulder. "Dennis, just this once, try to rise above yourself. And in any event, Alison is quite pretty."

I remembered how Isobel was good at the lie.

She led me around the floor. I was getting better, keeping off her toes. I concentrated on moving my feet to the rhythm. One, two, three, four. An old gummer tried to ditch his wife and cut in on me for a turn with Isobel, but his wife fiercely held on and the old guy didn't have the strength to break away.

"I've given Alison fair warning about you," Isobel said. "I don't want her to see your face the first time, and turn to flee for her life."

"That's nicely put."

"What I mean is, you have the face of a brawler. Cauliflower ear, big chin, a bumpy, out-of-kilter nose. Spiky haircut."

"My mother, the lady in that photo frame, loves my face."

Isobel said, "It has never occurred to Alison, cloistered at Mayer Hall at Tulane University, working away on the finer points of Austen, that a person might actually have calluses on his eyebrows. I've had to prepare her."

"Terrific."

"And I've told her you are smart and funny and lively." She grinned again.

The band swung into an elevator version of a John Denver song. The musicians were watching Isobel, every damn one of them. The clarinet player swiveled back and forth in his seat so that his clarinet was always pointed at her as she and I moved across the floor. The bass player's mouth was open, standard for a bass player.

"You've gone two minutes without mashing my toes," Isobel said, "so now it's your turn to lead."

I did so, concentrating. She was weightless, floating in front of me. I moved smoothly, but I think it was mostly her skill allowing me to think I was dancing well.

Isobel said, "Now after several dances, you and Alison may dance more closely. None of your typical pawing, just a slight contact."

She drifted closer, and now my chest was touching her. She moved her hand from my shoulder to the back of my neck. She pinched my neck. "What's this?"

"Is that a trick question? It's my neck."

She squeezed the back of my neck, none too gently. "I mean this slab of hard flesh. It's muscle, isn't it? Why does anyone need so much muscle in his neck?"

"To keep my head upright, I suppose."

"A head—even your head, Dennis, filled with bone and nonsense. only weighs so much."

I counted to myself, not paying too much attention to what she was saying. *One, two, three, four,* trying to remember the pattern.

"Don't flex your chest, Dennis."

"I'm not," I said.

She pressed into me a little. "You are, too."

"That's just me. I've got more muscles than you are accustomed to out at Mayer Hall at Tulane University."

She put a hand on my chest and squeezed the pectoral muscle. "I'm allowed to do this because I'm your manager." She tried to sink her fingers into my chest muscle. "And I'm still taking your personal inventory." She pressed my right deltoid. "Your chest is like armor plate, Dennis." She kneaded it. "Women like softness."

"Well, you've got Charles. That's plenty of softness."

Then she moved her hand to my left trapezius, squeezing the muscle at the base of my neck. "Dennis, this is going to intimidate Alison. She isn't accustomed to muscle. You'll frighten her if she brushes up against you while she is dancing."

One, two, pivot, three four, pivot again. I focused on my feet. My new shoes had tassels on them, if you can imagine.

"And feel this." She put both of her hands on my shoulders, and squeezed the muscles there, which are nicely developed because as a boxing coach will tell you, a thrown punch begins at the shoulder. "There is honestly no reason to be built like this, Dennis." She inhaled slowly, then ended by clucking sternly.

We glided across the dance floor. I was doing pretty well keeping my feet out of her way. *One, two, pivot, three, four, pivot.* One of the old couples danced so close to us I could smell their dentures.

She moved her hands down to my biceps. "What possible good is all of this muscle? It just stretches out your shirts."

"I no longer buy my own shirts. The syndicate does. So I don't worry about it."

I had been concentrating, trying to keep myself untangled from her feet, and trying to move in time to the music, staring at the far walls so as not to be distracted, but now I lowered my gaze to Isobel.

She was looking up at me, studying me intently, her lips slightly parted.

Finally she said, more a whisper, "This is part of my inventory of you." She dropped a hand to my belly, and ran her fingers along the muscles there. "There is simply no reason in the modern world to have a stomach that is corrugated, Dennis."

"A thousand sit-ups a day since I was sixteen years old."

"Muscles are out, Dennis. You should be fashionably thin, like Charles."

"Quiet. I'm counting time to the band." *One, two, three, four.*

Her hand slid down to my left thigh where she prodded the muscle.

I could feel her breath as she spoke into the curve of my neck. "It's my considered judgment that to be attractive to women, you need to lose thirty pounds of muscle."

"Skinny boxers are like slow sprinters."

I was doing fairly well. One, two, three, four, right along with the music. Many years skipping rope and working the speed bag were paying off. Joe Louis would've made short work of learning the waltz, you can bet.

She asked, "May I survey the density of your gluteus maximus?"

One, two, three, four. I tried not to dip my shoulders, and was careful not to hug Isobel to me, like I would some girl in a bar, though she was now standing pretty close. Real close, in fact. Right up against me.

One, two, three, four. "My butt? There's only muscle there, too, pivot, three, four, pivot. Hey, this is easy." I guided her across the dance floor.

Her hand went around to my posterior. She tested it, pressing lightly, then with more energy.

"Honestly, Dennis," she breathed into my neck. "I don't know when I've been so disgusted." She pressed her hand into my bottom again and kept it there. "What possible use is a rump that's this solid?"

We danced, the old guys looking at me with undisguised envy.

The song ended, and the clarinet player said into the microphone, "We'll be right back after a short break."

A break from what, I wanted to ask. After a long moment, Isobel slowly released me. We moved across the dance floor toward the diners.

I looked at her. "You need to get a little more exercise."

"Why do you say that?" Isobel's voice seemed strained. She crossed her arms, hugging herself as she walked toward our table. She was scowling for some reason. She didn't look at me.

"That wasn't much of a workout, teaching me to do the waltz, with slow music and all," I said. "But your face is red, like you've run two miles."

"I'm in great shape." With her fingers she dabbed at moisture on her forehead.

I remembered to pull out her chair. I lowered myself to the chair next to her.

"Teaching you anything is hard work." She still wouldn't meet my gaze. "It'd make anyone's face red." She was looking at the door from the hallway into the dining room. "Here come Daddy and Charles. Now I'll be able to dance without getting my toes maimed."

I looked around for a waiter.

She rose from her chair, but before leaving to greet them, she said, "I'm going to have to give Alison a new and more stern warning about you. She has no idea how to handle a big glob of muscle." She smiled in a small way, sort of an embarrassed smile.

She walked toward her father and fiancé. The air was oddly cooler after she had left.

10

"He's not going to give you the poem," I said.

"We made a deal, and I've done my part. I've danced my last dance out in French Town. Now he owes me the poem."

Isobel was behind the wheel of her black Mercedes, which she drove like a Camaro.

"There's the number," she said, and stomped on the brakes.

The house's address was in brass on a white post. We turned off the county road, crossed a ditch drainpipe, then drove down an asphalt driveway. This was bayou country, and moss hung from oak and hickory trees that dotted fields on both sides of the driveway.

At one time cattle may have grazed in the soggy fields, but now hackberry and crabgrass and saltmarsh willows had reclaimed them. Wild petunias grew along a row of rotted fence posts. Cypress trees lined the edge of the field to the west, meaning water was nearby.

Moe Barnes had a big spread. We wound around for three hundred yards, passing old stumps that had wild orchids growing from them, and banks of crabapple trees. We crossed two small bridges over branches of the bayou. I could smell the dank water. A blue heron honked, a strangling sound. I don't like swamps, generally.

"If he was going to give you the poem," I said, "he would've done so last night after your last performance."

"That's why you're here, Dennis." Isobel turned the steering wheel back and forth. "You're going to make sure we walk out of there with that poem."

We passed under the boughs of an ancient oak tree, rounded the last curve and came to a wide asphalt parking lot near, which was a five-car garage. Wild azaleas and brown-eyed Susans bordered the parking lot. To the north, across the expanse of asphalt, was a walkway that led to a small pedestrian bridge over a pond. Isobel parked the car, and I opened the door and stepped out into the bayou heat. Almost instantly, my back was wet. Clubmoss hung from the tree boughs, and airplants were stuck on tree trunks. A cardinal let loose with its fluty cheer, cheer, cheer. The air smelled of blossoms and rot.

We stepped onto a pedestrian bridge, a masonry and wood structure, not more than twenty feet across with low safety rails. Crane fly orchids grew near the water. A collection of concrete yard sculptures was near the banks: a deer, a gnome, a sundial and some others. I peered down into the murky water, which was dappled with orange-blooming lilies. The water rippled suddenly, and I saw a flash of fin or belly, some predator, I was sure. I shuddered.

We left the bridge, and came to Barnes's home, which was surrounded by a lawn trimmed as neatly as a golf green. The one-story house was Mediterranean, with pink stucco walls and a red tile roof. A large weeping willow tree cast shade on the front yard.

Isobel was wearing a blue plaid Irish linen shirt, open at the front, over a cotton T-shirt, and white linen cropped pants. She carried a small leather handbag. Her brown sandals clicked along the pavers. We walked under the porch. The double doors were massive, and made of oak, with a stained glass tulip bouquet in the middle of each door. Instead of a button, a chord hung to one side of the door. When she pulled it, a bell rung from deep inside the building.

After a moment, Moe Barnes opened the door, smiling at us with his horse teeth.

"A gangster opens his own door?" Isobel asked. "Since when?"

Moe Barnes looked her up and down. "I hardly recognize you with your clothes on."

"I want my poem." She was fairly hissing.

Barnes looked at me and laughed, a grating sound from deep in his chest. "Last I heard, you were sleeping in a Dumpster outside my club."

I didn't say anything.

"He's your muscle, Professor?" Barnes asked. "He can stay outside with the mosquitoes while we talk."

Isobel replied, "If he doesn't come in, I don't come in."

Barnes considered this for a moment, then said, "Sure. We can all have a nice little visit."

His words were a series of stertorous gasps, and his double chin wagged left and right as he spoke. He was wearing yellow suspenders that held up black slacks, and much of his yellow socks showed. On his feet were gray dock shoes. His eyes were set back deeply in his pudgy face. He came up only to my chin but his shoulders and arms were beefy, and his thighs pressed against the fabric. His belly hung over the top of his pants.

Walking with a limp, he led us through his house. We passed the living room, which was filled with faux-Tiffany lamps, one advertising Ipana toothpaste and another Moxie Drugs in leaded glass. Also in the living room were about two dozen pairs of andirons, some made of bronze and others of wrought iron, along one wall. Squeezed together in a bookcase were maybe a hundred German beer steins. In the hallway, lined up like soldiers, were antique filling station pumps, some with illuminated glass globes on top.

He spread his hands and said, "EBay is going to bankrupt me."
Barnes showed us into his den, where a floor-to-ceiling bookshelf held a collection of Mr. Peanut coin banks, Mr. Peanut salt and pepper shakers, a Mr. Peanut five-piece set of serving dishes, and a dozen Mr. Peanut glow-in-the-dark lamp fobs. A boom box was also on the bookshelf.

He sank into a chair behind a massive mahogany desk, and he spread his hands out, palms down. On a side table were displayed fifteen brass and beveled glass carriage clocks. On another table were three dozen old salve tins, and on the wall above the tins was a framed advertising flyer from one of the salves, "Do You Have Piles? DeWitte's Carbolized Witch Hazel Salve."

He caught me looking at his collection. "What does 'carbolized' mean, do you think?"

I shrugged. "Sometimes I eat candy bars that have been carmalized, but carbalized doesn't ring a bell."

"Don't you have a dictionary?" Isobel demanded. "You've got everything else."

He smiled sourly. "You don't need a dictionary to do what I do."

"My poem shouldn't even be touched by a gangster."

He smoothed his desk top with his palms, a gesture of equanimity. "I'm sixty-four years old, which is too old to be called a gangster by anybody."

Intent on getting us killed, Isobel replied, "You're only fifty-four, if you don't count the time you've been in prison."

His upper lip curled. "I want to talk business."

Isobel had filled me in on Moe Barnes. Moe's father, Ike Barnes, had been king of the loan sharks in St. James Parish, and had run a policy racket, and was a bootlegger, too—anything that was profitable and illegal and out in the country, away from New Orleans, where the big boys were.

When Ike Barnes disappeared one day, his body was never found and a dozen rumors about the disappearance sounded credible. Moe inherited his father's rackets, which consisted of the allegiance of half a dozen small-timers who didn't have a high-school diploma among them. When he was younger, Moe Barnes was a cock-of-the-walk who didn't know his limits, and when he decided to expand his bayou loan sharking operation into New Orleans, just a little bit into the Kenner neighborhood out near the airport, Leo LeClerque, whose territory it was, didn't view Barnes's ambition in a kindly way.

Leo caught Barnes on his turf one night, and drove a Cadillac over Barnes's legs, shattering them. This was thirty-five years ago, and Moe Barnes had walked with a gimp ever since, and he had never returned to New Orleans, not once in all the years, even though his home was only fifty miles from the city.

He said, "I've bought a club in New Orleans."

"I thought Leo LeClerque taught you a lesson about moving into New Orleans," Isobel said.

"LeClerque died two weeks ago." Barnes smiled with cold pleasure. "He passed away peacefully in his sleep, unfortunately."

On Barnes's desk were eight pink glass cockatoos lined up in a row near the telephone. Each bird sat on a glass perch above a glass stand and was fourteen inches high with a pink and white glass tail that curled under in a circle below the perch, the feathers and all of it in glass. The desk's writing surface was tan leather inlay, and its front panel was intricately carved, and displayed a serpents riding on a wave, horses at full gallop, snails on grape leaves, and other scenes I couldn't make out.

Barnes scooted back in the chair, and opened the desk's drawer to pull out an envelope. Isobel's breath caught.

"Here it is, Professor." He wiggled the envelope temptingly in the air. "But I want to renegotiate our deal."

"Give me my poem." Her voice was percussive. "I've earned it."

Barnes said, "Those two fools, Soapy Fay and Donnie Lafitte, brought me this poem as a return on some favors I had done for them, getting Soapy out of a fix with the law. They said a real class act would work for me if I dangled this poem in front of her, a poem written by one of her dead relatives."

Isobel stared at Barnes.

"So I took them up on their offer," he said, "and soon I had Dr. Lizzie fans busting down my doors trying to get into my club."

"I've done my part of the deal." Isobel's voice was diamond-hard.

Barnes made a steeple of his fingers. "That poem means a lot to you, doesn't it, Dr. Lizzie? But who is Horace Eap, I asked myself."

I could sense Isobel tightening.

"I looked him up in the encyclopedia. Couldn't find him. Then I went down to the library, and did some looking around. Still couldn't find a trace of Horace Eap, and couldn't find any poetry by him, either."

She said, "*The Lost Land* is the only poem he ever wrote. It was never published, and it's my professional opinion that it isn't very good, that it is amateurish and rather child-like. I mean, look at the repetitive use of words. That alone should tell you why Horace never made it as a poet."

Barnes said. "It didn't have much rhyming, either. Ain't poems supposed to rhyme?"

"But Horace is a relative of mine. He's my great great grandfather."

Barnes nodded over his fingertips.

Isobel pulled a photograph from her handbag. She passed it over the desk to Moe Barnes. The back of the photo was yellow with age.

She said, "This is Horace Eap. He was a lieutenant in the Confederate army."

Isobel had come prepared. She had purchased the photograph at a Royal Street antique store, and had no idea who the soldier was.

"I see the resemblance." Barnes studied the photo. "Same shifty eyes."

I glanced at Isobel. Her eyes were shifty.

The gangster said, "But you've gone to a lot of trouble to get some poem that you yourself, Professor, says isn't very good, and—"

Isobel interrupted with heat, "I want to join the Daughters of Confederate Army Poets Society, and they won't admit me unless I have that poem."

"The Daughters of Confederate Army Poets Society?" he repeated.

"I must have that poem to be admitted into the society."

What a whopper. I caught myself about to roll my eyes, same thing Isobel always did. Surely the gangster would burst out laughing. But the lie was laid out without hesitation and with a natural anger, and was utterly convincing.

Isobel was coiled and ready to leap out of her chair at Barnes's throat. I lightly placed my hand on her arm to steady her.

Barnes returned the photo to her. "I see why you want the poem so badly. Daughters of the Confederate Army Poets Society and all. Maybe we can do a deal."

"We've already done a deal," she said.

He turned to me. "Soapy and Donnie somehow think you and I cheated them, that they didn't receive fair value for their Eap poem. They saw how much money Dr. Lizzie made for me, and now they are mighty upset. They may know better than to take me on, but they are looking for you. So I give you that warning as proof of my friendship."

I nodded.

"My new club is called the French Kiss," he said. "I'm going to have a gala re-opening celebration, and I'm going to have the hottest dancer in the south. And that's you, Dr. Lizzie."

"I'm done with dancing, and I'm done with you." She held out her hand. "Give me my poem."

Moe Barnes placed the envelope on the desk top, squaring it in front of his ample belly, then held up his thick hands, framing his words. "I've got a big new reader board out front of the French Kiss. On opening night, it'll say, 'Professor Lizzie Lectures You on the Bump and Grind.' What do you think?"

"You promised me the poem."

"You'll have your own dressing room. A nice big costume allowance. Two days off a week. Medical and dental, the works. And my club is right near Tulane. Maybe we can draw some of your students."

Isobel's eyes were locked on the envelope.

Barnes said, "I've hired hundreds of dancers over the years, but I've never had anybody fill my club night after night like you did, Professor. There's something about you. Your looks, your moves, your ... fire. You are magic, and you're my ticket to New Orleans."

Without taking her eyes off the envelope, Isobel said, "Dennis, now is the time to do your part of our deal. Grab the poem and let's get out of here."

Mo Barnes placed his hands across his ample stomach and smiled, and in through the den door came his nephew, Spazz Sprague, carrying a pistol. Sprague was a large-boned man with blank black eyes and eyebrows that grew together over his nose. He was wearing jeans and red shirt with a Cat's Meow emblem on the chest. The Cat's Meow is a karaoke joint in the Quarter. The pistol was a small automatic almost hidden in the fellow's hand. He stepped close and wiggled the pistol at me. This was the fellow who had clipped me with a sap at the Pink Lady.

"Let's not be hasty, Professor," Barnes said. "You haven't heard all of my deal."

As I've mentioned before, the hand is quicker than the eye. My left hand lashed out, a tight arc with my entire body behind it, and smashed into Sprague's gun hand, and sent the pistol sailing across the room. At almost the same instant, I threw a right cross, and my fist caught him square on the nose. He was out cold standing there, and he collapsed as if the carpet had been yanked from under his feet. The pistol clattered against a bookshelf, then fell to the floor. I snatched the envelope from the desk, and all this took less than two seconds. Moe Barnes's eyes widened, but he didn't have time for any other reaction.

I grabbed Isobel's arm and dragged her out of the den, and then we ran through the house, passing all of Moe Barnes's collections. We opened the front door and ran along the walkway. I glanced over my shoulder. No one was following us. We stopped on the bridge over the bayou. A redwing blackbird called from the bushes along the damp shore. The bayou was steamy.

Isobel threw back her head and laughed, quick notes of victory. She held her hands over her head as if she were crossing a finish line. Her grin hung ear to ear.

"We did it," she crowed. "Edgar Allan Poe's lost poem is mine."

She did a little victory jig, shuffling her feet, and spread her arms and lifted her face to the sun, ready to receive the world's adulation. She breathed, "At last, at last, at last. It's mine."

Smiling along with her, I handed Isobel the envelope. She held it like a piece of the true cross.

"The things I have gone through to get this. All the work, and all the struggle." She glanced quickly up at me, and her smile turned puckish. "Tolerating you, for one thing." She slit open the envelop with her fingernail. "But you earned your keep back there, Dennis."

Then she slowly drew out the paper. It wasn't faded and yellow, as I might have expected, but was new and bright.

Isobel read aloud, "'The poem is in my safe deposit box. Come on back, and we'll talk. Best regards, Moe.'"

Isobel's face whitened to the color of a skull. She brought her eyes up, but they were unseeing. She stared off into the bayou. Her mouth worked without a sound. Moe Barnes's note fluttered to the bridge deck.

"Isobel?" I asked.

A wash of red swept over her face, a startling change of color, and her lips turned down into a snarl, and her gaze snapped to me. Her eyes were bullets. A primal scream of rage came from her. No Dervish ever gave a more fearsome battle cry. And she slammed both her palms into my chest and pushed me over the low rail.

I cartwheeled off the bridge and fell eight feet into the brown water.

•

Charles Brooks must have known the owner because our table at Nola was on the first floor at a window. I had arrived a few minutes early and was wearing some of my new finery, so the waiter showed me to the table, though I could sense his reluctance, him sneaking looks at my cauliflower ear and assorted calluses and scars.

I had been sitting only a few minutes, fiddling with my fork when Isobel and Charles arrived, towing my date for the evening. The young lady was one of Isobel's doctoral students, you'll recall, and when she first saw me she didn't wince, which is always a plus.

I stood and smiled and held out my hand as Isobel introduced us. Her name was Alison Karl, and her smile faltered when her gaze found my ear. I'm accustomed to it. As we lowered ourselves into chairs around the table, Isobel placed her hand on Alison's arm as if to brace her.

"You're a boxer?" Alison asked. She was trying not to stare at my tissue-filled ear, but her eyes clicked back and forth between it and my eyes.

"Sometimes I'm a boxer but most times I'm just a punching bag."

She smiled tentatively.

"You're not going to be a boxer if I can't get you a fight," Isobel said, frowning. "I had thought, using some of Daddy's connections, I could line up a good bout. He was on the Louisiana Boxing Commission a long time ago. Too long ago, it turns out. I was trying to get a fellow named Sammy Dresser."

I laughed and shook my head. Dresser was a Tennessee fighter, and Ring Magazine said he was number six in the country. "There's no chance Sammy Dresser will take on the likes of me. He wants quality opponents so that when he beats them his ranking will rise."

Isobel said, "You are a quality fighter, and you are getting even better thanks to diligent efforts on the part of your manager, me. I'll keep working on getting you a fight. Don't worry." But she sounded worried.

"I don't spend much time with athletes." Alison's words carried a wistful tone. "My life is sort of bookish right now."

Her chestnut-colored hair was held behind her head with a tortoise shell clip. Her face was narrow, and her eyes were large and brown and lively. Her chin was finely sculpted. Her lips were full and red, and her cheekbones prominent. Around her long and elegant neck was a thin strand of gold with a single pearl lying in the cleft of her throat. She was wearing a crepe sheath dress with floral beading on the short sleeves. She was looking at my ear less and less. The waiter came to our table.

Speaking French, Charles ordered a bottle of wine, but when the waiter shook his head politely, Charles switched languages, with a triumphant glance at us.

Isobel's jet hair was all around her head, flying away like it did, elegant and crazy at the same time, with curls and sweeps, gleaming under the light. She was wearing a black dress with no sleeves. Three thin silver bracelets were on her left wrist. Her engagement ring glittered in the light.

She smiled. "I told Alison that even an education at a fine university like Tulane cannot fully prepare her for the ordeals waiting for her out in society. So her date with you tonight will round out her education."

Alison laughed, still staring at me, studying me as if I were behind glass at a museum.

The waiter returned to pour a taste of wine into Charles's glass. Charles swirled the wine around inside his glass, sniffed it, tasted it loudly and pronounced it satisfactory. The waiter filled our glasses.

"I've really been looking forward to tonight," Alison said. "Out at the university, there's a lot of eighteen and nineteen-year-olds. Kids, really, with no experience and nothing to say."

"I've had a lot of experience, and still don't have much to say."

She laughed as if I were witty.

"And I'm fascinated by boxing," Alison said." I can't imagine anybody getting into a ring, ready to fight."

Isobel wrinkled her nose at Alison's eagerness.

"With me, I fight or I don't eat." I sipped the wine. "Get beat up or starve, is my choice."

I apparently had never been funnier. Alison laughed as if I were Jay Leno. Isobel rolled her eyes.

We ordered dinner, Alison choosing something called a Lafayette boudin, which was stewed in beer, onions and cane syrup. I recognized almost nothing on the menu, so I ordered the same thing, hoping for the best.

Alison leaned a little toward me, her chin cupped in her palm. "I'd like to go to one of your fights some day."

"If you sit in the first six rows," Isobel said, "you get too much of Dennis's blood on you, is my experience."

Charles was wearing a blue silk tie and French cuffs. He regaled us with a story about one of his patients who had eighty-three warts on the back of her left hand, "and when I got done with her, her hand resembled Verdun."

Verdun is a World War I battlefield. I looked it up later. Our salads were served. I could've sworn mine had dandelion leaves in it. I ate it anyway.

Alison hardly waited until Charles was done speaking before again turning to me, "Do you live around here, Dennis?"

"Not too far."

"In an apartment? What's it like?" She removed her hairclip and shook out her hair, which fell to her shoulders. Her brown hair was streaked with honey and caramel hues.

"Honestly," Isobel said under her breath.

Alison apparently didn't hear her, as she was concentrating on me.

"It's not much. A room, a narrow bed, a beat-up dresser, a tipsy chair. From the roof of my building, I get a good view of Mardi Gras."

When Alison finished her wine, Charles refilled her glass. The skin doctor was a convivial host, shifting the conversation back and forth, but Alison was deft at returning it to me, and she asked question after question about boxing and my career. I didn't stretch the truth too much, just minimizing the amount of time I'd spent on my back.

"Your life is just so exotic," Alison gushed.

.Isobel scoffed loudly.

A word about my plunge into Moe Barnes's pond. I hit that dark water, and with Barnes's reputation for feeding foes to crocodiles well in my mind, swam to shore and would've left Mark Spitz in my wake I was moving so fast.

When I scrambled up the embankment, assorted pond weeds hanging from my sodden clothes, Isobel was already back in the car. I removed my shirt, plucked the plant life from it, wrung it out and put it back on. Then I entered her car, about to cuss her out for her foolishness.

Both her hands were on the steering wheel. Her face was preternaturally calm, and she was so still I was tempted to take her pulse. She stared out the windshield without blinking, maybe without breathing. Finally she said, "I have a new plan, Dennis," her lips scarcely moving. I didn't inquire about it at the time because her plans usually involved me in some uncomfortable way. We drove away from Barnes's house, ignoring his invitation to return.

The main courses arrived, and the air filled with the scents of spices. Isobel joined Charles in leading the conversation here and there, touching on the theater, to which I could contribute nothing, then to movies. When Charles said the funniest movie ever made was Lina Wertmueller's Pasqualino Settebellezze, I replied he had never seen Laurel and Hardy move a piano up a flight of stairs.

Alison blurted, "It's so authentic."

"What's authentic?" I asked.

"Your life."

Isobel said in a low voice, "Alison, take a few sips of water, why don't you?"

Whenever Alison could, she returned the conversation to me, leaning toward me, and trying to cut the table into two conversations. I glanced at Isobel, and could tell she was not amused.

Alison said she had received a masters in comparative literature from UCLA, and now was working on her doctorate so she could teach literature to college students. She told me the reason she wanted to do this, but it made so little sense that it didn't register on me so I carry no memory of it.

Alison asked me if I had any ambition. Actually, she phrased it, "Tell me about your dreams." And I replied that I was going to be heavyweight champion someday. She thought I was serious, and I didn't have the heart to correct the impression.

I'm less skilled with women than I am with boxing, so that tells you something. I do know, though, to ask questions, listen intently and keep my hands to myself. Alison must have taken this modest level of civility for charm and intrigue, because during desert— Alison ordered a Creole chocolate cream cheese brownie—she asked if I wanted to go somewhere after dinner and have a drink. Meaning, she wanted to ditch Isobel and Charles.

A tuck of suspicion formed on Isobel's brow.

I smiled. "Sounds like fun."

Alison leaned closer. "Maybe you have something to drink at you're apartment."

I had one bottle of water and two cans of Coke in my refrigerator. I didn't get the impression she was particularly thirsty, though.

Isobel had followed this little exchange, her fork hovering over her apple buttermilk pie. Her expression reflected utter bafflement. "This can't be happening." Isobel's face was pinched with disapproval. "Dennis, you've done something to anesthetize Alison."

"I've only had a glass and a half of wine, spread out over the entire meal," Alison argued.

"You've been working too hard on your thesis, Alison, and your judgment isn't as critical as it should be. Studying Austen's dialectic will do that to anyone."

Charles paid the bill with a credit card. As we rose from the table, Alison put her arm in mine. Isobel's mouth turned down. And when we left the restaurant and Charles and Isobel walked toward his car parked twenty yards down the street, Alison gently pulled on my arm.

She asked, "You said your apartment is nearby?"

Isobel turned on her heels. She grabbed Alison's wrist, and ordered, "You come with us."

"What?" Alison protested.

Isobel tugged on her, but Alison gripped my arm tightly.

"I'm your faculty advisor," Isobel scolded, "and going off to Dennis's apartment is an utterly foolish thing for you to do. You, who are trying to understand Austen, for God's sake."

Alison couldn't maintain the grip on my arm, and she slipped off.

"It simply won't work, you and Dennis," Isobel said, dragging her student along the sidewalk with surprising strength.

Alison had to work her legs to keep from toppling. "Hey, let go, Isobel."

"I would be remiss in my duty to you, Alison, were I to let Dennis inveigle you back to his apartment."

"I did the inveigling, Professor. I'm an adult. Let me go."

Half pushing and half dragging Alison toward the car, Isobel said, "I couldn't live with myself, knowing Dennis had lured you back to his place."

"Professor, listen to me. I'm twenty-eight years old and ..."

Charles's eyebrows were high on his head. Isobel shoved Alison into the backseat as if she were loading a clothes dryer.

"Alison, you will thank me in the morning." Isobel slammed the door shut.

Shaking his head, Charles climbed into the Mercedes and started the engine. Isobel caught my gaze. A grin slid across her face, and then it broadened into a dazzling smile full of mischief and knowing and victory.

She got into the car and it pulled away, leaving me on a French Quarter sidewalk, my hands deep in my pockets.

11

"The poppy symbolizes sleep," Charles Brooks whispered to me, "and the hand with the finger pointing up means that the dead hope for heaven."

"This place gives me the willies," I replied.

"And the rose symbolizes purity," Charles added. "And it's appropriate here because Kathleen Autrey was purely a lunatic."

Charles and Isobel and I, and maybe five hundred other mourners were gathered around the Autrey family tomb at the Lafayette Cemetery in the Garden District. The barrel-vaulted tomb had been made of brick, then plastered over, and the symbols had been carved into the plaster. At the end of the tomb was a flat pediment on which was an empty concrete vase, a symbol for something else, I'm sure, though Charles didn't mention it.

Isobel wore a long black dress and a black hat. She stood next to her father Lawrence, who stared down at the coffin, and he looked smaller than the last time I had seen him. An Episcopalian priest was speaking to the mourners, though I was able to tune him out.

Rows of tombs were separated by avenues wide enough for funeral processions. Some of the tombs had pitched roofs, some resembled sarcophagi, others were massive tables resting on pillars above the burial receptacle. Long rows of wall vaults were on the cemetery's perimeter.

Generations of a family would use the same vault. The remains of a body placed in the vault decades ago would be pushed to the back of the structure where the bones fell to a receptacle below, and then the vault would be ready for the newly-deceased. Bodies aren't placed below ground in New Orleans because the water table is too high. Isobel's mother was in the coffin, and was about to be slid into the vault.

"Do you know what Isobel's mom died of?" I whispered.

"The medical examiner isn't sure," Brooks said. "It might've been suicide or it might've been an accident."

"What happened?"

"She fell or jumped out of a window."

"My Lord," I exclaimed, though in a low voice. "Was she suicidal? How could her hospital not know it?"

"If it was Kathleen Autrey who went out the window, it was probably suicide. But if Kathleen was Greta, the Flying Norse Valkrie, it was an accident. The examiner has concluded it was probably an accident."

"What makes him think so?"

"Kathleen was wearing a costume breastplate and a blond, braided wig when she died. Bought them from a catalogue. So she might've been trying to fly, which makes it an accident."

Isobel was silently weeping, and her shoulders were bucking. She dabbed a handkerchief to her cheeks. Her father's eyes were moist, and he occasionally shook his head, trying to deny his wife's death, and maybe some of her life. He had lost weight, and his black suit was baggy on him. The skin over his face was pulled taut. His wispy white hair was tugged by an idle wind.

The mourners were mostly old New Orleans society, but a number of politicians were also tomb-side, including the mayor. Several newspaper reporters were making notes or quietly speaking into miniature digital recorders. Lawrence had once been mayor, and he and Kathleen had been prominent Garden District residents, and their charitable giving was well-known. Although Kathleen's illness had prevented her from participating in New Orleans society for many years, the city's political and social powers were at this bone-yard service in force to show their gratitude. And perhaps they suspected old Lawrence Autrey could still pull strings just as he could in the old days, and so they needed to show respect.

The sun was high overhead, and the granular light was pressing me down. Shimmers rose from the paths, and heat radiated off the tombs. I felt as if I were in a rotisserie. My shirt was damp from neck to belt. The minister finally wound down, and Isobel and her father turned away from the tomb. The body would be placed inside later, and the tomb re-sealed. Mourners gathered around, offering handshakes and hugs and a few words of sympathy and encouragement. Isobel whispered "Thank you" again and again.

The mourners gradually went their own ways, and Isobel took her father's arm to guide him along a cemetery path. We turned south at the Lafayette Hook and Ladder Company No. 1 tomb. I walked next to Charles, not knowing if I was welcome to follow, but having nothing else to do.

We passed a Gothic revival tomb where the mortal remains of Robert Huyghe were deposited in 1877, and the twin tombs of Benjamin and Cristoval Toledano which had a black iron picket fence around them. The old man was averting his eyes from these grim structures, keeping his wet gaze on the path.

We were almost to Sixth Street when Moe Barnes stepped out from behind a tomb. He was grinning as if this were a party. His nephew, Spazz Sprague, followed him, his right hand near his open jacket's zipper. It was too hot for a jacket, so I supposed he had a pistol in there, the same weapon he had pointed at me last week. I was gratified to see the white bandage across the bridge of his nose. He stared at me, his eyes alert with malice.

Isobel stopped as if she had bumped up against a wall. She blurted, "What are you doing here?"

"I invited you to come back to my house, and you didn't, so I had to come to you," Barnes said. "I don't usually work that way."

"Who is this fellow?" Lawrence Autrey asked.

Isobel said quickly, "Charles, take father home, please."

Brooks led the old gent away, and he was too dispirited to ask any more questions or to look back over his shoulder at Barnes. I moved closer to Isobel, and grinned narrowly at the flunky, Spazz Sprague.

Crescents of sweat were under the arms of Barnes's white jacket. His white straw hat was pushed back on his head. His nose was red and bulbous, appearing about to pop in the heat. In one hand was a handkerchief.

"Too bad about your mother," Barnes said. "I heard her radio was missing a few knobs, if you know what I mean."

"What do you want?" Isobel asked.

"You're no longer interested in your poem, Professor?" Barnes asked.

"I'm mourning my mother. How dare you ..."

Barnes said, "I got a new deal for you."

"I'm not ..."

I think Isobel was going to add "interested," but the word wouldn't form. She had told me that her mother's death had given her a new perspective, but it had sounded like she was trying to convince herself, not me.

"I'm feeling generous," Barnes explained in his gravely voice. "So there's no dancing for you in my new deal."

She hesitated. "What then?"

"You should've told me your buddy here was an up-and-coming prize fighter." He lifted his hat brim to draw the handkerchief across his forehead. "You should've told me he just beat Sonny Smith and Antoine Doaks."

"The fewer words I have with you, the cleaner I feel," Isobel said.

"Your boyfriend, an over-the-hill carnival fighter, is suddenly a contender, Professor."

"The very thought of Dennis Jones being my boyfriend makes the hair on the back of my neck stand up." This crack was for my benefit. "What's your new deal?"

Barnes turned to me. "You must be real proud, Jones. A late-in-life run at the title." He clucked his tongue. "Everybody should be so lucky."

I was proud, truth be told, more than I had let on to Isobel, and maybe more than I had admitted to myself. I once had dreams, me climbing into the ring to face the heavyweight champion, and then knocking him silly. Holding the title belt above my head as I danced around the ring. But those fantasies were long ago, and had been lost somewhere during my desultory wandering. Meeting Isobel and her father and Charles Brooks had rekindled my ambitions. Sure, it was foolish, at age thirty-four, to think of a championship, but when the Civil War began, U.S. Grant was selling nails in a hardware store in Galena, Illinois. And, sure, Isobel was an intriguer in it for herself, and a kook besides. But my life needed some scheming, and Isobel provided plenty of it. I had begun to dream again.

"So the deal is this," Barnes said, sweat seeping from under his hat and flowing down the crevices of his face, "You fight Sammy Dresser."

"I can't get a fight against Dresser," I said, sounding defensive. Dresser would murder me in the ring, pure and simple. "He's the sixth-ranked heavyweight. He doesn't want anything to do with me.

My manager—" I nodded at Isobel—"has tried."

Barnes pulled his loose lips into a smile. "I've got contacts your manager, her being a professor and all, doesn't have." He pronounced it *perfesser*. "I spoke with Dresser's manager. The fight has already been arranged."

"A fight with Sammy Dresser?" I asked, hardly comprehending it.

"All he has to do is fight this Sammy Dresser, and I get my poem?" Isobel asked.

Barnes slowly moved his chin back and forth. "I'm going to have a lot of money on this prizefight. He has to fight Dresser."

"Sure, I'll fight Dresser," I said.

Barnes added, "And you have to beat Dresser."

"What are the chances of that?" I laughed. "I'll be lucky to last one round."

"The bookmakers will set the odds at five or six to one. I'm going to put a lot of money on you, the underdog. You've spent your career kissing the canvas, but with your last two fights you've caught a wave, Jones. I don't understand it but I'm going to ride it."

"Dresser will crush me like a cigarette butt."

The gangster turned his gaze to Isobel. "If your boyfriend doesn't win the fight, Professor, I'm going to use your poem to wipe my Oldsmobile's dipstick."

I was about to make another self-deprecating and entirely accurate remark about my boxing abilities, but Isobel put her eyes on me. Once again, light seemed to fade all around, except the spectral spotlight shining on her, making her eyes gleam like blue crystals, and her hair roil and toss and giving off red sparks and dark smoke. The skin on her cheeks and jaw shimmered and glowed. And fears I had about a fight with the sixth-ranked heavyweight flew out of my head like bats from a cave.

"I can beat Sammy Dresser," I said. "Count on it."

•

"I loved my wife, you know that?" Lawrence Autrey's frail frame seemed lost in the burgundy leather chair. His toy soldiers were all around. "I never cheated on Kathleen, not once in forty years of marriage, even near the end, when sometimes during my visits with her at the sanitarium she would confuse me with a piece of prime rib, and stick a fork into my arm."

Such was the intimacy of these revelations that I suspected Isobel's father had forgotten who was in his den with him: just me. Late afternoon sun was blocked by heavy drapes. The lights were low, and most of the illumination came a green-shaded banker's lamp next to the old man. The light washed away the little coloring he had. He sat with his hands on his lap, with deep shadows for eyes and a dark slash for a mouth, entirely still except for the slight work of his lips as he talked, as if any other movement would drain away the little life remaining in him. Isobel and Charles were away on some errand regarding Kathleen's death.

"And do you know why I never had an affair in those forty years? Never even contemplated one?"

"No, sir." I wondered if Lawrence, unburdening himself in his grief, would regret this conversation tomorrow, like a drunk regrets last night's accusations.

"Because our love was pure."

"Pardon, sir?"

"I've given this a lot of thought over the years. I don't believe I could have loved anyone else on the entire planet."

"Maybe not," I said. "I like to think that's how the world works, anyway."

"That Kathleen and I found each other those forty years ago. An incredible series of coincidences led us to each other, a pattern of events that could never be replicated, not once again in the course of human history—was sheer luck, not fate, but utter and benevolent luck."

I suggested, "If you've got something to drink, I'll pour you one."

"In the bookshelf next to Gettysburg. The bottom cabinet has some cognac. Two fingers in a snifter for me, and help yourself."

I found the liquor, and poured four fingers for him and just a splash for myself. He balanced the glass on his knee, and didn't sip it.

"I love my daughter Isobel. I want for her in a marriage what I had with Kathleen. A one-in-a-billion love." He was silent a moment, then he asked, "Dennis, what do you think of Isobel's fiancé, Charles?"

For once in my life I tried to compose an answer, rather than just putting my mouth into gear. "Charles is smart and he's kind and he has a good profession." Not bad. And I believed it, too.

"Does he strike you ... How shall I say this? As something of a dink?"

"A dink?"

He sighed heavily. "He's got all the credentials. He and Isobel are the perfect pair. Everybody says so, and I would believe it too, except ..." His words faltered.

"Except what, Mr. Autrey?"

"Except that Charles is a dink. His hands are too soft and he speaks French given any excuse and he carries a small mirror in his pocket and he injects himself with Botox to rid himself of wrinkles even though he's only in his thirties and doesn't have many wrinkles."

"Those are small things, aren't they?"

"And he has his nails manicured and he knows more about wine than any other person in New Orleans and he owns four polo ponies."

"Other than those things, he seems solid, sir."

Charles Brooks had taken obvious pleasure in my win over Antoine Doaks, and so I felt obliged to defend him.

Lawrence said, "He has a compilation of habits and mannerisms and interests that are going to drive me right into Kathleen's sanitarium."

"No son-in-law is perfect," I offered.

"Isobel is all I have left."

Except for this mansion and millions of dollars, but I refrained from pointing that out. I knew what he meant. I hurt for the old guy, him sitting there, all crumpled in his chair.

He said, "I don't think Isobel is finding in Charles what I found in Kathleen. And I've spoken to Isobel about it once or twice, in as straight forward a manner as I could, and she quickly turned my opinions aside."

"I've noticed she is a bit headstrong," I said by way of understatement.

"Do you know why Isobel is marrying Charles?"

"She loves him, I believe."

"She has determined it is time to get married, and Charles is at hand. And Charles is New Orleans's most eligible bachelor, and she can get him, and so she is doing so."

"Maybe she loves him," I tried again.

"I'm going to intercede," the old gentleman said, not so much to me, but to this grand den, maybe to all his miniature soldiers. "I'm going to find her someone else, and in fact I'm already working on it."

"You are? Do I know him?"

He said nothing for a long moment, and I thought he had nodded off, but then he said, "No, you don't know him. Someday you'll meet him, though, and you'll be pleased for Isobel."

There was a touch of mystery in his words, as if he were offering me a puzzle. I sipped my cognac, and didn't think about it for more than a minute. I was determined to sit there as long as Lawrence needed someone to talk with. I owed it to the old guy. His civility had been a rare thing in my life.

He fell asleep after a while, and I gently pulled the snifter from his hands and placed it on a lamp table before I left him.

•

"You want to eat at this dump?" Isobel exclaimed, turning the car into the lot at my direction. "Have I made no progress? Has the School of Isobel done nothing for you?"

Hankie's Hot-to-Trot was a crawfish joint on the road to Houma, where Isobel's aunt, Kathleen's sister, lived in an old house with a wandering porch. Isobel had traveled there to spend a few hours with her aunt by way of comforting her, and I had gone along just to fill the passenger seat. We were on our way back to the city and were hungry.

The restaurant, if it could be called that, was in an old storefront that had been a Rexall Drugstore. The yellow Rex was still on the window, but the all had been scraped off with a razor. High on the window was an amateurishly painted Hankie's Hot-to-Trot, and under that, Craws and Hot Sauce.

I stepped aside so Isobel could enter the restaurant, but she said, "You first," so I led her in. The place had six tables, a few chairs for each table, and not much else except a display case of bottled hot sauces. The case was on the wall near the cash register and contained maybe a thousand bottles. Most of the labels were in reds and oranges and yellows, the colors of fire. We sat at a table, and on it were several more bottles. One was a hot sauce name named Quick Death. Others were Atomic Fireball, Pure Hell and Mule Kick. The labels had cartoons, most showing what would happen should we try the sauce. One label showed an exploding head. Also on the table was a bottle of Tabasco, the only sauce I'd touch. Some of these sauces were so hot they'd burn skin.

Isobel sat across from me at the small table. The floor was green linoleum, turned up near the walls. A broom was in a corner. A swinging door led to the kitchen, and another door was to the toilet. A sign near the cash register read, We Made A Deal with the Bank: They Don't Serve Food and We Don't Cash Checks.

A waitress in a splattered apron pushed her way through the kitchen door. She was wearing flip-flops and jeans. She gave us a tired smile. We were the only patrons in the place.

I ordered, "Two Buds and two pounds of crayfish, please."

"Two pounds?" Isobel said. "We can't eat two pounds of anything."

"That's just my order. You want any?"

She hesitated, then said, "I'll have a few of yours."

Isobel was wearing a lightweight white cotton sweater and tan cotton shorts. She glanced around as if planning an escape route.

After the waitress returned to the kitchen, Isobel said, "I've noticed you've started hanging around with Charles."

"He and I had dinner last night, is all. A couple of sandwiches."

The waitress arrived with our beers. She spread out a newspaper on the table but didn't set out utensils or plates, just paper napkins and a small bowl. I took a large swallow of beer. Normally I wipe my mouth with the back of my hand after the first swallow of anything liquid, but the School of Isobel had taught me to refrain from this comforting ritual.

"Something wrong me with me having dinner with Charles?" I asked.

"Not at all," she said quickly. "It's just that he likes to hobnob, and not usually with boxers. He has a network of friends and contacts that he always works. Lunches and phone calls and birthday cards. He's like a politician."

I shrugged. "Charles likes to talk, and I don't mind listening if someone else is paying for the sandwich."

"I think it thrills him to hang out with a guy who has a cauliflower ear and calluses on his knuckles."

The waitress carried an aluminum pot to our table. She dumped out dozens of red and steaming crawfish onto the newspaper.

Crawfish are sometimes called crayfish. Some places, though not in New Orleans, they are also called crawdads. They resemble tiny lobsters, and taste like them too, except for an additional hint of the Louisiana muddy bottom. I poured Tabasco into the bowl, dipped a crawfish into it, and ate half of it, then tossed the legs and head to a corner of the newspaper, Isobel watching with some disgust.

"Do you have any friends in New Orleans?" she asked.

"Sure."

"Like who? Name some friends."

I hesitated. "Well, there's James 'Amazing Grace' Jefferson."

"Tell me about him."

"He sings Amazing Grace on street corners in the Quarter. He knows lots of songs but it's the only song he sings because it fills his can with cash. He's got great pipes, and he should be singing at the Met. He and I have coffee sometimes."

"Anybody else?"

I reached for another crawfish. "Why are you asking?"

"Why is it you go through life acquiring so little? No possessions, few friends, no home worthy of the name, nothing."

"I travel light."

"There's more to it than your flippant answer."

I tried to make my voice sound bored. "What would that be?"

"You are afraid."

"I've agreed to get into the ring with Sammy Dresser, and you call me afraid?"

"You're afraid of any kind of attachment."

I sucked out the juice from the head of another crawfish. "I'm mostly afraid of being psychoanalyzed by a professor of literature."

"You walk away from anything that requires the slightest commitment. Here's the lesson your troubled childhood taught you: you can't lose anything if you don't have anything."

"Have a crawfish," I suggested.

"So you risk nothing."

"The School of Isobel has a psychology department?"

"The School of Isobel doesn't want you to shy away from our deal, doesn't want you to run away. I don't have my Poe poem yet."

Ah. There was her angle. "I'll do my best, don't worry."

"Will your best be good enough?"

I shrugged. She finally lifted a crawfish, holding it as if it were a dainty teacup.

"I think you can beat Sammy Dresser," she said after a while. "Maybe with a little help."

I couldn't keep bitterness from my voice. "Sammy Dresser is going to make me look silly in the ring. You think otherwise because you don't know anything about boxing."

"My father was a member of the Louisiana boxing commissioner for many years, one of his many civic posts. It was an honorarium, and he was lending his name to the sport, but he tried to learn the sport, and so did I."

"Like I said."

She hadn't touched her beer, and now she returned the crawfish to the pile. She said nothing for a while, and I ate crawfish, enjoying the silence.

I tried again, "You should try the crawfish."

"I'd love to." She again stared at the things. "But I simply don't want to."

I sucked the meat out of a few more, first dipping each one in sauce. After two or three, I'd wash them down with beer.

She studied me as I ate. She might've been staring at the butcher's scale, making sure she received every ounce of hamburger she was paying for.

I guess she couldn't stand to see me have so much fun because she finally said, "Why don't you try using a napkin on your chin once in a while."

I replied, "Learning table manners and wearing new shirts and having dinner at the Fortune Club don't interest me much."

"What does interest you, Dennis?"

"Boxing," I replied with some heat. "It's been my curse that it's the only damned thing I care about."

"The only thing?" She smiled. "Not so."

I sipped my beer. "What do you mean?"

"You are interested in me." Isobel stared at me, daring me to contradict her. "I can tell." She smiled, dazzling the room with her teeth. "I can always tell."

I mopped my mouth with a napkin. "I'm interested in you for the same reason I read *Ripley's Believe it or Not.*"

Her brows lowered themselves a fraction.

I reached for another crawfish, maybe my fortieth. "For the same reason I'm happy to know that someone in Fort Worth has a flea trained to walk on a tiny tightrope, I'm interested in you."

She flicked her hand, discarding my comment. "I can't let your attraction to me get in the way of our deal."

"My attraction to you?"

"It could cloud your judgment, the little there is of it."

"What're you talking about, my attraction?"

"It's happened before, you know. I've addled someone's head. One time while I was sitting next to Harry Fry while he was driving, I kissed him, and he drove off the road into a ditch. This was back when we were in high school."

I was slowing down on the crawfish. I picked up a bottle of Mule Kick hot sauce from the table. I fiddled with it.

"Another time, on our front porch—I guess this would be when I was fifteen—I kissed Dukey Maillard under the porch light, and he wet his pants."

I turned the Mule Kick in my hand.

"I don't doubt Harry and Dukey thought the kisses were fun, but neither wanted anything to do with me again. I wonder why." Her expression indicated she well knew the reason. "And you've heard the rumors about my fiancés not being able to keep up with me."

"I don't listen to rumors."

"Now I've done it to you, without even a kiss."

"You've done nothing to me except entertain me." I made a point of studying the hot sauce label, which showed a mule on his front legs, sending its rear hoofs into the rump of some fellow who had just sampled the sauce.

"Can you deny that you feel a certain chemical reaction when I'm near you?"

"Is fright a chemical reaction?"

"You get stirred up every time you see me."

"That's pure bunk."

She lit into me with one of her smiles. "You think you are hiding your attraction to me but you aren't. You don't have the strength or energy to hide it."

"I can't hide my opinion of you. You're a nutball."

"It's chemical, so let's do a chemistry experiment," she suggested.

"What sort of experiment?"

She pushed back her chair and rose from the table. She came around to me. "Stand up, Dennis."

When I rose from the chair, she came up to me and put her hands on my shoulders.

"Relax." Her eyes were blue and bottomless.

"I'm always relaxed."

"But brace yourself."

"I'm always braced."

She slid her hands along my shoulders and placed them behind my neck. She rose on her toes and moved against me and she brought my head to hers. Then she placed her lips on mine.

I have no memory of the kiss, nothing at all. My mind went blank, I believe because she short-circuited it somehow. I don't know how long the kiss lasted, what exactly Isobel did with her lips and whatever else she might have used—nothing.

My recollection returns as she moved away from me, grinning, and holding me still with her eyes.

"Well?" she asked.

"I didn't feel a thing." Which was true. It's hard to feel things you don't remember.

She scoffed, "Sure, you did."

I shook my head. "Nothing."

"You can tell me the truth."

"Not a thing."

Her face lengthened. "Impossible."

I smiled. "I must be made of sterner stuff than Harry and Dukey."

Her eyes narrowed. She surveyed me for several more seconds. She was apparently astonished at this failure. She abruptly brushed by me and strode to the restaurant's door.

I instantly brought up my right hand. It was covered with hot sauce and glass shards. Sauce was dripping onto the floor. The bottle of Mule Kick had been in my hand when Isobel kissed me, and during the kiss I had apparently squeezed my hand with such force that the bottle had shattered. I had no recollection of that, either. But now sharp pain came from my palm, where glass fragments had cut me in two or three places. Pain was increasing by the second as Mule Kick seeped into the cuts.

Dripping hot sauce, I ran toward the restroom door, intent on washing my hand and plucking glass from it. My hand felt as though a chainsaw were working on it, the peppers in Mule Kick eating away at the exposed nerves.

Even so, even with fiery pain in my hand, I was already wondering how I would hide these wounds from Isobel.

12

"Come on, this isn't a party," Old Al Higgens yelled. "Show me what you've got."

I threw a combination at the heavy bag, focusing on the left cross, sending my fist into the canvas. Standing behind the bag and bracing it with his body, Old Al was jarred by the force of the blow.

"You're asleep on your feet, Dennis," he said. "Just set him up with the jab and the right. Then put it all into the left hand."

Perspiration was running down my face and into my eyes and down my arms. My workout trunks were as wet as if I were swimming. My shoes were squishy from catching sweat rolling down my legs.

My effort still wasn't good enough for Old Al. "Launch it from your feet, Dennis. Everything you've got for another three minutes, then you'll get a break."

I tried another. One, two three, laying it into the bag. This was my fourth consecutive three-minute round with Old Al and the heavy bag, sixty seconds off in between rounds, Al looking at his wristwatch so I didn't get an extra second of rest. My arms were burning.

"Sammy Dresser is going to take some hitting," he said. "Show me your stuff."

I sent another combination into the bag, rattling Old Al, sweat stinging my eyes. Old Al owned the gym, which was above a twenty-four-hour doughnut shop on Magazine Street. The gym always smelled of sweat socks and maple bars. The place was officially called Higgens' School of the Fistic Science, but fighters called it Old Al's. Everything in the place was worn out and patched. The heavy bags were covered with duct tape. The jump ropes were frayed. The leather speed bags were shiny from use. More tape was around the ring ropes. Cracks were in the mustard-colored plaster walls. Boxing posters from the 1950s and 60s hung on some of the walls, and they were curled and yellowed.

One showed a photo of Old Al, then called Jersey Al Higgens, with his fists up and savage determination on his face. Old Al had fought for the welterweight title in the late 1960s, and, as he liked to say, "I was asked the question." He couldn't answer it. The fight lasted two-minutes.

Old Al himself was as beat-up as his gym. His brows were so low they were a roof over his eyes. His nose was almost the size of a tennis ball, and was fleshy, with hair growing from the pours. He had some hair left on his head, but not much, and it was colorless and always matted to his scalp. His chin was prominent. "Too much a target," he liked to say. Wrinkles were everywhere, even on his nose. He was missing teeth, and his smile resembled a picket fence.

Ten others were working out in the gym, two sparring in the ring, several working the bags, one skipping rope and the rest using the free weights at the end of the room near the windows. The sounds of a boxing gym—the skipping, punching, shuffling, grunting, the drum roll of the speed bags, the jingle of the turnbuckles and the bag chains—are both soothing and inspiring.

I tried another combination, drops of sweat spinning off me as I landed the punch.

Old Al grunted when the bag bumped into him. "From your feet, Dennis. Throw it from your feet. "

I was tiring quickly, Old Al making sure of that. I was about to launch another series of blows at the bag when I noticed that the gym had gone quiet. Old Al looked around the bag toward the door, and I followed his gaze.

Isobel Autrey had walked into the gym. Medusa had no greater effect. The boxers froze as they saw her, their gloved hands hanging, the jump rope dangling, barbells stilled, speed bags swinging more and more slowly, then stopping.

She strode toward me. Isobel's hair was glistening and black, and her eyes were startlingly blue and her smile was broad and knowing. She walked with a bit of cocky swagger. She knew she was being examined by a bunch of sweaty men, and was confident of their conclusions, I suppose. She was wearing a red cotton V-neck T-shirt and a black button-front skirt. Old Al's gym was faded and smelly, tattered and worn, but Isobel had just added an electric dash of elegance and spirit.

She walked up to me. "You're not sweating enough."

"I'm wet, head to foot."

Old Al cleared his throat pointedly. I introduced them. Isobel took Al's hand, looked into his eye, and shot him a smile that gave him another twenty years. He stood with one hand on the heavy bag, the other gripping Isobel's hand, and couldn't move or say a word.

The boxers in the gym slowly reclaimed their wits. Cecil Rodrick, who liked to call himself the Iron Shovel for reasons no one knew, had been sparring in the ring, and he grinned and called out, "Dennis isn't man enough for you, miss. But I'm here, ready and willing."

She barbecued him with a grin. "When I've whittled Dennis down to a toothpick, I'll give you a call."

Rodrick laughed and clapped his mitts together. Others in the gym hooted and whistled.

Old Al said in his raspy voice, "Dennis, let me know when you want to get back to work." He walked toward the ring.

She turned back to me. "How can you stand this place?"

I surveyed the room. Some of the boxers had returned to their workouts while others still gaped at Isobel. Old Al began coaching a young flyweight, reminding him to keep his elbows close to his ribs. Another boxer was hitting hand pads held up by his work-out partner. Everyone in the room, save Old Al and Isobel, glistened with sweat. Everyone pushed himself. Everyone was trying to sharpen skills. Everyone saw a championship belt in the future and a new home for his mom.

"I love this place," I said. "It's my home."

"You haven't been in New Orleans long enough to call anywhere home," Isobel remarked.

"A gym like this is my home, I don't care what town it's in."

She lifted at eyebrow.

"I feel better when I'm in a gym than anywhere else," I added.

"This place?"

"I know all these boxers," I said, "and I know all about them, even if I don't know their names and even I've never spoken with them."

"That hardly makes it a home."

"And I know all this equipment, all the bags and ropes and

barbells, and the sparring ring. Watch this." I led her to the speed bags.

The bag was inflated leather with Everlast imprinted on it, and it hung idly under the rebound board. I stepped up to it, putting my chin just outside of the bag's widest reach. I lifted my fists and lit into it, instantly putting the bag into rhythmic motion, my fists against the leather and the bag against the board producing a loud tattoo.

The speed bag was my element. I knew everything about it. I could do anything with it. I had named my patterns. Greased Lightning. A Hundred More for the Gipper. Buddy Rich. I ran off several patterns, one blending into the next, using my knuckles front and rear, using my elbows and backhand, a couple of times even bouncing the bag off my forehead. The bag could hardly be seen, it was moving so fast. My fists whirred in front of my face. I had been working out on the speed bag for twenty years, and I was good at it, much better on the bag than I am in the ring, in fact.

"You are showing off," she said over the sound of the bag.

"Every time I get around you, I get aggravated." I slid into my Drums Along the Mohawk routine, the bag jumping off my fists. "But every time I work the speed bag, I become entirely calm, sort of a trance."

She snorted nicely.

I continued to pound the bag. "So right now, with you here aggravating me and the speed bag calming me, I'm in a nice state of equilibrium."

"I watched you for a few innings from the door," Isobel said. "You're not working hard enough. It occurs to me that someone who plans on beating Sammy Dresser needs to train harder."

"They are rounds, not innings." I slapped the bag, stopping it. "And that's a bonehead thing to say, me not working hard enough. My workouts are none of your business."

"Until you get me my poem, everything about you is my business."

My fear of Sammy Dresser—there was no other word for it; I was afraid of him—had been steadily working on me. I had made a deal with Isobel, and until that moment had been determined to carry out my end of it, even if it meant being destroyed in the ring. I'd be another Benny Paret, who in 1962 was beaten to unconsciousness by Emile Griffith, and who died ten days later. Until she walked into Old Al's gym just then, I had been ready to get into the ring against Dresser. But Isobel's arrogance, and her ignorance of what was important to a boxer, and her cavalier willingness to toss me into the ring against a fighter who would in all likelihood hurt me badly abruptly enraged me.

"And where were you last night?" Isobel demanded. "I called your apartment at eleven o'clock, and you weren't there."

"I was out having fun."

"This is no time for fun." She crossed her arms in front of her.

"I was replenishing all yesterday's sweat with a some beer."

"You aren't taking your fight and my poem seriously. You are being lazy and undisciplined."

I was still panting from the workout, beads of sweat coursing down me, my arms and shoulders aching, and this woman was calling me lazy?

She said, "I want you to work harder."

I fairly yelled, "I quit."

Her eyes ate me. "You quit what?"

"Our deal is off." I was so mad I was sputtering. "I quit your big plan, and I quit you."

"You and I have made a bargain, and we have a deal with Moe Barnes."

"No deals. No way. I'm done being your chump."

I could feel Old Al's boxers again turning toward Isobel and me.

Her voice sounded like steam escaping. "You'll regret this, Dennis."

I spread my gloved hands. "When will I regret it? When I'm celebrating the fact that Sammy Dresser isn't going to get the chance to kill me?"

"No," she spat out. "Right now."

She was fast for someone so smart. She wound up her leg and delivered a ferocious kick to my shin. And I mean it felt like a mule had laid into me. This wasn't a woman's kick, or a poet's kick, or a professor's kick. It was a mule's kick.

I cried out, and reached down for my battered shin and held it, and then I started to bounce around on one foot, calling out, "Ouch, damn, damn, ouch." And on and on, hopping and spinning.

The boxers lit up with laughter, Old Al laughing so hard he spit out his bridgework.

Isobel marched to the gym's door, where she turned around and pointed at me. "My house, tomorrow." Her voice sounded like a hammer hitting an anvil. "Ten o'clock. Be there, Dennis." She disappeared through the door.

I tried my leg, but it still felt like it was in a bear trap. I hopped toward the shower, the boxers' laughter chasing me.

•

I fought Sammy Dresser, and the fight didn't last long.

The match was again in Slidell, at the community college gym, but this time the place was full. Moe Barnes and his nephew Spazz Sprague sat ringside, gazing up at me as I stood in my corner, Barnes's chunky face beaming with satisfaction.

Barnes now fancied himself a sport, I suppose. He wore a lime green sports coat and a white silk tie. One hand was around a box of popcorn, and the other was clenching into a fist, the releasing, then clenching, as if he were practicing clutching all the money he would win when I sent Sammy Dresser down for the count. He smiled up at me, full of benevolence. In the next seat, Sprague glowered at me. He hadn't gotten over me laying him out with a sucker punch in front of his uncle and mentor and employer, Moe Barnes.

I glanced across at Sammy Dresser. He was from Memphis, and had been fighting since he was twelve. His skin was the color of teak, a golden brown, and his arms and chest and abs looked as hard as teak, too. His hunter's eyes were on me. I was determined to give him all I had, let him know he had a match on his hands, let him know that Dennis Jones was a fighter. I would only last three or four rounds, I figured, but if I fought with skill and ferocity maybe Sammy Dresser would remember me, even if the fight world would not.

While the announcer made the introductions, I danced in place to keep warm. Isobel was at ringside, and so were her father and Charles Brooks. She studied me, contempt and amusement on her face. I don't think Lawrence or Charles knew of my difficulty with Isobel two days ago at Old Al's gym. They were smiling and chatting, and whenever one of them caught my eye, he gave me a thumbs-up or an okay with his fingers.

Coral Thibideaux was there, too. She was wearing a loud yellow sarong and a matching turban, looking entirely exotic. I wondered what weirdness she was up to this time. She was studying me, too.

In Isobel's hand, as she sat ringside, was a check made out to me with the dollar amount left blank. Yes, when I had visited her the next morning—damned if I know why I bothered—she had simply resorted to bribery. No talk of managing me, of turning my life around, none of that nonsense. No beguiling smiles. No witty barbs aimed at me. She had been all business.

She said that she would pay me two thousand dollars per completed round, plus another five thousand if I beat Dresser. Of course, I didn't stand a chance of earning much of that money, but if I stayed on my feet a few rounds, I'd make the rent money for a while.

And then she would take it from there, would deal with Moe Barnes herself, she had promised. She would give me the check in the dressing room after the fight, and she and I would be done with each other.

Fine by me. A few thousand dollars to me, then goodbye Isobel, it's been charming, and out the shower room door I was going to go, her check in my hand, leaving her behind for good. I had played this satisfying scene in my head a hundred times the past two days.

And what about my indignant rage at Isobel's callus and ignorant comments regarding not training hard enough for the fight? The truth was, I had won a few fights lately, sure, but I knew that my boxing days were about over, that my championship dreams were just that: airy daydreams not grounded in any sort of reality. I was a canvas-back and would always be one. Against Sammy Dresser, I was out of my league.

But, despite my brain-numbing fear, I wanted a shot at Dresser. I couldn't go ten rounds with the likes of Sammy Dresser, not in a million years. I was going to do my damnedest, then quit boxing for good. Dresser would surely ask me the question, that same question Old Al had been asked when he fought for the welterweight championship. I wanted to know if I could answer it.

I met with the ref and my opponent center ring. I stared right back into Dresser's eyes. He looked away in an instant of weakness. I was going to beat him like a rug for a couple of rounds, for as long as my legs would hold me up. I didn't need to save anything for later. He was going to have a hellacious few minutes. We returned to our corners.

And there, mounted atop the ring post, was an animal's skull. A small animal, maybe an opossum or a weasel, the bone gleaming white under the ring lamp. I looked around at Coral. Her face was impassive, and she shrugged for my benefit. Her partner in this scheme, Isobel Autrey, was still staring at me.

The bell rang. The crowd cheered, and out I went, my gloves up, my chin down, my elbows in. Sammy Dresser circled to my right. I flicked off several of his jabs. They were slower than I would've supposed.

No, not so. He wasn't slower. Rather, I was faster. Something had sped me up. My fists were blurs. Perhaps from the instant I saw the animal's skull, I had been accelerated and was now slipping quickly through time, unimpeded by the dreary clock.

I didn't see any point in answering Dresser jab for jab, so my first move was the one-two-three Old Al Higgens had drilled me on.

My left and right set up Dresser, and then my left cross found his temple. He went down as if he'd been thrown through a tavern door to the sidewalk.

Isobel leaped to her feet and stared at the fallen Sammy Dresser as the referee yelled the count. Her expression was one of rapture. At long last, she would get her Poe poem. Confused by this sudden turn of events—Sammy Dresser stretched out at my feet—I walked to a neutral corner.

Dresser rolled onto his back and held an arm across his eyes as if shading them from the spotlight. When the count hit ten, the ref crossed the ring to lift my hand. I was the victor. Dresser's trainer and cut man rushed into the ring to bend over him.

I had won the fight? Against Sammy Dresser? What in hell had just happened?

Moe Barnes's doughy face was molded into an gleeful grin. He clapped his hands, then held his arms over his head. He yelled congratulations I couldn't hear over the cheers of the crowd. Spazz Sprague smiled grimly at me. I suppose he was planning our next encounter. My making a fistful of money for his uncle didn't make up for my humiliating him, I guessed.

Still standing in my corner, the applause rolling over me mixed with much nasty booing for Dresser, I glanced down at Isobel. Her face had softened. Had she known I would win? Had Coral, with her weasel skull, promised a victory?

I lifted my gloves in a gesture of goodwill and understanding. I called out, "I won the fight. Didn't I say I would?" That ought to make her laugh.

But Isobel couldn't hear me, not with all the crowd noise. She smiled at me, and for an instant tenderness touched her features. Then she turned to Moe Barnes, her hand out for her poem. Barnes shook his head at her and continued grinning. He held out his hands.

The poem wasn't in them. His flabby lips worked. He was welshing on the deal, and proposing a new deal for Isobel, trying to make some new bargain.

She stiffened so quickly I thought I could hear the vertebrae in her back crackle. She wildly swung her hand at Barnes, but from the next seat Spazz Sprague caught her fist and turned it aside. Barnes said a few more words. He wiped his mouth with his fingers. Maybe he had been drooling over the money he had just won. Then he patted her shoulder, and she recoiled as if he had used a hammer. He turned to walk down the aisle, his nephew following him.

Her precious Edgar Allan Poe poem was still far away.

She jerked her gaze around to me, then savagely tore up my check, as if it had been me, not Barnes, who had just reneged on the deal. Furious and shaking, she tore the paper until it was too small to tear further, and then she threw bits of paper onto the floor. She marched down the aisle toward the stairs to the exit. Lawrence and Charles appeared puzzled, their gazes going back and forth between me and her. Finally Charles shrugged and hurried after Isobel, the old man following.

I slipped under the top rope, and jumped down to the gym floor, then walked up the aisle. The only person of my acquaintance who remained in the gym was my cut man, Arturo Lopez, and he had his hand out, wanting his fee as if I had squirreled it away in my shoe and was going to pay him on the spot.

I ignored him, but he followed me to the dressing room, his hand out all the way.

13

So I didn't get any money from Isobel, and I spent my ring prize mostly on back rent, so I needed some cash. I sometimes worked for O'Donnell Temps, and O'Donnell would send me out on bouncer and doorman jobs. I stood at whatever door I was sent to, nicely patting people down so they wouldn't bring in booze, politely lifting purses to see if a young lady might be packing, keeping out drunks and toughs. Most people looked at my face and didn't give me trouble, and it's a hard life when you make your living frightening people with your face.

One evening it would be a high school dance, the next the boarding gate at one of the river's sternwheelers, the next a club that was having its grand opening—that sort of thing. This is how I earned my provender in New Orleans when I couldn't get a fight.

So a couple of days passed after my split with my so-called manager Miss Isobel Autrey. She was so angry she couldn't distinguish between Moe Barnes and me, and I had telephoned Lawrence Autrey, and Isobel wasn't speaking to her father or her fiancé, either. Everybody was depriving her of the Poe poem. I was at the convention center alongside the river a bit south of the Quarter, working the door at the North American Professional Magician's Convention. Magicians aren't your Yankee Stadium bleacher bums, so this was easy work, me just checking the magicians' name tags as they entered the hall to make sure they had paid their registration fees.

The magicians arrived in groups of three and four, and many paused at my door to show off bits of their acts in front of their friends. I was the only non-magician in sight, so I was their mark. Dressed in a lumpy suit, one magician paused long enough to pull a mouse out of my ear. Not to be outdone, his pal who wore huge floppy shoes, a ten-inch wide paisley tie and a red kitchen-mop wig, and whose nametag identified as Bertrum the Magical Clown—handed me back my wristwatch, the first I'd noticed it had been missing. Then Mandy the Mentalist paused to declare that she could read my mind. She squinted her eyes, her hand on my forehead like a faith healer, and then announced there was nothing in my head to read, which received big boffos from her magician friends.

This was a seminar and trade show, and the room inside was filled with displays. American Saw-the-Lady-in-Half Company was showing off its colorful coffin-sized boxes and huge lumberman's cross-cut saws. Top Hats Inc. was selling black mourning coats tricked out with hidden pockets and sleeve springs. All Thumbs Company was displaying three hundred fake plastic thumbs and fingers in all shades and sizes, I suppose for hiding things under. All sorts of noises came from the room: chicken squawks, exaggerated clown laughs, mysterious Egyptian music, oompah horns and slide whistles.

Six fellows asked me if I would mind letting them put me into handcuffs, to which I replied each time, "Yes, I'd mind." The Amazing Torch paused by the door long enough for me to check his registration card and for him to set himself on fire, and I mean a blaze that leapt from nowhere and covered him from his knees to his hair, brilliant yellow and blue flames dancing all over, and was just as suddenly out and gone, leaving no burns anywhere and the Torch not charred in the least. I have no idea how he did it. I didn't have an idea how any of them did it.

Dressed in a wild red and black checked sports coat that made him look like a taxi, and white buck shoes and sunglasses, a magician held two knives in his hands, and with a broad gesture plunged one into his belly. Then he pulled the blade away and held it up for inspection, looking around to see if any fellow magicians had seen it. At last, a trick I knew: the blade collapsed into the handle. Kid's stuff. His name was Buddy the Knife Man.

As I checked his registration, he said, "Watch how this works." And he plunged one of his knives into me. This wasn't a trick knife. The blade sank deeply into my chest. Pain shot through my like a bolt. Down I went.

•

When I awoke I was lying on my back, tubes running in and

out of me. After a while a doctor came in to tell me that the knife had plunged through my pectoral muscle, been deflected by a rib, and slid alongside my trachea, missing my subclavian vein, but puncturing my lung. The surgeon had fixed me up, he assured me, though I didn't feel fixed up, the pain making my neck and chest feel as if they were on fire.

I had been unconscious in the St. Charles General Hospital operating room, then the recovery room, and then in the hospital room here almost twelve hours. The surgeon said I'd need about five days in the hospital, then I could go home.

Behind me was a headwall with an examination light and outlets for medical air, nitrous oxide and oxygen. A blood pressure gauge was on the wall, and an IV stand and bag were near my shoulder. I was told that James Jefferson came by to sing Amazing Grace, all the nurses gathering in my room to listen, but I was still unconscious, and have no memory of it.

That day in the hospital, I drifted in and out of consciousness, the pain medication, of which I needed plenty, knocking me out sometimes. When I was awake, I had to listen to my roommate, a grizzled old carcass who had just had a foot amputated due to diabetes-caused gangrene, which he thought gave him license to bend my ear all day.

The old guy's name was Dietz, and I never learned whether Dietz was his first or last name. He had more theories than Carter had pills such as claiming Halloween was a plot by the French to sap the vigor and intellect of American youth. With his tortured and phlegmy voice, Dietz laid out for me in dense detail his conspiracies.

My only defense was to lie there, as still as lead, lest the slightest movement on my part encourage Dietz to even greater extravaganzas of conspiracy.

I had my own conspiracy to deal with, the one to murder me. I should've taken a closer look at Buddy the Knife Man at the convention door. I was sure it was Moe Barnes's nephew, Spazz Sprague. The guy had despised me ever since I had swatted his pistol aside and popped him on the nose. I'd made Sprague seem silly and useless while his Uncle Moe, his employer and tutor, looked on.

I doubted Moe Barnes had okayed Sprague knifing me because I had just won a bunch of money for Barnes in the Sammy Dresser fight. It had been a solo act of revenge. Buddy the Knife Man's blade had been aimed for my heart, but had bounced off a rib.

After dinner on my first day in the hospital—it was also to be my last day, as you'll shortly see—I was sipping a tasteless broth through a straw when Dietz abruptly interrupted his theory that depletions of salmon stock in Pacific Northwest rivers is caused by Irish peat burner, to ask me who the lady was who had visited me that morning.

I asked in a foggy, weak voice, "Someone visited me?"

"You were still out cold," Dietz said. "You never woke up."

"What'd she look like?"

"She looked like trouble."

Isobel had visited me? I asked, "Dark hair, slender, big blue eyes, very pretty but in sort of a dangerous way?"

"That'd be her," Dietz said. "She came into the room and saw you lying there, tube up your nose and all and she started crying, really leaking, and when she bent over to kiss you she had to wipe her tears off your face."

Last I had seen of Isobel, standing there ringside, she was so angry with me she was vibrating head to foot like a tuning fork.

I was so weak I had to concentrate to get my next words out. "Did this lady say anything?"

"She was crying and carrying on, and she said, 'Oh Dennis, it's all my fault, please don't die,' and 'My Lord, Dennis, what have I done?' a couple of times."

"She did?" I was pleased Isobel had figured out it was all her fault.

"And then she said, around all her bawling, that if you were awake she'd strangle you, after what you did to her."

"She wanted to strangle me?"

Dietz went on, "But then she said, her burbling away and wiping her tears with a Kleenex, that she couldn't strangle you now because you were hurt and in the hospital, and life wasn't fair, her missing her big chance to strangle you, and she was weeping all the while."

I asked, "Which did she want more, could you tell? Me alive or me dead?"

"About a toss-up, I'd say."

I groaned as a new wave of pain burst from my wound. I pressed the button that gave me another shot of pain killer through the needle in my arm.

Dietz added, "Then the nurse came in and shooed her away, saying you wouldn't be awake for quite awhile."

I took a couple more sips of broth, then a doctor appeared above my head. He was wearing a mask and a surgical cap and a white apron.

"You've become infected," the doctor said. "We need to operate right away."

A second fellow, also wearing surgical garb, showed up on the other side of my bed. He nodded gravely, then kicked the brake lock on my bed. This fellow had a mammoth belly under his apron.

"What do you mean?" I asked. "I'm sure the surgeon got all the infection during the operation."

The two of them pushed my bed toward the door, the first one swatting aside the curtain. I was rolled past the nurses' station. Nobody was there.

"Hey," I yelled. "What's going on? I don't—"

One of them hissed, "You and that dame and Moe Barnes swindled us out of our Eap poem."

One of them slammed his hand over my mouth, pressing me down. I couldn't see anything but passing doors as they hurried me along the hallway, then into a freight elevator. One of my new attendants lowered his surgical mask. The counterfeiter stared down at me, Soapy Fay, the one with the shaved head and the tattoos.

The other fellow was Donnie. The elevator whirred and clanked. Donnie said, "So you've been knifed. Where exactly?"

With that he stabbed my stomach with his thumb, like he was sinking it into a plum pie.

I flinched.

He giggled. "Not there, I guess."

Then he thrust his thumb through my hospital gown and into my stab wound. The stitches ripped out of my skin. I screeched and tried to rise, but Soapy's meaty hand grabbed my jaw and shoved me back onto the bed. He kept his hand over my mouth as they rolled me out of the elevator and along a hallway. We passed several people, but none glanced down at me, my attendants Soapy and Donnie leaning over me with apparent concern.

They rolled me to the emergency entrance. I tried to grab Donnie's arm, but I was weak and he brushed my hand away. No ambulances were parked at the loading area, and no other vehicles except a ten-year-old Ford. Soapy and Donnie rolled me up to it, then opened the trunk.

Soapy said, "So you and Moe Barnes thought you would cheat us out of our poem, letting us think it was just some old guy's scribbling, but that poem was written by Horace Eap, and it's worth thousands."

"Barnes has made big bucks from the poem, using it to get that professor to dance out at the Pink Lady. The poem must be worth a fortune. We were scammed out of it."

They grabbed me by the feet and shoulders, and tossed me into the trunk, cramming my legs into a corner.

I managed to squeak out, "I don't work for Moe Barnes. His flunky stabbed me."

"We don't care who stabbed you." Soapy Fay's voice had a smoker's rasp. "You and Barnes swindled us out of our big-bucks poem."

Donnie added, "We could've had a major score with that poem, and you and Barnes stole it from us."

He grabbed a bottle of Captain Morgan spiced rum from a cardboard box in the trunk. The lid slammed shut.

I gasped from the agony of my re-opened chest. The engine turned over, then the car started down the road. I could hear Donnie laugh. It was close in that trunk, me not being able to unbend in the slightest, my head bouncing against a jack. I was lying on lengths of chain, it felt like. The links prodded my skin, and rattled when the car hit a pothole. I was bunched up, and the pain went in circles, around and around, coursing down my hips and legs, then leaping from my feet to my head and then down my shoulders again and again.

Through the seatback came Donnie's muffled voice. "This is going to be pure cool, Soapy. Pass me that bottle."

I was in that trunk maybe an hour. Blood from my knife wound trickled down my shoulder. I gasped for breath. I fought nausea.

Soapy laughed shrilly. "Teach him to mess with Soapy Fay. Him and Moe Barnes thought they could screw us out of our Eap poem and get away with it."

The pain in my chest and shoulder never relented. Every time the car rounded a corner, my head banged against the fender well. Donnie and Soapy laughed crazily much of the time, and each demanded the other pass the bottle again and again. When the car veered side to side, both counterfeiters brayed with laughter. I heard their bottle shatter when it hit the pavement. One of them must've tossed it out the window when it was empty.

A siren suddenly came from behind the car, the wail rising and falling. For a moment I thought my rescue was at hand, but Soapy yelled, "We can't be pulled over with that bastard in the trunk," and then the car sped ahead.

Even though I braced myself, my head bumped against the tire jack and the trunk's sides as the car spun left, then right, then left again. When it bounced, I was tossed up against the trunk hood, then fell back onto the chains. I heard branches scrape the sides of the car. Donnie barked out something. The car lurched and bucked, then came to a stop.

Soapy yelled, "We got to get out of here."

The doors opened, and I could hear the two counterfeiters running away through brush. Its siren blaring, the police car sped by, chasing Soapy and Donnie. The sound receded, and then faded entirely. I had been left alone.

I pushed myself around, my head against the box of rum bottles. My shoulder dispensed massive doses of pain. I raised my knee to my chin, then savagely sent my foot into the partition between the trunk and the cab. The jolt of pain made me shudder. I kicked again, then again, trying to ignore the agony in my chest and shoulder, my jaw clamped tightly against the pain. I kicked through the partition, shoving the seatback forward, then crawled with much scraping and groaning and inching along into the back seat.

After a moment I found the strength to climb out of the car but my legs collapsed and I fell to the mud, and I could do nothing but lie there for a moment, gasping in agony. The western sky was purple. Night was coming.

I turned my head, and even that small motion hurt. Illuminated by up-lights, a large sign at the entrance to a parking lot read Gator-Rama. Also on the sign was the legend: 100s of Gators. Another sign read Meet Gatorzilla: 25 Feet of Eatin' Fury. And another: Fresh Hush Puppies and Gator Hot Dogs. I had heard of this place, Gator-Rama, a tourist trap on the old state road to Baton Rouge. The counterfeiters had been planning to feed me to the gators, it looked like.

The smell of alligator dung and the damp, hot weather made the air seem molten. I began to walk. I have no clear recollection of how long I wandered or which direction I traveled. My only memory is of a terrible thirst and the agony in my shoulder. I had come from a hospital bed, so I was wearing no shoes, and my feet began to bleed. I tried putting out my thumb to get a ride from several cars that passed me, but in my blood-soaked hospital gown and bare feet I looked like an escapee from Bedlam. I plodded along, delirious some of the time, in pain all of the time.

I found myself on a narrow road with bushes on all sides, and that's where I fell to my knees and pitched forward onto the gravel.

•

When I opened my eyes I was lying on a bed in a small room that had cotton drapes over the only window. A sheet lay over me. A nicked-up dresser with a mirror was against one wall. A few bottles of perfume were on the dresser. An open closet door displayed jeans and blouses and shirts and skirts.

That's as far as my observations got before a grenade of pain exploded in my chest, and at the same instant I smelled burned meat. I arched my head down to look at my chest. Burn marks were around the stab wound, and the wound had been crudely sutured with dental floss. My head fell back. The hollow sound of pounding came from outside, someone at work outside the room, maybe. I bit down, trying not to cry out in agony. Tears of pain blurred the ceiling.

An enormous man wearing bib overalls and carrying a barrel stave walked into the room.

He stared at me, then said, "My name is Leroy Kelton. I'd hold out my hand, but you probably don't have the strength to shake it." His words filled the room, and were deep and echoing. "How you doing?"

"I don't know." Compared to his voice, mine sounded like a kazoo.

"Well, I fixed you up." The fellow moved further into the room. He was built like a river barge. His hands were gnarled and his arms were as thick as tree trunks. His belly was heroic, moving out in front of him, leading the way.

"How'd I get my chest burned?" I asked. "I thought I was only stabbed."

He looked down at me. His face was a big hambone with a broad nose and wet, pendulous lips and a purple burn scar under an ear, a face life had chewed on. "I cut out the dead meat in your wound, then burned out all the germs. Sewed it up myself."

"You didn't take me to a doctor?"

"Lookie here." He held up his right hand. Two fingers were missing. "I lopped off one finger sixteen years ago, and another four years ago. Both times I sneezed as my ax was coming down and so missed my target, if you can understand. I fixed myself right up. Didn't need no doctor. You, neither. You're sewed up tight as a cat's butt."

I asked, "What're you going to do with that club?"

He looked down at his hand, and seemed surprised to find the piece of wood there. "This is a stave. I'm a cooper. Been one all my life."

"What's a cooper?"

His brows went lower. "A barrel maker. My daddy was one, and so was his daddy."

When I nodded, the hole in my chest flooded me with pain.

"You live around here? I'll get you home, soon as you can move."

"I can't go home."

"Why not?"

"Some people are looking for me."

"The police? I don't want nothing to do with the police." He shifted the barrel stave from one hand to the other.

"Not the police."

They knew they hadn't killed me, so Soapy and Donnie were certainly hunting me, if they weren't in jail for drunk driving.

Kelton's expression shifted as he pondered. "You can stay here a couple days, I guess."

I tried to nod, but the small movement made the pain in my chest flare up again.

He reached into the pocket of his overalls to pull out a bottle. "Eat this medicine." He held it out to me.

"What is it?"

"It fights infection."

He handed me the pill bottle I squinted at the label.

"This medicine is for Pal," I said. "Who is Pal."

Kelton replied, "My dog."

"This is dog medicine?"

"It's all I got."

He helped me open the bottle, and I swallowed a dog pill.

"My dog died, but I hope those pills work better for you."

I asked, "How did you burn out all the rot in my wound?"

"Heated up a spoon handle over a fire, stuck it in the hole in your chest, and wiggled it around," Kelton said. "Smelled like death, I don't mind saying."

"Still does, actually."

"You got to eat," he rumbled. "Keep up your strength. My wife'll cook up something." As he left the room, he used the barrel stave to whack the doorframe.

I lay there, I don't know how long. The hammering outside my room went on and on. I struggled up to look out the window. A pile of white-oak staves was next to a tin-sided building with a forty-foot chimney that was spewing black smoke into the air. Leroy Kelton was loosely arranging staves in a steel ring. He pounded them into position with a wood club. He worked quickly, a loose-staved barrel forming in minutes.

I fell back onto the bed, my stab wound filling me with hurt. The pillow carried a nice odor, a woman's scent, which mingled with the smell of barbecue coming from my chest. Stuck to the mirror over the dresser was an *In Style Magazine* cover. A boom box was also on the dresser.

Half an hour later, Leroy brought me a bowl of chicken soup, and he said he would spoon it into my mouth if I couldn't do it myself, but I allowed as how I could manage. He told me this was his daughter's room, but she was away at school, at LSU, the first person in his family ever to go to college. He beamed when he said it, and I congratulated him.

I lay in that bed six days. Leroy tended to me, and so did his wife, a big, handsome woman named LuAnne, who would bring a chair up alongside my bed and fill my ear for two hours at a stretch. I ate some dog medicine every day.

On the seventh day, I put some clothes on that LuAnne had left for me on a hanger. She had even found a pair of tennis shoes that fit me. I was out of the bed two hours that day, and five the next. I was getting better. My wound didn't leak, and it was healing. Leroy was right: he had burned out all the germs.

One day I found myself standing next to the pile of barrel staves. Leroy was hammering staves into the ring, carefully adjusting one stave after another, which is called barrel raising.

"You got to be careful," Leroy said. "We don't want any pregnant barrels."

That's the cooper's term for a barrel where stave stands out too much.

After a few minutes, he asked, "Want to try?"

I took his mallet, and he showed me how to place the next stave in the ring. Each barrel has about thirty staves. I brought the mallet up and down, my shoulder not feeling too badly. I hammered eight staves into place before I wore out and my wound began to hurt. Leroy had to take all eight out of the ring and do them again. Coopering is a skill.

Leroy and LuAnne weren't in any hurry to have me leave. I started working at the cooperage, not too many hours at first. I toted barrel staves over to the ring. Then I worked the steam tunnel, where the staves are softened so they won't break when the hoops are put around them. Then I worked the furnace. Most of whiskey's taste comes from the barrel where it is aged.

During my stay with the Keltons, Leroy was doing an alligator char, where the inside of the barrel is burned about thirty seconds so that it becomes scaly and black. He explained that temperature and humidity variations during the passing seasons cause the liquid to enter and exit the porous staves, gaining taste from the wood's sugars.

After that first week I moved out of the daughter's bedroom, and took up lodging on the back porch, feeling I was less a bother that way.

The porch was open to the weather but screened off against bugs, of which Louisiana has eighty percent of the world's supply. I got stronger every day. Leroy offered to put me on the payroll, along with his three other employees but I declined. Their room and board and kindness were more than enough pay.

Leroy and I would sit out on the porch at night, him smoking a cigar. He was a life-long Chicago Cubs fan, saying that when he was a kid he listened to them on a home-made crystal radio, though he admitted that "waiting for them to have a good season is like wiping my butt with a hoop: it's endless." We sat on that porch evening after evening, listening to the night, and solving the world's problems. I don't ever remember being more at peace.

Except, that is, for my thoughts about Isobel. I kept them to myself, staring out at the night. But one evening, Leroy abruptly asked, "You got a girl anywhere? Some girl who might be wondering where you been lately?" he asked.

I rubbed my chin. "My so-called manager may have wondered where I've been, but she's pretty busy and I might not've crossed her mind all that often."

"Your boxing manager is a woman?" he asked.

"I'm not sure how it happened."

"You've got the hots for her?"

"Her name is Isobel Autrey, and I've come to believe she's a few peas short of a casserole, if you take my meaning." I put scorn into my voice. "And no, hell no, I don't have the hots for her."

Leroy stretched out his legs. A glass of iced tea was on a table next to the radio. "Well, I'm out here, and the frogs are croaking and the moon is out, and I'm drinking iced tea with a slice of lemon in it, and I'm listening to the Cubs lose another game, and I'm believing that you've got the hots for her."

I asked, "Leroy, you know anything about poetry?"

He sipped his tea. "I don't study poetry as much as a barrel maker should, I admit."

"Let me ask you a hypothetical question."

"Fire away," he said in his sousaphone voice.

"How much money would you give for a poem?"

"Pay money for a poem?" Leroy's tone was as if I had asked if he could flap his arms and fly up into a tree.

"A poem by a famous poet, a poem that's been lost for 150 years. How much money would you pay to be the person who discovered the poem after it had been lost for so many years?"

"Oh, I don't know." Leroy rubbed his big folded cheeks. He was wearing green suspenders and a plaid Pendleton shirt. "Maybe fifteen dollars. Twenty, tops."

"Would you risk your status in your profession for such a poem?"

He said, "Leroy Kelton barrels are the best that can be bought along the lower Mississippi, and every distiller in these parts knows it. I wouldn't put that reputation at risk over some words on a piece of paper, I don't care how good they rhyme."

Isobel was doing just that, imperiling everything in a gamble to claim a few old words on old paper. I'm not sure whether I liked Isobel. Her number one priority was herself, and Lord help anyone who wandered into her way. I had no doubt that somewhere along the line, had I hung around her long enough, I would've had her boot prints on the skin of my back.

And she was a kook. She hid it behind her wit and her big smile and her laugh, but the cheese may have slid off her cracker long ago, you have to admit.

My thoughts had been along these lines during my entire time at Leroy and LuAnne Kelton's home. Some of my pain had been from the stab wound, and some from this confusion about Isobel, but I was healing both ways, I thought.

Leroy poured more tea for both of us

I said, "Leroy, it's about time I get back to my life."

He turned his big head my direction. "No need to rush off."

"I'm all healed up, thanks to you and LuAnne. If I stay any longer, I'd just be hiding."

"I don't figure you for a hider."

"I'll leave tomorrow, if that won't leave you short-handed at the cooperage."

He shook his head, his dewlaps wagging. "How about coming back for Thanksgiving. LuAnne makes a pecan pie you'll think about for years."

"I'll show up hungry."

Leroy swished the tea in his glass, and the ice cubes clinked together. "You going to visit those two fellows who kidnapped you from the hospital?"

"I've been thinking on it."

"Want some help? I can work a barrel mallet pretty good."

I shook my head.

"You'd miss out on LuAnn's pecan pie, you go out and get yourself killed, Dennis."

"My life lately has taught me one thing, Leroy." I grinned at him. "I take a lot of killing."

14

Old Al Higgens let me borrow his car, and I filled the trunk with Quik Set concrete bags, ten of them weighing fifty pounds each, so the rear end of Old Al's Ford was sunk down to the axles as I drove down Palona Street looking for an address.

I passed several haggard palm trees. Weeds grew in sidewalk cracks. Many of the one-story clapboard houses that lined the street suffered from peeling paint, scuffed front doors and tilted porches. Junkyard dogs roamed the street. The lawns were either overgrown and dandelion-choked or trampled to dirt by children's feet. I had to maneuver around parked cars, most of them as shabby as Old Al's Fairlane. Lots of kids were on the street, skateboarding and biking and fooling around, so I drove slowly.

I spotted it, a tiny house that looked like a face, with a door in the middle and a window on each side. Ragged curtains were drawn over the windows. The house had once been yellow but was now faded and was stained from gutter runoff. A leaning television antenna was on the shingled roof. The screen door was torn, and a flap of wire mesh hung down.

The house didn't have a driveway so I pulled up in front. A mockingbird loosed a trill as I got out of the car. I walked across the unkempt grass, then alongside the house to the back door. The backyard was an impenetrable thicket of weeds growing around a cast-off kitchen stove and a rusted car axle.

I looked left and right, didn't see anyone, brought up my foot, and smashed it into the doorknob. The door popped open. I hurried through the house, looking into each room, but no one was there. Then I returned to Old Al's car, opened the trunk, and lifted out two bags of Quik Set. I threw them over my shoulders and returned to the house's back door. Carrying them through the tiny kitchen,

I then threw the sacks down on the bathroom floor. I made that trip four more times, carrying two sacks of ready-mix concrete each time. On my last trip, I also brought out a number-two idiot stick—a shovel—and brought it into the house, too.

In the bathroom I ripped open three Quik Set bags and dumped the powdery gray contents into the bathtub. The bathroom had a tub, a sink and a toilet with no room to spare, so it was close in that room, me working up a sweat and fine particles of concrete dust churning up from the tub. I turned on the tub faucet, and stirred the concrete with the shovel. I added another bag of concrete, then another, folding the concrete paste into the water again and again, until I had a nice sludge that filled the bathtub almost to the rim. To test its consistency, I placed the shovel into the mix, and it stayed upright. I pulled out the shovel and scraped off dabs of concrete from the blade. I balled up the empty Quik Set sacks and tossed them out the back door. I was ready.

I returned to the living room, a shabby place even by my standards. The only thing new in the room was a television set that must have had a 50-inch screen, and a six-foot-tall karaoke machine. Over a tattered sofa was a poster of the metal group AC/DC attached to the wall with staples. I sat down carefully on the sofa, which was tilty because of a missing leg.

I waited. An hour passed. I went back into the bathroom to add a little water to the concrete so it wouldn't set up. Another hour passed, and I did the same thing, keeping the concrete at the consistency of mud. Nightfall came and I still waited, the shovel across my lap. I didn't turn on a light.

Then I heard footsteps on the porch outside the front door. Carrying the shovel, I stood quickly and moved behind the door. The door opened, and even in the faint moonlight coming through the door, I recognized the Hooters T-shirt. I swung the shovel at the round head, and the flat of the blade struck with a dull clap.

The counterfeiter, Soapy Fay, fell heavily to the floor. His partner Donnie Lafitte made it half-way through his turn—him intending to make a dash for it—when my shovel found his head, sounding like a melon hitting the floor. He toppled, senseless.

I dropped the shovel and grabbed Soapy by the wrists and pulled him toward the bathroom, none too gently. He skidded along on his big belly. I tugged him into position alongside the tub, then lifted his shoulders, balanced him on the rim, then brought up his feet and dumped him onto the concrete. He groaned softly.

Then I returned for Donnie. I pulled him into the bathroom, and lifted him up and over the bathtup rim. He weighed half what his partner did.

They both sank a little into the muck, but not enough, so I got the shovel from the living room and used the handle to prod them down into the cement, pushing their feet and knees and Soapy's great belly down, and making sure their hands were well under the surface. I left only their heads in the air. It was tight in that tub, with both men, a tangle of arms and legs. With the shovel, I arranged the concrete evenly, smoothing it out with the blade. The tub was now over-full, and concrete oozed over the rim and fell onto the linoleum.

I sat on the toilet lid. After three or four minutes, Soapy came to, and he stared at me, his eyes round in his round face. When he tried to raise a hand up through the viscous concrete, I placed the shovel blade on the bridge of his nose.

"If you move, I'll sink this shovel into your brain. And if you talk, I'll do the same." I leaned a little more onto the handle, creasing the skin on his nose.

Donnie's eyes opened. He was about to protest, but must've seen my grim face.

I said, "You both lie there quietly, and don't tempt me."

They believed me. I sat down on that toilet. After an hour, I got a toothbrush from the cabinet above the sink and carved my initials into the concrete near his chin.

Then I waited some more. Three more hours passed. They didn't say a word, and didn't so much as flare their noses.

At the end of those hours, I stabbed the shovel at the concrete near the faucet. The blade bounced off. The mix had set.

"Next time I'm not going to be so nice," I said.

And I left them there, closing the bathroom door behind me. I went out of the house by the fractured back door, got into Old Al's car and drove back to the Quarter.

•

"It's a beauty, isn't it?" Isobel's father asked me.

"Sir, I trust your judgment," I replied. "But on this, I'm not so sure."

He laughed heartily. "Like much in life, Dennis, the beauty is under the hood."

We were in the six-car garage in the back of his home in the Garden District. Two BMWs and a Suburban took up some of the space, but also in the garage was the old rattle-trap he had just called a beauty.

His eyes glittered with amusement as he ran a hand along the fender. "You don't see it, yet?"

"Afraid I don't, sir."

"Call me Lawrence, will you? You remind me of the county jail, where you sir this and sir that."

It was my turn to laugh. "As if you've been in the county jail."

He glanced meaningfully at me. "This is a 1936 Ford five-window coupe. Rather dilapidated, wouldn't you say?"

The Ford had swooping front fenders and running boards. The headlights were mounted on the fenders. The tires were wide whites. The coupe might have been olive green at one time, but rust and fading and scuffs and small dents had made it hard to determine the original color.

I said, "Looks a little rusty, and it's got some dings on it."

"Doesn't look like much, does it?" he asked.

"It's an old car." I wondered what Lawrence's point was. "Needs some body work and paint."

"Look at the lock on the rumble seat. It's been caved in, like a sledge hammer hit it. Try to open it."

The chrome trunk button and its surrounding frame were wrinkled, and the button wouldn't budge under my thumb. "Can't."

"That's not by accident."

"The trunk handle was smashed on purpose?" I asked.

"Go ahead." Lawrence opened the driver's door. "Climb in. Start it up."

I looked at him. He was smiling widely. He was on the verge of revealing some great secret. I hadn't an idea what it might be.

I slid into the seat. When I turned the key, nothing happened.

"Do the key, but also punch the starter button on the floor."

I'd never heard of a starter button. I found it near the clutch. I pressed it with my left foot.

The starter clicked over, and then the engine kicked in. I jumped in the seat at the sound, a deep bass rumbling that was painfully loud in the garage.

Lawrence yelled gleefully, "Try the accelerator."

I gently pressed the pedal. The engine wound up quickly. The throaty scream made the car tremble and put my eardrums on the verge of imploding. The garage's windows shimmered. I'd heard quieter jet engines.

Lawrence pantomimed turning off the engine. I twisted the key. After the engine died, I could hear him laughing, entirely delighted.

"Let me show you something," he said after I got out of the car.

He opened the hood. "It's not the stock engine. It's a big new lead-sled Cadillac motor. At least, it was new when I was driving the Ford. Over three hundred horses."

I leaned over the radiator to examine the engine.

Lawrence added, "Two carburetors, drilled out pistons, altered cam, big electric system added on, dual exhausts, and four-speeds on the floor. Heavier brakes. The only thing on this old car that is run-down is the exterior, and that's so cops wouldn't pay it no never mind. I've driven this car one-hundred-ten miles-an-hour, at least, that's my guess as the needle was pegged out."

Had stuffy, wealthy Lawrence Autrey just said, "Pay it no never mind?"

"You did all this?" I asked. "You made it a hot rod?"

"My pappy did," Lawrence explained. "The reason you can't—" He pronounced it *cain't*. "—get into the rumble seat is 'cause he smashed 'at handle to make it hard so no cop, just for fun, opens 'at trunk."

"There's a rumble seat in there?" I asked.

"Once 'twas. Now 'ere ain't nothin' in 'ere but space. You get to 'at trunk by takin' out 'at driver's seat."

"Your pa was a bootlegger, as I remember."

"He'd move his shine in 'is rig. And when I got to be thirteen year ol', my pa reckoned I could move hootch as well as him. An' I did. I'd leave them police flat on they asses." PO'lice. "I'd be in Memphis afore 'at engine got warm."

I stared at him. He was still there in his blue blazer and tasseled loafers. But he had begun to sound like the backwoods.

"Why are you talking funny all of a sudden, Mr. Autrey?"

"I ain't talkin' funny. 'Is is how I learnt to talk." He pronounced I tawk.

"I'm not getting it, sir."

The old guy closed the Ford's hood. "The manner with which I have spent the last forty years speaking is an utter affectation, Dennis."

Suddenly he was again the Lawrence Autrey I knew. Flinty diction, big words.

He said, "For decades, I've kept a little secret from my family."

"And you're going to tell me?"

"My wife and daughter and almost everyone else in New Orleans think my father was the great bootlegger and liquor runner, and they think he left me an inheritance that allowed me to rise above my family's bayou background."

"That's not how it happened?" I asked.

He brushed unseen dust from his blazer sleeves. "My father didn't leave me much more than this car and some equipment and some contacts." He smiled with pleasure at his impending revelation. "The truth is that I made my own fortune. I'm from the deep bayou. I ran rum for years after my dad died. I was good at it, at one time having sixty people working for me, doing the cooking and running. And then I branched out into importing rum from Cuba. That's where the big money was made. And I spent some time behind bars."

"Isobel doesn't know this?"

He shook his head. "She thinks I was born with this Garden District, old money, tut-tut-tut accent."

"You're good at that accent, for sure."

"Isobel thinks my father made all the illegal money, and got out of the hootch business and was a wealthy businessman before I was born. In truth, I was a bayou cane-liquor maker for many years, and a rum smuggler for many years after that. And then I worked long and hard to get out of my illegal liquor business and build a reputation here in New Orleans."

I scratched my chin, wondering why he was telling me all this.

Lawrence said, "As part of it, I reinvented myself. I learned to tie a tie. I got rid of ain't and cain't. I learned not to plant my elbows on the table when I eat. I learned a thousand things, working assiduously at it. I became a gentleman."

"You are saying you are a fraud?"

He smiled. "Some people might view it that way. I have a more benign view of what happened: people can change. I am today precisely what you see before you, a Garden District gentleman."

"So what's your point?

"You can take the boy out of the bayou, and you can also take the bayou out of the boy." He put his hands in his blazer pockets in that yacht-skipper manner that aggravates everyone who doesn't own a yacht. "I had a good laugh two days ago, drinking my coffee and reading the morning newspaper."

He'd eventually get to his point, I figured.

"There was a story about one Soapy Fay and one Donnie Lafitte who were found in a bathtub under a ton of hardened concrete. It seems they had been yelling for a day and a half, and finally a boy over the back fence heard him and told his parents, and they called the paramedics. It took three hours to chip them out."

I tried not to smile. Lawrence Autrey had telephoned me four days ago, offering to help locate the two counterfeiters. When I had asked him how he could possibly find them, he had replied that he had contacts from the old days. Sure enough, he had called the next day, telling me where I might find Soapy and Donnie.

He laughed. "That was a bad day for Soapy and Donnie because when the medics pulled them from the tub, the police were waiting, and they arrested them on an outstanding warrant for skipping bond before a trial for counterfeiting. You have anything to do with that, Dennis?"

"Some, maybe."

Lawrence affectionately patted the hood of his souped-up Ford, then led me from the garage out into the sun. The backyard was about half an acre, and filled with magnolia trees, white gardenia blossoms, purple asters, daylilies, and an expanse of lawn where a croquet rig had been set up. An elderly gardener was weeding near the back door to the house. The driveway led to the street out front. Bees worked the flowers, hundreds of bees.

"My point is, Dennis, that you can transform yourself, just like I did. I went from bootlegger to Garden District gentleman. You can go from—what? A loser to a winner."

Then I understood. "You're suggesting that I renew my partnership with your nutty daughter?"

He worked his seamed face into a grin. "Exactly."

"I didn't break off our partnership. She did."

"She was aggravated and despondent, so much so that she blamed you for Moe Barnes dangling the poem in front of her, then yanking it away again. Somehow she also blamed me, and Charles, and the dean of the Tulane English Department, and the chairman of the Federal Reserve."

"She's naïve, believing a gangster will keep his end of a deal," I said.

"I suppose you are right."

"It's her fault, not mine." I sounded childish.

"That poem has clouded her judgment, Dennis."

We stepped toward his back door. Chrysanthemums lined the brick walkway. His mouth was pursed, and he seemed deep in thought.

He turned to me. "Isobel will never be happy without that poem."

"I've gathered that much."

"And I'll never be happy unless she's happy. That's the father's curse. Moe Barnes has contacted her again. Once more, he has offered her the poem. Now that you've beaten Sammy Dresser, you're even hotter as a boxer. You win another big fight and he'll give her the poem."

I unbuttoned my shirt. The scar was red and angry. I pointed at it. "This is new, this scar. I took a six-inch shank for your daughter, and it almost killed me. It was Moe Barnes's nephew who did it. I almost got killed, thanks to your daughter."

"Isn't blaming Isobel for being knifed as silly as Isobel blaming you for losing the poem?"

Well, that quieted me.

Lawrence said, "Barnes wants a new deal because he can make considerably more money now that you are better known and ranked higher after the Dresser fight. The bettors are paying attention. Your fights will carry a bigger waging pool."

"I'm ranked higher?"

He smiled. "After beating Sammy Dresser, you're the fifth ranked heavyweight in the country right now. Didn't you know that?"

"I've been bleeding too much to pay attention to boxing."

He smoothed an eyebrow with a finger. "Moe Barnes wants you fighting again. He wants you to take on a higher-ranked opponent."

"What are you proposing?" I asked.

"The syndicate will continue with your reformation. We'll make you a winner. If not necessarily in the ring, then in life."

"It still sounds screwy."

"I transformed myself, and so I know how to do it. Have you ever heard of William Hazlitt?"

"No, sir."

"He was an English fight fan and essay writer, and he said in 1822 that it was not impossible for a prize fighter to be a gentleman. I agree with him. We can turn you around."

"I'm sort of afraid of Isobel."

"Lots of people are," her father said. "Will you do it? You fighting again in a match arranged by Moe Barnes is the only way she'll get her poem."

"I'm more inclined to help you than her, frankly." I rubbed my big chin. "Isobel hasn't agreed to it?"

"Last I saw her, she had made a cornhusk doll of you and Moe Barnes, and was taking them to Coral Thibideaux."

Odd pains began shooting down my back, as if I were being stabbed again, thinking about Coral and her voodoo parlor. I've always been susceptible to suggestion, and that's the hell of it. I shook myself, and the pains subsided.

"But I think Isobel is beginning to realize her anger at you was misplaced. You did your part, defeating Dresser. It was Barnes who reneged, and who didn't give her the Poe poem."

I didn't say anything.

"I'm apologizing for Isobel."

"Did she ask you to?" I pressed the knife scar. It was still tender.

"Not exactly."

"So this is all your idea?"

"Isobel might apologize someday," he said. "Stranger things have happened."

We walked a few steps, side-by-side.

Then Lawrence said, "If Isobel proposes that you renew your deal with her, at least listen, will you?"

"A deal with someone who has taken a cornhusk doll of me to a voodoo lady?" I said.

I left him there, and he waved goodbye. Then he stepped toward the gardener, I suppose to give him instructions.

I walked alongside the house, then down the street toward the streetcar stop to get myself back to the Quarter. It was hot out there, summer in Louisiana, but I was thinking about the prospects of a new deal, and being in Isobel's hands again.

I was shivering.

15

The tunnel was too low to stand upright, so I moved along in a crouch, carrying the bucket and dragging a shovel. Black galoshes were on my feet, and with each step they sank through the crust into the rotted muck below. The air was so foul—a fetid, stench that rose from the muck in waves—that I breathed through my mouth, but the rank odor filled my head anyway. I swallowed quickly, trying to keep my breakfast in my belly.

"Hurry up down there," came from the shaft at the north end of the tunnel. It was the straw boss, who liked to yell more than he liked to work. "You must think you're on vacation in that tunnel." He laughed coarsely.

With the shovel, I dug into the crust, then scooped it into the bucket. A new wave of revolting odor enveloped me. At my elbow was a conveyor belt that ran the length of the tunnel. The belt ran on top of a series of steel rollers powered by electric motors. The belt was idle, and only a few wheat grains lay on it, along with the wheat dust that also covered all the machinery. The tunnel was about fifteen feet wide and two hundred feet long, and dimly lit by bare bulbs on the ceiling. I slopped more of the muck into the bucket, then carried it a few feet to the rope, which had a hook on it.

I secured the bucket, then called up, "Okay, take it up."

"About time."

The bucket rose into the shaft. I'd never before been in a place that smelled so bad it made me sweat, but this tunnel was doing it. After being stabbed, I couldn't get any more door work from O'Donnell Temps, the dispatcher telling me he didn't favor murder attempts on his jobs. And I needed some money, so I got a job at Southern Farmers Warehouse, which owned grain elevators, this one on the Mississippi's banks several miles upriver from the Quarter. When I worked the shovel, I felt only a twinge from my stab wound. I was almost fully healed.

The bucket descended again. "Fill 'er up," came from the straw boss, the fellow who had hired me so he wouldn't have to do this scut work himself, down here in the tunnel.

I shoveled more goop into the bucket. The tunnel ran underground below the elevators. To transfer grain from one of the huge storage structures or to a ship, a below-grade hatch would be opened, and the grain would slide down to the conveyor belt, where it was hauled along underground to an enclosed bucket belt, where the grain would be lifted up ten stories, then dumped into a spout where it fell down into the hold of a bulk cargo ship moored alongside.

I hooked the bucket onto the rope again. Up it went. Over the course of a season, dust gathered at the bottom of the tunnel from the grain being carried along on the belt. The tunnel seeped water due to the high ground water. The water mixed with dust, creating mud. Then spilled grain sprouted, and quickly died due to lack of sunlight. Then it rotted, forming a crust on top, with muck below, like an apple cobbler.

Added to this were dead rats and mice that found their way into the tunnel and couldn't get out. The sulfurous vapors could peel chrome from a bumper. Spider webs were thick along the concrete ceiling, and my hair kept brushing them off, where they hung to my shoulders. I gagged and spit, and made my way toward the ladder, splashing with every step.

The bucket came back down, bumping my arm. I yelled up into the shaft, "I've got to get out of here."

"The hell you do," the straw boss yelled back. "I didn't hire you so you could loaf."

"I'm getting sick down here," I said.

"Happens to everybody, first dozen times or so." He laughed. "Once you puke, you'll be okay."

The bucket twitched on the rope, the straw boss working the rope as if it were a fishing line, trying to tempt me to fill it with the muck. I jabbed the shovel at the crust.

"Dennis, come up here."

The voice brought me up with such surprise that I banged my head on the tunnel's ceiling.

"Dennis, can you hear me?" It was Isobel, her voice echoing down the shaft. "Come up here."

I looked upward. She was peering down the shaft, and the straw boss was there, too, bent over the square hole, puzzlement on his face.

So I put the shovel aside and climbed up, muck dripping from my galoshes. The ladder was nothing but rebar bent to resemble staples. I arrived at the surface, which was a driveway for grain trucks. The driveway was under a corrugated tin roof. Wheat arriving at this elevator was sent to European and Caribbean ports.

The straw boss had his arms crossed in front of him. He wore denim overalls and a scowl. At his knee was a wheelbarrow, where he had been pouring the muck from the bucket. I breathed the sweet air.

Isobel's nose was wrinkled. "What are you doing down in a hole?"

"Working for a living. You ought to try it some day."

"Teaching poetry is working for a living."

"You teach poetry?" The straw boss laughed. "Where do I get in line for a job like that?"

She looked at him. "First you have to be able to recite the alphabet." She grabbed my arm and said to him, "Dennis quits this job."

"I can't quit," I protested. "I've got to make the rent or I'll be out on the street."

"You're back on the syndicate's payroll."

The straw boss's mouth worked under his sparse mustache. "Lady, you can't quit for him."

"You bet I can." She pulled me away. "I'm his manager."

"A day laborer needs a manager?" the straw boss asked. "Jones, if you quit, I've got to go down into that tunnel myself."

Isobel pulled me along the driveway, over the truck scales. The scaleman's office was to the our right. Isobel was wearing a striped cotton pullover sweater—the stripes were several shades of blue— and black jeans. A purse was over her shoulder.

I looked back up the driveway and hollered, "Keep my job open for a couple of minutes, will you, boss? I'll go back down into the tunnel when I get done with this lady."

Or, more likely, when she got done with me. The straw boss

cursed as we left him. Holding onto my arm, Isobel guided me out into the sun.

"My father made me renew our deal," she said. "I didn't want to have anything to do with you again, but such is his power over me that here I stand in the warehouse district speaking with someone who smells like he's been lying dead in the sun too long."

"I'll bet your father worked harder convincing me than convincing you."

"That's preposterous. I have an iron will."

"So do I." If you tell a lie, make it a whopper, I always figure.

She shook her head. "Your will is made of whatever was in that bucket back there." Then her eyes lit up and she laughed, a carillon of sound. She squeezed my arm. "I hate to admit it, Dennis, but I haven't had as much fun since you've been away."

"I wasn't away. I was fighting for my life."

Now she was serious. "I visited you that first day, but you were still anesthetized, and when I came back the next day you were gone, and nobody knew where you were. I looked for you, but you had vanished. I was worried sick."

We walked down the truck ramp. Her car was parked in the lot in a line of workers' pick-up trucks. The elevators were behind us, rising a hundred-fifty feet above the ground, resembling enormous silos lined up along the river.

"I have a theory." Isobel looked up at me. "Want to hear it?"

"No, to tell the truth." Gravel crunched below our feet.

"It's this: the trouble in your life is because of your mother."

I tried to laugh derisively but it didn't come out the way I wanted. "I have almost no memories of my mother."

"But you have some?"

"I absolutely refuse to talk about my mother."

"Tell me what you remember about her?"

I asked, "Why don't you ever listen to what I'm saying? I don't want to talk about my mother."

"You told me you don't remember her face. What do you remember?"

We came to her car. Heat shimmers rose from the gravel. Some of the shimmers seemed to course up her body, making it pulsate and steam. I blinked my eyes. No, maybe not. Lit by the high white sun, her hair was so black it was steel blue.

Her eyes flashed. "Come on, Dennis. Open up a little."

I pulled at my ear lobe. "When my father was cursing her after she left, he would call her Susan."

"Have you ever looked for her?"

"Why would I do that?" I spit out. "She ditched me when I was a little kid. When people ditch me, I never look for them. Never."

She drew herself up. "You weren't going to look for me after I walked out on your last fight, were you? You were through with me."

"You're damn right."

"I was angry. Just like you are angry at me for being knifed."

I was silent.

"I wasn't holding the knife. Buddy the Knife Man stabbed you, not me."

After a moment, I said, "Moe Barnes has contacted you again, your dad told me. You just want me to fight again so you can get your poem. That's what this is all about."

She ignored me. "So what are your memories of your mother?"

Why argue with her? I always lose. "I have two."

"Just two?"

"One is from Christmas. I must've been three, maybe even younger. I remember the tree, all the dazzling lights, and my mom is standing there putting ornaments on the tree."

"I thought you said you have no memory of her face."

"I don't. Her back is to me. It's the smallest of memories, just a flicker, maybe only three or four seconds worth, and no matter how I nudge that recollection, I can't get my mother to turn toward me to let me look at her face."

Her voice softened. "What's the other memory?"

"We are walking somewhere, her and me. I don't know where, but I'm holding her hand, high above me. I'm on a sidewalk. And she laughs and says, 'Denny, don't drag me toward the curb. You're like a puppy, pulling all the time.' My mother's voice is strong and clear and recognizable. I've played it a million times in my head. So I know her voice but not her face."

"Do you know her maiden name?" Isobel asked.

I shook my head. "Why are you asking questions about her?"

Isobel didn't answer. She dug into her purse for car keys. "I have a new plan."

I complained, "Every time you get a plan, I get a wound."

"Don't whine, Dennis." She brought out her keys. "It's unseemly." She opened the driver's side door, then looked at me again. "Get in the car."

"Every time I get into the car with you, something bad happens."

"You're still whining. Get in the car."

"Not a chance. I'm going back to work, back into the tunnel. I've thought about it. I don't want anything to do with your so-called syndicate."

She smiled. "I've got some big news for you, Dennis."

"I'm not getting into the car with you, doesn't matter what your news is."

"You've got another fight lined up."

"After getting stabbed, thanks to you, I may have retired from boxing." Then I simply couldn't help myself. "Who's the fighter?"

"Gentleman James Norton."

I hesitated. Had she just said Gentleman James Norton? The third-ranked heavyweight?

"Gentleman James Norton?" I blurted. "Really?"

I hurried around the car to the passenger door, opened it, and crawled in, Isobel laughing lightly as I did so.

•

"Don't be nervous," Isobel advised.

"I'm not nervous." I was carrying a thick file. "Compared to my upcoming fight with Gentleman James Norton, this interview is going to be easy."

"Above all," she said, "don't be yourself."

We were in Gibson Hall, the administration building at Tulane University. The building resembles an English baronial palace, and faces St. Charles Street where streetcars pass by, including a streetcar named Desire. Isobel mentioned our names to a receptionist, who showed us into the dean of admission's office. The little plaque on the door revealed that the dean's name was Jay Harper.

She introduced me, and he smiled as he shook my hand but I could tell he was working hard to keep perplexity from his face. His eyes clicked to my cauliflower ear. I'm used to it. He also took in my knotted nose and my beaten brows and the cross-hatch scar along my jawbone. I was wearing slacks and a sports coat the syndicate had purchased for me.

Harper waved us to chairs in front of his desk. "You are considering applying for admission to Tulane, Dennis?"

I leaned across the desk to hand him my file. "I hope to apply to transfer to Tulane as a junior."

The dean lifted my documents up and down. "This is the thickest student file I've ever seen."

Isobel said, "Dennis hasn't applied yet, Jay. We simply want your reading on his chances. If there's no possibility he'll be admitted, we won't waste everybody's time."

Jay Harper opened the file which contained a loose pile of transcripts, employment records and such like that I had assembled at Isobel's request. The dean had thinning hair and a lofty forehead. His eyes were wide apart on his face, giving him an open and honest expression. His lips were thin and bloodless. He wore a tweed jacket and a narrow wool tie.

On the back desk behind his chair were photos of his wife and children, a laptop computer, and an engraved plaque, some award he had received. An autographed baseball was under a plastic display dome, and next to it was a photo of Harper in a baseball uniform. He was younger in the photo, still in his twenties. Loose-leaf binders filled the shelves above the back desk.

"What would you be hoping to major in here at Tulane?" Harper asked.

"Whatever doesn't require any science, math, or liberal arts classes. I've had some difficulty with those in the past."

Isobel clucked her tongue softly, a warning to me.

"That narrows your fields," Harper said equably. "Forgive me for asking, as I'm sure it's here somewhere in this stack, but precisely what school are you transferring from, Dennis?"

"I last attended Blue Springs Community College."

He said, "I'm sorry, but I haven't heard of that particular institution."

"It's near Independence, Missouri," I explained.

"And what was your course of study?"

"I took a course in self-acupuncture."

He stared at me.

"I had a buzzing in my ear," I said, "after a fighter hit me with a horseshoe hidden in his glove. I couldn't get rid of the buzz for two months, so I took an acupuncture course, which I figured was cheaper than paying a doctor."

Isobel scowled at me for some reason.

"Did it work?" The dean glanced again at my tissue-filled ear.

I shook my head. "I learned how to do it, but I couldn't ever get up the gumption to stick a needle into my ear. The buzzing went away a couple of weeks later during a fight in Leavenworth, when my head bounced off the ring post on my way down to the canvas. When I woke up, no buzzing."

Harper smiled. "Your boxing explains certain angles in your face."

Isobel said, "Dennis is now the fifth-ranked heavyweight in the country."

Harper's eyebrows rose. "Really? I'm impressed." He tapped my documents. "And what other courses did you take at Blue Springs?"

"None."

"So you were at another school prior to Blue Springs?"

"Well, before Blue Springs, I took a welding course offered at Joplin Technical School."

Isobel cleared her throat rather loudly, trying to send me a message, maybe.

"A welding course?" The dean dug a little further into the stack. "In a mechanic's shop?"

"Not in a shop," I said. "The class was held in a gymnasium surrounded by razor wire."

Harper asked, "You were in prison?"

"Jail," I replied. "A jail is different from a prison. This was just the Newton County jail, a little place, cute by incarceration standards."

Harper glanced at Isobel, who was staring out the window toward St. Charles.

Then Harper asked, "And what were you in jail for?"

"For three days."

"I mean, what sent you to jail?"

"A judge sent me to jail."

He ran a hand through his hair, as if checking to see if he'd lost any more of it recently. "I mean, what crime were you convicted of?"

"It was hardly a crime," I answered. "It was an unlicensed pugilistic competition, is what the complaint said. In some places, you can't put on a fight without having a license."

He formed his fingers into a steeple, and stared at me over them. "Have you ever been in jail for anything other than unlicensed boxing?"

I scratched my jawbone. "One time I was caught with a fingernail file."

"You were shoplifting? Stealing a fingernail file?"

"I had the file in my mouth, just a small one."

He again looked at Isobel, who wouldn't meet his eyes. "Why was a nail file in your mouth?"

"Up in Gary, Indiana I was fighting a bum named Red Lasser, who kept head-butting me."

Isobel began vigorously scratching her arm.

I said, "So Red Lasser is banging his head on me whenever he can, so between rounds three and four I tell my cornerman to get me something sharp. He borrowed a nail file from a lady spectator in the first row, and slipped it to me while he was holding a water-bottle up to my mouth."

"What did you do with the file?" the dean asked.

"I pinned it between my lower teeth and my mouth guard. The bell rang for round four, and the next time that bum got his head next to me, I slashed at his forehead with the file."

"That wouldn't do much damage, would it? A scratch?"

Isobel said, "Honestly, Jay, you can't be interested in this."

"Not in and of itself," I replied. "But Red started bleeding, and the forehead bleeds a lot, and the blood spilled down over his left eye."

Harper smiled. "So he couldn't see your punch. I get it."

"He never saw my right hook coming, and I'm surprised you didn't hear the smack down hear in New Orleans. Red went down as if the hangman had opened the trapdoor, and when he was carried from the ring, the tops of his shoes were dragging on the canvas."

Harper shook his head pleasantly. "I turned out for the boxing club in college."

"How'd it go?" I asked.

"Turns out I have an aversion to being hit in the face."

Isobel's voice could have etched glass. "Could we please get on the with the interview, Jay and Dennis? You'd think we were sitting in a tavern, trading sports stories."

The dean squared my documents. "Dennis, have you been

imprisoned for anything other than boxing-related offenses?"

"Not once. But I get into the ring with Gentleman James Norton, I might be arrested for stupidity."

"You have a fight lined up with Gentleman James Norton?" the dean asked.

"He's next on my card." I indicated the photo of Harper in the baseball uniform. "You played for the Indianapolis Indians?"

He glanced over his shoulder at the photo. "You recognize the uniform?"

"The Brewers' triple-A affiliate. I saw them play a couple times when I was up in Indianapolis. Victory Field is a great place to see a game. Hot Indiana summer night. Cold beer and a dog. Bunch of players really showing their stuff, trying to earn a shot at the next level. Can't be beat."

"Honestly, Dennis," Isobel said.

"I never made the majors," Harper said in the tone of an undertaker. "I tried for five years at the Triple-A level. Couldn't make the jump."

"Neither have I." I laughed again. "But I'm still working on it." I rose from the chair. "Jay, this whole deal, meeting you and applying here at Tulane, was cooked up by Isobel. I know I don't have a chance at getting into Tulane, so I'll stop wasting your time."

"With that attitude, you'll never beat Gentleman James Norton," Harper said.

"Yeah. You're right."

He said, "Tulane is a selective school but admission is not entirely based on transcripts from educational institutions. We also look at achievement and character. And background, such as what an applicant has had to overcome."

"Well, I've got a lot of background."

"And you've got some good schools in that stack of transcripts. LSU and Washington University and some others," he said, "I advise you to make a formal application for admission, Dennis."

I looked at him a moment, waiting for him break out in laughter and wink at Isobel. But he didn't. I waited some more, and he still didn't.

"All right, I'll apply." I looked at my watch. "But right now I'd like to apply for a sandwich and a beer somewhere."

"Dennis, will you for once refrain from talking about your

physical needs?" Isobel said. "You're at an important interview."

As if he couldn't help himself, the dean again looked over his shoulder at the photo of himself in an Indianapolis Indians uniform, a quick glance. I wondered how much time he spent staring at the photograph and dreaming of lost opportunities.

"You want to join me, Jay?" I asked. "I'll tell you all I know about boxing over the beer, and then you can tell me all you know about baseball over the sandwich."

He paused, but only for an instant. Then he quickly rose from his chair. "I know just the place over on Magazine Street. Terrific Reubens on rye."

I followed him out of the office.

"Honestly, Dennis," Isobel said, hurrying after us. "Can't you stick to my script just once in your life?"

16

A pencil in her hand, Isobel stared down at the practice SAT I had taken that morning. She had been grading it. "Have you ever taken an algebra class?"

"Lots. Algebra is my life."

"As I suspected, your knowledge of algebra and my dog's knowledge of algebra are precisely the same. But I'm ready."

She disappeared toward the kitchen, the wiener dog following her, its nails clattering on the hallway's slate floor.

Isobel had spent four days reducing my two-inch stack of transcripts—twenty-two different educational institutions—to an application to Tulane. She termed the application "marginally presentable."

Isobel returned down the hallway. Following her was Coral Thibideaux.

"Hi, again, Dennis." She beamed me with a full-wattage smile. She was carrying a cooking pot and two bottles.

In Isobel's hand was a wood rack, maybe a spice rack, something you would put inside a cupboard to hold pepper and cloves. A drinking glass was in her other hand "You understand, Dennis, everything you are about to do is for your own good."

"I'm not about to do anything."

"Oh yes, you are," Isobel replied. "I'm your manager. You have to do what I tell you."

"I'm happy just sitting here doing nothing."

Isobel remarked, "That's one of your problems, Dennis."

"I've been back in the kitchen cooking all morning long," Coral said, placing the pot on the table in front of me. Her long, crimson Mali-cloth dress almost reached the floor. Perhaps twenty thin silver bracelets hung from her left wrist, and they chimed together as she moved. Her black hair was in cornrows that fell past her shoulders. Steam rose from the pot. Isobel placed the spice rack on the table. I fought the urge to flee.

"Now, what I'm cooking up is a miracle drink." Coral poured liquid from one of the bottles into the pot. "I've reduced the ingredients to this broth, stirring while it sat over the heat, adding bits of this and that."

I looked into the pot. The liquid was thick and brown. "It smells like a grain elevator tunnel."

Coral lifted one of the small bottles from the spice rack. "To keep the mix fresh and potent, some items must be added at the very last minute."

The bottle appeared to be ancient, with rough glass and a stained cork stopper, nothing the Safeway would carry. Coral produced a measuring spoon, and tapped out some of the spice or whatever it was into the spoon, then dumped it into the pot.

"I've got to be careful," she said. "Three too many grains of this, and you would die in agony."

"I'm not going to drink whatever you've cooked up, Coral. No offense."

Isobel said, "It's for your own good."

"What is it?" I said by way of delay.

"It's Elixir 42, the Jamaican Brain Boost."

"I'm not going to drink it, no way."

"Now, now, Dennis," Coral said smoothly. "Everyone needs a boost now and again."

"A brain boost? What's it supposed to do? Make me smarter?"

"Technically, no." Coral reached for another bottle from the rack. "The brain is fettered by many ideas, many inhibitions and many limitations, most of them learned and most of them removable."

"I like my inhibitions and limitations," I said. "I'm comfortable."

Coral poured a few dried leaves from the bottle into the pot. "From what Isobel tells me, you have an ingrained hindrance against doing the smart thing."

"What's that mean?" I looked accusingly at Isobel.

Isobel explained, "Dennis, when you come to a fork in the road, where one road sign says 'Smart Thing To Do,' and the other road sign says 'Stupid Thing To Do,' you unfailingly go down the stupid road."

"You may have some chemistry in your head that forces you to take the stupid road." Coral stirred the pot with a wooden spoon. "That's what my little drink will remedy. After you finish my course of therapy, when you come to the junction, you'll take the smart road."

I said, "Coral, please don't be upset by this question to Isobel." I turned to my so-called manager. "You don't believe this nonsense, do you? An intelligence potion?"

Isobel didn't answer.

"I mean, this is voodoo, isn't it?" I remembered her and Coral, and the old lady at the tending a little fire at Coral's shop. I remembered Coral's little voodoo tricks at my fights, the ashes and the grease. Maybe Coral had recruited Isobel into a voodoo cult. "It's wacky."

Isobel asked, "What's more wacky, Dennis? Coral and I trying a tad of voodoo, or you trying to be heavyweight champion?"

The question didn't make sense, but I couldn't figure out how her analogy broke down. Maybe if I knew more algebra.

I peered again into the pot. "I'm not drinking that sludge, I know that much."

Coral added a few drops of a purple fluid from a jar. "This will shrink the moron synapses and expand the genius synapses. It will set your intelligence free."

"You'll notice an immediate improvement," Isobel added.

"I would notice an immediate improvement if I didn't listen to you two crazy women."

"Looks delicious, doesn't it?" Coral asked.

I looked again over the rim of the pot. The fluid resembled marble with different ingredients swirling together in a pattern, greens and browns and blues. Steam from the mixture wrapped around my head. It had a decayed, threatening scent.

"Have either of you drunk this stuff?" I asked.

"We don't need it," Isobel answered.

"We don't have moron shackles wrapped around our brains." Coral used a spoon to half-fill a glass.

"Isobel, why don't you give it to your dog?" I asked. "There's never been a wiener dog born who couldn't use a smart potion."

She clucked her tongue. The dog was sitting on the rug behind her, looking like a tube-sock.

Coral held out the glass to me. "Drink this and be free."

"No way."

"Your Neanderthal synapses will vanish," Isobel said. "The SAT will be child's play. And no longer will you slap your forehead with your palm."

"I'm going to the gym for a workout," I said. "So long, ladies."

Isobel took the glass from Coral. I walked out of the room into the hallway. Along one wall was a fifteen-foot-long George III four-pedestal mahogany table. On the wall was a painting by the Seventeenth Century Flemish artist Jacob Jordaens. The painting was titled Repast in the Drawing Room, and was mostly blacks and browns and dark reds, and made the hallway gloomy. Isobel followed me.

I reached for the door, but Isobel's hand caught mine on the doorknob.

She said, "You aren't leaving until you drink this." She held the glass up to my nose.

"I'm not thirsty." I said. "And I'm going to the gym."

I tried to turn the door knob, but Isobel's hand clamped down hard. Then she stepped close and bored into my brain with her eyes, and I was only aware of their blue with the tiny black flecks. The blue filled in my head, an expanding galaxy, soaking my mind with her purpose, and chasing away my resistance. I don't know how she did it. Voodoo, maybe.

She pushed the glass into my yielding hand. The contents were warm. I looked down into the glass, but could still only see the blue of her eyes.

"Drink, Dennis."

So I lifted the glass to my mouth and drank. It went down like motor oil, thick and slow. Helpless, I drank every drop.

My throat tingled, and the bottom of my tongue felt metallic. My head finally cleared itself of the vast blue, and I could make out Isobel and Coral and the hallway. Isobel's eyes were back in their sockets, not in my brain anymore. I handed the glass back to her, and she let me open the door.

She was smiling widely at me. "You won't be sorry."

I stepped out onto the porch. "That tasted like horse piss."

"See, Dennis?" Isobel said gaily just before closing the door. "You're getting smarter already."

•

My life began to change. The *Times-Picayune* ran a story on me, three columns on the front page of the sports section, big photo and all. And then two television stations, WDSU and WWL, did spots on me, both with the same angle: an aged boxer's new run of success. I watched both segments. I hope I'm less punch-drunk in person than I sound on TV.

Little things began to happen, and here's a day's worth, from a day just after the newspaper article and TV reports came out.

That morning I opened my apartment door to find a fifteen-pound, fully-cooked honey-roasted ham in the hall, with a note that said, "Congratulations on your upcoming match. Please visit Arquel's Meats in the French Market."

I went to my morning workout at Old Al's gym. Below the mottled sign in the window which read Higgins School of the Fistic Science was a new banner, Home of Battlin' Dennis Jones. When I entered the dressing area, I found that I had a new locker, which Old Al had spray painted blue. In bright white lettering on the locker was Battlin' Dennis Jones. The boxers working out in the gym called me champ.

Normally I might have to wait a few minutes for a speed bag or a heavy bag or to use the weights, but the guys working out saw me coming and got out of my way, letting me use their speed bags and the other training tools, and they did so with a nod and a smile.

When I tried to tell them they shouldn't interrupt their workout for me, they wouldn't hear it. When I sparred with Cecil Rodrick, the Iron Shovel, a small crowd gathered ringside to watch. And after Cecil and I finished our rounds, and I climbed out of the ring, a fellow from Ring Magazine asked if he could interview me. He had brought along a photographer, who wore two cameras around his neck and an equipment bag over his shoulder.

After the interview and photo shoot, I left the gym, and a Jaguar was parked in front of the building. A fellow emerged from the car to ask if he could examine my cauliflower ear. He was a plastic surgeon, he said. I stood there while he fingered my ear a moment, and then he offered to operate on it, making it look almost normal. The doctor said he would perform the surgery free of charge if I would let him publish the results in some medical journal. I told him I was fond of my lumpy ear, if only because it was conversation piece. But I said I would think about it, and took his card.

When I visited the Acme Oyster House on Iberville for lunch, the proprietor said the first four dozen oysters were on the house. I managed to eat only three dozen. He took a photo of me while I was scarfing down the oysters.

I returned to my apartment to find an enormous UPS box waiting in the hallway. Normally I never received packages, not even at Christmas. I had no parents and no siblings, so nobody ever sent me gifts. Excited as a child, I lugged it inside, then ripped it open. The box contained three pairs of boxing gloves in assorted weights, two pairs of leaded speed bag gloves, a pair of punch mitts, two headquards (one with cheek protectors, one without), three pairs of black leather ring shoes, size twelve ... (How did the sender know my size?) A weightlifter's leather belt, a dozen pairs of glossy ring shorts, six jump ropes, two of those little deals that you squeeze to give you a stronger grip, six cotton headbands, two dozen pairs of white cotton socks, three jock straps, six single mouth guards and six double mouth guards.

Every item was imprinted with the Everlast logo. I was giddy. Had I ever had the occasion to make up a Christmas wish-list, every single one of these items would have been on it. Also inside the box was a letter from Everlast Worldwide inquiring if I would enter into an endorsement deal.

A few moments later, I left my apartment for my daily run, crossing Rampart and entering Louis Armstrong Park. That day five kids—thirteen and fourteen years old, I guessed, who had seen me jogging in days past, were waiting for me.

"Can we run with you, Champ?" they called out.

"I don't know." I jogged along. "Can you?"

Turns out they could, at least for the first mile. Each time we crossed a road, the kids' Nikes and Adidas shoes would clatter loudly. Metal taps had been placed on the toes and heels of the athletic shoes. These kids were tap dancers, who made pocket change by dancing in the Quarter, hoping passersby would toss coins into small cardboard boxes the dancers placed on the street.

After the first mile the kids waited by the park entrance while I put in another three miles, ending with ten 100-yard sprints that left me gasping. By that time they had produced paper and a pen, so I signed autographs, them insisting I add Battlin' to my name. I told them I was a long way from being a champ, but they called me that anyway.

That evening I passed by the Gumbo Eatery on St. Peter Street, and stopped on the sidewalk to stare at the menu on the window, a habit I had gotten into, pausing at restaurants in the French Quarter, enjoying figuring out what I would eat if I had any money. I was studying the menu when the maitre d' hurried out onto the sidewalk, I first thought to chase me away.

He asked, "Does anything on the menu look good to you, Mr. Jones?"

Instead of asking him how he knew my name, I said, "It all looks good."

"Please step inside. The best table in the house is waiting for you."

"Some other time, maybe. I'm light in the pocket today." Every day.

"Please accept a meal as a gift from the management. And perhaps you'll mention the Gumbo Eatery someday if an interviewer asks about New Orleans restaurants."

"The chicken andouilli gumbo sounds mighty good," I said as the maitre d' led me into the restaurant. Andoulli is a Cajun sausage, about as tasty a thing as there is on this earth.

Later that evening I stopped in at Jelly's for a beer. A band called the Creole Jukes was playing, and I had hardly settled into my chair before a young lady asked me to dance, which doesn't happen too often. She introduced herself as Brianna. Her blond hair hung to the middle of her back, and it swung back and forth as she moved, and boy, did she move.

So I danced two songs with her, her smiling and looking at me all the while. She leaned close several times to ask if there was a lot of prize money in boxing. I'm not sure how she knew I was a boxer, other than seeing my ear. Or maybe she had seen me on TV. When I thanked her and returned to my table, another girl was waiting there and she, too, asked me to dance. Her name was Adrian, and I was the most interesting fellow she had ever met, apparently. She clung to me with much ingenuity but I was finally able to break away after three songs.

An hour later I had danced with seven or eight different women, and was exhausted. From several of them I had received frank offers regarding how I might spend the rest of the evening but I turned them down, with thanks, due to my training schedule. The bartender wouldn't let me pay for any of the beer I drank.

So a touch of celebrity had come my way. I enjoyed it but I knew it wouldn't last, not with me preparing to get into the ring with Gentleman James Norton. I don't think Isobel had figured that Norton was going to knock me into the next time zone. She'd never get her poem, counting on me to win that fight.

•

Once in a while a person stumbles across a piece of information that he fervently wishes he hadn't, some bit of news he doesn't know what to do with, and finally figures out he can't do anything with other than to let it sit there in his head getting more and more sour.

Charles Brooks had invited me out to the Knights of the Arcadian Peacock's clubhouse. Apparently some of the knights had remembered my face from that day when I was bartending at Charles's pantomime branding, and then had seen me on TV or in the newspaper and had asked Charles to bring me out for a lesson in the manly sport of boxing.

So I showed them a few things in their gym, which was filled with stair machines, stationary bicycles and some new exercise equipment I'd never seen before. Dainty stainless steel dumbbells were in a rack along a mirrored wall.

Charles introduced me to Ben Smyth, whose father owned eight newspapers in assorted Gulf Coast towns, and Bob Chevenement, whose family were contractors, and had just erected the forty-two-story Louisiana First Federal Bank building on Graveler Street in the CBD. And I met Dwight Madelin, whose family had founded Madelin Switch, now called Madelin Technologies, the international distributor of electrical and communications equipment. They had purchased sixteen-ounce gloves, and I showed them a few boxing moves. It was a seriously guy thing, and the Arcadian knights— throwing jabs and hooks, me correcting their form—had the time of their lives, it seemed.

Then the knights and I changed into street clothes and went upstairs to the clubhouse bar. Drinks were served around. I sipped a Beck's beer and did my best to entertain them with stories, them doing a little vicarious living, somehow thinking that getting regularly beaten up was a romantic way to spend a life.

After a few minutes Charles asked, "Can you catch a ride with Ben back to the Quarter, Dennis? I've got to get back to town right away. No time for another drink."

He left the bar, and the knights continued to ask me about boxing. The bar's windows looked out to clubhouse's front entrance, to the driveway. I glanced out when a Ford Explorer drove up.

That's when I learned my bad piece of information. Charles Brooks emerged from the club's door out into the sunlight. The Explorer's driver was Jenny Blake, also known as Bambi LaTour, the exotic dancer who had taught Isobel to strip. When she rolled down the window, Charles smooched her through the window frame, then walked around to the passenger side to climb into the Explorer.

They drove away together.

I like Beck's beer, but the rest of that bottle was exceptionally bitter.

Part Three

"Falling in love consists merely in uncorking the imagination and bottling the common sense."
-Journalist Helen Rowland.

17

I began suspecting Isobel of treachery that very same day.

I was headed back to my apartment in the Quarter, strolling along, and was maybe half a block from my door on the other side of the street when I saw Isobel and another man emerge from my apartment building. Quite a few folks were on the sidewalks. She looked around furtively, then grabbed the man's arm and led him quickly away, glancing several times over her shoulder as she did so. The fellow was carrying a camera. He walked calmly as if accustomed to subterfuge. She didn't see me. They turned onto Dumaine Street and disappeared from my view.

Surprise and disappointment welded me to the sidewalk. What were they doing in my apartment building? Isobel claimed to be my manager. What would she be doing in my apartment, then leaving it sneakily, as if looking out for cops, or for me? Why would she be so underhanded?

When I could move again I walked to my building, through the door into the hallway, then climbed the stairs. My apartment door was locked, as I had left it. I inserted the key, turned it, and opened the door.

At first glance nothing seemed amiss, though I could smell her perfume, a hint of lilac in the air, and it tightened my throat. She had been in my apartment, had somehow gotten through my locked door. I turned a circle, not seeing anything out of the ordinary. In her earlier visit, Isobel had pretty much cleaned out my apartment in her effort to reform me. I had utterly nothing of interest or value in the place.

I must have a good nose, despite its appearance, as I could follow her scent. It was stronger near the desk. Items on the desktop were just as I had left them: an empty Coke can, an old wind-up alarm clock, a couple of boxing magazines, and some dust. The desk only had two drawers. In the top one I kept an assortment of stuff, such as athletic tape, a broken Timex watch I had worn for ten years and couldn't bear to throw away, a Mercedes radiator ornament I had found while out jogging—junk like that.

In the second drawer, along with back issues of *Ring Magazine*, were three manila envelopes where I kept documents, and which I had carried from place to place in my travels without much thinking about them. I might've been fooling myself about Isobel's scent now, but it seemed to be coming from this second drawer. I pulled out a manila envelope. I had never sealed it. I peered inside. It contained four or five expired drivers' licenses, my social security card, several old credit cards, a health plan card from a short time when I could afford a plan, voter registration cards from a dozen towns, some old library cards—that sort of thing.

I opened the second envelope that contained old photos, a thin annual from a junior high school I attended for a year, some medical records, including an emergency appendectomy performed when I was in my early twenties, and a wad of other paper. I sifted through the items. I wasn't precisely sure of all this envelope had contained but it didn't appear anything was missing.

The third envelope held the items the Clallam County coroner up in Port Angeles had sent me after my father's head got reshaped between two logs. I had looked through it quickly many years ago, hoping there might be some money or a safe deposit key, but no such luck. His union card, army discharge papers and his dog tags, social security card, and a few letters were in the envelope. Didn't look like anything was missing there either.

I returned the envelopes to the drawer, then went over to my bed and stuck my hand under the blanket. No, Isobel hadn't short sheeted my bed. Then why had she snuck into my apartment, and who was the fellow she was with? If she had wanted something in my apartment, why didn't she just ask me? I would've gladly given her anything she wanted among my meager possessions. I hadn't a clue what was going on.

My throat was tight with disappointment and fear. I had begun to think of Isobel as my champion, someone who, however bizarre and self-serving with her chase after the Edgar Allan Poe poem, still had my best interests in mind. Maybe I had it wrong. She was sneaking around, up to some mischief, and I could only be harmed by it.

Angry and confused, I sat in the chair in front of the desk, my mouth turned down. After a while I noticed that I had crumpled up the Coke cans to the size of a walnut.

•

Getting married in New Orleans is a complicated matter, apparently. Isobel Autrey and Charles Brooks' social calendar in the weeks leading up to the wedding was crowded. Much of New Orleans society wanted to host them, but this night was Isobel's father's turn. To celebrate their engagement, Lawrence put on a dinner and dance—ball is a better word, I suppose—for two hundred of the Autrey and Brooks families' friends, and he did so in his Garden District mansion.

Dinner was served in the back yard, where caterers and party planners had erected tents and put down a portable wood dance floor. Twenty musicians, Hal Holiday's Big Orchestra, played everything from Benny Goodman to Bruce Springsteen.

Then at ten o'clock, all the guests walked several blocks to Isobel's home for late desert. It was a colorful procession, and I was among them, wearing a tuxedo and a red tie the syndicate had purchased for me. I had come up in the world, from bartending at the Knights of the Arcadian Peacock's lodge to attending Lawrence Autrey's Garden District soiree for his daughter.

I was pleased to be along, because I was going to see more of Isobel's house than she would want me to see. She could be sneaky. So could I.

The parade of guests followed Isobel and Charles along the walkway, then up the steps to the porch and into her house. I walked alongside Isobel's father and another gentleman who asked me a dozen questions about boxing, and he wasn't the first. I had been invited as a curiosity, I believed.

Florists had transformed the interior of Isobel's house into a garden. Grapevine trellises had been placed at the doors, with vines and flowers curled along the arches. Long-stemmed magenta roses were in vases throughout the dining and living rooms and along the hallways. White lilies were in other vases. Freesias along the fireplace mantles were emitting their heady scent. White-coated waiters moved among the crowd. A dessert buffet was in the dining room. A string quartet was parked in front of the living room's bay windows. I don't mind string quartets, except for the sounds they make.

Isobel posted herself in the hallway, greeting everyone who entered her home, even though she had just spent three hours with them at her father's house. She was wearing a vampire red satin gown with a deep neckline and spaghetti straps. I drifted into the living room.

Lawrence Autrey had been following me all night, introducing me to one old codger after another, telling them about my boxing accomplishments, leaving out ninety-five percent of my rocky career, of course. I met a retired federal appeals court judge, an ex-ambassador to Belgium, a deposed nobleman from Austria, six direct descendants of Robert E. Lee, and the inventor of the inflatable fracture splint. They gazed up at me with their wet, blinking, yellow eyes, their ears filled with hair. I smiled, willing to go along with Lawrence showing me off. Isobel's father had taken to me. I don't know why.

Charles was surrounded by the Knights of the Arcadian Peacock, and they were laughing uproariously at something. All of the knights had already consumed a few drinks, which I had begun to think was the main reason the Knights of the Arcadian Peacock existed. The women wore long gowns filled with beading, lace inserts and embroidery. The hands and forearms of a few of the older women were covered in long white gloves.

The living room contained the largest Persian carpet I had ever seen, with greens and golds and deep reds. The furniture was a mix of old and new, with a few modern stainless steel floor lamps and brown leather chairs. On the mantle was a one-hundred-fifty-year old French gilt-over-brass clock where the clock face was framed by winged cherubs. A bushel-sized vase of roses rested on a walnut side-table that had the angry faces of lions carved into its leg knobs.

"Have I ever mentioned that I rowed in college?" an elderly gentleman asked me, peering over the rims of his spectacles.

"No, sir, you haven't."

"Are you sure I haven't mentioned it?"

"I just met you twenty seconds ago." I smiled. "I would've remembered."

He nodded and glanced at his scotch and soda. I asked him how he knew the Autrey family, and he began a long explanation that bored my clackers off. After several moments, I tuned him out, just nodding once in a while.

I had much to think about. I had witnessed Isobel's fiancé kiss the exotic dancer Jennifer Blake. I've been kissed enough so I know the whole catalogue of kisses except, of course, the kiss a mother gives her son. Charles's smooch was one of familiarity, not the first time he had kissed Jennifer, and not the most intense kiss he had ever given her, either. It was a kiss that relayed how happy he was to see her, and a kiss that promised more later.

Had I missed something? Wasn't Charles engaged to be married to one Isobel Autrey? Wasn't that the reason I was in Isobel's living room just then, reeling from an old geezer's cologne as he talked on and on about him and Lawrence in the old days? Wasn't this gala affair a celebration of Isobel and Charles's impending marriage? What was Charles doing giving a stripper a juicy smack? is what I was wondering.

That kiss had tormented me. What should I do with the information, I kept asking myself. Maybe Isobel was marrying a cad, a guy who would fool around with one woman while engaged to another, while going to all these pre-wedding events. Didn't I owe Isobel the information? Just report it and let her decide what to do with it.

But my quandary had been solved by seeing Isobel and that other fellow sneak out of my apartment building. To hell with her, tiptoeing around like that. She was out for herself. I suppose I had never doubted that, but this was proof positive. So let Charles and Isobel figure out their own relationship. They deserved each other. I didn't owe them anything.

Still, I was curious. And this event perhaps gave me a way to discover some answers. Finally the old gummer ran out of gas, and I excused myself, heading through knots of guests, then into the hallway as if intent on using the back bathroom off the kitchen, but then I checked over my shoulder. No one was looking. I ran up the back stairs. In the old days they were called the servants' stairs. I found myself in an upper hall. I turned a corner toward the front of the house. That's where Isobel's bedroom would be.

Snooping is undignified, but she had snooped on me and that had suspended whatever dignity and decorum I had regarding her. I passed an oak coat rack in the hallway, and walked by two bedroom doors and a bathroom door. Sounds of the party came up the wide and winding main stairwell. I pushed open the door to the master bedroom and stepped inside, and instantly knew this was Isobel's room. The bust of Edgar Allan Poe on a dressing table gave it away.

The sculptor had expertly brought forth from a chunk of marble Poe's protruding eyes, pointed chin, prim little mustache and air of impending madness. On the wall above the table, on one side of a large beveled mirror, was a framed letter from Poe, his signature large and plain at the bottom of the sheet of paper. The letter was to a New York publisher, inquiring if the publisher had received a manuscript, sent four months before.

Tortoiseshell hairbrushes and assorted small bottles of perfume were on the table, along with a lacquered wood jewelry box. Along a wall was a japanned cabinet-on-stand made of rosewood with silver hinges. Her bed was large, and covered by a red and green plaid comforter. A green jade elephant—must've weighted twenty pounds—was on a display stand near the window. Its trunk was raised high, and its tusks were made of ivory. Such a thing would cost more than an English professor earned in a year, was my guess. Charles had let it slip that Lawrence Autrey had been giving Isobel large sums of money every year as part of Lawrence's estate planning. I breathed slowly through my nose. The room carried Isobel's scent.

I wasn't here just to root aimlessly around in Isobel's private things. I had a plan. The fellow I saw emerge with Isobel from my apartment building was a professional. A professional what, I wasn't sure. I could tell from the few seconds I saw him walk, and from the deference Isobel seemed to give him as they moved along the sidewalk. A person becomes a professional when his services, whatever they are, command a fee. Isobel was paying him, I was fairly certain.

As I walked toward a small desk under a window, I cocked my head. The sound of soft footfalls came from the hallway, headed my way. I glanced at the door handle. It turned slowly. I crouched behind Isobel's bed. The door opened slightly.

A giggle came from the other side of the door, then the whispered words, "Not here, Freddy, for Pete's sake." A woman's voice.

Then a whisky-driven, hoarse voice came in return, "Why not, babe?"

The door opened further. I was crouched behind the bed, but visible to anyone who bothered to look. I didn't recognize the couple.

"This is Isobel's room." The woman looked into the bedroom, but only for an instant, missing me. "It would be scandalous for us to—"

"That bed is probably like brand new," interrupted the man, laughing. "I heard the only thing Isobel does is sleep in it."

"You sound bitter," his date said. "Isobel turn you down, too?"

"You aren't a real New Orleans male until Isobel Autrey has refused you. It happens to the best of us." He laughed again. "But no problem, sweetie. I've got you."

The woman said in a gravel voice, "Not tonight, you don't."

She slammed Isobel's door, and I could hear her march away. He groaned in frustration, and followed her down the hall.

I hurried across the room, feeling like a thief, though I had no intention of stealing anything. The small desk was under a mounted and framed black feather, maybe a crow's, but it would've been the largest crow I'd ever seen. Nothing of interest was on the desk. I quickly opened the drawers. Files in long rows, and odds and ends.

I walked across to the closet. The house had probably been built without closets, back in armoire days. But the room adjoining Isobel's bedroom had been made into a walk-in closet, and contained rows of dresses and suits, half a dozen chests of drawers, banks of shoe holders and accessories racks.

I found what I wanted on the floor near the entrance: Isobel's purse, a black-and-tan, over-the-shoulder rig that looked as if it had been made of some endangered species. I dug around in it, trying not to allow the purse's contents to register on me because I didn't care to know about Isobel's private matters, except this one thing. I found her checkbook and pulled it out.

Isobel and the professional had been in my apartment two days ago. I turned her check register for that day. She had paid twelve bills that day, including her bank cards and utility fees. Not what I was looking for. I turned the register to see checks written a day earlier. I recognized all the payors: a drugstore, the Tulane book store, a Mercedes repair shop, a florist shop and others.

I went back another day, then another. Then came a payor in the register I didn't know, a check written seven days ago to one Jon Cal Murray in the amount of three thousand dollars.

The name and the sum leapt out of Isobel's check register. I was confident Jon Cal Murray was the professional. Jon Cal Murray. I would remember the name.

I returned the checkbook to Isobel's purse, left the room and headed down the back stairs to return to the party, which was winding down.

Isobel was again at the door, this time saying goodnight, her father at her elbow. An old guy with a polished, bald head, and who claimed to have sparred with Rocky Marciano, began filling my ear, and every time I tried to leave, he caught my arm and took off with another story. Pretty soon only a few guests remained, Isobel and Lawrence seeing them on their way. Then Lawrence escorted out the old fellow I had been listening to, and Lawrence didn't return himself. Suddenly just Isobel and I and the caterers remained. She and I were in the marbled hallway. The caterers were cleaning up.

Isobel smiled. "Three down, three to go."

"Three more parties?" I asked. I hadn't spoken with her all evening. I tried to quell my anger about this Jon Cal Murray.

"But I'm not hosting them, so they'll be easier." She stepped toward the sitting room. Her beaded crimson dress clung to her, accentuating her every move. She combed her black hair with her fingers, lifting the thick strands out, then letting them fall.

"Goodnight, Isobel," I said, still in the hallway.

She pivoted on a two-inch heel. "You're leaving?"

"It's late."

"Sure, but I'm wired. Hosting does that to me. I won't be able to sleep for hours."

"Maybe Charles will talk you to sleep. He has that effect, I know."

She gestured quickly, as if trying to discard sticky tissue. "The knights took Charles out for a celebratory nightcap. Or maybe to one of their endless rituals. Maybe this time they'll pretend to brand his tongue."

Isobel must have heard about the branding ritual. She always knew more than I guessed she knew.

"But I want to talk with you, Dennis. And this is a good time."

"It's midnight. I'm tired."

"Midnight is the perfect time to discuss Edgar Allan Poe."

"I have no interest in talking about Edgar Allan Poe," I said.

"Then we can discuss you."

"I have as little interest in talking about me as I do Poe."

"Ah," she said magisterially, "but I do. At least until I get my poem."

She seized my arm and pulled me into the sun room. A waiter was clearing away empty glasses that had accumulated on the wrought-iron table near the window. As if she were wearing jeans and a T-shirt rather than an elegant, ankle-length gown, Isobel plopped herself down on the sofa, leaned back and spread her feet, stretching the fabric. She patted the cushion next to her. Warily, I sat down.

She locked her hands behind her head. "I'm still working on your history. Tell me how you became interested in boxing."

I didn't say anything. I tried to undo my bow tie, tugging at it with no success. Isobel reached over and pulled it loose with a practiced motion. Her father had helped me knot it earlier that day.

"I need to fill in a few blanks in your past," she explained.

I wasn't feeling friendly toward Isobel, not even civil, not with her spying on me. I tried to come up with something clever and cutting, and I might have done so, five-thousand blows to the head ago.

She said, "The syndicate has hired a publicist for you. Have you seen the press release about your fight with Gentleman James Norton?"

"'Jones's hand speed makes him a deadly inside fighter, and he is a savage counter-puncher who can dance out of trouble,' is what it says. You hired some fiction writer."

She laughed in that way that always brought my head up, sounding like a clarinet running up a scale. "The publicist is building the gate. So, how did you come to boxing?"

At that moment her scent invaded my nose, that touch of dark lilac, and I'm not sure what happens to my brain when that happens, so instead of the truculence that I wanted to show her, I readily replied, "It was Bazooka bubble gum."

She waited a moment, then said, "I'm not following you, not for the first time."

"That big roll of Bazooka, five or six chunks stuck together, comes

with a comic. It was the best thing a twelve-year-old ever tasted."
I stopped, and tried to regenerate my anger at Isobel, but she patted
my knee.

"Keep going, Dennis."

"My father never had any money, not after he drank it all on
Friday nights after payday, so he never gave me an allowance. I could
go a month without seeing a quarter. But every time I did somehow
obtain twenty-five cents—and I have a memory of every time I did,
it was so rare—I would spend it on a big roll of Bazooka. And I never
had the willpower to ration myself. I'd stuff it all into my mouth at
once, all five portions. My cheeks bulged, all that bubblegum flavor
would flow through me, and I'd be wonderfully happy."

"Bazooka could do that to you? You have a low happiness
threshold."

"I'd buy it at Mike's Candy Shop in Anacortes. Mike would stand
there behind the counter and he would crack wise, such as calling
Good & Plenties, Bad & Not Enoughs. Each time I had a quarter, I
would linger over Mike's counter looking at all the candy as if I had
a decision to make, but I always went for the Bazooka."

Isobel's wiener dog pranced into the room. He stopped midway
across the carpet, plopped himself down and began licking his
patoot, one leg up in the air as if saluting me.

"One day while standing there I heard this tappety-tappety tap
coming from the ceiling," I went on. "I asked Mike what the sound
was, and he said there was a gymnasium upstairs. So chewing my
huge wad of pink gum, I climbed the outside stairs and entered
Swabby's Boxing Club, just looking around. One guy was working
the speed bag, and an older fellow, the gym's owner, Swabby, was at
his elbow, talking to him. Nobody else was in the gym. It was a small
place in a small town."

My eyes were on the dog. I've actually seen people kiss their dogs
on the lips. Not after this little performance, they wouldn't. I waited
for Isobel to prompt me. She said nothing. The dog kept cleaning
away, his long body bent almost in two.

So I said, "Swabby saw me walk through the door, and called out,
'Can you throw a left hook?' I didn't know what a left hook was, and
was about to retreat back down the stairs but Swabby grabbed me
and led me to an equipment rack, then shoved two gloves on me,
saying 'I got a fighter who needs a sparring partner. You only throw

left hooks. Keep your right hand near your chin. He isn't going to throw any punches. He's going to just block your hooks.' So Swabby led me to the ring."

Suddenly I was aware of a touch of Isobel's hair brushing my neck, then a little more of it, some strands lying on my shoulder. And I felt her lean into me, just slightly.

I asked, "How much cleaning does a wiener dog's butt need, do you think?"

Isobel didn't say anything but I could feel her press against my arm and shoulder.

"So the owner showed me what a hook was, and I climbed into the ring, and the owner said, 'You hear me, Tommy? You're just blocking this kid's left hook. No hitting him. Got that?' Tommy smiled and nodded, and put up his mitts."

Then Isobel leaned fully into me, shoulder to thigh. I still didn't turn toward her, not knowing what to make of this development. The beads of her dress pushed against my skin, and her thigh was tight against mine. Her ebony hair was slowly surrounding my head. I could see it in most directions, and I could feel it against my cheek and neck. The dog slurped away.

"So I threw a few hooks, and this guy Tommy flicked them aside. Then I put a little effort into it, lashing my left fist at him. He didn't take too kindly to this, so he landed his own hook square on my chin."

Then I felt Isobel's breath on my neck, warm and damp.

"My big ball of Bazooka shot out of my mouth and skittered across the floor. For a second I stared at it. Twenty-five cents was a huge expenditure for me, and that bubble gum was the most pleasure I would find in any given month."

Isobel's hand gently landed on my thigh.

"Enraged, I turned on Tommy and smacked him left and smacked him right, walking right up his legs. And finally I punched him through the ropes."

I waited a moment, wondering what Isobel was doing. She was full against me now, and I could feel the heat coming from her, her skin and her breath, and her hair all against my head acting as a blanket, holding the heat in.

When she didn't ask what happened next, I said, "Tommy fled to the dressing room. Swabby asked if I could come back the next day, said he would show me how to do it right. I crossed the ring, lifted the Bazooka off the floor, put it back into my mouth and said, 'Sure.'"

Isobel leaned harder against me, and now her lips were against my neck. I could feel them.

"Isobel? I really don't think we should do this. I mean, what would Charles say about this?"

She didn't reply. The wiener dog finally finished his bath, and began watching us, his tongue hanging out a long way, small wonder after where that tongue had been. I turned to Isobel, twisting my shoulders, and as I did so she slid slowly across my chest, so that I had to catch her lest she fall to my lap.

"Isobel?"

Her eyes were closed, and her lips were slightly parted. She was breathing in soft drafts. Five minutes ago she was wired. Now she was asleep.

I decided to leave her there on the sofa, but when I tried to shift out from under her, slowly so as not to wake her, she groaned sleepily, then raised a slender arm and put it around my neck. Her eyes fluttered open, but then closed. She again started to slide sideways, so I put an arm around her. She breathed in small sighs. Then her other arm came up and around my neck. I had Isobel Autrey in my arms.

I sat there many minutes, holding her, her lips inches from mine, her breath smelling of cinnamon. At one point I was surprised to find myself lightly stroking the curve of her neck, so I stopped that quickly. When her breathing deepened, I gently took her arms from around my neck and squeezed out from in front of her, laying her softly on the sofa. I found a crocheted afghan over one of the chair arms in the living room, and I placed it over her.

Then I quietly slipped out the front door, more perplexed than when I had arrived. And unaccountably worked up.

18

The house was a one-story brick rambler on a small lot. I was around back, standing in an alley, watching the house for a moment. I was going to have a talk with the professional.

Jon Cal Murray was a private investigator. Once I had his name finding him was a snap. He had a quarter-page add in the Yellow Pages setting forth his services, such as skip tracing, surveillance and debugging. The ad listed his office address. Finding his home address was almost as easy. I had waited outside his office building and followed him home, having borrowed Johnny Dykes's beat-up Cutlass, the one with so many rust spots it resembled a Dalmatian. I stayed a long way behind Murray as I tailed him, and I don't think he saw me. He drove straight to his home without any dodging around.

I wasn't just going to knock on his door, as that might result in a pistol being pointed at my head. I'd try the back door. Maybe it was unlocked. If not, I'd come up with another plan once I'd scoped out the house.

The lock on my apartment door hadn't given Murray any hesitation, so he deserved it. I was going to march into his house, grab him by the shirt collar and demand to know what he and Isobel had been doing in my apartment. Perhaps I should've just asked Isobel, but I knew how well she could bend the truth, and I also knew that my mind did peculiar things when she was near. It'd be easier to get it out of this Jon Cal Murray.

I started to climb over the hurricane fence that separated his back yard from the alley. Honeysuckle had claimed the fence entirely, and the air was filled with its scent, and I had to feel though the foliage for handholds on the fence. The grass in the back yard had been beaten down, and there were three filthy tennis balls and a piece of a tattered rug lying on the dirt. A white-flowering pear tree was in the yard, looking unkempt, with suckers rising from the main branches. I topped the fence and dropped into the yard, and took a step toward the back door.

Then I heard a quick scuffling coming from the side of the house, a locomotive sound. And it was getting louder quickly.

As if propelled from a slingshot, a dog burst from the shadows and charged toward me. And I don't mean a vanilla dog like a golden retriever or a yellow lab. This was a hell-dog, a hundred-thirty-pound, slit-eyed, chewed-ear, black-haired, tightly-wrapped, homicidal mass of muscle and fangs, and it was aimed right at me.

Fortunately, I'm a trained athlete. I leapt back up the fence, my legs churning, searching for a toe hold, and I frantically pulled myself toward the fence top. I admit to yelping in fear. I almost made it.

I learned later the thing was a Rotweiler. I got one leg over the top of the fence, and was about to launch myself to the ground on the other side when the monster caught my foot. I felt a puncture wound, maybe two. Straddling the fence, I frantically shook my leg. The dog twisted and spun, his legs digging backwards as he tried to drag me back into his yard for a chew. Its eyes glowed like red coals. I hadn't thought dogs could smile, but this dog was grinning like a demon, ecstatic with my pending destruction.

I pitched myself down toward the alley, hoping the dog would fall back of its own weight into his yard. Instead, the fiend scrambled up the fence, still attached to my foot. Over the fence it came, falling down onto me. It still wouldn't let go of my foot, and it was savagely shaking its head back and forth, the move dogs use to break their prey's neck. I tried to crawl away but the Rotweiler back-pedaled, pulling me back toward the fence. The dog didn't so much growl as hiss and burble, and his spit flew in all directions. My shoe was filling with blood, and stabbing pains were shooting up my leg.

I rolled to sitting, and grabbed a handful of dirt and pebbles and flung them at the animal's eyes. It startled him. He didn't let go entirely, but for an instant he decreased the pressure. I furiously kicked its nose with my other foot, and only then did he release me. I scurried to my feet and rose to sprint away.

I made it two steps. The beast hurled itself at me, aiming at my neck, but catching only the back of my shirt collar. Trying to bring me down, the dog gyrated wildly as he hung from my shirt. His hot breath on my neck was like the blast from a blacksmith's bellows.

The dog yanked and yanked and pawed my back, seeking purchase, hoping for another, higher snap with his jaws, this one on my neck.

I ran as if I were on fire, the dog hanging from my shirt. A woman on a porch who had been sipping iced tea called to her husband in the house, and pointed at me.

At a telephone pole, I spun in a circle, and swung the dog smartly into the pole. He yipped, but didn't let go. Buttons popped on my shirt, one after another, so that the shirt was hanging from my arms. I moved away from the pole and spun again, this time winding myself up. Then I stepped near the pole as I rotated, and sent the animal into the pole again. He hit with a gratifyingly loud smack. Then I spun again, and he sailed into the telephone pole yet again. This time he let go of my shirt and dropped to the ground.

He didn't even look over his shoulder at me as he ran away, headed back to his owner's house. I breathed deeply, like a man who has just received a pardon. My shoe was squishy with blood. I limped down the sidewalk, my shirt hanging from me. The Cutlass was just down the block.

The old lady called, "Shame on you, treating a dog like that."

•

In the course of an hour I went from being chased by a dog to being chased by a gangster. I had caught the bus headed back to town, hopping off on Canal. I hadn't looked at my foot yet, but despite the dog's ferocity it hadn't done much damage, I could tell. My shoe had absorbed most of it, and I hoped the syndicate would buy me another pair.

Still, I was limping as I walked by the big Marriott Hotel in the Quarter, then passed Roux Fun, a strip joint where a female tout standing outside the door automatically brought down her shirt front, exposing herself to me and smiling invitingly, just as she had done daily for the past month. I never went in, and I don't think she expected me to after so many times passing her door. It was just her way of saying hello.

I was about to enter my apartment building when a silver Oldsmobile pulled up to the curb. The window slid down to reveal Spazz Sprague, the guy who had sent a shank into my chest at the magician's convention.

So I lit out of there, sprinting down the sidewalk as best I could on my punctured foot. I'm tougher than the flunky's knife, I had proven, so I supposed this time he had brought a gun to finish the job.

"Hey," he called out after me. "Mr. Barnes wants to talk."

Yeah, right. I dodged a street sign, and ran down the sidewalk, ignoring the pain in my foot. I could hear the Oldsmobile's engine wind up. I passed two painters working on a bar's façade, and pushed myself through a group of college students who were gawking at French Quarter sights. Breathing hard and pumping my arms, I ran around a Lucky Dog and sprinted across an intersection.

"Hey," came again from behind me, Sprague hollering out his window, following me in the car. "Wait a minute."

Isobel had told me that Moe Barnes had made another deal with her, but the last time I had anything to do with his nephew I had been knifed. Running crazily, I stepped onto a soiled and discarded Pampers . The adhesive stuck to my shoe, and the diaper flapped along as I ran.

I turned onto Bourbon, ran passed three doors, then ducked into the New Orleans Souvenir Shop, and rushed passed stacks of T-shirt and bins of Marde Gras coins and necklaces. Feathered masks and orange and blue boas lined the walls. I sprinted down an aisle between displays, pushing by some folks who were browsing, and then out the back door into a tiny courtyard that was half-filled with pallets. I leaped up to grip the top of a rickety slat fence, then hauled myself over into another courtyard, this one littered with discarded rain gutters, boards and pipes, and other construction debris.

I ran between two buildings, my arms pumping and me laughing crazily because I had ditched them. I ran out onto the sidewalk. But the Olds had beaten me there and pulled up to the curb. The window was open and Sprague was pointing a pistol at me. His greased-back hair glittered in the sun. The car's back door opened. The diaper was still attached to my shoe. I scraped it off.

"Get in," Sprague ordered from the driver's seat.

My alternative was being gut-shot, I supposed, so I lowered myself into the back of the car, sinking into black leather. The interior of the car smelled of old cigars.

Moe Barnes was sitting there in the back seat, his double chin ballooning out as he nodded at me. "I heard my nephew Spazz here used his knife and carved you up some. I had a talk with him, and docked him three days' wages."

Spazz snickered from the front seat.

Barnes said, "Dennis, you and I need to talk."

I replied, "I don't have anything to say to you, Barnes."

"Yes, you do," came from the front seat, a woman's voice.

A black-haired woman turned to look at me over her shoulder and smile. It was Isobel.

•

The following may not have happened. That is, everything that occurred in the basement after Lawrence Autrey opened the basement door, said, "Good luck, son," patted me on the back, and sent me down those stairs into the darkness might have been only the result of some faulty wiring in my head, prompted by overpowering stimulus. Or it may have happened. I'm not sure.

Isobel's dad and I were in his large kitchen. The shiny chrome refrigerator was the size of a bank vault. Charles Brooks had cleaned out and sewn together the two puncture wounds on my foot. He gave me a tetanus shot, but when he suggested I get a rabies inoculation—fifteen shots in the belly—I said I'd take my chances.

Wearing a white apron, Lawrence stirred a pot on the stove. "Do you know when I first realized I had escaped poverty?"

I shook my head.

He pointed at a woven basket on the counter, which was filled almost to overflowing with fruit. "When I could afford oranges and bananas and apples, and could eat them whenever I wanted, then I knew I had finally left the swamp."

"Well, you're a long way from the swamp, sir."

"You and Moe Barnes had a talk, I hear."

"He grabbed me off the street yesterday. He has a new deal for Isobel."

"Win the fight against Norton, and she gets her poem? Forgive me for saying, but it doesn't sound like she'll get her poem."

I shook my head. "All I've got to do is last six rounds against Norton, and he'll hand her the poem. So he says."

"Barnes is round wagering?"

That's where a wager is placed on how long a fighter will last. The boxer doesn't have to win the fight as long as he lasts that number of rounds. In some parts of the country it's called a shade wager.

"Barnes thinks he knows boxing," I said. "He says he's seen tapes of Norton's recent fights, and that I can't beat Norton, but Barnes says he can still make a ton of money if I can last six rounds."

Knowing I only had to go half the fight would give me a huge advantage over Gentleman James Norton: I didn't have to save myself for later. I could put everything into those six rounds, while he was still reserving some of his energy for the late rounds.

Lawrence reached for an apple. "And if you don't last six rounds?"

"Barnes will chuck Isobel's poem into a bonfire, he says."

"Can you stay in the ring with Gentleman James Norton for those eighteen minutes?"

"Lately I've been doing pretty well. I seem to speed up, and everything else slows down. I can take a punch. Maybe I can last six rounds."

"Nobody thought you would defeat Sammy Dresser."

"That was pure luck." I rubbed my cauliflower ear. "Or maybe something else I haven't figured out. Weird things happened during that fight. Such as, I won it. Where's Isobel?"

"She's down in the basement. She and some friends."

"How come she invited me over to your house, if I can ask?" I looked at the basement door with some trepidation. "I mean, I don't need any more smart potion, if that's what Isobel has in mind. I took the SAT a couple days ago and I think I did okay."

His eyes brightened with amusement. "She said you need some of her will power."

"What's that mean?"

"Isobel believes that you need a singular focus and a steely determination in your fight with Norton. So she's going to transfer some of herself to you."

"That's a scary prospect, sir."

"Indeed." He chewed his apple. "Would you like something to drink before you go. Scotch and soda, maybe?"

"Go where?"

"Down to the basement, Dennis."

"I'm going down into the basement?" I paused. "What's down there?"

"I don't know, but whenever I came into a room all day today, Coral and Isobel would stop talking."

"I don't like to think of myself as a coward, sir."

"It's for your own good. I'd go, were I you."

When I didn't say anything, he took it for agreement. He walked me to the basement door.

Lawrence said, "Let me know how it goes." That's when he pulled open the basement door, said, "Good luck, son," and gave me a pat on the back meant to buck me up.

The stairwell to the basement was dark. I reached for a light switch, found one, flicked it, but nothing happened. Smoke rising from the basement and the darkness hid what lay below.

"Isobel?" I called out, stepping cautiously down the stairs. "Is something on fire?"

"Hello, Dennis," came from the bottom of the steps. It wasn't Isobel but I recognized the voice.

Coral Thibideaux was waiting for me at the end of the banister. Her grin was wide and her turban was crimson, as was her ankle-length wrap.

"What're you doing here?" I asked.

"I'm your guide."

I nervously pulled at my ear lobe. "What are you and Isobel up to, Coral?"

"You are about to witness a transference."

"I don't want anything to do with that." I hesitated. "What is it?"

"You must last six rounds against Gentleman James Norton so that Isobel can get her poem. We are going to see that you do."

She hooked my arm in hers. "Walk with me, Dennis." She smelled of cloves.

Smoke drifted along the dark hallway. A ping pong table was folded up against a wall, near several older-model bicycles, maybe Isobel's when she was a child.

"Is this more of your horse urine nonsense, Coral? I'm not drinking any more of that particular mixture, I guarantee you."

"Aunt Bea knows what she's doing. Do you want to last six rounds?" She didn't wait for my response. "This is the only way."

She pivoted me into a room, and I stopped dead just inside the door. The place was filled with fog, thick white strands of translucence that stirred and mixed together. It wasn't smoke I had been seeing but rather this artificial fog. I guessed there was a fog machine somewhere inside the room. Through the haze I could see the indistinct outline of votive candles spread across the floor in a five-pointed star pattern, maybe two hundred candles in all, and the flames trembled in a draft.

The room was filled with a peculiar low sound, a bass rushing noise, like a distant water fall, and the sound was punctuated by bird shrieks—maybe parrots—and throaty reptilian rumbles, the sound of frogs or alligators. These swamp sounds were being pumped into the room by several stereo speakers along a wall. And the odor in that room was heady and intense, an earthy herbal smell as strong as if I had my nose in the swamp's moist dirt. The smell invaded me, filling me, and I was abruptly light-headed and a bit wobbly.

I half-stepped back, the beginning of a full retreat, but Coral re-gripped my arm, tighter this time.

She murmured, "Steady, Dennis. This won't hurt." Then I think I heard her add under her breath, "Much."

In the middle of the star of candles sat the leathery old woman who had been at the bayou ritual Charles and I had witnessed. This was Bea, the same lady who was at Coral's shop, tending her fire. Her thin white hair floated above her head, revealing patches of brown scalp. The old woman's loose dress appeared to be made of gunny. She was graveyard thin, lost in the dress. Her nose was broad, and flat up against her face as if pressed and held there. Bea's mouth was moving, forming words, but she made no sound. She stared at a pattern of small bones on a woven mat in front of her. In the heavy fog she drifted in and out of my sight, as if she were an apparition.

Coral guided me into the room. We stepped into a thick bank of fog, and the strands whirled around us. She led me to the tip of the star, facing the old woman, who didn't look up from her bones.

"Stay here," Coral ordered.

She drifted away, disappearing in the haze, and I was left there, facing the old woman, who reached out with her talons and rearranged the bones. The candles threw numberless shadows, making the concrete floor appear to ripple as if it were water. The candles lit the old lady from below, dappling her face with soft shadows.

The air in the room had thickened, and carried such a strong scent that it caught in my throat. It was making me loopy. I had the sensation of lifting off the floor to hover above it, and the old lady seemed to be radiating, a pulsing red light coming from her skin and her dress. The swamp sounds grew louder. Fog hid the ceiling and walls, and I could see only the candles forming the star and old Bea in the center. They blurred in my vision. The room seemed to rotate, me still hovering in the air.

Holding something in her hand, the old woman rose and walked toward me. She moved stiffly, with small steps. Her eyes were hooded and black, and sunk deeply into her lined face. She was full of years, and broadcast an immense authority and calm. I wanted to sprint away from there, but my legs wouldn't obey my orders. The swamp sounds and the intense odor and the rippling shadows chased away useful thoughts.

She held a cup under my nose. Her eyes were locked on mine. I had no choice but to drink from the cup. The liquid had no taste, nothing that could compete with the room's fetid smell. The haze shifted, and I saw a pot bubbling away on an electric burner against the wall. I emptied the cup and passed it back to her. She returned to her bone pile in the center of the star.

A window opened in the fog. Isobel was standing at another tip of the star. She was wearing a long white gown that had a deep neckline and was made of some nearly-diaphanous fabric that clung to her, revealing every curve. Her black hair seemed to be alive, moving and curling. She was staring at me but gave no indication she saw me. Her hands hung at her sides. Her mouth was painted a livid red, and her eyes were living crystals of blue. The old woman walked between the candles toward Isobel, and placed both of her bony hands on Isobel's chest.

I must report as best I can what happened next, and at the same time announce that it could not have happened. The old woman dug her hand into Isobel's chest just above the dress's neckline, opening it up like she would a purse. And she pulled out a small bone, one of Isobel's bones. Isobel didn't even wince. And then with a swift motion of her hand, the old lady zipped Isobel's chest closed, leaving not a trace, no blood, not a wound, not a scar, nothing. I saw it with my own eyes.

Carrying the bone, maybe a rib, the old woman again crossed the burning star. Her eyes were fastened on mine. I was terrified but I was also oddly content to be floating in front of her, the candles glimmering gently, the odor changing, becoming more flowery, Isobel drifting in and out of the fog. The room hummed like the swamp. Deep, primitive sounds.

Bea came up to me, the gleaming white bone in her hand. She

whispered some incantation. Then she took Isobel's bone in both her hands, placed the tip of it against the skin of my chest just below my throat, and pushed the bone through my skin into my chest, where it disappeared. This, too, I saw with my own eyes. I didn't feel a thing.

The old woman returned to the center of the star, and knelt down to again study her arrangement of bones on the floor, me apparently forgotten.

Coral Thibideaux came out of the fog and took me by the elbow. My feet found the concrete, and I could walk again. Coral led me from the room. My mouth was dry. My shirt was sodden.

I croaked, "Coral, what—"

She led me from the room out into the basement hallway. "Some things it's best you don't know about."

I touched my chest, where the bone had entered me. It was normal. No wound, not even a scratch. I flexed my shoulder. It didn't feel like I was carrying an extra bone in there.

At the stairs, Coral said, "We'll see each other again, Dennis."

I managed to mumble, "Not if there's a God in heaven."

I was weak. I climbed the stairs slowly, leaving Coral in the basement. I opened the door to the kitchen. Lawrence Autrey was sitting in the breakfast nook eating a sandwich.

"How'd it go down there, Dennis?" he asked, chewing.

"I'm not sure, sir." I touched my chest again. My fingers searched the skin. There had to be a puncture wound there, but there wasn't.

"You hungry?" He pointed to the kitchen counter. "I made a tuna salad sandwich for you. And there's some soup in the pot. I've got a bowl and a spoon there."

I was suddenly famished, overwhelmed with hunger. I filled a bowl with soup, then grabbed the sandwich.

Lawrence patted the back of the seat next to him. "Have a chair."

I sat next to him, then took an enormous bite of the sandwich. I asked, "Does Charles Brooks know everything about your daughter, you think? I mean, does Charles know what he is getting into, marrying Isobel?"

"*Caveat emptor*, is my theory."

"What's that mean, sir?"

"It's Latin." He smiled at me. "Let the buyer beware."

•

Most prize fighters don't talk trash during a fight, figuring there's no point enraging the enemy. Gentleman James Norton was an exception, and he came out of his corner at the bell mouthing off from the start.

"How'd you get on the card, shorty?" were the first words out of his mouth. "I'm going to chew my manager's ass, putting you on the same card as me."

He caught me with a sharp jab, snapping my head back. He circled to his left, smiling at me, revealing his crimson mouth guard.

Norton said, "I got me a red-hot date in forty minutes, shorty, and I've got to be showered and out at the curb by then."

He stalked me around the ring. He jabbed again, brushing my ear with his glove. Norton was three inches taller than me, which I suppose gave him license to call me shorty. His biceps looked as if they had been inflated with a bicycle pump. He had no neck that I could detect, just a bald head planted on massive shoulders. His eyes were well back in his head, mean little eyes. I tried a jab but he flicked it off and scoffed loudly at my impudence.

The bout was at the Shreveport Civic Arena, and there was a considerable gate, maybe seven thousand folks in attendance. Judging from the cheers during the introductions, I had only seven supporters in the hall: Isobel and her father Lawrence, Charles Brooks, Coral Thibideaux, my cut man Arturo Lopez, and Moe Barnes and his nephew Spazz.

Norton was a home-town favorite, having graduated from C.E. Byrd High School in the town. Several photographers leaned over the canvas to steady their cameras.

Norton played around, feinting in an exaggerated way, which brought hoots of appreciation from his fans. He jabbed me at will, taunting me all the while. I didn't connect with his face once during the first round.

In the previous two weeks, I had been working out ferociously, spending hours at the gym and on the road, getting ready for this fight, but when the bell ended the first round, I was already sweating heavily and a cut had opened above my right eye, a bad sign.

I sat on the stool in my corner. From her ringside seat, Isobel smiled encouragingly at me. She was nervous, I could tell. Maybe Moe Barnes had the poem in his pocket, ready to hand over to her at the end of the sixth round. Coral stared at me, her face revealing nothing.

Arturo pressed the slash above my eye with a cotton swab, then applied styptic. He said something in Spanish. I hoped it was, "This cut isn't too bad." He applied more Vaseline to my face.

The bell sounded for the second round, and I moved warily to the center of the ring, prepared for more punishment. Norton moved in, that same cruel grin on his face.

Then that same peculiar thing happened, that same quickness overtook me. I feinted with my left, then popped Norton squarely on the nose. He half-stepped back but caught himself, and rushed forward again.

Norton's movements seemed constrained, as if he were being hindered by invisible webs. At least, that's the way it appeared, compared to my swiftness. Maybe my extra bone, inserted into me by that wrinkled old lady in Lawrence's basement, was making me quicker. Norton lowered his right hand, cocking it at a leisurely pace, it seemed to me in my speeded-up mode. And for an instant his head was exposed. I sent a left hook into his temple. He tottered but caught himself. Boos came from the crowd.

Norton glanced desperately at his corner. His face registered both fear and surprise.

He turned back to me. He tried a combination but I slipped away, then jabbed him twice, and then sent a wicked left hook into his ear. He fell to the canvas.

I walked to a neutral corner. The audience shouted its disdain. The ref began the count.

I glanced at my fans. Charles Brooks and Lawrence Autrey were on their feet, smiling widely and clapping their hands. Lawrence's expression indicated he never had any doubt that I would handily beat Norton.

Isobel wasn't paying any attention to me. She was empty-handed. No Edgar Allan Poe poem. Her mouth pulled back in rage, she leaped from her chair and would've had her hands around Moe Barnes's fleshy neck had not his flunky gotten between them. In a rage, she yelled at Barnes and tried to hit him with her fist.

Barnes was laughing, and he managed to slide out of his chair and make for the stairway. He glanced back at Isobel and shook his head, grinning. Spazz Sprague held off Isobel until Barnes was safely away, then he roughly shoved her back down into her seat and followed his uncle.

Isobel was gasping with anger. Once again she had been duped. Once again she had put her faith in a bargain with a gangster, and had come up short. She grabbed her thick hair with both hands as if to yank it out, and then her eyes slowly closed and she slumped back in her chair, a limp posture of utter defeat. Coral put an arm around Isobel, comforting her.

I had a victory to celebrate. The ref crossed the ring to raise my hand. Some of the crowd had switched allegiances, and began cheering for me. They had just witnessed a huge upset. I walked around the ring, hands held aloft. Cameras flashed.

I looked again at Isobel. Now she was sitting there with her arms crossed, glaring at me as if I had somehow double-crossed her. But I had completed my part of the deal, hadn't I? I hadn't just lasted six rounds. Against all odds, I had defeated Gentleman James Norton.

I'd deal with Isobel later. I walked around the ring again, arms still in the air, and more people cheered.

I would've enjoyed it, too, had not the heat of Isobel's stare been cooking the back of my head.

19

"I've given her a sedative," Charles Brooks said. "She'll be fine."

"She doesn't look fine." I glanced again at Isobel's haggard face. "She looks like she blew a fuse."

"Charles?" Isobel called, her voice hollow and dreamy. "Are you there?" She was staring at the wall above Charles's head.

"Right here, dearest."

Isobel lowered her gaze. "How do you do that, Charles? One minute you are gone, and the next you are here. It's another of your talents, isn't it? You are a talented man."

"It's a Valium," Charles said to me in a low voice. "She's not used to it."

"And who is that with you, Charles? It's the boxer, isn't it? What happened to your face, Boxer?"

"I've been boxing." Gentleman James Norton's fists had purpled my jaw under my ear, and the walnut-sized swelling around the cut above my eye had an ochre tinge.

Isobel said, "So here I am, a respectable Garden District woman, and I've fallen in with a run-down boxer and a double-crossing gangster."

"Don't take her comments seriously, Dennis," Charles whispered. "It's the drug."

Isobel continued, "And I'm engaged to a guy who removes warts for a living. How's that for being in a fix?"

Charles said, "On second thought, maybe I won't give her another half a pill."

I must now report what happened here to me physically, as honestly as I remember it, but it was a puzzling experience, and I hope I get it right, because it plays an important part in what happened later.

I was abruptly aware that my heart was beating fast, as if I were jogging. I could feel the pulse in my neck. And I had begun to sweat, my forehead beading up. I wiped away the dampness with my hand. And my mouth was dry. I was thirsty. The air was dense, exotic, as if I were in a hothouse. I had no idea what was happening. And Isobel was glowing, a red light emanating from her, as if she were neon.

The room seemed bathed in this red light.

I whispered, "Do you see that, Charles? That red light from Isobel?"

"What are you talking about?"

"The light Isobel is throwing off. See it?"

He looked at me, an eyebrow raised. Maybe Gentleman James Norton's punches had addled me. I gulped air.

Charles asked, "Dennis, you okay?"

After a moment my heartbeat returned to normal, and I could generate some saliva. Maybe I was punch drunk. Isobel's red light faded.

Isobel went on, "The minute Gentleman Whatever fell to the mat, Moe Barnes turned to me and said, 'I've got a new deal for you.' So he reneged on me, just like that. I wanted to kill him but I wasn't carrying any weapons." She inhaled slowly. "I'll never get my poem."

"Am I involved in the new deal?" I asked.

Charles said, "From Isobel's ranting and shouting before the tranquilizer took effect, I gathered that Moe Barnes thinks that you might get a bout with Tug Johnson."

Roman "Tug" Johnson? The undisputed heavyweight champion of the world?

"Dillon Anders has just pulled out of his scheduled heavyweight fight with the champion," Charles explained. "So HBO and Tug Johnson have an open date. Two weeks from now. They've got some TV time to fill. Can you be ready?"

"I don't even rate as the champ's sparring partner," I said.

"You just defeated Gentleman James Norton," Charles said. "You're a credible opponent now."

Isobel snorted, as unladylike a sound as I imagine she had ever made. "Tug Johnson is going to kill you. How'm I supposed to get my poem?"

"How does Moe Barnes have anything to do with Tug Johnson's

fights?"

Charles said, "He knows a lot of people. He might be able to arrange a fight with Johnson."

"Edgar Allan Poe and me should've been connected in history forever," Isobel muttered. "And now it's lost. Why can't I weep?"

"You're on drugs is why, sweetie." He kissed her on her forehead.

I walked with him into the hall, then through the door into the evening. Red passionflower grew along the fence bordering Isobel's front yard. Bottlebrush lined the wide brick walkway. The air was heated and sticky. The sun was just setting, and its tired light colored only the tops of the trees.

At the sidewalk, Charles asked, "Where're you headed, Dennis?"

"Back to the Quarter eventually. Can I buy you dinner?"

"Not tonight, thanks."

We had walked several yards down the street when I noticed his pace was slowing.

His voice peculiarly oily, Charles asked, "You catching a streetcar, Dennis?"

"I feel like being out in the air. I'll walk with you a ways."

"Well, actually, my car is down that way, and I'm not headed downtown. I'm going the opposite way."

I wanted to talk to Charles, the head of my syndicate, about a potential fight with Tug Johnson, a giddy prospect. "I'll walk you to your car."

"Well, Dennis, actually, I'm being picked up here in a moment, and then ..."

"I'll wait. I don't mind."

"Actually, there's really no need ..." His voice trailed away.

Then I saw the problem, and it was a big one. Parked at the curb two houses away was Charles's Mercedes, and in the passenger seat was the stripper, Jenny Blake, her straw-blond hair and wide mouth clearly visible through the windshield. She slumped a little in her seat, and raised a hand to hide some of her face.

"Well, nuts," I said.

Charles inhaled sharply through his teeth. Then he tried, "I'm just giving her a ride, and ..."

I quickly held up my hand to stop the lie. "I saw you give her a big smooch when she picked you up at the Arcadian Knights' clubhouse."

He was silent. He looked down at the sidewalk.

I said, "We need to talk, Charles. You need some advice."

"I don't need advice from a boxer." His words weren't meant to be hurtful, and sounded more like a long sigh. "Ah, hell. I don't know what to do."

"I know what you should do, absolutely."

"You do?" he asked with pathetic eagerness. He looked at his car, then back me, and then he held up a finger to Jenny Blake, indicating he would be a moment.

I took his elbow and steered him back the way we had come, just a few steps.

"What's gotten into you, Charles? You're engaged to Isobel Autrey, last I heard."

With a finger, he touched the corner of his mouth "Yes, of course I am."

"Then what're you doing romancing Jenny Blake?"

He tried a conspiratorial gesture. "I can't help it."

"What do you mean?"

"When I'm around Jenny, I'm intoxicated. I'm dazzled by her. She makes me tingle. Her mouth, the curve of her shoulder, her belly button. Isobel has an outie, did you know?"

"How would I know that?"

"Jenny's long thighs with the tan skin, her luscious ..."

"I get the picture."

"All my life I've dated Garden District girls." His voice was sour. "My mother and father made sure of it. They simply weren't going to allow their son to besmirch their position in New Orleans' society by marrying underneath himself. God, Dennis, if you only knew the pressure."

"I can imagine." No, I couldn't. My father never pressured me. He just beat me.

"Jenny is a blast of fresh air."

"You love Isobel Autrey. She loves you."

He nodded too vigorously, as if trying to convince himself.

"You are being married in less than a month."

"Of course." He added with distaste, "It's the social event of the year in New Orleans."

"Let's look at the equation." I held up my hands like a scale. "On the one hand, you have a woman, Isobel, who is beautiful."

"Yes." He held up a finger, to count them out.

"And extremely intelligent," I said.

He held up another finger. "Yes."

"Well-educated."

Another finger.

"And wealthy."

Another finger.

I said, "But something of a lunatic."

He lowered a finger, deducting it from the total.

"And with Jenny, you have a woman who is beautiful," I said.

He brought up his other hand and held up a finger. "Yes."

I asked, "And what else?"

He thought for a moment. "She's ambitious. She wants to work in clubs in Chicago. She says it'd be an important career step."

I rubbed my chin.

"Dennis, she lights me up," the skin doctor exclaimed. "I've never experienced it before. She puts on these private dances for me and …" The memory seemed to overwhelm him, and he stopped mid-sentence, his eyes gleaming. "You have no idea."

"Charles, you've done a lot for me, the syndicate and all, taking me out to the Arcadian Knights, buying me clothes. I trust your advice."

He glanced at the Mercedes.

"And you can trust me, trust my advice right now," I said. "I'm on your side."

"Well, that's easy for you to say, because …" He fell into glum silence. Then he admitted, "Yeah, I know."

"You need to shake off your infatuation with the dancer."

"Yeah, I know."

"How many women like Isobel are there in the world? She's not my type, Lord knows, but every other bachelor in New Orleans would kill to be engaged to Isobel Autrey."

He ran his fingers through his dark hair.

"You are promised to Isobel, and she is promised to you. This thing with the stripper is goofy."

He stared at his shoes.

I prompted him, "So what are you going to do?"

He sighed heavily. "I'll tell Jenny about my engagement to another woman."

"Jenny doesn't even know?"

He shook his head. "I'll tell her, and I'll stop seeing her."

"You won't regret it. You'll look back in a year, and shake your head at how close you came to blowing it."

He gripped my arm. "You'll keep this between us?"

"Me and the fencepost."

"I mean, it'd really hurt Isobel to know about Jenny, and about my ... my weakness."

"I won't say anything."

He shook my hand. He turned toward his car. I crossed the street in the direction of the streetcar line.

I was headed back to the Quarter to Jelly's to do a little celebrating. Not for defeating Gentleman James Norton. Rather, in my back pocket was a thick letter. I was going to show it to my friends at the bar, and let them buy me a beer.

I had been admitted to Tulane University, damned if I hadn't.

•

"May I ask you a question, champ?" I was sitting on a folding chair in a waiting room near the main conference hall at the Windsor Court Hotel just off Canal Street a couple of blocks from the river. "What are you doing here?"

Tug Johnson laughed. "I'm more an entertainer than a boxer, and this fight—believe me, Dennis—is going to be big entertainment."

Outside the door in the conference room, loud preparations were being made for our weigh-in. In this small side room where we were, Johnson's management team was in a circle near the buffet table. I didn't have a management team, only my cut man, Arturo, who was helping himself to chips and salsa from the spread. I was wearing boxing trunks under a terry-cloth robe. Johnson's robe was made of silk.

He said, "You've had more press this past couple weeks than I've had in my entire career, I think." He laughed again. "Good for you."

Tug Johnson looked big on television and big in newspaper photographs, and even bigger in person. He had me by four inches, not only in height, but also in biceps measurement. And while I had good pecs and lats, they were nothing like Johnson's. I felt tiny sitting next to the champ.

"Here's another question from a longtime fan," I said. "How do you shave your head every day without cutting yourself?" Johnson's scalp was the color of an eight-ball. It reflected light. His opponents said Johnson's head had the density an eight ball, too, for all the effect hitting it had.

He grinned. "I have a guy who does that for me. Comes in every morning. After this fight, you'll be able to hire him, too, you want."

I was receiving only a fifth of the championship fight payout, the rest going to Johnson. So the minimum I would earn for the fight would be three million dollars. I couldn't even grasp the concept, couldn't even think about that much money.

"How'd you do it, man?" Johnson shook his head. "I mean, I've never seen such publicity. My team hardly had a choice but to schedule you once Dillon Anders dropped out."

"I had nothing to do with it," I replied. "A run-down old canvas back has a shot at the title. The media thought it was a good story, I guess."

"You know how many times I've been on the cover of *Sports Illustrated* in the four years I've been champ?"

"Lots, I'd imagine."

"One time, until this week's issue, which makes it two times, except that I had to share the cover with you."

I laughed and so did he. A fellow wearing a tan suit and a cobalt blue tie rushed up to ask Johnson if he would sign several publicity photos for some kids out in the ballroom. He was one of Johnson's entourage, which by my count numbered about twenty, including his manager and trainer, personal photographer, masseuse, driver, nutrition advisor, two bodyguards, and assorted gofers, all milling about in the room. Arturo the Cut Man was the only one there who worked for me. Waiters offered drinks to everyone. Two doormen kept the riffraff out.

Isobel and Charles were in the room talking to the Windsor Court's manager, who Charles knew. Coral Thibideax was with them. Isobel had announced that Coral was now my natural physician, and Isobel had asked her to join us. Tug Johnson sported a diamond stud in his right ear.

My ring date with the heavyweight championship of the world came about this way. Dillon Anders dropped off the card because of a pulled hamstring he suffered while doing stair wind sprints. HBO needed to quickly fill an important slot. Here I was, a well-past-his-prime circuit fighter who suddenly had beaten Sammy Dresser and Gentleman James Norton. ESPN, *Ring Magazine*, Time and *Newsweek*, CBS Sportsline, they all showed up, and a dozen big-city newspapers, too.

They interviewed anybody who had ever met me, including Old Al Higgens and my sometime sparring partner Cecil "Iron Shovel" Rodrick, James "Amazing Grace" Jefferson, the bartender at Jelly's, and the deputy up in Newton County who had arrested me, who told the reporter I was a "decent enough fellow, no rattling his cup on the bars, that sort of thing." The reporters dredged up that I had once crossed Australia on a train, from Sydney to Perth, fighting for purses in every little drover town along the way.

"Are you keeping all the suck-ups away from you?" the champ asked.

"I suddenly have a lot of people who want to be around me, I'll guarantee you that. I give them a grin and turn them away."

With all the publicity, more strange things were happening to me. A fellow tracked me down at Jelly's one night, and offered to be my valet. I asked him, why in the world do I need a valet? He snapped his finger at the bartender and yelled out, "Bring the champ a beer here." He turned back to me. "That sort of thing. Man, think how great that will be." I sent him on his way.

Another fellow showed up at my apartment door with five thousand dollars in cash in his hand, asking me if he could publish a boxing card—one of those sets that in the old days came with a flat piece of bubble gum so hard it could break your teeth—with my face on it. I signed the contract and took his cash.

The *Times-Picayune* ran a contest to give me an appropriate nickname. Among the entrants were the Crescent City Crusher, the Mississippi Mauler, Slow Old White Guy, and The Fighter From The Least Irritating French Place On Earth. The winning nickname was the Bayou Bruiser, which had been submitted by over a thousand readers.

I once enjoyed hanging out on a Bourbon Street corner, leaning up against a post watching the day go by, especially after a workout, just winding down. I couldn't do that anymore because crowds would gather, folks asking me questions, touching me, demanding autographs and asking if they could pose next to me for a snapshot.

Photos of my face were all over New Orleans; newspapers, TV, posters, and the sides of Darigold milk trucks, me holding up a tall glass of milk, for which I received another five thousand dollars.

I thought these crowds were fun for a day or two, but then I purchased a straw hat and a pair of large sunglasses. This simple disguise worked most of the time.

The folks at my hang-out, Jelly's, left me alone mostly, except for two or three women who would throw themselves at me each night. Different women every night, hoping I might be their lunch tickets. Isobel had forbidden me to have anything to do with women before the fight, saying it would irreparably weaken me. I scoffed at this, but Charles added, "As a medical man, I advise you to forego such pleasures until after the bout." So I turned aside these young ladies, not without difficulty.

Old Al began charging admission to his gym. Every day a hundred or more spectators showed up, many of them from the press. They watched me work out, and passed comments back and forth. Oscar de la Hoya was in town, came by the gym, and coached me from the corner during a sparring match.

New Orleans had adopted me as its son. The press likened me to the city itself. I had heart. Just like the city, I had taken blow after blow, yet I always rose again from the mat. Or so folks liked to believe. I was just an over-the-hill circuit fighter, and I knew it.

The best thing that had happened was happening just then, getting to sit next to the heavyweight champion of the world, and exchanging a few words. Johnson was 52-2 in his professional career, the two losses coming when he was young. He also possessed an Olympic gold medal. Johnson had dominated the heavyweight division for so long now that he was being compared to Joe Louis.

Coral approached us. "I know you get bothered all the time, Mr. Johnson, but could I have your autograph for my husband."

"My pleasure," he smiled as he took her pen and a piece of paper.

Coral was wearing black pants and a blue blouse with a necklace made of tiny shells and steel bells and other trinkets. It jingled when she moved. Her mass of precise black cornrows fell to the middle of her back.

I introduced Coral to the champ, then said, "Coral is my voodoo doctor."

Johnson looked up. "What do you mean?"

She grinned. "I've just done a few things to help Dennis."

Johnson eyes narrowed. "Help him how?"

Her smile broadened, and now it was teasing. "I've increased his strength and stamina, using some methods I know."

The champ leaned forward in his chair. "You mean, voodoo things? You've done some voodoo rituals?"

"I'm a fourth-degree dark-spirit geomancer," Coral explained. She told me later she invented this title on the spot.

"She added an extra bone to me," I said. "Shoved it right through my skin, the bone taken from a very tough customer."

Johnson sounded alarmed. "Hey, that can't be legal. And it's unfair, having an extra bone." Then brought his chin up and smiled. "You're setting me up, isn't that right? This is just to get inside my head, give me some doubt."

Coral raised an eyebrow. "We'll see." She turned to rejoin Isobel and Charles.

"Adding a bone." He laughed derisively. "Man, you had me going."

"I don't believe it, either," I said.

He laughed again.

I added, "Except that I saw it with my own eyes."

He stared at me, no longer laughing.

One of the hotel's security men approached. "Mr. Jones, there's a man outside who claims to be your manager, and asks to see you."

"I don't have a manager," I said. "What'd he say his name was?"

"Billy Dupree."

I laughed. "That old carnie? Kick the bum out."

The security man had taken a step back to the door, when I said, "No, wait a minute. Show Billy in. I want him to see me sitting next to the champ."

Tug Johnson smiled. Someone else passed him several cards to sign. He obliged nicely.

Billy Dupree was escorted into the room. His pudgy face was even more florid than usual, as if he had climbed several flights of stairs. He wiped sweat from his forehead with a well-used handkerchief. His belly filled his white shirt, and the shirttails ballooned down, hiding his belt. His sports coat was shiny, and was yellow or green, depending on how the light hit it. He came up to me. He smelled vaguely of pickles. The security man stood by.

"Dennis," he said. "I've been waiting for your call."

"I telephoned several times about that four hundred dollars you owe me. You didn't bother to call me back."

"You need a manager, Dennis."

I said, "Billy Dupree, this is Tug Johnson."

The two men shook hands.

Dupree nervously said, "Sure, hi, champ. I'm a big fan of yours."

I said, "I don't need a manager, Billy, and certainly not an old swindler like you."

Dupree patted the back of his neck with the handkerchief. "Every fighter needs a manager. Someone's got to oversee the business. You can't do it yourself."

"I'm doing fine so far."

"You need someone to handle the press, and your appointments, and your endorsements." He hitched up his pants. "A fighter needs a pro like me in his corner. Ain't that right, champ?"

"That's right," Johnson said.

"Beat it, Billy," I said mildly. "I'm done with you for good."

"Well, you think about it, Dennis. Will you?"

"Not for a second," I said. "Don't let the door knob hit your butt on the way out."

Dupree looked entirely defeated, his hang-dog face hanging even more than usual.

He finally said, "An honor meeting you, champ." Dupree turned to go, the security man escorting him to the door.

Tug Johnson said, "Our fight is scheduled for the Superdome, Dennis,"

"Yeah?"

"We need to fill it, and that's a tall order—what? With seventy thousand seats in the dome. Everything we can do to build the gate, we need to do."

"I'm not following you, champ."

Johnson flipped his thumb toward a nattily dressed fellow. "See my manager over there, the one with the Italian suit and the silk tie? He's got a Stanford MBA. He's as slick as goose crap. That's the way my whole operation is. It's run like a corporation. Polished in every detail."

"I've heard."

"But this guy, this Billy Dupree. Cheap suit, big pink nose, greasy hair, all the sweat, the beat-up brogans, the turned-up collar, the swamp accent. You take him on as your manager, his photo will be in all the papers. The two of you will look like you wandered in from the 1940s. What a contrast it'll be, my sophisticated operation versus this bayou bumpkin Billy Dupree."

"I think I see."

"It's another angle. It's one more burst of publicity. It's one more reason to buy a ticket."

I rose, crossed the floor to the security man, and asked him to go get the big fellow who had just left. I didn't have to wait long, as Dupree had been out in the ballroom with the crowd waiting for the weigh-in.

Dupree came in through the door, wearing a wide smile, displaying his remarkably yellow teeth.

I said, "All right, you're my manager."

"I knew you'd come around." He gleefully rubbed his hands together.

"Ten percent is your cut. But the checks come directly to me, and I issue you your ten percent. The money doesn't go to you first."

"Sure, sure. Anything." He was beaming.

He followed me back toward the champ.

Tug Johnson said, "An extra bone. Who're you kidding?" He sounded worried.

The weigh-in's organizer appeared at the door to loudly announce, "We're ready, ladies and gentleman. The first to appear will be the challenger, Mr. Jones."

I followed Billy Dupree through the door into the ballroom. Loud applause filled the room. I had to squint against the TV lights and the flash bulbs. Trailing behind me were my cut man Arturo and Isobel and Charles and Coral.

I had an entourage now. I was coming up in the world.

20

That evening I was at the bar at Jelly's, chatting with the bartender between dance sets. The Swamp Soul Kings had just finished their zydeco version of Never Hit Your Grandma with a Shovel. The dancers were back at their tables. The cobra was still wrapped around the mongoose on the backbar.

I had danced a few songs and signed a few autographs. The bartender had filled my beer mug a couple of times. The patrons were looking at me, some of them pointing. They knew I was the contender.

Isobel Autrey appeared at my elbow, and I admit to barking out in surprise and fear. She stared at me. Her mouth was parted, and a delicate line of perspiration was on her forehead. Her black hair was all about, coiled and twisted and looking as if it were trying to escape. She was wearing a cranberry red silk jacket that was open down the front, revealing a black cotton camisole. Her pants were black and pleated.

She said over the noise of the bar patrons, "I had a talk with Coral yesterday."

No "hello" or "How are you, Dennis?" She held her hands behind her back, and appeared deep in thought.

"How does she get all the skin off her weasel skulls, do you think?" I sat down on a bar stool. "I about fainted, seeing that skull on the ring post. That lady worries me."

Isobel said, "Your new bone isn't going to be enough, Coral tells me."

"What do you mean?"

She saw the crack on the naugahyde covering the next bar stool, and remained standing. "Defeating Tug Johnson will take more than a weasel skull and one small bone from me."

"Well, I'm at my limit regarding your bones. One of them is enough for anybody."

Someone plugged in the jukebox. A waiter walked by carrying two orders of nachos. An overhead fan churned cigarette smoke.

"Coral has told me what I must do, and I'm prepared." Isobel rose on her toes, her hands still behind her back, resembling Gen. Patton addressing his troops. "It has been a life of sacrifice, and if I must continue to give, I shall. I am not one to complain."

A young lady approached. She had auburn hair and was wearing a halter top that defied the known laws of physics, and asked me to dance to the jukebox. I said I would be happy to, once I had heard all this other lady had to say, but I didn't expect that to take long, indicating Isobel with my thumb. The auburn-haired girl grinned promisingly, then returned to her friends.

Isobel said, "Coral tells me that Tug Johnson will easily defeat you."

"That's not really late breaking news. I know that, and everybody knows that."

"Coral said there is nothing that she, alone, can do. But there is hope."

I glanced over at the auburn-haired girl in the halter top. She was smiling at me. I said, "At Jelly's, there's always hope."

"These were her very words: 'Isobel, you need to step up or step back.'"

"That's my boxing motto, too. Step up and get smacked."

"To obtain my poem, I need to increase my commitment, Coral said. There's no other way."

"Increasing your commitment?" I sipped my beer. "What does that mean?"

"It revolts me" She inhaled deeply. "But I have no choice."

I lifted a few peanuts from the bowl on the bar and flipped them into my mouth.

"Dennis, is there somewhere we can be alone?" Isobel asked.

I couldn't read anything in her expression, but I could see those blue sparks in the back of her eyes, flickering there as if she were generating electricity, getting ready to zap me again like a bug light.

"Is this going to hurt?" I asked, only partly kidding. I leaned over the bar. "Rafael, let me use the manager's office, will you?"

Rafael lifted a key from near a cash register and handed it to me. I led Isobel along the bar, and passed several tables. The washboard player was showing off his percussion set to a couple of patrons, tapping a thimble against a tiny cymbal mounted on the board. We walked by the jukebox, then into a hallway where the restrooms were, passed the employee's time clock, then to the door at the end of the hall. The door was painted glossy black, and a fluorescent red sign tacked to it read, "Keep Out." I opened the door with the key. Isobel followed me inside.

I said, "I'm as ready as I'll ever be for my fight with Tug Johnson, if that's what you're worried about."

"You aren't quite ready, Dennis." Her voice was crabbed with distaste. "But you will be in a few minutes."

The manager's office was tiny and cluttered. A laptop computer, a printer, and a pile of unopened bills were on the desk, along with half a dozen empty Pepsi bottles and a metal Army surplus lamp, which issued a thin light that couldn't compete with the overhead light. The trash can near the desk was overflowing.

Along a wall were framed photographs of bands that had played at Jelly's over the years. The shag rug was whorehouse red. Two dented file cabinets were along the wall under a poster of Rocky and Bullwinkle. A snare drum was on a spavined sofa. Fabric covering the sofa's arms was worn down to the threads, the stuffing visible beneath. Stored in a corner was a box of spare drumsticks. A Hamm's Beer clock was on a wall.

Pushing the snare drum aside, I sat down, and I could feel the sofa's abused springs. Isobel closed the door, and took a long pull of air, hissing it between her teeth. She leaned back against the door, and brought her eyes to me. She bit her lower lip and then blinked slowly, and she swayed a little, as if on the verge of fainting.

"Are you cold?" I asked.

She looked at me vaguely, as if trying to place me.

"You are buttoning your jacket. It's hot in this little room, if anything."

She looked down, and seemed surprised to see her jacket halfway buttoned up. She undid the buttons, then looked at the red rug a moment. She swallowed three times in quick succession, as if forcing something back down her throat.

Ever so slowly, Isobel's expression changed. Her eyes hardened and her mouth softened. She looked at me through her lashes. Out on Jelly's stage, the guitar player ran through a riff, and it was followed by applause. The band's break was ending.

"Do you find me attractive, Dennis?" Isobel's voice was just above a whisper.

"Yes, sort of like I think a cougar is attractive. Lovely eyes, cute nose, but lots of fangs and claws."

"Have you ever thought of ..." She paused, and her lips moved soundlessly several seconds before she added, "... of pursuing me?"

"I've thought of setting a pack of hounds after you, like I would a cougar, yes." I thought this comment mighty snappy, but she didn't appear to hear it.

Isobel pursed her mouth, and she was apparently lost in thought, then she slowly turned to press the button on the knob that locked the door. She flicked off the overhead light, leaving the office lit only by the feeble desk lamp.

She said in a low voice, one I think she meant to be soothing, "Coral said a bone just wasn't enough to beat Tug Johnson. You need more, Dennis." She stepped in my direction.

I pushed myself back on the sofa. The drum fell to the floor with a rattle. "What do you mean, 'more?'"

"All." She moved closer.

"How much is all?"

"It's one hundred percent."

"How many bones is that?" I asked. "I don't want to carry around too much extra weight."

Her cheeks had gained a ruddy hue, and she wet her lower lip with her tongue. Her black hair moved around her head, curling and snaking.

"Coral isn't outside that door, is she?" I asked. "I mean, that woman would scare the stripe off a skunk."

"It's just you and me, Dennis."

She hovered above me. I swear, that electric shimmering started again, rippling up and down, tiny charges of red light that caressed her, coursing along her curves and making her glow like an ember. This was my imagination, I was sure. She had that effect on me, making my eyeballs untrustworthy.

She lowered herself next to me on the sofa, and said, "You smell like beer."

"Had I been drinking Tang out there at the bar, I'd smell like Tang."

She gently put her hand on my knee. "I don't want you to read anything into this, other than that I'll do anything for my Poe poem."

"How do you do that with your eyes, Isobel? Are you wearing battery-powered contact lenses with little lights in them or something?"

"That's in your head, Dennis, along with the rest of your thirty-four years of twaddle." She drew her fingers lightly along my leg. "Even this is in your head, me touching you."

"Feels real enough to me." I had begun to perspire, I don't mind admitting. Isobel often did that to me, when she got too close.

She said, "When I deny all this tomorrow, it's the same as being an hallucination right now."

Outside the door and down the hall, the band started their next set with a jump-jive number called Where'd That Hair Come From?

Isobel leaned toward me, both of us on the lumpy couch, and I ventured another look into her eyes. They were endlessly blue and sparking and full of life. Her lilac scent flowed over me.

"Isobel, I'm beginning to understand what you have in mind. And I can't."

She was close enough now so that I could feel her warm breath on my cheek. "I'll make you. You are powerless before me."

"You are engaged to be married to Charles and I don't have anything to do with engaged ladies. It's a point of honor with me. And, no, you can't make me."

She was yet closer, and the tips of her fingers ran along my thigh. She whispered, "Charles's idea of romance is naming the freckles on my back. I've got Mercury and Venus and Saturn and Bashful and Sleepy and Grumpy and a bunch of others. He likes to recite them in a kiddy voice, poking them with a finger."

"Isobel ..."

"So you don't have much competition in terms of technique, if that's what you are worried about."

"It's not that ..."

"If I don't give myself entirely to you tonight before midnight, you won't be able to defeat Tug Johnson." She looked at the Hamm's clock. "It's 11:30. Time is running out."

"Come on, Isobel. Coral is telling you nonsensical things, and making you do things you'd never otherwise do, like pressing into me like this, and making me stupid with your eyes and your scent when you are an engaged woman. Coral is just playing with your head."

"Kiss me, Dennis."

It wouldn't have taken much effort on my part, kissing her, as her lips were an inch away. Her eyes were still open, and I couldn't break her gaze, and she was paralyzing me with them. Her palm pressed my chest, then kneaded my right pec.

"I'm not going to kiss the mouth of another man's fiancée." My voice was reedy.

So she kissed me. A gong went off between my ears, overwhelming my better judgment. I could feel her cool lips and then her warm tongue. Her hand went around my neck, and her other hand slid down my shirt to lift it so she could slip her hand underneath and draw her fingers along my chest.

She moved her mouth to my ear, and once again she nipped it, though not so hard as to draw blood this time, and then she took little bites on my cheek and jaw, and ran her red lips under my eyes and along my nose and down my cheek. She moved against me, pushing me back and down on the sofa. I wanted to yell a protest but I couldn't get my chest and throat to work. My face was wrapped in her hair. She kissed me again and explored my mouth, and I felt her shudder.

Then she brought her head up and laughed, an earthy sound, something from the swamp. "Dennis, I don't know when I've been so appalled." She laughed again, that velvety, burbling sound. "Take a big breath, and hold on."

And then ... Well, I'm not too sure. At that point I forgot about Charles Brooks and honor and Coral Thibideaux and voodoo and Tug Johnson and Edgar Allan Poe.

Isobel TKO'd me, is what happened, and I don't remember a whole lot of it. I think I enjoyed myself but it's hard to say. She didn't injure me or anything, not like I would've guessed. I'd like to think Isobel had a good time, though once she gasped out, "Oh my God, all my years of education ... and look at me." But I suppose there are several ways to interpret this comment.

She left the office just before midnight, just as the band was playing one of my favorites, Fatty Ties His Shoes. I would've walked her out and to her car, but my legs wouldn't work, and maybe I should've shaken her hand, but by then my arms didn't work either, and I would've said goodbye and see you around, but there wasn't even enough energy left in me to push those few words out of my mouth.

The last thing I heard from her before she closed the office door on her way out was her clarinet laugh.

•

The Superdome sold out, seventy thousand people, and they all stood and hollered and whistled and clapped when I made my appearance and walked down the aisle toward the ring. I'd never before heard such a sound, as loud as a jet engine. Spotlights illuminated me, making it hard to see beyond Billy Dupree's back as I followed him. We were escorted by policemen, and our progress was slow. The crowd kept roaring.

Dupree called over his shoulder, "Give them a wave, Dennis."

So I did, raising my gloved fist. The noise increased, a surge of sound so loud it had a weight, pressing me down. I passed a tower made of scaffolding on which was mounted a television camera. I shuffled along, following my manager, the procession slowed by folks in the aisle. Arturo Lopez was behind me, carrying a water bottle and his bucket of swabs, Vaseline, styptic, nose spray, razor blades, smelling salts and tape.

We reached the ring, and the three of us climbed up, Billy Dupree having trouble squeezing his belly between the ropes. He was wearing a Panama hat, which had become his trademark this past week. The crowd cheered.

Tug Johnson had been right: my manager Billy Dupree was now as famous as I was, his harvest moon face in all the papers, along with his wit. "Tug Johnson has as much chance of winning this fight as he does getting a French kiss from the Statue of Liberty." That kind of thing. New Orleans loved him. I stood in my corner, Dupree and Lopez near me.

Then the champ made his appearance at the top of the aisle. Johnson received hearty applause, but also jeers and boos, as I was the hometown lad. His entourage made its way toward the ring. There must have been a hundred of them. As he always did, the champ wore a towel over his head, draped down to his shoulders, partially hiding his face, his sinister trademark. He was wearing a red silk robe. Mine was still terry cloth.

Tug Johnson slipped into the ring, as did many of his attendants. Isobel and Charles and Lawrence were in the second row, behind the photographers, and some of the Arcadian nights were with them. Coral Thibideax sat next to Isobel.

The ring announcer went into a long spiel that I didn't listen to, me surveying the huge crowd, some with homemade posters that said Go Bayou Bruiser. I glanced at Isobel. She was glowing red again, that eerie crimson glimmer, as if she were an oven burner. Maybe she was blushing as she looked up at me. Charles and her father were talking together. They didn't notice Isobel's glow.

Moe Barnes and his flunky nephew Spazz Sprague were on the other side of the ring. Barnes was grinning and talking to one person after another who were sitting around him, maybe his gangland friends. He was round wagering again. All I had to do was last five rounds, and Isobel would get her poem. So he said.

My stomach rolled over. Pure fear is what it was. I was gripping the top rope, and my gloved hands were trembling so much the rope was jiggling. I looked at the crowd, desperately hoping that they would all slow down, that is, I would speed up like I had in the prior fights. But the audience chatted and took photographs and ate popcorn, all in normal time. I had a bad feeling that my supernatural ability to speed up, and my luck, had deserted me.

Evander Holyfield walked toward me, grinning, with both hands out to shake my gloves. Then, as the ring announcer called their names, Ken Norton came over, then Joe Frazier, saying words of encouragement to me, then crossing the mat to Tug Johnson. The loudest roar of the night came when Muhammad Ali came in between the ropes and raised his hands. He patted me on the shoulder, winked at me and said, "Give it all you got."

The ring cleared out, leaving only the referee, Tug Johnson and me, and we met in the center of the mat. The ref gave his instructions. Because of the crowd's roar, I couldn't hear a word he said, but I presume it was a warning against doing any of the things I often did to win a fight, such as groin punching. Tug Johnson smiled at me. He didn't play the stare-down game, probably thought it beneath him. Man, he was big. He was wearing a three-day beard, same as me. Our faces were slicked up with Vaseline.

We returned to our corners. I danced lightly. Billy Dupree tapped my shoe, encouraging me. The bell rang, the crowd bellowed, and I went forward to meet the champ.

We didn't waste any time. I threw a jab just as we met in the center of the ring, and he returned one, a simple jab hitting me on the forehead about as hard as I'd ever been hit. I stepped back, then circled left, away from the wrecking ball he called his left hand. He went with me, going to his left. I tried to call forth my speed, so as to slip faster through time than anyone else in the place, but time was stubborn, and I was caught in the same stream of seconds as everyone else.

I sent a left at him again, but it was normal speed and he flicked it aside. He was wearing a gold-colored mouthpiece. He juked, then went to his left, and I had to turn with him. I again willed myself to speed up. Again, nothing doing. Isobel and Coral hadn't been able to work their magic. I sent a hapless one-two at him, and hit nothing but air. Then he drove a jab into my forehead again. It felt like a hammer.

I launched another jab, and he slipped inside and hit me in the stomach so hard I suffered an instant of total paralysis, as if I'd caught a cannon ball with my belly. Then his left hook came around and crushed my head right about at my ear, and I blacked out on my feet.

The official timer claimed the fight lasted sixty-eight seconds. I have no memory of being carried from the ring.

•

When I regained consciousness, I was lying on a cot in the dressing room, a doctor shining a light into my eyes. When I tried to get up, he pushed me back down, but I swatted aside his hand and sat up anyway. My insides felt as if a stick of dynamite had gone off just above my belt, so painful that I could only lean forward and dry heave. The doctor apparently decided he preferred more appreciative patients, so he left me there on the cot, saying, "I'll keep the reporters away from you a while. There's a hundred of them out there."

I could hear muted footfalls and stadium seats snapping up into their folded position as spectators left their seats, headed toward the exits. I'm sure they all felt cheated. Sitting on the edge of the cot,

I let my head rest on my palms. My right eye was blurred, and one of my ears was ringing, a high-pitched mosquito's hum. The doctor must have removed my gloves.

Arturo was on a bench in front of the lockers, but he knew he couldn't do anything for me, so he stayed there. My new manager, Billy Dupree, was nowhere to be seen, though he would show up for his cut, I was sure. Dupree had inadvertently done me a service when I traveled the circuit with him, teaching me not to enter a ring before I got paid. Three million dollars, less the federal tax withheld by the promoter, was already in my bank account. I was a wealthy man, even if I would be peeing blood for a week. I closed my eyes. Tiny sparks of light danced behind my eyelids. My mouth had that familiar taste of canvas.

"How are you doing, Dennis? Are you okay?"

I looked up to see Lawrence Autrey crossing the tiled floor. I tried to say something but my mouth was dry, and it came out a croak. Charles Brooks followed him. Charles patted my shoulder, then they sat on a bench across from me.

"You received the full Tug Johnson treatment, I'm afraid," Lawrence added.

When I shifted even slightly, my innards made a peculiar swooshing sound, as if things were loose in there.

"I'm sorry, Dennis." Tears were in Lawrence's eyes.

I might've tried to nod but it hurt to even try to move my head. I touched my ear where the champ's fist had found me, then my jaw and neck. Nothing was free from pain.

"Isobel is distraught," Charles said. "She can hardly speak."

My chest didn't seem to work. I couldn't get any words out.

Charles said, "As Moe Barnes marched up the aisle, he yelled at Isobel that he had just lost a one million dollar wager, and that he was going to put the poem into the fire tonight. I feel awful for her. And for you."

I lifted a water bottle from the floor under my cot and managed to bring up a few drops of water through its straw. It hurt to do so.

"Well." Lawrence dabbed at a tear. He sat for a moment more but could think of nothing to say.

Charles's head was bowed, and his hands were clasped together. He couldn't come up with anything, either.

Lawrence finally said, "We'll see you soon, Dennis."

The old fellow led Charles from the dressing room. Arturo Lopez opened my locker and produced my check book. He handed a pen to me. He steadied the checkbook on my lap while I wrote him a check for five thousand dollars. I didn't have the strength to tear the check from the book so he did it for me. He smiled at me, grabbed his bucket and left me there.

An hour ago I had been a contender. And now, once again and forever, I was the carnival fighter, the canvasback, the saloon pug. I slowly lay back down on the bench and closed my eyes.

•

Carrying a cardboard box, Isobel appeared at my apartment the next morning. I let her in, and without a word she walked to the sink, pulled a bottle of Butch Wax out of her box and placed it on the counter. Then from the cardboard box came a three-pack of J.C. Penny underwear. She tossed them into the dresser.

"I'm releasing you from my care, and am returning you to your previous life," she said in a pavement voice. "No more School of Isobel for you. And so you'll need all your tacky, cheap stuff around you again."

"I'm too sore to listen to you, Isobel."

"Oh no, you're not."

"Last night I was destroyed by someone who knew how to do it so I don't need you here to do it again this morning."

She dug into the box. "Here's a fifty-cent black plastic comb." She placed it on the dresser. "And here's a rabbit's foot, and here's a bunch of rubber bands so you can restart your collection."

I sat back down on the bed. I ached all over, my beating from Tug Johnson still echoing in my bones and muscles. Vision in my right eye was still hazy, but the ringing in my ear had gone away. The champ had hit me so hard in the stomach that everything between my Adam's apple and my knees was still throbbing.

Isobel was wearing khaki pants and a black shirt. Out came a copy of *Sports Illustrated*. She tossed it onto the dresser.

"And here's a cheap wristwatch." She spit out the words. "And a Binaca, and a gold chain for your neck, and a cheesy girlie wall calendar, and a little black phone book for the phone numbers of all the slatterns you meet down at that saloon of yours, everything you'll need to return to the same old squalid clueless you."

"All those voodoo rituals with Coral were a bunch of crappola," I said. "The skulls and the brown drink and the candles and the ritual to give me an extra bone—that was just sleight of hand, wasn't it? It all added up to nothing."

"And here is a flea-bitten old blanket, just like your old one." With a flourish, she produced it from the box, then flung it at me on the bed.

I ducked it, and it hit the wall behind me. "And if you believed any of that stuff with Coral, you're goofier than I thought."

She produced something else from the cardboard box. "Here's a pair of nose hair clippers."

"And that's plenty goofy, believe me."

"We all need a center to our existence," she adopted the tone of a schoolmarm, "Some item that represents our core, something that is a distillation of our very essence, and these nose hair clippers can be yours." The clippers clattered onto the dresser.

"Listen, Isobel ..."

"No, you listen to me." She pointed at me. "I did my part. I did everything in my power, and it should have been enough. You should have defeated Tug Johnson. You should've at least last five rounds. And I should've had my poem."

"Well ..."

She strafed me with her eyes. "You didn't fight hard enough."

"I lost to the heavyweight champion of the world, one of the greatest fighters who ever lived, and that's letting you down?"

She exclaimed, "I gave you everything I had. Everything. And you failed me."

"I tried, Isobel. I just didn't have the horsepower to take on the world champion."

She dropped the cardboard box onto the floor. "And you don't have the horsepower to keep me in your presence one second longer."

"Isobel ..."

"You'll never see me again, Dennis Jones, and that's the only hopeful thought I've had since last night's fight."

She marched across the room. She was making this peculiar keening wail of anger and frustration, and charged out the door, slamming it behind her.

Maybe I should've gone after her and tried to do more explaining, but I hurt too much and it wouldn't have worked anyway. So I sat there trying not to move because any motion whatsoever called forth a new wave of pain. I stared at the far wall for a moment as the realization sank in: I wouldn't be seeing Isobel any more.

She was a nut, sure, but even so I'd grown fond of her. More than fondness, maybe. With Isobel, it was hard to tell how I felt. When she was near, I was often nervous and sweaty, and I could feel my heart pounding, and my mouth would dry up. Of course, the same things happened to me at the dentist. Much of my reaction to Isobel was primitive, I was sure, generated from my brain stem, an instinctive fight-or-flee response.

I rubbed the back of my neck, trying to knead the pain away. I don't remember Johnson hitting me there, but lots of places hurt where he hadn't hit, so thorough had been the beating. Isobel just wasn't my notion of someone to love. I favor women who can be charmed. I like women you can put a few moves on and who don't get it, or at least pretend they don't get it. Women who laugh at your jokes, and not at you. Women who are intelligent but who don't kill you with it. Women who don't have a current running through them like an electric fence.

So why was I sitting there, still thinking about Isobel? When I looked at her, I saw a finagler, a wire-puller, an operator, a hustler. A lot of other words came to mind—not anyone I would ever fall for. I'm wary of such people who are always in the process of setting you up. When they are done with you, you've been made a sucker.

I had not ever seriously thought of Isobel and me together, not really, not more than a passing daydream if even that, I mean it. Why waste even my daydreams? She was a Garden District daughter, a product of the finest upbringing and education. She was the perfectly lifted chin, the eloquently turned phrase, the amused and knowing glance. Compared to Isobel, I was a belch in church.

Ah, well. You can't lose something you never had. I rubbed my forehead, scrubbing away thoughts of Isobel. I breathed deeply, and my chest ached. My chest, not my heart, I was sure.

I glanced at the door, but it was still closed and she was still gone.

21

Someone peaked from behind a curtain in Moe Barnes's front room—maybe his nephew Spazz Sprague, maybe Barnes himself—and this is what he saw through the window.

A big cherry-red Paccar semi was rumbling down Barnes's driveway in front of his house. The truck was pulling a low-boy trailer, and on the trailer was a Caterpillar D8N, a yellow crawler dozer. Mounted on the front of the Cat was a semi-U dozer blade. On the rear of the Cat, a jackhammer was attached to a backhoe's arm, instead of a dipper bucket. The Caterpillar was massive, eleven feet tall and ten feet wide, and weighed thirty-eight tons.

That person peeking through the window would have seen the truck and trailer come to a stop, and then a driver open the cab door and climb down, carrying a folding map and wearing a baseball cap, his head low. The Paccar's engine idled, the exhaust cap flapping. The driver unfolded the map, scratched his head in puzzlement, then turned to look back at the country road, took several steps toward the road to see if he could spot a sign, then turned around, studying the map, his head down and his face hidden by the cap's brim.

The driver walked slowly toward Moe Barnes's house, still examining the map. He crossed the bridge over the stream. Bayou was all around; tall trees and vines and still water. The driveway led to a garage. Clearly lost out here in the bayou, the truck driver turned the map forty-five degrees as he walked along a cobblestone path that split the grass yard. A martin house was mounted on a pole in the side yard. An enormous weeping willow tree dominated the front yard, to the east of the walkway.

His head still lowered to study the map, the truck driver knocked on the house's front door. Immediately the door opened, and Spazz Sprague growled, "Get that equipment out of the driveway."

"If you'd just help me find State 22, I'd appreciate it."

Sprague opened the door wider, and took a menacing step toward me. "Didn't you hear me?"

The driver was me, of course. I wound up my right fist behind the map, and I put my legs and shoulders and anger into it, and there was plenty of anger. This punch erupted from the center of the earth and tore through magma and granite. It slammed Sprague on his forehead. He never saw it coming. I had a roll of quarters in my hand, and that helped considerably. I caught him before he fell. As quietly as I could, I dragged him out onto the sidewalk, then over to the willow tree. He was out entirely, spit coming from a corner of his mouth. I left him at the base of the willow.

I rushed into the hallway. I'd been in Moe Barnes's den before, as you'll recall, me and Isobel, and it appeared to be where he spent almost all of his time, surrounded by his collections. I sprinted down the hall, trying to make as little noise as possible.

Barnes was there, behind his desk in the den. His boombox was tuned to a music station, Engelbert Humperdink singing something about perfect love, and Barnes hadn't heard a thing. Startled, his head came up and his eyes widened, and then he tried to reach into a drawer for a pistol, I imagine. I hurled myself around his desk and grabbed him by his shirtfront, and lifted him out of his chair and hauled him over his desk, and then I roughly pushed him back into his bookshelf, and fifty Mr. Peanuts fell to the floor.

He grunted, and he grunted again when I hit him in the solar plexus. He crumpled up, his breath stuck in his chest. I grabbed his hands and dragged him out of the den, along the hallway, then through the door into the front yard to the willow tree. Spazz Sprague was lying there where I had left him. I tossed my baseball cap aside. I can't stand wearing them.

From the semi's cab I brought out a large roll of duct tape. When I got back to the willow tree, Sprague had started to move, so I kicked him in the head. Barnes's eyes were opening, but he was gasping and hacking as if he were having a heart attack, which didn't concern me. I lifted Sprague by his hair and pushed him up against the willow's trunk. I quickly taped his hands together behind the tree trunk. Then I did the same to Moe Barnes, so they were next to each other.

Barnes could finally cough out, "What are you doing?"

"I'm determining whether you are capable of learning a lesson."

Sprague's eyes opened. They found me. I walked to the trailer, then lowered the equipment gangplanks, one for each tread. I climbed up to the Caterpillar's cab. Some older Cats have a small gasoline motor used to start the diesel engine, but this one had batteries and an electric starter. I turned over the engine, engaged the gears, and drove the tractor off the lowboy and onto the driveway.

Crawler tractors don't have steering wheels. Rather, two clutch handles are at the driver's knee, one for each track. If you disengage the right treads, the left treads will turn the tractor to the right. And each track has a brake pedal for even tighter turns. So I used the right clutch handle and right brake pedal, and the tractor turned around almost in less room than its length. The treads clattered on the pavement. You'll remember that I had once been a heavy equipment operator, so I knew how to do this.

Barnes and his nephew were carefully studying the Caterpillar. Sprague's wise-guy expression had disappeared. His greased hair stuck out at odd angles, courtesy of my foot.

I aimed the giant tractor at Barnes's home, and I pulled the lever to raise the huge blade. The tractor neared the front door, then swerved toward a corner of the house. The blade hit the corner, and didn't slow in the slightest as it ripped into the house. Pink stucco shattered, and the wood framing behind it cracked and splintered. The roof sagged, and red tiles spilled onto the yard. The Caterpillar crawled over the new debris, then I spun the tractor around, and aimed it again at the house.

This time I wiped out the front of Barnes's home, crushing the stucco and wood under the treads. Pieces of rubble shot into the air. Dust rose and spread. The sound was of fracturing wood and the big diesel engine. More of the roof slumped. A bathroom disappeared under the treads. Furniture was flattened. I turned away from the wreckage, spun the Cat, and headed back in, hitting the house square. Walls fell inward, and the tractor rose up on the debris, pulverizing it. The steel treads clanked. The blade blew through walls. Compared to highway grading, this was easy work for the Caterpillar. In what was once the living room, the tractor flattened Barnes's andiron collection.

The blade pushed aside the collapsing roof, and plowed into a bedroom. A bed disappeared under the tracks. Then I crushed a sideboard and a leather chair. I spun the tractor on top of the broken plaster and boards and tile, then set off in another direction, smashing a wall. I came to the kitchen, and crushed the refrigerator and stove, smashed all the cabinetry and tore out a pantry, squashing cans of tomato sauce and bottles of wine. I turned the tractor again, and this time the Cat found the den.

All the Mr. Peanuts were ground down to nothing. The glass cockatoos vanished under the treads. Barnes's massive mahogany desk—the one with the tan leather inlay and the carved serpents on the front—was smashed flat as lath. More of the roof came down, red tiles everywhere. I counted three chimneys as they toppled. A satellite dish was squashed. Water seeped out from under the mound of debris.

The Cat's diesel roaring, I took out several other rooms, and finally no interior or exterior walls remained standing. Then I had the Caterpillar criss-cross the rubble several times, grinding it down, flattening everything. Dust flew up. In the rubble I saw a few of Barnes's antique filling station pumps that weren't flat yet, so I spun the Cat around and around on top of them, crushing them down to two dimensions. Fractured remnants of his German beer stein and carriage clock collection were everywhere.

Then I lowered the enormous blade to dig around where the den used to be, pushing aside the broken furniture and plowing into the downed walls, digging and pushing with the steel dozer blade. And I found what I was looking for.

Moe Barnes kept a safe at home, of course. No gangster deposits money in a bank account, or even a bank safe deposit box, where a court can abruptly freeze the assets. Amid all the rubble, it was too late to tell which wall the safe had been in, but there it was, a gun-metal gray cube, probably eighteen inches by eighteen inches, with a blue combination dial on the front. I lowered the blade and pushed the safe through the wreckage, having to back up several times when it slipped further down into the debris. The blade skidded the safe along until it cleared the broken wood and stucco. I used the dozer blade to push the safe toward the willow tree, right up to Barnes and Sprague.

The gangster's face was drained of color. Even his rosy nose had paled. Sprague's mouth had gone slack, and he stared gape-jawed at the proceedings.

I spun the Caterpillar one-hundred-eighty degrees, and pivoted the cab's chair so I could look out toward the boom and arm. I manipulated the controls, and the jackhammer was lowered to the safe. The tool, which is what you call the jackhammer's business end, touched the safe. I pressed the trigger.

The tool hammered the safe with repeated blows, sounding like a machine gun. The strongbox squirted out to one side, and I had to reposition the arm, and this time I pressed the tool harder against the safe, pushing the safe an inch or two into the turf before I pulled the trigger. The jackhammer struck the safe again and again, a powerful stuttering. After a few seconds, the safe's door popped open.

I raised the hammer arm, and left the Cat's engine idling as I jumped down from the cab, then dug into the safe and brought out a dozen or so stacks of hundred dollar bills. I tossed them aside. Several diamond rings were in the safe, and eight Rolex wristwatches. I flipped them onto the grass. Next I brought out a white, letter-sized, unsealed envelope. I opened it and pulled out a yellowed piece of paper.

I read aloud, "The Lost Land." At the bottom of the page, under maybe forty lines of verse, was EAP.

Barnes whined, "You could've asked me. I would've negotiated some more. You didn't have to squish my glass cockatoos."

I studied the page. Poe had scratchy handwriting, and there were a few black ink spots at the bottom of the page where his quill had leaked.

I returned the poem to the envelope, and put it into my jeans' back pocket, making a mental note not to sit on it on my way back to town.

I stepped close to Moe Barnes. "I want you to listen closely to me. The next time I see you, I'm going to beat you to death with my own hands."

Barnes was silent.

I added, "I don't care if I'm in a crowded bar or in a grocery store or in a church or on the sidewalk in front of a police station. The instant I see you, I'm going to beat you to death, no matter how many witnesses see it. Your life depends on you believing me."

He didn't say anything, but finally he nodded. I think he understood I was serious.

Then I put my scarred face right up to the Sprague's nose. "The same thing goes for you. If I ever see you again, nothing will stop me from using my fists, and I'll pound you until you are dead. I swear to you I'll do it. Do you understand?"

After a quick sideways glance at his boss, the Sprague's chin dropped a fraction of an inch, a sleight nod.

I grinned meanly. "Good. We understand each other."

I turned to go. It was only a matter of minutes before I had loaded the dozer onto the trailer. I turned the rig and trailer around, using much of Barnes's grass, careful not to get near the martin house. I drove the truck down Barnes's driveway back toward the road. The poem was on the truck's passenger seat.

I looked into the rear-view mirror. Barnes and his nephew were still tied to the tree. They'd eventually wiggle and squirm their wrists out of the knots. I hadn't tied them that tight. There's only two ways to handle gangsters. Scare them almost to death or kill them. I'm no killer—most of my ring opponents would attest to that—so I had frightened them. I was successful. I never saw Barnes or Sprague again.

I turned the rig toward New Orleans, heading back to the equipment rental yard. I wondered what I'd do with my Edgar Allan Poe poem.

•

Coral Thibideaux stung me, and I don't mean in a metaphorical sense. I mean she stuck me with a sharp object, and she did so on purpose for a reason I couldn't fathom, and I'll get to that in a minute.

I was lying on my bed, all my clothes on, my fingers laced behind my head, staring at the far wall, hoping the black mark on the wall was truly a mark and not a cockroach, and reviewing the last few days. I had done some smart things and some stupid things in the week following my fight with Tug Johnson.

The smart things included taking my winnings to a Merrill Lynch broker, the whole wad, less taxes. I figured I would never again come across two million dollars, which was what I had left after taxes and Billy Dupree's ten percent and Arturo Lopez's five grand. I was determined to conserve it. I hadn't purchased a car. I hadn't bought a home or moved into a more expensive apartment. I hadn't treated myself to a surround-sound stereo system or a flashy wristwatch. I hadn't spent any of it. I wasn't going to end up as a greeter at Caesar's Palace.

Another smart thing was to enroll in an intensive math tutoring course, getting ready for fall, when I would be entering Tulane University. After having sifted through my thick stack of college, junior college, trade school and jail transcripts, Tulane had decided it could grant me credit for two years. I would enter the university as a junior. I was going to give Tulane my best effort.

One of the dumb things was to call Tug Johnson's manager to see if a rematch could be arranged. I was laughed off the phone. Johnson already had his next match lined up, and I was boxing history. I should've known.

My moment in the spotlight was over. Newspaper reporters had already stopped calling. Crowds didn't form when I walked along a sidewalk in the Quarter. Restaurant owners no longer eagerly showed me to their best tables. The milk company removed my face from its trucks. Spectators no longer came to Old Al's gym to watch me workout. Gangs of kids didn't follow me when I jogged. I didn't miss any of it, except maybe the kids.

On the floor next to my bed was that day's *Times-Picayune*. I lifted it once again to read the story about Isobel and Charles's upcoming wedding, which would take place at two in the afternoon on Saturday at the Trinity Episcopal Church on Jackson Avenue in the Garden District, the Reverend John Derbyshire performing the service. Three hundred guests would be present. A banquet at Lawrence Autrey's home would follow the ceremony. The newlyweds would leave that evening for their honeymoon on St. Croix in the Caribbean.

I tossed the newspaper aside. Isobel and Charles deserved each other. I had the Poe poem in my jacket pocket. I had read the poem several times. It was titled *The Lost Land*, as you know. Even I, an utter layman regarding poetry, could see its shining worth. It ranked with Poe's *The Raven*, I was sure. *The Lost Land* was a singular masterpiece of the English language.

I sat up and put my feet on the floor. I missed old Lawrence, and all his little soldiers and his scotch and his Tobacco Road hot rod. I had childishly fantasized him being my father, being raised by

Lawrence instead of the puke who had been my real father.

And I missed Isobel. I'm not sure why. She was a jolt of energy. When I was with her, I routinely shook my head in wonderment. Who knew what she would say next, what crazy thing she would do next? And she was astonishingly lovely with her flying black hair and her flashing blue eyes, her mad grin, her full-throated laugh. A man could gaze upon her, and believe the world a better place than it was.

But she was such a schemer. She had played me for a fool, letting me think I was a real fighter, setting me up to be a chump in the ring against Tug Johnson. I despise being a sucker, a pigeon, an easy mark. I would never have anything to do with her again.

Except for one thing. I had one small errand to perform.

So I lifted myself off the bed, gathered my coat. It was raining. I left my room and went down the stairs to the street level. I opened the door and Coral Thibideaux was standing there, her hand on the door handle about to enter the building.

"Hello, Dennis." She grinned widely at me.

"What do you want, Coral?" She was one of Isobel's minions. I didn't owe her much civility.

"A short talk with you."

I stepped out onto the sidewalk, and she followed along. She was wearing a sapphire-blue turban and a black blouse and a long black skirt.

"I'm done with everything and everyone related to Isobel, and that includes you, Coral. I was badly treated."

"So you seem to think."

She gripped my arm as we walked along, which I thought peculiar as we didn't know each other well. I liked this handsome woman, though. I would miss Coral, too.

She said, "Sometimes, Dennis, you need to just relax and see how the day unfolds."

And at that instant I felt a sharp pain on the back of my hand, the one she was holding. I flinched, then pulled my arm free. My hand was bleeding.

"What the hell, Coral?" I pressed my finger onto the tiny wound. "What'd you do that for? You just cut me, for Pete's sake."

Still grinning—and I mean that woman had a powerful grin— she looked at me straight in the eyes. "Dennis, try to have more fun.

You're too tense."

She laughed merrily, then turned to walk quickly back down the sidewalk, headed the other direction. I had a notion to follow her and demand an explanation but she'd never give me one. She was just strange with all her voodoo nonsense, and she was of no account to me any more. I wiped away the drops of blood.

The rain had lessened, though the streets were still glistening. I caught a streetcar out to the Garden District, and walked toward Isobel's home. I waited down the block for a few minutes, making sure no one was coming or going.

Then I quickly walked to her house, climbed up to the porch, and slipped Poe's *The Lost Land* through the mailbox slot.

•

Friday night, the evening before Isobel and Charles's wedding, I was having a sandwich and a couple of beers at Jelly's. With me at the table was James "Amazing Grace" Jefferson and my manager-of-sorts, Billy Dupree, who had surprised me by offering to take me to dinner after he collected his $300,000, his ten percent of my purse.

After we sat down at a table, Dupree had tucked his napkin into his shirt collar, and I wouldn't have expected anything else.

"So you say you've never boxed before?" Dupree asked James Jefferson.

"I'm a singer, not a boxer."

We were all eating poor boys and drinking Abita Amber.

"I can make you a boxer," Dupree offered. "Take me only a couple of weeks. You'll be better than Dennis here ever was. You could ride the circuit with me. Make big money."

I laughed, though I wasn't in the mood for humor. "James makes more money singing Amazing Grace than I ever made on the circuit with you, Billy."

Dupree reached for his pint. He had mayonnaise smears on his big mudslide of a face. He drained off half the pint.

I had received an invitation to Charles Brooks' bachelor's party, which was being held that night out at the Knights of the Arcadian Peacock's clubhouse. Dwight Madelin and Robert Chevenement and the other knights would be there, telling stories and drinking scotch and making lewd comments to Charles about his impending honeymoon. I despise bachelor parties, and I was particularly uninterested in that one. I didn't want anything more to do with

Charles or the knights.

The band lit into Forget the Night, Help Me Make It Through the Door, a zydeco number. The fiddler was taking the lead, really sawing her instrument. The squeezebox player was harmonizing on the chorus. Dancers were drifting out onto the small floor in front of the bandstand.

I was unaccountably sad. I should've been celebrating. I was newly wealthy. I was going back to school, and a very fine school at that. I was at my home-away-from-home, Jelly's. The music was good. Yet I was having trouble getting into the zydeco frame of mind. When he wasn't trying to swindle me, Billy Dupree was always worth a laugh, but not even his presence was lightening my mood. I couldn't place the source of my sadness. Maybe I hadn't exercised hard enough that afternoon. That often did it, putting me into a funk.

I hadn't been listening to Billy and James until Billy exclaimed, "They'd cheat a man singing Amazing Grace?"

James had to speak loudly, over the band. "I get lots of stuff put into my hat instead of money. Hair pins, gravel, bottle caps, anything that'll clink, so the person who just listened to me sing can walk away, me and everybody else thinking he put some money into the hat."

Billy said, "Stiffing a man who just sang Amazing Grace is tempting the Lord's revenge, is my thinking." He crammed more of his sandwich into his mouth.

"Dennis?"

The voice came from over my shoulder. I turned to see a woman standing there, seemed to be in her late fifties, with dark hair that had a badger's streak of gray. A nice looking lady with candid green eyes and a bobbed nose. Thin lines were around her eyes and at the corners of her mouth. She looked weary and full of anxiety. She tried smiling, but it faltered.

She asked, "Are you Dennis Jones?"

I could hardly hear her, what with zydeco filling the place. I rose from the chair. "I am. Can I help you, ma'am?"

"May I sit down?" she asked.

Her voice ran down my spine, rendering me momentarily senseless. I managed to pull out the chair for her. She sat down, looking at my face. How could this woman's voice have done that, made me blank out for an instant?

"Howdy, ma'am," Billy Dupree said. "Buy you a drink?"

She shook her head and touched a finger to the corner of an eye.

I sat down, and then found my voice. "Ma'am, is there something I can do for you? How do you know me?"

"Your friend Isobel Autrey just dropped me off out at the curb, telling me you were in here, that you were always in here on Friday nights."

"Isobel Autrey is no friend of mine," I said with feeling.

That lady's voice. Something about her voice. Was it some memory?

"I believe she is a friend of yours, Dennis." The lady had to dab at her tears. She hadn't taken her eyes off me since she sat down.

I shrugged. "Isobel can think what she wants."

The lady leaned forward and put her hand on my arm. "Dennis, I'm your mother."

22

I was reading a copy of *Money Magazine*, an article about investing. It advised that I should diversify and be conservative, which made sense, same thing my Merrill Lynch broker had told me—when a knock came on the door.

"Is that you, mom?" I called out. I had never heard anything more exotic and emotional than my own voice saying those words right than. Smiling widely, I rose from the chair.

Through the door came, "It's me, Lawrence Autrey."

I opened the door. Lawrence was wearing a tuxedo with a standing collar, a white tie and a waistcoat under the morning coat. A boutonnière was on his lapel. He looked regal.

He entered my small apartment. I waved him to my only chair.

"Aren't you supposed to be at your daughter's wedding?" I asked.

He glanced at his wristwatch. He was wearing French cuffs. "It's still an hour away."

"That's cutting it a little close, isn't it?'

He shrugged. "How'd it go with your mother?"

"It went great." I sat on the bed. "How in the world did Isobel find her?"

He smiled. "She hired a private investigator, a specialist in skip tracing."

"That fellow I saw leave my apartment with Isobel?" The fellow whose dog almost ate me whole?

"You saw them?" He laughed. "Isobel needed any information you had about your mother, so she and the detective broke into your apartment with a pick, then rifled your documents."

"Why didn't she just ask me to see them?"

"She didn't want to get your hopes up, Dennis. Finding your

mother was a long shot. And she wanted it to be a surprise."

"You could've knocked me over with a spitball."

"When the detective searched your documents he found a social security form amidst all the other papers in the file in your desk," Lawrence said. "The form had been sent to your father at some point. It listed your mother as living in Portland, Oregon, though not giving an address. With that lead, the detective traveled to Portland, and he found her."

My mom had been living in Portland all these years. She had done well for herself, had worked her way up in the Fred Meyer organization, the big retail chain based in the Northwest. She now managed a huge store there. She had told me her story.

As I had known, my father beat her until she couldn't stand it any longer. For some perverse reason, instead of letting me go with my mother, he had told her that if she ever tried to get her son, or even visit him, he would kill her. He was that filled with meanness. She had been so roughly treated by my father that she believed him.

After two months in Portland, she gathered the courage to call my father, demanding she be able to return to Anacortes to pick me up. My father, with a drunkard's boldness and persuasion, told my mother I had been run over by an automobile while on my tricycle. Said it was a hit and run, and the police didn't have any leads. He was convincing.

My mother lived all those years believing her only son was dead, and believing the person who had run over me with the car was probably my inebriated father.

Then a few days ago she had received a call from Isobel Autrey. Mom had said last night at Jelly's, "That was quite a call, Dennis."

Mom said she has lived a quiet life, grieving for me, but thanking God every day she had escaped her husband. She had never remarried. We had sat at Jelly's while she told me of her life, and I hadn't been able to squeak out more than a few words, just stared at her, Billy Dupree and Amazing Grace Jefferson smiling all the while, listening, too.

"Is Isobel upset with you, Dennis?" Lawrence asked.

"She was growling last time I saw her, if that's a clue."

"She might be over it. You got her the poem, after all."

"And I'm upset with her. It was a rotten thing to do, Mr. Autrey. Set me up like that, making me think I had a shot at the championship belt."

He patted his knees.

"Making me think I was actually a fighter."

"That's the worst of it, isn't it, Dennis? For a while your fantasies had come true. You were actually fighting like you had always dreamed you would."

I didn't like admitting such things. Most of my daydreams are no more realistic than a fifteen-year-old kid's.

I knew by then that my success against Doaks, Dresser and Norton had been caused by a rare confluence of events. My opponents—all three of them—had bad fights on those days. It happens in sports, inexplicably awful outings by otherwise first-rate athletes. Ask any Cy Young-winning pitcher who occasionally gets shelled and taken out in the first or second inning of a game.

Combine this with my rising to the occasion, and giving freakishly good athletic performances, perhaps due to the voodoo's placebo effect on me, or Isobel's nearness, or to my pent-up anger because of the years of boxing futility. I never speeded up in the ring, of course. It just seemed that way to me, just like when Ted Williams said he could often see the stitching on baseballs thrown at him at ninety miles an hours.

"It was like having your heart broken, wasn't it?" Lawrence asked. "Realizing you didn't, after all, have the talent to beat the champion."

I inhaled slowly. "Yes, it broke my heart."

He pursed his lips. "Well, I'm sorry."

"Your nutty daughter couldn't stay the hell away from me. I've never seen such a schemer."

Again he looked at his watch. "Will you do me a favor, Dennis? I want you to attend Isobel's wedding with me."

I laughed derisively. "No way."

"Humor an old man, will you?"

I was about to laugh again but I hesitated. I liked old Lawrence, no matter how manipulating his daughter was.

I said, "Well, I'm waiting for my mother."

"Susan is out in my car."

"My mom is in your car?" I exclaimed. "What's she doing there?

"She wants to see a Garden District wedding. And I've told her all about Isobel."

"Isobel swore she'd never set eyes on me again. I'm inclined to honor her wish."

He smiled. "You can sit way back in the church, over in a corner. She won't see you."

I chewed on my lower lip.

He rose from the chair, and put his hand on my elbow. "Put on a coat and tie. Come on, Dennis."

So I quickly changed clothes, Lawrence helping with the tie. I led him downstairs to his car, parked right in front of the building. My breath caught at the sight of my mother sitting in the front seat.

I had a mother.

She was there, right in front of me, smiling at me from the front seat of Lawrence's car. I grinned like a maniac. I wondered when that would stop happening.

•

We were on St. Charles, in the car heading for the church, when Lawrence said over his shoulder at me, "You know that detective Isobel hired to search for your mother?"

"He knows his business," my mother commented.

I awkwardly patted her shoulder. I'd eventually learn how to be affectionate with a mother, I presumed.

Lawrence said, "I was impressed with him, so I hired him, too."

"You and Isobel hired him?" I asked.

He shook his head, not taking his eyes off the road. His bony fingers were gripping the steering wheel. "I hired him on my own, after he had found Sue, and after he was no longer working for Isobel."

I thought for a moment, and then it came to me. I put the question delicately, "To see how the Isobel's and Charles's engagement was going?"

He laughed without mirth. "One of my friends was having dinner at the Knights' dining room a while ago, and he saw Charles kiss a young blond lady, and the next day my friend telephoned me to say with the consummate satisfaction of a gossip, 'Who did I see Charles Brook's kiss yesterday? I thought your daughter was a brunette.'"

So I hadn't been the only person to see Charles kiss Jennifer Blake that day.

"As a result, I had the detective, Jon Cal Murray, look around," Lawrence went on. "Just this morning he showed me photographs he has taken this past week. They show my future son-in-law and that bombshell dancer in all sorts of amorous embraces."

"Did you tell Isobel?" my mom asked.

"Sue, I have a duty to my daughter to insure she has all the facts."

I said, "I like Charles fine."

The old man argued, "If Charles does this kind of stuff during the week before his wedding, imagine what he'll do after they are married. My daughter deserves better."

As he parked the car near the church, Lawrence added, "I showed Isobel the photos this morning. The decent ones, anyway."

I flinched in sympathy with both Isobel and Charles. "That's a hard way to learn something about a fiancé, sir."

He laughed again, this time with some humor. "How would I have sugarcoated such news?"

"It's better to learn things about a person in advance," my mom said. "I know from hard experience."

Lawrence said, "It was too late to call the guests to uninvite them."

"What's Isobel going to do?" mom asked.

I saw Lawrence's unpleasant grin in the rear view mirror. "I don't know, but I thought you'd like to be here to see it."

We left the car, walked along the sidewalk a ways, then strolled up the Trinity Episcopal Church's front steps, my mother's arm in mine. She was wearing a lovely light blue dress and a pearl necklace. Lawrence led the way.

The church was built in 1851, was made of stucco over brick, and was topped by a helm roof. Trinity was known as the "church that makes bishops" because of the many leading spiritual leaders who had served there, including the Bishop Leonidas Polk, the Civil War's famous fighting bishop. We entered under a peaked gable.

Most of the guests had already arrived, and they almost filled the church. Lawrence waited in the anteroom for Isobel. I didn't see her anywhere. The flower girl and ring bearer waited in the narthex. I spotted Coral Thibideaux in a corner of the church, and she waved me over so I didn't have much choice but to join her. I guided mom along.

Isobel had decided she and Charles were too old to have a lot of attendants, so only two people waited at the altar: the priest and

Dwight Madelin, who was the best man. Both were fidgeting.

I sat next to Coral on the pew and whispered, "Please don't cut me again, Coral. I'm not as fond of shedding blood as my boxing career would suggest."

She grabbed my hand and brought it up so she could see the tiny wound. "Looks like you'll survive."

I introduced Coral to my mother. They were quickly leaning toward each other and laughing about something.

"You just can't walk out." This shout came from one side of the church, from a door near the alter. I recognized Charles Brooks' voice.

The guests turned toward the door.

"Watch me, buster." This was Isobel, her loud words echoing in the church.

Then she appeared at the door. She was wearing a light sweater and pants, not a wedding dress. A manila envelope was in her hand. She passed the altar, apparently on her way out of the church. Charles rushed after her, caught her, and spun her around, Isobel's hair flying.

He wagged a finger in her face. "I won't let you ditch me at the altar like you've done so many others, Isobel." His voice was strident.

"They deserved it, and so do you."

He raised his hands to encompass the room. "Look at all these people. You just can't leave them here. They are here for a wedding."

Isobel scanned the guests, then she said in a loud voice, "You're all welcome to come to my father's home for a party but don't call it a reception, because there isn't going to be a wedding."

The guests had been embarrassed to silence, but now a hubbub grew. A few people shouted questions at Charles. A man I took for Charles's father, wearing a tux, gestured wildly and yelled at his wife, his face the color of a pomegranate. He jabbed a finger in Isobel's direction.

Other guests stood. A few began to weep. Some shrugged, as if to say, "with Isobel Autry what were we to expect?" Sitting next to me, Coral Thibideax laughed. My mother raised her eyebrows questioningly at me, but I couldn't tell her anything.

Charles grabbed Isobel's arm and yelled, "I won't let you do this to me."

Her words had the cadence of a jack hammer. "Charles, if you don't back off, I'm going to walk down this aisle and pass out the contents of this envelope, one photo per row." Isobel held up the envelope. She had a small bandage on the back of her hand.

Charles gaped at the envelope. He swallowed hugely, I could see it from the back of the church. He was defeated and he knew it. Envelope in hand, Isobel disappeared through the sanctuary's side door.

The guests were roaring, on the verge of a riot. Curses and accusations and angry shrieks came from up front where Charles's family was. A woman I later learned was Charles's mother had collapsed and was being laid out on a pew so she could recover herself, someone fanning her with a hat. I turned to see Lawrence sliding along the pew toward us.

He said to Coral, "I've been to longer wedding ceremonies."

She smiled. "And I've been to shorter ones. Try the Baptists some time."

"What do you say we all go to the reception?"

Mom corrected him. "The party, rather."

"I'm paying for the food and beverages and entertainment and decorations, so we might as well enjoy it, bride and groom or no." He was puzzlingly cheery. This disastrous episode involving the Autrey family would be gossiped about in the Garden District for decades, yet it apparently didn't bother Lawrence in the least.

He and Coral and my mother slid along the pew to the aisle.

When Lawrence looked back at me, I said, "I'm going to sit here a while."

So he placed himself between mom and Coral and escorted them from the sanctuary. After a while the last of the baffled guests made their way out of the church. I sat there alone in the sanctuary. After half an hour the priest approached to ask if I wanted to talk about anything, and I replied not today. He said the doors to the church and his office were always open if I changed my mind. I said I'd visit sometime.

So I stayed in the church for a while, looking at all the flowers and candles, sometimes thinking about my mother, but mostly thinking about Isobel Autrey.

•

"A musical note is not a training bag," Amazing Grace Jefferson said. "Sing it. Don't punch it."

I laughed. Five minutes ago, halfway through his second beer, Amazing Grace had decided I needed to learn to sing. That the band was playing a zydeco number at one-hundred-twenty beats per minute at ninety decibels didn't prevent him from trying to teach me Amazing Grace. He was wearing a purple shirt. He had nicked himself shaving his head that morning, and a small slice was in the skin above his right ear.

When I tried a few notes, warbling pathetically, he grimaced. "You've been hit too many times in the voice box, Dennis. You need to learn another skill, one that doesn't use your voice. Typing, maybe."

Jelly's was crowded with the Friday night gang. I was drinking Diet Coke. Ever since my fight with Tug Johnson, beer had tasted sour. So I had called Charles Brooks's office, intending to ask him if there was some bodily organ that governed taste, because I was sure that Johnson had broken mine, and maybe it could be fixed.

Ten days had passed since the fight and I still ached when I moved. Charles's receptionist had told me the doctor was not in the office that week, and I had charmed the receptionist into telling me that Dr. Brooks and his girlfriend Jennifer were in Hawaii. Being ditched at the altar wasn't bothering Charles as much as I would have imagined.

At Jelly's I still enjoyed a little residual celebrity, and had been asked to dance several times that night, but I had politely refused, saying I was still hurting from the fight. One of the girls nodded her understanding and added, "I was at the Superdome. That beating would've killed anybody else." I took it as a compliment.

A strobe light was making Amazing Grace appear in stop-motion. The dancers were flinging themselves around. The bartender rang a brass bell near the cash register, meaning he had just received a tip.

"Will you dance with me?" The question came from over my shoulder, right at my ear.

I turned in the chair to see Isobel. I think I gasped, but I couldn't be sure over the sound of the band. Her eye lights were on, those flickering blue sparks, but otherwise she didn't look threatening.

"Stand up, Dennis." She put a hand on my shoulder. "Dance with me."

I pushed myself up from the chair. She led me onto the crowded dance floor, and even though it was an up-tempo number, she stepped into me. For a moment I tried to hold her at a distance the proper way, as she had taught me at the Fortune Club. But she slipped inside and pressed herself against me.

Her hand was on the back of my neck, and she said into my good ear. "I'm celebrating tonight."

"Celebrating what?"

She was tight against me. "The Authentication Division of the American Poetry Society has issued a preliminary ruling that *The Lost Land* is indeed by Edgar Allan Poe. They examined not only the language of the poem, but the handwriting, the paper and the ink. Extensive lab tests. And they studied all my evidence regarding when and why it was written, and why it had been hidden from sight for so long. There isn't any doubt in any of the experts' minds that it is an Edgar Allan Poe poem."

"You knew it was authentic all along, didn't you?"

"And now the academics know it. My written description of my search for the poem that I submitted to them had only a small omission."

"An omission?"

"I left out all mention of you."

I pulled my head away a little to look at her.

She was smiling. "The announcement of the poem's discovery will be made next Wednesday. *Time* and *Newsweek* and *People* have already been informed, and they are going to run big articles."

"You'll be famous, just like you wanted."

"Tulane's English Department is putting on a huge gala in my honor. The governor and both Louisiana senators will be there. The governor is going to present me with the Louisiana Medal of Honor, and Tulane's president will announce that I've been appointed to the Truman Capote Chair of Literature."

I said, "You owe me an apology."

"For what?"

"For everything."

"For getting you a fight with the world champion, which earned you three million dollars? For helping you get into Tulane? For finding your mother? For what, exactly?"

I turned with the music, and she turned with me. She was up

against me like ham on rye, her lips at my ear. The flowery scent of her hair was all around. I could sense the befuddlement descending on me, same thing that always happened when Isobel was too close. I didn't know what it was, some peculiar toxic chemistry she had, maybe on her skin, like a stinging nettle.

I said, "I deserve an abject across-the-board, cover-all-the-bases, I-grovel-before-you apology for all I've been through since I first laid my pepper-stung eyes on you."

She laughed into my neck. "Daddy and your mother are at a reception at the Museum of Art."

"The two of them? Really?" I moved with the music, and concluded profoundly, "Well, that's something to think about."

I felt the bandage on the back of her hand. "What happened to your hand?"

"Coral put a tiny cut in it, and took some blood."

'You, too? She did the same to me."

"I know."

"What's she up to?"

"Something about getting your and my blood together, and adding some other stuff: nine rose petals, nine dozen drops of red wine, nine crushed cloves and nine melted Sugar Babies."

"What did she do with this mixture?"

"At her request, I drank it."

"You should know better than to do anything Coral asks."

"Have you gotten more handsome in the past couple of days, Dennis? And sort of more lovable? How has that happened? I wonder." She laughed softly. "And you've been glowing red. Have you noticed it?"

The band segued to their signature song, You're the Reason Our Kids Are So Ugly. Isobel took this as her prompt to squeeze tighter against me. A five-dollar bill couldn't have passed between us, ankle to forehead.

Her lips were on my ear as she said, "Charles is in Hawaii, I hear. With his girlfriend, Jennifer."

I didn't say anything.

"It wouldn't have worked anyway, Charles and me."

"Are you rationalizing?"

"I don't know whether my giddiness these past few days has been because of the poem or because I discovered a good reason to send

Charles packing."

"Well, I'm sorry for you. It must've been hard."

"Not hard at all. Since I've met you, Charles has seemed … oh, I don't know—too simpy. Do you know what I mean?"

"Maybe."

"And, since I've met you, Charles has seemed too sophisticated, and too intelligent, and too gentlemanly, and too well-dressed, and too wealthy, and …"

"Enough, please."

"Daddy didn't want me to marry Charles. He'd been hinting at it for months but he finally generated the courage to tell me, just as he handed me those awful photographs."

"He mentioned something along those lines to me, about Charles not being right for you."

She said, "He thinks you, Dennis Jones, of all people—would make the best match for me."

"Well, that's something terrifying to think about."

"When he told me, I almost broke my face laughing," she said into my neck. "He has been paying Coral, did you know that? Hiring her for voodoo services."

"No way your dad believes in voodoo."

"He said he was just covering all the angles."

Suddenly my earlobe flashed with pain, and I flinched but Isobel held me close.

I tried to move my fingers to my ear to see if there was blood but she gripped my hand. The nip reverberated up and down my body.

I demanded, "Isobel, why do you do that?"

"I don't know why I do it."

"Damn it, that hurts. Between you and Tug Johnson, I've about been destroyed."

"Don't be flattered. Half the men in the Garden District are missing earlobes."

We swayed with the music. The small dance floor was crowded, and I had to dodge elbows and backsides.

She put both her arms around my neck, still moving with me to the music. "Do you know what your problem is, Dennis?"

"I'm dancing with a nutball is my main problem."

"Your problem is that you just haven't had enough School of Isobel." Now her lips were on my cheek. I could feel their feathery touch. "You need a couple more semesters. I have much to teach you, much to show you."

"I barely survived the first semester."

"Oh, you'll survive." She laughed, right into my cauliflower ear. "But I'll make sure it's close."

• • •

James Thayer

Multi-published author, James Thayer, says he doesn't write with a theme in mind; however, "The good guy always wins, but it's close." A lawyer and novelist, he is currently a novel writing instructor at the University of Washington.

Thayer is an occasional contributor to *The Weekly Standard*. He has written twelve previously published books through companies like Simon & Schuster, Crown Publishing and Putnam. *The Boxer and the Poet: Something of a Romance* is James Thayer's thirteenth novel. He and his family live in Seattle.

YOU MIGHT ALSO ENJOY THESE OTHER TITLES FROM BLACK LYON PUBLISHING ...

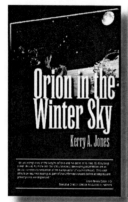

Breinigsville, PA USA
20 December 2009
229534BV00001B/42/P